PENGUIN M

THE

FRANZ KAFKA

Franz Kafka was born in Prague in 1883, the son of a rich
Jewish Czech merchant. After studying literature and
medicine for a short time, he turned to law, which he
believed was the profession that would give him the greatest
amount of free time for his private life and for his writing.
He took his doctorate in law at Prague University, obtained
a job with an insurance company, and later became a clerk
in the semi-Governmental Workers Insurance Office. In later
years the necessity of earning his living by routine office
work became an intolerable burden, and he broke away
altogether, settling down in a Berlin suburb to devote himself to writing. In 1914 he became engaged, but broke it off,
feeling unable to face marriage. He made one more attempt
to marry, but it was discovered that he was suffering from
tuberculosis and he went to a sanatorium. His unsatisfactory
love affairs, his relationship with his father, a self-made man
who cared nothing for his son's literary aspirations, and
his own inflexible intellectual honesty and almost psycho-
pathic sensitivity finally broke down his health, and the
'hunger years' of post-1918 Berlin added the finishing
touches. He died in 1924. Although he was a Czech, Kafka's
books were all written in German. Seven of them were published during his lifetime. *The Trial* first appeared after the
author's death in 1925, *The Castle* in 1926, *America* in 1927,
and *The Great Wall of China* in 1931.

Cover design by André François

THE TRIAL

Franz Kafka

WITH AN EPILOGUE BY
MAX BROD

PENGUIN BOOKS

Penguin Books Ltd, Harmondsworth, Middlesex
AUSTRALIA: Penguin Books Pty Ltd, 762 Whitehorse Road,
Mitcham, Victoria

—

Translated from the German – *Der Prozess*
(first published 1925) – by Willa and Edwin Muir
First published in England 1935 by Victor Gollancz
Reissued in 1945 by Martin Secker & Warburg Ltd
Published in Penguin Books 1953
Reprinted 1955, 1960, 1962, 1963

—

—

Made and printed in Great Britain
by Hazell Watson & Viney Ltd
Aylesbury, Bucks
Set in Linotype Granjon

Contents

I   THE ARREST – CONVERSATION
    WITH FRAU GRUBACH THEN FRÄU-
    LEIN BÜRSTNER   7

II   FIRST INTERROGATION   39

III IN THE EMPTY INTERROGATION
     CHAMBER – THE STUDENT – THE
     OFFICES   58

IV   FRÄULEIN BÜRSTNER'S FRIEND   85

V   THE WHIPPER   94

VI   K.'S UNCLE – LENI   102

VII ADVOCATE – MANUFACTURER –
     PAINTER   126

VIII THE COMMERCIAL TRAVELLER –
     DISMISSAL OF THE ADVOCATE   184

IX   IN THE CATHEDRAL   218

X   THE END   245

     EPILOGUE   252

I

The Arrest – Conversation with Frau Grubach then Fräulein Bürstner

SOMEONE must have been telling lies about Joseph K., for without having done anything wrong he was arrested one fine morning. His landlady's cook, who always brought him his breakfast at eight o'clock, failed to appear on this occasion. That had never happened before. K. waited for a little while longer, watching from his pillow the old lady opposite, who seemed to be peering at him with a curiosity unusual even for her, but then, feeling both put out and hungry, he rang the bell. At once there was a knock at the door and a man entered whom he had never seen before in the house. He was slim and yet well knit, he wore a closely fitting black suit, which was furnished with all sorts of pleats, pockets, buckles, and buttons, as well as a belt, like a tourist's outfit, and in consequence looked eminently practical, though one could not quite tell what actual purpose it served. 'Who are you?' asked K., half raising himself in bed. But the man ignored the question, as though his appearance needed no explanation, and merely said: 'Did you ring?' 'Anna is to bring me my breakfast,' said K., and then with silent intensity studied the fellow, trying to make out who he could be. The man did not submit to this scrutiny for very long, but turned to the door and opened it slightly so as to report to someone who was evidently standing just behind it: 'He says Anna is to bring him his breakfast.' A short guffaw from the next room came in answer; one could not tell from the sound whether it was produced by several individuals or merely by one. Although the strange man could not have learned anything from it that he did not know already, he now said to K., as if passing on a statement: 'It can't be done.' 'This is news indeed,' cried K., springing out of bed and quickly pulling on his trousers. 'I must see what people these are next door, and how Frau Grubach can account to me for such behaviour.' Yet it occurred to him at once that he should not have said this aloud and that by doing so he had in a way admitted the stranger's right to an interest in his actions; still, that did not seem important to him at the moment. The stranger, however, took his words in some such sense, for he asked: 'Hadn't you better stay here?' 'I shall neither stay here nor let you address me until you have introduced yourself.' 'I meant well enough,' said the stranger, and then of his own accord threw the door open. In the next room, which K. entered more slowly than he had intended, everything looked at first glance almost as it had done the evening before. It was Frau Grubach's living-room; perhaps among all the furniture, rugs, china, and photographs with which it was crammed there was a little more free space than usual, yet one did not perceive that at first, especially as the main change consisted in the presence of a man who was sitting at the open window reading a book, from which he now glanced up. 'You should have stayed in your room! Didn't Franz tell you that?' 'Yes, yes, but what are you doing here?' asked K., looking from his new acquaintance to the man called Franz, who was still standing by the door, and then back again. Through the open window he had another glimpse of the old woman, who with truly senile inquisitiveness had moved along to the window exactly opposite, in order

to see all that could be seen. 'I'd better get Frau Grubach —' said K., as if wrenching himself away from the
two men (though they were standing at quite a distance
from him) and making as if to go out. 'No,' said the man
at the window, flinging the book down on the table and
getting up. 'You can't go out, you are arrested.' 'So it
seems,' said K. 'But what for?' he added. 'We are not
authorized to tell you that. Go to your room and wait
there. Proceedings have been instituted against you, and
you will be informed of everything in due course. I am
exceeding my instructions in speaking freely to you like
this. But I hope nobody hears me except Franz, and he
himself has been too free with you, against his express instructions. If you continue to have as good luck as you
have had in the choice of your warders, then you can be
confident of the final result.' K. felt he must sit down, but
now he saw that there was no seat in the whole room except the chair beside the window. 'You'll soon discover
that we're telling you the truth,' said Franz, advancing
towards him simultaneously with the other man. The
latter overtopped K. enormously and kept clapping him
on the shoulder. They both examined his nightshirt and
said that he would have to wear a less fancy shirt now,
but that they would take charge of this one and the rest
of his underwear and, if his case turned out well, restore them to him later. 'Much better give these things
to us than hand them over to the depot,' they said, 'for
in the depot there's lots of thieving, and besides they sell
everything there after a certain length of time, no matter
whether your case is settled or not. And you never know
how long these cases will last, especially these days. Of
course you would get the money out of the depot in the
long run, but in the first place the prices they pay you

are always wretched, for they sell your things to the
best briber, not the best bidder, and anyhow it's well
known that money dwindles a lot if it passes from hand
to hand from one year to another.' K. paid hardly any
attention to this advice, any right to dispose of his own
things which he might possess he did not prize very
highly; far more important to him was the necessity to
understand his situation clearly; but with these people beside him he could not even think, the belly of the second
warder – for they could only be warders – kept butting
against him in an almost friendly way, yet if he looked up
he caught sight of a face which did not in the least suit
that fat body, a dry, bony face with a great nose, twisted
to one side, which seemed to be consulting over his head
with the other warder. Who could these men be? What
were they talking about? What authority could they represent? K. lived in a country with a legal constitution,
there was universal peace, all the laws were in force; who
dared seize him in his own dwelling? He had always
been inclined to take things easily, to believe in the worst
only when the worst happened, to take no care for the
morrow even when the outlook was threatening. But that
struck him as not being the right policy here, one could
certainly regard the whole thing as a joke, a rude joke
which his colleagues in the Bank had concocted for some
unknown reason, perhaps because this was his thirtieth
birthday, that was of course possible, perhaps he had only
to laugh knowingly in these men's faces and they would
laugh with him, perhaps they were merely porters from
the street corner – they looked very like it – nevertheless his
very first glance at the man Franz had decided him for the
time being not to give away any advantage that he might
possess over these people. There was a slight risk that

later on his friends might possibly say he could not take a joke, but he had in mind – though it was not usual with him to learn from experience – several occasions, of no importance in themselves, when against all his friends' advice he had behaved with deliberate recklessness and without the slightest regard for possible consequences, and had had in the end to pay dearly for it. That must not happen again, at least not this time; if this was a comedy he would insist on playing it to the end.

But he was still free. 'Allow me,' he said, passing quickly between the warders to his room. 'He seems to have some sense,' he heard one of them saying behind him. When he reached his room he at once pulled out the drawer of his desk, everything lay there in perfect order, but in his agitation he could not find at first the identification papers for which he was looking. At last he found his bicycle licence and was about to start off with it to the warders, but then it seemed too trivial a thing, and he searched again until he found his birth certificate. As he was re-entering the next room the opposite door opened and Frau Grubach showed herself. He saw her only for an instant, for no sooner did she recognize him than she was obviously overcome by embarrassment, apologized for intruding, vanished, and shut the door again with the utmost care. 'Come in, do,' he would just have had time to say. But he merely stood holding his papers in the middle of the room, looking at the door, which did not open again, and was only recalled to attention by a shout from the warders, who were sitting at a table by the open window and, as he now saw, devouring his breakfast. 'Why didn't she come in?' he asked. 'She isn't allowed to,' said the tall warder, 'since you're under arrest.' 'But how can I be under arrest? And particularly in such a ridiculous fashion?' 'So now you're beginning it all over again?' said the warder, dipping a slice of bread and butter into the honey-pot. 'We don't answer such questions.' 'You'll have to answer them,' said K. 'Here are my papers, now show me yours, and first of all your warrant for arresting me.' 'Oh, good Lord,' said the warder. 'If you would only realize your position, and if you wouldn't insist on uselessly annoying us two, who probably mean better by you and stand closer to you than any other people in the world.' 'That's so, you can believe that,' said Franz, not raising to his lips the coffee-cup he held in his hand, but instead giving K. a long, apparently significant, yet incomprehensible look. Without wishing it K. found himself decoyed into an exchange of speaking looks with Franz, none the less he tapped his papers and repeated: 'Here are my identification papers.' 'What are your papers to us?' cried the tall warder. 'You're behaving worse than a child. What are you after? Do you think you'll bring this fine case of yours to a speedier end by wrangling with us, your warders, over papers and warrants? We are humble subordinates who can scarcely find our way through a legal document and have nothing to do with your case except to stand guard over you for ten hours a day and draw our pay for it. That's all we are, but we're quite capable of grasping the fact that the high authorities we serve, before they would order such an arrest as this must be quite well informed about the reasons for the arrest and the person of the prisoner. There can be no mistake about that. Our officials, so far as I know them, and I know only the lowest grades among them, never go hunting for crime in the populace, but, as the Law decrees, are drawn towards the guilty and must then send out us warders. That is the Law. How could there be a mistake in that?'

'I don't know this Law,' said K. 'All the worse for you,' replied the warder. 'And it probably exists nowhere but in your own head,' said K.; he wanted in some way to enter into the thoughts of the warders and twist them to his own advantage or else try to acclimatize himself to them. But the warder merely said in a discouraging voice: 'You'll come up against it yet.' Franz interrupted: 'See, Willem, he admits that he doesn't know the Law and yet he claims he's innocent.' 'You're quite right, but you'll never make a man like that see reason,' replied the other. K. gave no further answer; 'Must I,' he thought, 'let myself be confused still worse by the gabble of those wretched hirelings? — they admit themselves that's all they are. They're talking of things, in any case, which they don't understand. Plain stupidity is the only thing that can give them such assurance. A few words with a man on my own level of intelligence would make everything far clearer than hours of talk with these two.' He walked up and down a few times in the free part of the room; at the other side of the street he could still see the old woman, who had now dragged to the window an even older man, whom she was holding round the waist. K. felt he must put an end to this farce. 'Take me to your superior officer,' he said. 'When he orders me, not before,' retorted the warder called Willem. 'And now I advise you,' he went on, 'to go to your room, stay quietly there, and wait for what may be decided about you. Our advice to you is not to let yourself be distracted by vain thoughts, but to collect yourself, for great demands will be made upon you. You haven't treated us as our kind advances to you deserved, you have forgotten that we, no matter who we may be, are at least free men compared to you; that is no small advantage. All the same, we are prepared, if you have any money, to bring you a little breakfast from the coffee-house across the street.'

Without replying to this offer K. remained standing where he was for a moment. If he were to open the door of the next room or even the door leading to the hall, perhaps the two of them would not dare to hinder him, perhaps that would be the simplest solution of the whole business, to bring it to a head. But perhaps they might seize him after all, and if he were once down, all the superiority would be lost which in a certain sense he still retained. Accordingly, instead of a quick solution he chose that certainty which the natural course of things would be bound to bring, and went back to his room without another word having been said by him or by the warders.

He flung himself on his bed and took from the wash-stand a fine apple which he had laid out the night before for his breakfast. Now it was all the breakfast he would have, but in any case, as the first few bites assured him, much better than the breakfast from the filthy night café would have been, which the grace of his warders might have secured him. He felt fit and confident, he would miss his work in the Bank that morning, it was true, but that would be easily overlooked, considering the comparatively high post he held there. Should he give the real reason for his absence? He considered doing so. If they did not believe him, which in the circumstances would be understandable, he could produce Frau Grubach as a witness, or even the two odd creatures over the way, who were now probably meandering back again to the window opposite his room. K. was surprised, at least he was surprised considering the warders' point of view, that they had sent him to his room and left him alone there, where he had abundant opportunities to take his life. Though at the same time he also asked himself, looking at it from his own point of view, what possible ground he could have to do so. Because two warders were sitting next door and had intercepted his breakfast? To take his life would be such a senseless act that, even if he wished, he could not bring himself to do it because of its very senselessness. If the intellectual poverty of the warders were not so manifest, he might almost assume that they too saw no danger in leaving him alone, for the very same reason. They were quite at liberty to watch him now while he went to a wall-cupboard where he kept a bottle of good brandy, while he filled a glass and drank it down to make up for his breakfast, and then drank a second to give him courage, the last one only as a precaution, for the improbable contingency that it might be needed.

Then a shout came from the next room which made him start so violently that his teeth rattled against the glass. 'The Inspector wants you,' was its tenor. It was merely the tone of it that startled him, a curt, military bark with which he would never have credited the warder Franz. The command itself was actually welcome to him. 'At last,' he shouted back, closing the cupboard and hurrying at once into the next room. There the two warders were standing, and, as if that were a matter of course, immediately drove him back into his room again. 'What are you thinking of?' they cried. 'Do you imagine you can appear before the Inspector in your shirt? He'll have you well thrashed, and us too.' 'Let me alone, damn you,' cried K., who by now had been forced back to his wardrobe. 'If you grab me out of bed, you can't expect to find me all dressed up in my best suit.' 'This doesn't help you any,' said the warders, who as soon as K. raised his voice always grew quite calm, indeed almost rueful, and thus contrived either to confuse him or to some extent bring him to his senses. 'Silly formalities!' he growled, but immediately lifted a coat from a chair and held it up for a little while in both hands, as if displaying it to the warders for their approval. They shook their heads. 'It must be a black coat,' they said. Thereupon K. flung the coat on the floor and said – he did not himself know in what sense he meant the words – 'But this isn't the capital charge yet.' The warders smiled, but stuck to their: 'It must be a black coat.' 'If it's to dispatch my case any quicker, I don't mind,' replied K., opening the wardrobe, where he searched for a long time among his many suits, chose his best black one, a lounge suit which had caused almost a sensation among his acquaintances because of its elegance, then selected another shirt and began to dress with great care. In his secret heart he thought he had managed after all to speed up the proceedings, for the warders had forgotten to make him take a bath. He kept an eye on them to see if they would remember the ducking, but of course it never occurred to them, yet on the other hand Willem did not forget to send Franz to the Inspector with the information that K. was dressing.

When he was fully dressed he had to walk, with Willem treading on his heels, through the next room, which was now empty, into the adjoining one, whose double doors were flung open. This room, as K. knew quite well, had recently been taken by a Fräulein Bürstner, a typist, who went very early to work, came home late, and with whom he had exchanged little more than a few words in passing. Now the night-table beside her bed had been pushed into the middle of the floor to serve as a desk, and the Inspector was sitting behind it. He had crossed his legs, and one arm was resting on the back of the chair.

In a corner of the room three young men were standing looking at Fräulein Bürstner's photographs, which were stuck into a mat hanging on the wall. A white blouse dangled from the latch of the open window. In the window over the way the two old creatures were again stationed, but they had enlarged their party, for behind them, towering head and shoulders above them, stood a man with a shirt open at the neck and a reddish, pointed beard, which he kept pinching and twisting with his fingers. 'Joseph K.?' asked the Inspector, perhaps merely to draw K.'s distracted glance upon himself. K. nodded. 'You are presumably very surprised at the events of this morning?' asked the Inspector, with both hands rearranging the few things that lay on the night-table, a candle and a matchbox, a book and a pin-cushion, as if they were objects which he required for his interrogation. 'Certainly,' said K., and he was filled with pleasure at having encountered a sensible man at last, with whom he could discuss the matter. 'Certainly, I am surprised, but I am by no means very surprised.' 'Not very surprised?' asked the Inspector, setting the candle in the middle of the table and then grouping the other things round it. 'Perhaps you misunderstand me,' K. hastened to add. 'I mean' – here K. stopped and looked round him for a chair. 'I suppose I may sit down?' he asked. 'It's not usual,' answered the Inspector. 'I mean,' said K. without further parley, 'that I am very surprised, of course, but when one has lived for thirty years in this world and had to fight one's way through it, as I have had to do, one becomes hardened to surprises and doesn't take them too seriously. Particularly the one this morning.' 'Why particularly the one this morning?' 'I won't say that I regard the whole thing as a joke, for the preparations that have been made seem too elaborate for that. The whole staff of the boarding-house would have to be involved, as well as all you people, and that would be past a joke. So I don't say that it's a joke.' 'Quite right,' said the Inspector, looking to see how many matches there were in the matchbox. 'But on the other hand,' K. went on, turning to everybody there, he wanted to bring in the three young men standing beside the photographs as well, 'on the other hand, it can't be an affair of any great importance either. I argue this from the fact that though I am accused of something, I cannot recall the slightest offence that might be charged against me. But that even is of minor importance, the real question is, who accuses me? What authority is conducting these proceedings? Are you officers of the Law? None of you has a uniform, unless your suit' – here he turned to Franz – 'is to be considered a uniform, but it's more like a tourist's outfit. I demand a clear answer to these questions, and I feel sure that after an explanation we shall be able to part from each other on the best of terms.' The Inspector flung the matchbox down on the table. 'You are labouring under a great delusion,' he said. 'These gentlemen here and myself have no standing whatever in this affair of yours, indeed we know hardly anything about it. We might wear the most official uniforms and your case would not be a penny the worse. I can't even confirm that you are charged with an offence, or rather I don't know whether you are. You are under arrest, certainly, more than that I do not know. Perhaps the warders have given you a different impression, but they are only irresponsible gossips. However, if I can't answer your questions, I can at least give you a piece of advice; think less about us and of what is going to happen to you, think more about yourself instead. And don't make such an outcry about your feeling innocent, it spoils the not unfavourable impression you make in other respects. Also you should be far more reticent, nearly everything you have just said could have been implied in your behaviour with the help of a word here and there, and in any case does not redound particularly to your credit.'

K. stared at the Inspector. Was he to be taught lessons in manners by a man probably younger than himself? To be punished for his frankness by a rebuke? And about the cause of his arrest and about its instigator was he to learn nothing?

He was thrown into a certain agitation, and began to walk up and down – nobody hindered him – pushed back his cuffs, fingered his shirt-front, ruffled his hair, and as he passed the three young men said: 'This is sheer nonsense!' Whereupon they turned towards him and regarded him sympathetically but gravely; at last he came to a stand before the Inspector's table. 'The advocate Hasterer is a personal friend of mine,' he said. 'May I telephone to him?' 'Certainly,' replied the Inspector, 'but I don't see what sense there would be in that, unless you have some private business of your own to consult him about.' 'What sense would there be in that?' cried K., more in amazement than exasperation. 'What kind of man are you, then? You ask me to be sensible and you carry on in the most senseless way imaginable yourself! It's enough to drive me mad. People first fall upon me in my own house and then lounge about the room and leave me to rack my brains in vain for the reason. What sense would there be in telephoning to an advocate when I'm supposed to be under arrest? All right, I won't telephone.'

'But do telephone if you want to,' replied the Inspector, waving an arm towards the entrance hall, where the telephone was, 'please do telephone.' 'No, I don't want to now,' said K., going over to the window. Across the street the party of three were still on the watch, and their enjoyment of the spectacle received its first slight check when K. appeared at the window. The two old people moved as if to get up, but the man at the back blandly reassured them. 'Here's a fine crowd of spectators!' cried K. in a loud voice to the Inspector, pointing at them with his finger. 'Go away,' he shouted across. The three of them immediately retreated a few steps, the two ancients actually took cover behind the younger man, who shielded them with his massive body and to judge from the movements of his lips was saying something which, owing to the distance, could not be distinguished. Yet they did not remove themselves altogether, but seemed to be waiting for the chance to return to the window again unobserved. 'Officious, inconsiderate wretches!' said K. as he turned back to the room again. The Inspector was possibly of the same mind, K. fancied, as far as he could tell from a hasty side-glance. But it was equally possible that the Inspector had not even been listening, for he had pressed one hand firmly on the table and seemed to be comparing the length of his fingers. The two warders sat on a chest draped with an embroidered cloth, rubbing their knees. The three young men were looking aimlessly round them with their hands on their hips. It was as quiet as in some deserted office. 'Come, gentlemen,' cried K., it seemed to him for the moment as if he were responsible for all of them, 'from the look of you this affair of mine seems to be settled. In my opinion the best thing now would be to bother no more about the justice or injustice of your be-

haviour and settle the matter amicably by shaking hands
on it. If you are of the same opinion, why, then —' and
he stepped over to the Inspector's table and held out his
hand. The Inspector raised his eyes, bit his lips, and
looked at K.'s hand stretched out to him; K. still believed
he was going to close with the offer. But instead he got
up, seized a hard round hat lying on Fräulein Bürstner's
bed, and with both hands put it carefully on his head, as
if he were trying it on for the first time. 'How simple it all
seems to you!' he said to K. as he did so. 'You think we
should settle the matter amicably, do you? No, no, that
really can't be done. On the other hand I don't mean to
suggest that you should give up hope. Why should you?
You are only under arrest, nothing more. I was requested
to inform you of this. I have done so, and I have also observed your reactions. That's enough for to-day, and we
can say good-bye, though only for the time being, naturally. You'll be going to the Bank now, I suppose?' 'To
the Bank?' asked K. 'I thought I was under arrest?' K.
asked the question with a certain defiance, for though his
offer to shake hands had been ignored, he felt more and
more independent of all these people, especially now that
the Inspector had risen to his feet. He was playing with
them. He considered the idea of running after them to
the front door as they left and challenging them to take
him prisoner. So he said again: 'How can I go to the
Bank, if I am under arrest?' 'Ah, I see,' said the Inspector, who had already reached the door. 'You have misunderstood me. You are under arrest, certainly, but that need
not hinder you from going about your business. You
won't be hampered in carrying on in the ordinary course
of your life.' 'Then being arrested isn't so very bad,' said
K., going up to the Inspector. 'I never suggested that it

was,' said the Inspector. 'But in that case it would seem there was no particular necessity to tell me about it,' said K., moving still closer. The others had drawn near too. They were all gathered now in a little space beside the door. 'It was my duty,' said the Inspector. 'A stupid duty,' said K. inflexibly. 'That may be,' replied the Inspector, 'but we needn't waste our time with such arguments. I was assuming that you would want to go to the Bank. As you are such a quibbler over words, let me add that I am not forcing you to go to the Bank, I was merely assuming that you would want to go. And to facilitate that, and render your arrival at the Bank as unobtrusive as possible, I have detained these three gentlemen here, who are colleagues of yours, to be at your disposal.' 'What?' cried K., gaping at the three of them. These insignificant anaemic young men, whom he had observed only as a group standing beside the photographs, were actually clerks in the Bank, not colleagues of his, that was putting it too strongly and indicated a gap in the omniscience of the Inspector, but they were subordinate employees of the Bank all the same. How could he have failed to notice that? He must have been very taken up with the Inspector and the warders not to recognize these three young men. The stiff Rabensteiner swinging his arms, the fair Kullich with the deep-set eyes, and Kaminer with his insupportable smile, caused by a chronic muscular twitch. 'Good morning!' said K. after a pause, holding out his hand to the three politely bowing figures. 'I didn't recognize you. Well, shall we go to our work now, eh?' The young men nodded, smiling and eagerly, as if they had been waiting all the time merely for this, but when K. turned to get his hat, which he had left in his room, they all fled one after the other to fetch it, which seemed to indicate a certain embarrassment. K. stood still and watched them through the two open doors; the languid Raben-steiner, naturally, brought up the rear, for he merely minced along at an elegant trot. Kaminer handed over the hat and K. had to tell himself expressly, as indeed he had often to do in the Bank, that Kaminer's smile was not intentional, that the man could not smile intentionally if he tried. Then Frau Grubach, who did not appear to be particularly conscious of any guilt, opened the front door to let the whole company out, and K. glanced down, as so often before, at her apron-string, which made such an unreasonably deep cut in her massive body. Down below he decided, his watch in his hand, to take a taxi so as to save any further delay in reaching the Bank, for he was already half an hour late. Kaminer ran to the corner to get a taxi, the other two were obviously doing their best to distract K., when suddenly Kullich pointed to the op-posite house door, where the tall man with the reddish, pointed beard was emerging into sight, and immediately, a little embarrassed at showing himself in his full height, retreated against the wall and leaned there. The old couple must be still coming down the stairs. K. was an-noyed at Kullich for drawing his attention to the man, whom he had already identified, indeed whom he had actually expected to see. 'Don't look across,' he said hur-riedly, without noticing how strange it must seem to speak in that fashion to grown-up men. But no explana-tion proved necessary, for at that moment the taxi ar-rived, they took their seats, and drove off. Then K. re-membered that he had not noticed the Inspector and the warders leaving, the Inspector had usurped his attention so that he did not recognize the three clerks, and the clerks in turn had made him oblivious of the Inspector.

That did not show much presence of mind, and K. resolved to be more careful in this respect. Yet in spite of himself he turned round and craned from the back of the car to see if he could perhaps catch sight of the Inspector and the warders. But he immediately turned away again and leaned back comfortably in the corner without even having attempted to distinguish one of them. Unlikely as it might seem, this was just the moment when he would have welcomed a few words from his companions, but the others seemed to be suddenly tired. Rabensteiner gazed out to the right, Kullich to the left, and only Kaminer faced him with his nervous grin, which, unfortunately, on grounds of humanity could not be made a subject of conversation.

That spring K. had been accustomed to pass his evenings in this way: after work whenever possible – he was usually in his office until nine – he would take a short walk, alone or with some of his colleagues, and then go to a beer hall, where until eleven he sat at a table patronized mostly by elderly men. But there were exceptions to this routine, when, for instance, the Manager of the Bank, who highly valued his diligence and reliability, invited him for a drive or for dinner at his villa. And once a week K. visited a girl called Elsa, who was on duty all night till early morning as a waitress in a cabaret and during the day received her visitors in bed.

But on this evening – the day had passed quickly, filled with pressing work and many flattering and friendly birthday wishes – K. resolved to go straight home. During every brief pause in the day's work he had kept this resolve in mind; without his quite knowing why, it seemed to him that the whole household of Frau Grubach had been thrown into great disorder by the events of the morning and that it was his task alone to put it right again. Once order was restored, every trace of these events would be obliterated and things would resume their old course. From the three clerks themselves nothing was to be feared, they had been absorbed once more in the great hierarchy of the Bank, no change was to be remarked in them. K. had several times called them singly and collectively to his room, with no other purpose than to observe them: each time he had dismissed them again with a quiet mind.

When at half-past nine he arrived at the house where he lived he found a young lad in the street doorway, standing with his legs wide apart and smoking a pipe. 'Who are you?' K. asked at once, bringing his face close to the lad's; one could not see very well in the darkness of the entrance. 'I'm the house-porter's son, sir,' said the lad, taking the pipe from his mouth and stepping aside. 'The house-porter's son?' asked K., tapping his stick impatiently on the ground. 'Do you want anything, sir? Shall I fetch my father?' 'No, no,' said K., and his voice had a reassuring note, as if the lad had done something wrong but was to be forgiven. 'It's all right,' he said and went on, yet before he climbed the stair he turned round for another look.

He had intended to go straight to his room, but as he wanted to speak to Frau Grubach he stopped instead to knock at her door. She was sitting darning at a table, on which lay a heap of old stockings. K. excused himself awkwardly for knocking so late, but Frau Grubach was most cordial and would hear of no apology, she was always glad to have a talk with him, he knew very well that he was her best and most valued boarder. K. looked round the room, it had reverted completely to its old state, the breakfast dishes which had stood that morning on the table by the window had apparently been cleared away. Women's hands are quietly effective, he thought. He himself might have smashed the dishes on the spot, but he certainly could never have quietly carried them away. He gazed at Frau Grubach with a certain gratitude. 'Why are you still working at this late hour?' he asked. They were both sitting at the table now, and from time to time K. buried one hand in the pile of stockings. 'There's a lot to do,' she said; 'during the day my time belongs to my boarders; for keeping my own things in order I have only the evenings.' 'I'm afraid I've been responsible for giving you extra work to-day.' 'How is that?' she asked, becoming more intent, the work resting in her lap. 'I mean the men who were here this morning.' 'Oh, that,' she said, resuming her composure, 'that didn't give me much to do.' K. looked on in silence while she took up her darning again. ('She seems surprised that I mentioned it,' he thought, 'she seems to think it not quite right that I should mention it. All the more need for me to do so. I couldn't mention it to anyone but this old woman.') 'It must certainly have made more work,' he said at last, 'but it won't happen again.' 'No, that can't happen again,' she said reassuringly, with an almost sorrowful smile. 'Do you really mean it?' asked K. 'Yes,' she said softly, 'and above all you mustn't take it too much to heart. Lots of things happen in this world! As you've spoken so frankly to me, Herr K., I may as well admit to you that I listened for a little behind the door and that the two war- ders told me a few things too. It's a matter of your happi- ness, and I really have that at heart, more perhaps than I should, for I am only your landlady. Well, then, I heard a few things, but I can't say that they were particularly bad. No. You are under arrest, certainly, but not as a thief is under arrest. If one's arrested as a thief, that's a bad business, but as for this arrest — It gives me the feeling of something very learned, forgive me if what I say is stupid, it gives me the feeling of something abstract which I don't understand, but which I don't need to understand either.'

'What you've just said is by no means stupid, Frau Grubach, at least I'm partly of the same opinion, except that I judge the whole thing still more severely and consider this assignation of guilt to be not only abstract but a pure figment. I was taken by surprise, that was all. If immediately on wakening I had got up without troubling my head about Anna's absence and had come to you without regarding anyone who tried to bar my way, I could have breakfasted in the kitchen for a change and could have got you to bring me my clothes from my room; in short, if I had behaved sensibly, nothing further would have happened, all this would have been nipped in the bud. But one is so unprepared. In the Bank, for instance, I am always prepared, nothing of that kind could possibly happen to me there, I have my own attendant, the general telephone and the office telephone stand before me on my desk, people keep coming in to see me, clients and clerks, and above all, my mind is always on my work and so kept on the alert; it would be an actual pleasure to me if a situation like that cropped up in the Bank. Well, it's past history now and I didn't really intend to speak about it again, only I wanted to hear your judgement, the judgement of a sensible woman, and I am very glad we are in agreement. But now you must give me your hand on it, an agreement such as this must be confirmed with a handshake.'

'Will she take my hand? The Inspector wouldn't do it,' he thought, gazing at the woman with a different, a critical eye. She stood up because he had stood up, she was a little embarrassed, for she had not understood all that he had said. And because of her embarrassment she said something which she had not intended to say and which was, moreover, rather out of place. 'Don't take it so much to heart, Herr K.,' she said with tears in her voice, forgetting, naturally, to shake his hand. 'I had no idea that I was taking it to heart,' said K., suddenly tired and seeing how little it mattered whether she agreed with him or not.

At the door he asked: 'Is Fräulein Bürstner in?' 'No,' replied Frau Grubach, and in giving this dry piece of information she smiled with honest if belated sympathy. 'She's at the theatre. Do you want to ask her something? Shall I give her a message?' 'Oh, I just wanted a word or two with her.' 'I'm afraid I don't know when she will be back; when she goes to the theatre she's usually late.' 'It's of no consequence,' said K., turning to the door, his head sunk on his breast. 'I only wanted to apologize to her for having borrowed her room to-day.' 'That's quite unnecessary, Herr K., you are too scrupulous, the Fräulein knows nothing about it, she hasn't been back since early this morning, everything has been put back in its place again too, see for yourself.' And she opened the door of Fräulein Bürstner's room. 'Thanks, I believe you,' said K., but went in through the open door all the same. The moon shone softly into the dark chamber. As far as one could see everything was really in its proper place, and the blouse was no longer dangling from the latch of the window. The pillows on the bed looked strangely high, they were lying partly in the moonlight. 'The Fräulein often comes home late,' said K., looking at Frau Grubach as if she were to blame for it. 'Young people are like that,' said Frau Grubach apologetically. 'Certainly, certainly,' said K., 'but it can go too far.' 'That it can,' said Frau Grubach, 'how right you are, Herr K.! In this case especially, perhaps. I have no wish to speak ill of Fräulein Bürstner, she is a dear, good girl, kind, decent, punctual, industrious, I admire all these qualities in her, but one thing is undeniable, she should have more pride, should keep herself more to herself. This very month I have met her twice already on outlying streets, and each time with a different gentleman. It worries me, and as sure as I stand here, Herr K., I haven't told anybody but you, but I'm afraid there's no help for it, I shall have to talk to the Fräulein herself about it. Besides, it isn't the only thing that has made me suspicious of her.' 'You're quite on the wrong track,' said K., with a sudden fury which he was scarcely able to hide, 'and you have obviously misunderstood my remark about the Fräulein, it wasn't meant in that way. In fact I frankly warn you against saying anything to the Fräulein, you're quite mistaken, I know the Fräulein very well, there isn't a word of truth in what you say. But perhaps I'm going too far myself. I don't want to interfere, you can say what you like to her. Good night.' 'Good night, Herr K.,' said Frau Grubach imploringly, hurrying after him to his door, which he had already opened, 'I don't really mean to say anything to the Fräulein yet, of course I'll wait to see what happens before I do anything, you're the only one I've spoken to, in confidence. After all it must be to the interest of all my boarders that I try to keep my house respectable, and that is all I'm anxious about in this case.' 'Respectable!' cried K., through the chink of the door; 'if you want to keep your house respectable you'll have to begin by giving me notice.' Then he shut the door and paid no attention to the faint knocking that ensued.

On the other hand, as he felt no desire to sleep, he resolved to stay awake and take the opportunity of noting at what hour Fräulein Bürstner returned. Perhaps when she did so it might still be possible, unsuitable though the hour was, to have a few words with her. As he lounged by the window and shut his tired eyes, he actually considered for a moment paying Frau Grubach out by persuading Fräulein Bürstner to give notice along with him. Yet he saw at once that this was an excessive reaction, and he began to suspect himself of wishing to change his lodgings because of that morning's events. Nothing could be more senseless, not to say useless and equivocal.

When he became weary of gazing out into the empty street he lay down on the sofa, after having slightly opened the door to the entrance hall, so that from where he was lying he might see at once anyone who came in. Until about eleven he lay quietly on the sofa smoking a cigar. But then he could not endure lying there any longer and took a step or two into the entrance hall, as if that would make Fräulein Bürstner come all the sooner. He felt no special desire to see her, he could not even remember exactly how she looked, but he wanted to talk to her now, and he was exasperated that her being so late should further disturb and derange the end of such a day. She was to blame, too, for the fact that he had not eaten any supper and that he had put off the visit to Elsa he had proposed making that evening. He could remedy both omissions still, it was true, by going straight to the wine restaurant where Elsa worked. He would do that later, he decided, after his talk with Fräulein Bürstner.

It was a little after half-past eleven when he heard

somebody on the stairs. Absorbed in his thoughts, he had been marching up and down the entrance hall for some time as if it were his own room, and now he fled behind his bedroom door. It was Fräulein Bürstner coming in. As she locked the front door she shivered and drew her silk shawl round her slim shoulders. In a minute she would be going into her room, where K. certainly could not intrude at such an hour; he would therefore have to speak to her now, but unfortunately he had forgotten to switch on the light in his room, so that if he were to emerge out of the darkness it would look as if he were waylaying her and at least must be somewhat alarming. No time was to be lost, so in his confusion he whispered through the chink of the door: 'Fräulein Bürstner.' It sounded like a prayer, not like a summons. 'Is anyone there?' asked Fräulein Bürstner, looking round with wide-open eyes. 'It's I,' said K., stepping forward. 'Oh, Herr K.!' said Fräulein Bürstner, smiling. 'Good evening,' and she held out her hand to him. 'I should like to have a word or two with you, will you allow me to do so now?' 'Now?' asked Fräulein Bürstner. 'Must it be now? A little unusual, isn't it?' 'I've been waiting for you ever since nine.' 'Well, I was at the theatre, you know, I had no idea you were waiting.' 'What I want to talk to you about didn't happen till to-day.' 'Oh, well, I have no serious objection, except that I am so tired I can scarcely stand on my feet. So come for a few minutes to my room. We can't possibly talk here, we should waken everybody, and I should loathe that for our own sakes even more than for theirs. Wait here till I have turned on the light in my room, and then you can switch off the light here.' K. did so, but waited until Fräulein Bürstner from her room again invited him, in a whisper, to come in. 'Take a seat,' she said, pointing to the sofa; she herself stood leaning against the foot of the bed in spite of her confessed weariness; she did not even take off her small but lavishly flower-bedecked hat. 'Well, what is it? I am really curious.' She crossed her ankles. 'Perhaps you will say,' began K., 'that there was no urgent need to speak about it now, but —' 'I never listen to preambles,' said Fräulein Bürstner. 'That makes it easier for me,' said K. 'This morning your room was thrown into some slight confusion and the fault was mine in a certain sense, it was done by strange people against my will, and yet as I have said the fault was mine; I want to beg your pardon for this.' 'My room?' asked Fräulein Bürstner, and she cast a critical eye round the room instead of looking at him. 'That is so,' said K., and now they gazed into each other's eyes for the first time. 'The actual manner in which it happened isn't worth mentioning.' 'But surely that's the really interesting part,' said Fräulein Bürstner. 'No,' said K. 'Well,' said Fräulein Bürstner, 'I don't want to pry into secrets; if you insist that it is uninteresting, I shall not argue the point. You have begged my pardon and I herewith freely grant it, particularly as I can find no trace of disturbance.' With her open palms pressed to her hips, she made a tour of the room. Beside the mat where the photographs were stuck she stopped. 'Look here,' she cried, 'my photographs are all mixed up! That is really horrid. So someone has actually been in my room who had no right to come in.' K. nodded and silently cursed the clerk Kaminer, who could never control his stupid, meaningless fidgeting. 'It is curious,' said Fräulein Bürstner, 'that I should be compelled now to forbid you to do something which you ought to forbid yourself to do, that is to enter my room in my absence.' 'But I have explained to you, Fräulein,' said K., going over to the photographs, 'that it was not I who interfered with these photographs; still, as you won't believe me, I have to confess that the Interrogation Commission brought three Bank clerks here, one of whom, and I shall have him dismissed at the first opportunity, must have meddled with your photographs.' In answer to the Fräulein's inquiring look he added: 'Yes, there was an Interrogation Commission here to-day.' 'On your account?' asked the Fräulein. 'Yes,' replied K. 'No!' cried the girl, laughing. 'Yes, it was,' said K. 'Why, do you think I must be innocent?' 'Well, innocent,' said the Fräulein, 'I don't want to commit myself, at a moment's notice, to a verdict with so many possible implications, besides, I don't really know you; all the same, it must be a serious crime that would bring an Interrogation Commission down on a man. Yet as you are still at large — at least I gather from the look of you that you haven't just escaped from prison — you couldn't really have committed a serious crime.' 'Yes,' said K., 'but the Interrogation Commission might have discovered, not that I was innocent, but that I was not so guilty as they had assumed.' 'Certainly, that is possible,' said Fräulein Bürstner, very much on the alert. 'You see,' said K., 'you haven't much experience in legal matters.' 'No, I haven't,' said Fräulein Bürstner, 'and I have often regretted it, for I would like to know everything there is to know, and law courts interest me particularly. A court of law has a curious attraction, hasn't it? But I'll soon remedy my ignorance in that respect, for next month I am joining the clerical staff of a lawyer's office.' 'That's excellent,' said K. 'Then you'll be able to help me a little with my case.' 'That may well be,' said Fräulein Bürstner; 'why not? I like to make good use of my knowledge.' 'But I mean it seriously,' said K., 'or at least half-seriously, as you yourself mean it. The case is too trifling to need a lawyer, but I could do very well with an adviser.' 'Yes, but if I am to be an adviser I must know what it's all about,' said Fräulein Bürstner. 'That's just the snag,' said K. 'I don't know that myself.' 'Then you've simply been making fun of me,' said Fräulein Bürstner, extravagantly disappointed, 'it was surely unnecessary to choose this late hour for doing so.' And she walked away from the photographs, where they had been standing together for a long time. 'But, Fräulein,' said K., 'I'm not making fun of you. Why won't you believe me? I have already told you all I know. In fact more than I know, for it was not a real Interrogation Commission. I called it that because I didn't know what else to call it. There was no interrogation at all, I was merely arrested, but it was a Commission.' Fräulein Bürstner sat down on the sofa and laughed again. 'What was it like, then?' she asked. 'Horrible,' said K., but he was no longer thinking of what he was saying, for he was completely taken up in staring at Fräulein Bürstner, who was leaning her head on one hand – her elbow was resting on the sofa cushions – while with the other she slowly caressed her hip. 'That's too general,' she said. 'What's too general?' asked K. Then he came to himself and asked: 'Shall I let you see how it happened?' He wanted to move about and yet he did not want to leave. 'I'm tired,' said Fräulein Bürstner. 'You came home so late,' said K. 'So you've gone the length of reproaching me, and I deserve it too, for I should never have let you in. And there was no need for it, either, that's evident.' 'There was a need for it. I'll make you see that in a minute,' said K. 'May I shift this night-table from beside your bed?' 'What an idea!' cried Fräulein Bürstner.

'Of course not!' 'Then I can't show you how it happened,' said K. in agitation, as if some immeasurable wrong had been inflicted upon him. 'Oh, if you need it for your performance, shift the table by all means,' said Fräulein Bürstner, and after a pause added in a smaller voice: 'I'm so tired that I'm letting you take too many liberties.' K. stationed the table in the middle of the room and sat down behind it. 'You must picture to yourself exactly where the various people are, it's very interesting. I am the Inspector, over there on the chest two warders are sitting, beside the photographs three young men are standing. At the latch of the window – just to mention it in passing – a white blouse is dangling. And now we can begin. Oh, I've forgotten about myself, the most important person; well, I'm standing here in front of the table. The Inspector is lounging at his ease with his legs crossed. his arm hanging over the back of the chair like this, an absolute boor. And now we can really begin. The Inspector shouts as if he had to waken me out of my sleep, he actually bawls; I'm afraid, if I am to make you understand, I'll have to bawl too, but it's only my name that he bawls.' Fräulein Bürstner, who was listening with amusement, put her finger to her lips to keep K. from shouting, but it was too late, K. was too absorbed in his role, he gave a long-drawn shout: 'Joseph K.,' less loud indeed than he had threatened, but with such explosive force that it hung in the air a moment before gradually spreading through the room.

Then there was a knocking at the door of the adjoining room, a loud, sharp, regular tattoo. Fräulein Bürstner turned pale but put her hand to her heart. K. was violently startled, it took him a moment or so to withdraw his thoughts from the events of the morning and the girl before whom he was acting them. No sooner had he come to himself than he rushed over to Fräulein Bürstner and seized her hand. 'Don't be afraid,' he whispered, 'I'll put everything right. But who can it be? There's only the living-room next door, nobody sleeps there.' 'No,' Fräulein Bürstner whispered in his ear, 'since yesterday a nephew of Frau Grubach has been sleeping there, a Captain. There was no other room he could have. I forgot all about it. Why did you have to shout like that? I'm all upset.' 'There's no need for that,' said K., and as she sank back on the cushions he kissed her on the brow. 'Away with you, away with you,' she said, hastily sitting up again, 'do go away, do go now, what are you thinking about, he's listening at the door, he hears everything. How you torment me!' 'I won't go,' said K., 'until you are a little calmer. Come to the far corner of the room, he can't hear us there.' She let herself be led there. 'You forget,' he said, ' that though this may mean unpleasantness for you, it is not at all dangerous. You know how Frau Grubach, who has the decisive voice in this matter, particularly as the Captain is her nephew, you know how she almost venerates me and absolutely believes everything I say. She is also dependent on me, I may say, for she has borrowed a fair sum of money from me. I shall confirm any explanation of our being together here that you like to invent, if it is in the least plausible, and I pledge myself to make Frau Grubach not only publicly accept it but also really and honestly believe it. You needn't consider me at all. If you want to have it announced that I assaulted you, then Frau Grubach will be informed accordingly and she will believe it without losing her confidence in me, she's so devoted to me.' Fräulein Bürstner, silent and somewhat limp, stared at the floor. 'Why shouldn't Frau Grubach believe that I assaulted you?' K. added. He was gazing at her hair, evenly parted, looped low, firmly restrained reddish hair. He expected her to look up at him, but she said without changing her posture: 'Forgive me, I was terrified at the sudden knocking rather than at any consequence of the Captain's being there. It was so still after you shouted and then there came these knocks, that was why I was so terrified, I was sitting quite near the door, too, the knocking seemed to be just beside me. I thank you for your offer, but I'm not going to accept it. I can bear the responsibility for anything that happens in my room, no matter who questions it. I'm surprised you don't see the insult to me that is implied in your suggestion, over and above your good intentions, of course, which I do appreciate. But now go, leave me to myself, I need more than ever to be left in peace. The few minutes you begged for have stretched to half an hour and more.' K. clasped her hand and then her wrist. 'But you aren't angry with me?' he asked. She shook his hand off and answered: 'No, no, I'm never angry with anybody.' He felt for her wrist again, she let him take it this time and so led him to the door. He was firmly resolved to leave. But at the door he stopped as if he had not expected to find a door there; Fräulein Bürstner seized this moment to free herself, open the door, and slip into the entrance hall, where she whispered: 'Now, please do come! Look' – she pointed to the Captain's door, underneath which showed a strip of light – 'he has turned on his light and is amusing himself at our expense.' 'I'm just coming,' K. said, rushed out, seized her, and kissed her first on the lips, then all over the face, like some thirsty animal lapping greedily at a spring of long-sought fresh water. Finally he kissed her on the neck, right on the throat, and kept his lips there for a long time. A slight noise from the Captain's room made him look up. 'I'm going now,' he said; he wanted to call Fräulein Bürstner by her first name, but he did not know what it was. She nodded wearily, resigned her hand for him to kiss, half turning away as if she were un-aware of what she did, and went into her room with down-bent head. Shortly afterwards K. was in his bed. He fell asleep almost at once, but before doing so he thought for a little about his behaviour, he was pleased with it, yet surprised that he was not still more pleased; he was seriously concerned for Fräulein Bürstner because of the Captain.

II

First Interrogation

K. WAS informed by telephone that next Sunday a short inquiry into his case would take place. His attention was drawn to the fact that these inquiries would now follow each other regularly, perhaps not every week, but at more frequent intervals as time went on. It was in the general interest, on the one hand, that the case should be quickly concluded, but on the other hand the interrogations must be thorough in every respect, although, because of the strain involved, they must never last too long. For this reason the expedient of these rapidly succeeding but short interrogations had been chosen. Sunday had been selected as the day of inquiry so that K. might not be disturbed in his professional work. It was assumed that he would agree to this arrangement, but if he preferred some other day they would meet his wishes to the best of their ability. For instance, it would be possible to hold the inquiries during the night, although then K. would probably not be fresh enough. At any rate they would expect him on Sunday, if K. had no objection. It was, of course, understood that he must appear without fail, he did not need to be reminded of that. He was given the number of the house where he had to go, it was a house in an outlying suburban street where he had never been before.

On receiving this message K. replaced the receiver without answering; his mind was made up to keep the appointment on Sunday, it was absolutely essential, the case was getting under way and he must fight it; this first interrogation must also be the last. He was still standing thoughtfully beside the telephone, when he heard behind him the voice of the Deputy Manager, who wanted to telephone and found K. barring his way. 'Bad news?' asked the Deputy Manager casually, not really wanting to know but merely eager to get K. away from the telephone. 'No, no,' said K., stepping aside but without going away. The Deputy Manager lifted the receiver and said, speaking round it while he waited to be connected: 'Oh, a word with you, Herr K. Would you do me the favour of joining a party on my yacht on Sunday morning? There will be quite a large party, doubtless some of your friends will be among them. Herr Hasterer, the advocate, among others. Will you come? Do come!' K. made an effort to attend to what the Deputy Manager was saying. It was of no slight importance to him, for this invitation from a man with whom he had never got on very well was a sort of friendly overture and showed how important K. had become to the Bank and how valuable his friendship or at least his neutrality had become to its second highest official. The Deputy Manager had definitely humbled himself in giving this invitation, even though he had merely dropped it casually while waiting at the telephone to get a connexion. Yet K. had to humble the man a second time, for he said: 'Thanks very much. But I'm sorry I have no time on Sunday, I have a previous engagement.' 'A pity,' said the Deputy Manager, turning to speak into the telephone, which had just been connected. It was not a short conversation, but in his confusion K. remained standing the whole time beside the instrument. Not till the Deputy Manager had rung off did he start out of his reverie in some alarm and say, to excuse his aimless loitering: 'I have just been rung up and asked to go

somewhere, but they forgot to tell me at what time.'
'Well, you can ring up and ask,' said the Deputy Manager. 'It isn't so important as all that,' said K., though in
saying so he crippled still further his first lame excuse.
The Deputy Manager, turning to go, went on making remarks about other topics. K. forced himself to answer, but
what he was really thinking was that it would be best to
go to the address at nine o'clock on Sunday morning,
since that was the hour at which all the law courts started
their business on week-days.

Sunday was dull. K. was tired, for he had stayed late
at his restaurant the night before because of a celebra-
tion; he had nearly overslept. In a great hurry, without
taking time to think or co-ordinate the plans which he
had drawn up during the week, he dressed and rushed
off, without his breakfast, to the suburb which had been
mentioned to him. Strangely enough, though he had little
time to study passers-by, he caught sight of the three
clerks already involved in his case: Rabensteiner, Kullich, and Kaminer. The first two were journeying in a
street-car which crossed in front of him, but Kaminer was
sitting on the terrace of a café and bent inquisitively over
the railing just as K. passed. All three were probably staring after him and wondering where their chief was rushing off to; a sort of defiance had kept K. from taking a
vehicle to his destination, he loathed the thought of chart-
ering anyone, even the most casual stranger, to help him
along in this case of his, also he did not want to be beholden to anyone or to initiate anyone even remotely in
his affairs, and last of all he had no desire to belittle himself before the Interrogation Commission by a too scrupulous punctuality. Nevertheless he was hurrying fast, so as
if possible to arrive by nine o'clock, although he had not

even been required to appear at any specified time.

He had thought that the house would be recognizable even at a distance by some sign which his imagination left unspecified, or by some unusual commotion before the door. But Juliusstrasse, where the house was said to be and at whose end he stopped for a moment, displayed on both sides houses almost exactly alike, high grey tenements inhabited by poor people. This being Sunday morning, most of the windows were occupied, men in shirt-sleeves were leaning there smoking or holding small children cautiously and tenderly on the window-ledges. Other windows were piled high with bedding, above which the dishevelled head of a woman would appear for a moment. People were shouting to one another across the street; one shout just above K.'s head caused great laughter. Down the whole length of the street at regular intervals, below the level of the pavement, were planted little general grocery shops, to which short flights of steps led down. Women were thronging into and out of these shops or gossiping on the steps outside. A fruit hawker who was crying his wares to the people in the windows above, progressing almost as inattentively as K. himself, almost knocked K. down with his push-cart. A phonograph which had seen long service in a better quarter of the town began stridently to murder a tune.

K. penetrated deeper into the street, slowly, as if he had now abundant time, or as if the Examining Magistrate might be leaning from one of the windows with every opportunity of observing that he was on the way. It was a little after nine o'clock. The house was quite far along the street, it was of unusual extent, the main entrance was particularly high and wide. It was clearly a service entrance for trucks, the locked doors of various warehouses surrounded the courtyard and displayed the names of firms some of which were known to K. from the Bank ledgers. Against his usual habit, he studied these external appearances with close attention and remained standing for a little while in the entrance to the courtyard. Near him a barefooted man was sitting on a crate reading a newspaper. Two lads were seesawing on a hand-barrow. A sickly young girl was standing at a pump in her night-jacket and gazing at K. while the water poured into her bucket. In one corner of the courtyard a line was stretched between two windows, where washing was already being hung up to dry. A man stood below superintending the work with an occasional shout.

K. turned towards the stairs to make his way up to the Interrogation Chamber, but then came to a standstill again, for in addition to this staircase he could see in the courtyard three other separate flights of stairs and besides these a little passage at the other end which seemed to lead into a second courtyard. He was annoyed that he had not been given more definite information about the room, these people showed a strange negligence or indifference in their treatment of him, he intended to tell them so very positively and clearly. Finally, however, he climbed the first stairs and his mind played in retrospect with the saying of the warder Willem that an attraction existed between the Law and guilt, from which it should really follow that the Interrogation Chamber must lie in the particular flight of stairs which K. happened to choose.

On his way up he disturbed many children who were playing on the stairs and looked at him angrily as he strode through their ranks. 'If I ever come here again,' he told himself, 'I must either bring sweets to cajole them with or else a stick to beat them.' Just before he reached the first floor he had actually to wait for a moment until a marble came to rest, two children with the lined, pinched faces of adult rogues holding him meanwhile by his trousers; if he had shaken them off he must have hurt them, and he feared their outcries.

His real search began on the first floor. As he could not inquire for the Interrogation Commission he invented a joiner called Lanz – the name came into his mind because Frau Grubach's nephew, the Captain, was called Lanz – and so he began to inquire at all the doors if a joiner called Lanz lived there, so as to get a chance to look into the rooms. It turned out, however, that that was quite possible without further ado, for almost all the doors stood open, with children running out and in. Most of the flats, too, consisted of one small single-windowed room in which cooking was going on. Many of the women were holding babies in one arm and working over the stove with the arm that was left free. Half-grown girls who seemed to be dressed in nothing but an apron kept busily rushing about. In all the rooms the beds were still occupied, sick people were lying in them, or men who had not wakened yet, or others who were resting there in their clothes. At the doors which were shut K. knocked and asked if a joiner called Lanz lived there. Generally a woman opened, listened to his question, and then turned to someone in the room, who thereupon rose from the bed. 'The gentleman's asking if a joiner called Lanz lives here.' 'A joiner called Lanz?' asked the man from the bed. 'Yes,' said K., though it was beyond question that the Interrogation Commission did not sit here and his inquiry was therefore superfluous. Many seemed convinced that it was highly important for K. to find the joiner Lanz, they took a long time to think it over, suggested some joiner who, however, was not called Lanz, or a name which had some quite distant resemblance to Lanz, or inquired of their neighbours, or escorted K. to a door some considerable distance away, where they fancied such a man might be living as a lodger, or where there was someone who could give better information than they could. In the end K. scarcely needed to ask at all, for in this way he was conducted over the whole floor. He now regretted his plan, which at first had seemed so practical. As he was approaching the fifth floor he decided to give up the search, said good-bye to a friendly young workman who wanted to conduct him farther, and descended again. But then the uselessness of the whole expedition filled him with exasperation, he went up the stairs once more and knocked at the first door he came to on the fifth story. The first thing he saw in the little room was a great pendulum clock which already pointed to ten. 'Does a joiner called Lanz live here?' he asked. 'Please go through,' said a young woman with sparkling black eyes, who was washing children's clothes in a tub, and she pointed with her damp hand to the open door of the next room.

K. felt as though he were entering a meeting-hall. A crowd of the most variegated people – nobody troubled about the newcomer – filled a medium-sized two-windowed room, which just below the roof was surrounded by a gallery, also quite packed, where the people were able to stand only in a bent posture with their heads and backs knocking against the ceiling. K., feeling the air too thick for him, stepped out again and said to the young woman, who seemed to have taken him up wrongly: 'I asked for a joiner, a man called Lanz.' 'I know,' said the woman, 'just go right in.' K. might not have obeyed if she had not come up to him, grasped the handle of the door, and said: 'I must shut this door after you, nobody else must come in.' 'Very sensible,' said K., 'but the room is surely too full already.' However, he went in again.

Between two men who were talking together just inside the door – the one was making with both outstretched hands a gesture as if paying out money while the other was looking him sharply in the eye – a hand reached out and seized K. It belonged to a little red-cheeked lad. 'Come along, come along,' he said. K. let himself be led off, it seemed that in the confused, swarming crowd a slender path was kept free after all, possibly separating two different factions; in favour of this supposition was the fact that immediately to right and left of him K. saw scarcely one face looking his way, but only the backs of people who were addressing their words and gestures to the members of their own party. Most of them were dressed in black, in old, long, and loosely hanging Sunday coats. These clothes were the only thing that baffled K., otherwise he would have taken the meeting for a local political gathering.

At the other end of the hall, towards which K. was being led, there stood on a low and somewhat crowded platform a little table, set at a slant, and behind it, near the very edge of the platform, sat a fat little wheezing man who was talking with much merriment to a man sprawling just behind him with his elbow on the back of the chair and his legs crossed. The fat little man now and then flung his arms into the air, as if he were caricaturing someone. The lad who was escorting K. found it difficult to announce his presence. Twice he stood on tiptoe and tried to say something, without being noticed by the man up above. Not till one of the people on the platform pointed out the lad did the man turn to him and bend down to hear his faltered words. Then he drew out his watch and with a quick glance at K., 'You should have been here an hour and five minutes ago,' he said. K. was about to answer, but had no time to do so, for scarcely had the man spoken when a general growl of disapproval followed in the right half of the hall. 'You should have been here an hour and five minutes ago,' repeated the man in a raised voice, casting another quick glance into the body of the hall. Immediately the muttering grew stronger and took some time to subside, even though the man said nothing more. Then it became much quieter in the hall than at K.'s entrance. Only the people in the gallery still kept up their comments. As far as one could make out in the dimness, dust, and reek, they seemed to be worse dressed than the people below. Some had brought cushions with them, which they put between their heads and the ceiling, to keep their heads from getting bruised.

K. made up his mind to observe rather than speak, consequently he offered no defence of his alleged lateness in arriving and merely said : 'Whether I am late or not, I am here now.' A burst of applause followed, once more from the right side of the hall. 'These people are easy to win over,' thought K., disturbed only by the silence in the left half of the room, which lay just behind him and from which only one or two isolated hand-claps had come. He considered what he should say to win over the whole of the audience once and for all, or if that were not possible, at least to win over most of them for the time being.

'Yes,' said the man, 'but I am no longer obliged to hear you now' – once more the muttering arose, this time unmistakable in its import, for, silencing the audience with a wave of the hand, the man went on: 'yet I shall make an exception for once on this occasion. But such a delay must not occur again. And now step forward.' Someone jumped down from the platform to make room for K., who climbed on to it. He stood crushed against the table, the crowd behind him was so great that he had to brace himself to keep from knocking the Examining Magistrate's table and perhaps the Examining Magistrate himself off the platform.

But the Examining Magistrate did not seem to worry, he sat quite comfortably in his chair and after a few final words to the man behind him took up a small note-book, the only object lying on the table. It was like an ancient school exercise-book, grown dog's-eared from much thumbing. 'Well, then,' said the Examining Magistrate, turning over the leaves and addressing K. with an air of authority, 'you are a house-painter?' 'No,' said K., 'I'm the junior manager of a large Bank.' This answer evoked such a hearty outburst of laughter from the Right party that K. had to laugh too. People doubled up with their hands on their knees and shook as if in spasms of coughing. There were even a few guffaws from the gallery. The Examining Magistrate, now indignant, and having apparently no authority to control the people in the body of the hall, proceeded to vent his displeasure on those in the gallery, springing up and scowling at them till his eyebrows, hitherto inconspicuous, contracted in great black bushes above his eyes.

The Left half of the hall, however, was still as quiet as ever, the people there stood in rows facing the platform and listened unmoved to what was going on up there as well as to the noise in the rest of the hall, indeed they actually suffered some of their members to initiate conversations with the other faction. These people of the Left party, who were not so numerous as the others, might in reality be just as unimportant, but the composure of their bearing made them appear of more consequence. As K. began his speech he was convinced that he was actually representing their point of view.

'This question of yours, Herr Examining Magistrate, about my being a house-painter – or rather, not a question, you simply made a statement – is typical of the whole character of this trial that is being foisted on me. You may object that it is not a trial at all; you are quite right, for it is only a trial if I recognize it as such. But for the moment I do recognize it, on grounds of compassion, as it were. One can't regard it except with compassion, if one is to regard it at all. I do not say that your procedure is contemptible, but I should like to present that epithet to you for your private consideration.' K. stopped and looked down into the hall. He had spoken sharply, more sharply than he had intended, but with every justification. His words should have merited applause of some kind, yet all was still, the audience were clearly waiting intently for what was to follow; perhaps in that silence an outbreak was preparing which would put an end to the whole thing. K. was annoyed when the door at the end of the hall opened at that moment, admitting the young washerwoman, who seemed to have finished her work; she distracted some of the audience in spite of all the caution with which she entered. But the Examining Magistrate himself rejoiced K.'s heart, for he seemed to be quite dismayed by the speech. Until now he had been on his feet, for he had been surprised by K.'s speech as he got up to rebuke the gallery. In this pause he resumed his seat, very slowly, as if he wished his action to escape re-mark. Presumably to calm his spirit, he turned over the note-book again.

'That won't help you much,' K. continued; 'your very note-book, Herr Examining Magistrate, confirms what I say.' Emboldened by the mere sound of his own cool words in that strange assembly, K. simply snatched the note-book from the Examining Magistrate and held it up with the tips of his fingers, as if it might soil his hands, by one of the middle pages, so that the closely written, blotted, yellow-edged leaves hung down on either side. 'These are the Examining Magistrate's records,' he said, letting it fall on the table again. 'You can continue read-ing it at your ease, Herr Examining Magistrate, I really don't fear this ledger of yours though it is a closed book to me, for I would not touch it except with my finger-tips and cannot even take it in my hand.' It could only be a sign of deep humiliation, or must at least be interpreted as such, that the Examining Magistrate now took up the note-book where it had fallen on the table, tried to put it to rights again, and once more began to read it.

The eyes of the people in the first row were so tensely fixed upon K. that for a while he stood silently looking down at them. They were without exception elderly men, some of them with white beards. Could they possibly be the influential men, the men who would carry the whole assembly with them, and did they refuse to be shocked out of the impassivity into which they had sunk ever since he began his speech, even although he had publicly humi-liated the Examining Magistrate?

'What has happened to me,' K. went on, rather more quietly than before, trying at the same time to read the faces in the first row, which gave his speech a somewhat distracted effect, 'what has happened to me is only a single instance and as such of no great importance, especially as I do not take it very seriously, but it is representative of a misguided policy which is being directed against many other people as well. It is for these that I take up my stand here, not for myself.'

He had involuntarily raised his voice. Someone in the audience clapped his hands high in the air and shouted: 'Bravo! Why not? Bravo! And bravo again!' A few men in the first row pulled at their beards, but none turned round at this interruption. K., too, did not attach any importance to it, yet felt cheered nevertheless; he no longer considered it necessary to get applause from everyone, he would be quite pleased if he could make the audience start thinking about the question and win a man here and there through conviction.

'I have no wish to shine as an orator,' said K., having come to this conclusion, 'nor could I if I wished. The Herr Examining Magistrate, no doubt, is much the better speaker, it is part of his vocation. All I desire is the public ventilation of a public grievance. Listen to me. Some ten days ago I was arrested, in a manner that seems ridiculous even to myself, though that is immaterial at the moment. I was seized in bed before I could get up, perhaps – it is not unlikely, considering the Examining Magistrate's statement – perhaps they had orders to arrest some housepainter who is just as innocent as I am, only they hit on me. The room next to mine was requisitioned by two coarse warders. If I had been a dangerous bandit they could not have taken more careful precautions. These warders, moreover, were degenerate ruffians, they deafened my ears with their gabble, they tried to induce me to bribe them, they attempted to get my clothes and underclothes from me under dishonest pretexts, they asked me to give them money ostensibly to bring me some breakfast after they had brazenly eaten my own breakfast under my eyes. But that was not all. I was led into a third room to confront the Inspector. It was the room of a lady whom I deeply respect, and I had to look on while this room was polluted, yes polluted, on my account but not by any fault of mine, through the presence of these warders and this Inspector. It was not easy for me to remain calm. I succeeded, however, and I asked the Inspector with the utmost calm – if he were here, he would have to substantiate that – why I had been arrested. And what was the answer of this Inspector, whom I can see before me now as he lounged in a chair belonging to the lady I have mentioned, like an embodiment of crass arrogance? Gentlemen, he answered in effect nothing at all, perhaps he really knew nothing; he had arrested me and that was enough. But that is not all, he had brought three minor employees of my Bank into the lady's room, who amused themselves by fingering and disarranging certain photographs, the property of the lady. The presence of these employees had another object as well, of course, they were expected, like my landlady and her maid, to spread the news of my arrest, damage my public reputation, and in particular shake my position in the Bank. Well, this expectation has entirely failed of its success, even my landlady, a quite simple person – I pronounce her name in all honour, she is called Frau Grubach – even Frau Grubach has been intelligent enough to recognize that an arrest such as this is no more worth taking seriously than some wild prank committed by stray urchins at the street corners. I repeat, the whole matter has caused me nothing but some unpleasantness and pass-

ing annoyance, but might it not have had worse consequences?'

When K. stopped at this point and glanced at the silent
Examining Magistrate, he thought he could see him
catching someone's eye in the audience, as if giving a
sign. K. smiled and said: 'The Herr Examining Magistrate sitting here beside me has just given one of you a
secret sign. So there are some among you who take your
instructions from up here. I do not know whether the sign
was meant to evoke applause or hissing, and now that I
have divulged the matter prematurely I deliberately give
up all hope of ever learning its real significance. It is a
matter of complete indifference to me, and I publicly em-
power the Herr Examining Magistrate to address his
hired agents in so many words, instead of making secret
signs to them, to say at the proper moment: Hiss now, or
alternatively: Clap now.'

The Examining Magistrate kept fidgeting on his chair
with embarrassment or impatience. The man behind him
to whom he had been talking bent over him again, either
to encourage him or to give him some particular counsel.
Down below, the people in the audience were talking in
low voices but with animation. The two factions who had
seemed previously to be irreconcilable were now drifting
together, some individuals were pointing their fingers at
K., others at the Examining Magistrate. The fuggy atmosphere in the room was unbearable, it actually prevented
one from seeing the people at the other end. It must have
been particularly inconvenient for the spectators in the
gallery, who were forced to question the members of the
audience in a low voice, with fearful side-glances at the
Examining Magistrate, to find out what was happening.
The answers were given as furtively, the informant gener-

ally putting his hand to his mouth to muffle his words.

'I have nearly finished,' said K., striking the table with his fist, since there was no bell. At the shock of the impact the heads of the Examining Magistrate and his adviser started away from each other for a moment. 'I am quite detached from this affair, I can therefore judge it calmly, and you, that is to say if you take this alleged court of justice at all seriously, will find it to your great advantage to listen to me. But I beg you to postpone until later any comments you may wish to exchange on what I have to say, for I am pressed for time and must leave very soon.'

At once there was silence, so completely did K. already dominate the meeting. The audience no longer shouted confusedly as at the beginning, they did not even applaud, they seemed already convinced or on the verge of being convinced.

'There can be no doubt –' said K., quite softly, for he was elated by the breathless attention of the meeting; in that stillness a subdued hum was audible which was more exciting than the wildest applause – 'there can be no doubt that behind all the actions of this court of justice, that is to say in my case, behind my arrest and to-day's interrogation, there is a great organization at work. An organization which not only employs corrupt warders, stupid Inspectors, and Examining Magistrates of whom the best that can be said is that they recognize their own limitations, but also has at its disposal a judicial hierarchy of high, indeed of the highest rank, with an indispensable and numerous retinue of servants, clerks, police, and other assistants, perhaps even hangmen, I do not shrink from that word. And the significance of this great organization, gentlemen? It consists in this, that innocent persons are accused of guilt, and senseless proceedings are put in motion against them, mostly without effect, it is true, as in my own case. But considering the senselessness of the whole, how is it possible for the higher ranks to prevent gross corruption in their agents? It is impossible. Even the highest Judge in this organization will have to admit corruption in his court. So the warders try to steal the clothes off the bodies of the people they arrest, the Inspectors break into strange houses, and innocent men, instead of being fairly examined, are humiliated in the presence of public assemblies. The warders mentioned certain depots where the property of prisoners is kept; I should like to see these depots where the hard-earned property of arrested men is left to rot, or at least what remains of it after thieving officials have helped themselves.'

Here K. was interrupted by a shriek from the end of the hall; he peered from beneath his hand to see what was happening, for the reek of the room and the dim light together made a whitish dazzle of fog. It was the washerwoman, whom K. had recognized as a potential cause of disturbance from the moment of her entrance. Whether she was at fault now or not, one could not tell. All K. could see was that a man had drawn her into a corner by the door and was clasping her in his arms. Yet it was not she who had uttered the shriek but the man; his mouth was wide open and he was gazing up at the ceiling. A little circle had formed round them, the gallery spectators near by seemed to be delighted that the seriousness which K. had introduced into the proceedings should be dispelled in this manner. K.'s first impulse was to rush across the room, he naturally imagined that everybody would be anxious to have order restored and the offending couple at least ejected from the meeting, but the first rows of the audience remained quite impassive, no one stirred and no one would let him through. On the contrary they actually obstructed him, someone's hand – he had no time to turn round – seized him from behind by the collar, old men stretched out their arms to bar his way, and by this time K. was no longer thinking about the couple, it seemed to him as if his freedom were being threatened, as if he were being arrested in earnest, and he sprang recklessly down from the platform. Now he stood eye to eye with the crowd. Had he been mistaken in these people? Had he over-estimated the effectiveness of his speech? Had they been disguising their real opinions while he spoke, and now that he had come to the conclusion of his speech were they weary at last of pretence? What faces these were around him! Their little black eyes darted furtively from side to side, their beards were stiff and brittle, and to take hold of them would be like clutching bunches of claws rather than beards. But under the beards – and this was K.'s real discovery – badges of various sizes and colours gleamed on their coat-collars. They all wore these badges, so far as he could see. They were all colleagues, these ostensible parties of the Right and the Left, and as he turned round suddenly he saw the same badges on the coat-collar of the Examining Magistrate, who was sitting quietly watching the scene with his hands on his knees. 'So!' cried K., flinging his arms in the air, his sudden en-lightenment had to break out, 'every man jack of you is an official, I see, you are yourselves the corrupt agents of whom I have been speaking, you've all come rushing here to listen and nose out what you can about me, making a pretence of party divisions, and half of you applauded merely to lead me on, you wanted some practice in fool-ing an innocent man. Well, much good I hope it's done you, for either you have merely gathered some amusement from the fact that I expected you to defend the innocent or else – keep off or I'll strike you,' cried K. to a trembling old man who had pushed quite close to him – 'or else you have really learned a thing or two. And I wish you joy of your trade.' He hastily seized his hat, which lay near the edge of the table, and amid universal silence, the silence of complete stupefaction, if nothing else, pushed his way to the door. But the Examining Magistrate seemed to have been still quicker than K., for he was waiting at the door. 'A moment,' he said. K. paused but kept his eyes on the door, not on the Examining Magistrate; his hand was already on the latch. 'I merely wanted to point out,' said the Examining Magistrate, 'that to-day – you may not yet have become aware of the fact – to-day you have flung away with your own hand all the advantages which an interrogation invariably confers on an accused man.' K. laughed, still looking at the door. 'You scoundrels, I'll give you all an interrogation yet,' he shouted, opened the door, and hurried down the stairs. Behind him rose the buzz of animated discussion, the audience had apparently come to life again and were analysing the situation like expert students.

III

In the Empty Interrogation Chamber – The Student – The Offices

DURING the next week K. waited day after day for a new summons, he would not believe that his refusal to be interrogated had been taken literally, and when no appointment was made by Saturday evening, he assumed that he was tacitly expected to report himself again at the same address and at the same time. So he betook himself there on Sunday morning, and this time went straight up through the passages and stairways; a few people who remembered him greeted him from their doors, but he no longer needed to inquire of anybody and soon came to the right door. It opened at once to his knock, and without even turning his head to look at the woman, who remained standing beside the door, he made straight for the adjoining room. 'There's no sitting to-day,' said the woman. 'Why is there no sitting?' he asked; he could not believe it. But the woman convinced him by herself opening the door of the next room. It was really empty and in its emptiness looked even more sordid than on the previous Sunday. On the table, which still stood on the platform as before, several books were lying. 'May I glance at the books?' asked K., not out of any particular curiosity, but merely that his visit here might not be quite pointless. 'No,' said the woman, shutting the door again, 'that isn't allowed. The books belong to the Examining Magistrate.' 'I see,' said K., nodding, 'these books are probably law books, and it is an essential part of the justice dispensed here that you should be condemned not only in innocence but also in ignorance.' 'That must be it,' said the woman, who had not quite understood him. 'Well, in that case I had better go again,' said K. 'Shall I give the Examining Magistrate a message?' asked the woman. 'Do you know him?' asked K. 'Of course,' replied the woman, 'my husband is the Law-Court Attendant, you see.' Only then did K. notice that the ante-room, which had contained nothing but a washtub last Sunday, now formed a fully furnished living-room. The woman remarked his surprise and said: 'Yes, we have free house-room here, but we must clear the room on the days when the Court is sitting. My husband's post has many disadvantages.' 'I'm not so much surprised at the room,' said K., looking at her severely, 'as at the fact that you're married.' 'Perhaps you're hinting at what happened during the last sitting, when I caused a disturbance while you were speaking,' said the woman. 'Of course I am,' said K. 'It's an old story by this time, and almost forgotten, but at the moment it made me quite furious. And now you say yourself that you're a married woman.' 'It didn't do you any harm to have your speech interrupted; what you said made a bad enough impression, to judge from the discussion afterwards.' 'That may be,' said K., refusing to be deflected, 'but it does not excuse you.' 'I stand excused in the eyes of everyone who knows me,' said the woman. 'The man you saw embracing me has been persecuting me for a long time. I may not be a temptation to most men, but I am to him. There's no way of keeping him off, even my husband has grown reconciled to it now; if he isn't to lose his job he must put up with it, for that man you saw is one of the students and will probably rise to great power yet. He's always after me, he was here today, just before you came.' 'It all hangs together,' said K., 'it doesn't surprise me.' 'You are anxious to improve things here, I think,' said the woman slowly and watchfully, as if she were saying something which was risky both to her and to K., 'I guessed that from your speech, which personally I liked very much. Though, of course, I only heard part of it, I missed the beginning and I was down on the floor with the student while you were finishing. It's so horrible here,' she said after a pause, taking K.'s hand. 'Do you think you'll manage to improve things?' K. smiled and twisted his hand round within her soft fingers. 'Actually,' he said, 'it isn't my place to improve things here, as you put it, and if you were to tell the Examining Magistrate so, let us say, he would either laugh at you or have you punished. As a matter of fact, I should never have dreamed of interfering of my own free will, and shouldn't have lost an hour's sleep over the need for reforming the machinery of justice here. But the fact that I am supposed to be under arrest forces me to intervene – I am under arrest, you know – to protect my own interests. But if I can help you in any way at the same time, I shall be very glad, of course. And not out of pure altruism, either, for you in turn might be able to help me.' 'How could I do that?' asked the woman. 'By letting me look at the books on the table there, for instance.' 'But of course!' cried the woman, dragging him hastily after her. They were old dog's-eared volumes, the cover of one was almost completely split down the middle, the two halves were held together by mere threads. 'How dirty everything is here!' said K., shaking his head, and the woman had to wipe away the worst of the dust with her apron before K. would put out his hand to touch the books. He opened the first of them and found an indecent picture. A man and a woman were sitting naked on a sofa, the obscene intention of the draughtsman was evident enough, yet his skill was so small that nothing emerged from the picture save the all-too-solid figures of a man and a woman sitting rigidly upright, and because of the bad perspective, apparently finding the utmost difficulty even in turning towards each other. K. did not look at any of the other pages, but merely glanced at the title-page of the second book, it was a novel entitled: *How Grete was Plagued by her Husband Hans.* 'These are the law books that are studied here,' said K. 'These are the men who are supposed to sit in judgement on me.' 'I'll help you,' said the woman. 'Would you like me to?' 'Could you really do that without getting yourself into trouble? You told me a moment ago that your husband is quite at the mercy of the higher officials.' 'I want to help you, all the same,' said the woman. 'Come, let us talk it over. Don't bother about the danger to me. I only fear danger when I want to fear it. Come.' She settled herself on the edge of the platform and made room for him beside her. 'You have lovely dark eyes,' she said, after they had sat down, looking up into K.'s face, 'I've been told that I have lovely eyes too, but yours are far lovelier. I was greatly struck by you as soon as I saw you, the first time you came here. And it was because of you that I slipped later into the meeting-hall, a thing I never usually do and which, in a manner of speaking, I am actually forbidden to do.' 'So this is all it amounts to,' thought K., 'she's offering herself to me, she's corrupt like the rest of them, she's tired of the officials here, which is understandable enough, and accosts any stranger who takes her fancy with compliments about his eyes.' And K. rose to his feet as if he had uttered his thoughts aloud and sufficiently explained his position. 'I don't think that could help me,' he said; 'to help me effectively one would need connexions with the higher officials. But I'm sure you know only the petty subordinates that swarm round here. You must know them quite well and could get them to do a lot, I don't doubt, but the utmost that they could do would have no effect whatever on the final result of the case. And you would simply have alienated some of your friends. I don't want that. Keep your friendship with these people, for it seems to me that you need it. I say this with regret, since to make some return for your compliment I must confess that I like you too, especially when you gaze at me with such sorrowful eyes, as you are doing now, though I assure you there's no reason whatever for it. Your place is among the people I have to fight, but you're quite at home there, you love this student, no doubt, or if you don't love him at least you prefer him to your husband. It's easy to tell that from what you say.' 'No,' she cried without getting up but merely catching hold of K.'s hand, which he did not withdraw quickly enough. 'You mustn't go away yet, you mustn't go with mistaken ideas about me. Could you really bring yourself to go away like that? Am I really of so little account in your eyes that you won't even do me the kindness of staying for a little longer?' 'You misunderstand me,' said K., sitting down, 'if you really want me to stay I'll stay with pleasure, I have time enough; I came here expecting to find the Court in session. All that I meant was merely to beg you not to do anything for me in this case of mine. But that needn't offend you when you consider that I don't care at all what the outcome of the case is, and that I would only laugh at it if I were sentenced. Assuming, that is, that the case will ever come to a proper conclusion, which I very much doubt. Indeed, I fancy that it has probably been dropped already or will soon be dropped, through the laziness or the forgetfulness or it may be even through the fears of those who are responsible for it. Of course it's possible that they will make a show of carrying it on, in the hope of getting money out of me, but they needn't bother, I can tell you now, for I shall never bribe anyone. That's something you could really do for me, however; you could inform the Examining Magistrate, or anyone who could be depended on to spread the news, that nothing will induce me to bribe these officials, not even any of the artifices in which they are doubtless so ingenious. The attempt would be quite hopeless, you can tell them that frankly. But perhaps they have come to that conclusion already, and even if they haven't, I don't much mind whether they get the information or not. It would merely save them some trouble and me, of course, some unpleasantness, but I should gladly endure any unpleasantness that meant a set-back for them. And I shall take good care to see that it does. By the way, do you really know the Examining Magistrate?' 'Of course,' said the woman. 'He was the first one I thought of when I offered you my help. I didn't know that he was only a petty official, but as you say so it must naturally be true. All the same, I fancy that the reports he sends up to the higher officials have some influence. And he writes out so many reports. You say that the officials are lazy, but that certainly doesn't apply to all of them, particularly to the Examining Magistrate, he's always writing. Last Sunday, for instance, the session lasted till late in the evening. All the others left, but the Examining Magistrate stayed on in the court-room, I had to bring a lamp for him, I only had a small kitchen lamp, but that was all he needed and he began to write straight away. In the meantime my husband came home, he was off duty on that particular Sunday, we carried back our furniture, set our room to rights again, then some neighbours arrived, we talked on by candlelight, to tell the truth we simply forgot the Examining Magistrate and went to bed. Suddenly, in the middle of the night, it must have been far into the night by then, I woke up, the Examining Magistrate was standing beside our bed shielding the lamp with his hand to keep the light from falling on my husband, a needless precaution, for my husband sleeps so soundly that not even the light would have wakened him. I was so startled that I almost cried out, but the Examining Magistrate was very kind, warned me to be careful, whispered to me that he had been writing till then, that he had come to return the lamp, and that he would never forget the picture I had made lying asleep in bed. I only tell you this to show that the Examining Magistrate is kept really busy writing reports, especially about you, for your interrogation was certainly one of the main items in the two days' session. Such long reports as that surely can't be quite unimportant. But besides that you can guess from what happened that the Examining Magistrate is beginning to take an interest in me, and that at this early stage – for he must have noticed me then for the first time – I could have great influence with him. And by this time I have other proofs that he is anxious to win my favour. Yesterday he sent me a pair of silk stockings through the student, who works with him and whom he is very friendly with, making out that it was a reward for cleaning the court-room, but that was only an excuse, for to do that is only my duty and my husband is supposed to be paid for it. They're beautiful stockings, look' – she stretched out her legs, pulled her skirts above her knees, and herself contemplated the stockings – 'they're beautiful stockings, but too fine, all the same, and not suitable for a woman like me.'

Suddenly she broke off, laid her hand on K.'s hand as if to reassure him, and said: 'Hush, Bertold is watching us.' K. slowly raised his eyes. In the door of the courtroom a young man was standing, he was small, his legs were slightly bowed, and he strove to add dignity to his appearance by wearing a short, straggling reddish beard, which he was always fingering. K. stared at him with interest, this was the first student of the mysterious judicature whom he had encountered, as it were, on human terms, a man, too, who would presumably attain to one of the higher official positions some day. The student, however, seemed to take not the slightest notice of K., he merely made a sign to the woman with one finger, which he withdrew for a moment from his beard, and went over to the window. The woman bent over K., and whispered: 'Don't be angry with me, please don't think badly of me, I must go to him now, and he's a dreadful-looking creature, just see what bandy legs he has. But I'll come back in a minute and then I'll go with you if you'll take me with you, I'll go with you wherever you like, you can do with me what you please. I'll be glad if I can only get out of here for a long time, and I wish it could be for ever.' She gave K.'s hand a last caress, jumped up, and ran to the window. Despite himself K.'s hand reached out after hers in the empty air. The woman really attracted him, and after mature reflection he could find no valid reason why he should not yield to that attraction. He dismissed without difficulty the fleeting suspicion that she might be trying to lay a trap for him on the instructions of the Court. In what way could she entrap him? Wasn't he still free enough to flout the authority of this Court once and for all, at least as far as it concerned him? Could he not trust himself to this trifling extent? And her offer of help had sounded sincere and was probably not altogether worthless. And probably there could be no more fitting revenge on the Examining Magistrate and his henchman than to wrest this woman from them and take her himself. Then some night the Examining Magistrate, after long and arduous labour on his lying reports about K., might come to the woman's bed and find it empty. Empty because she had gone off with K., because the woman now standing in the window, that supple, voluptuous warm body under the dark dress of rough material, belonged to K. and to K. alone.

After arguing himself in this way out of his suspicions, he began to feel that the whispered conversation in the window was going on too long, and started knocking on the table with his knuckles and then with his fist. The student glanced briefly at K. across the woman's shoulder, but did not let himself be put out, indeed moved closer to her and put his arms around her. She drooped her head as if attentively listening to him, and as she did so he kissed her loudly on the throat without at all interrupting his remarks. In this action K. saw confirmed the tyranny which the student exercised over the woman, as she had complained, and he sprang to his feet and began to pace up and down the room. With occasional side-glances at the student he meditated how to get rid of him as quickly as possible, and so it was not unwelcome to him when the fellow, obviously annoyed by his walking up and down, which had turned by now to an angry trampling, said: 'If you're so impatient, you can go away. There was nothing to hinder your going long ago, nobody would have missed you. In fact, it was your duty to go away, and as soon as I came in too, and as fast as your legs could carry you.' There was intense rage in these words, but there was also the insolence of a future official of the Court addressing an abhorrent prisoner. K. stepped up quite close to the student and said with a smile: 'I am impatient, that is true, but the easiest way to relieve my impatience would be for you to leave us. Yet if by any chance you have come here to study – I hear that you're a student – I'll gladly vacate the room and go away with this woman. I fancy you've a long way to go yet in your studies before you can become a Judge. I admit I'm not very well versed in the niceties of your legal training, but I assume that it doesn't consist exclusively in learning to make rude remarks, at which you seem to have attained a shameless proficiency.' 'He shouldn't have been allowed to run around at large,' said the student, as if seeking to explain K.'s insulting words to the woman. 'It was a mistake, I told the Examining Magistrate that. He should at least have been confined to his room between the interrogations. There are times when I simply don't understand the Examining Magistrate.' 'What's the use of talking?' said K., stretching out his hand to the woman. 'Come along.' 'Ah, that's it,' said the student, 'no, no, you don't get her,' and with a strength which one would not have believed him capable of he lifted her in one arm and, gazing up at her tenderly, ran, stooping a little beneath his burden, to the door. A certain fear of K. was unmistakable in this action, and yet he risked infuriating K. further by caressing and clasping the woman's arm with his free hand. K. ran a few steps after him, ready to seize and if necessary to throttle him, when the woman said: 'It's no use, the Examining Magistrate has sent for me, I daren't go with you; this little monster,' she patted the student's face, 'this little monster won't let me go.' 'And you don't want to be set free,' cried K., laying his hand on the shoulder of the student, who snapped at it with his teeth. 'No,' cried the woman, pushing K. away with both hands. 'No, no, you mustn't do that, what are you thinking of? It would be the ruin of me. Let him go, oh, please let him go! He's only obeying the orders of the Examining Magistrate and carrying me to him.' 'Then let him go, and as for you, I never want to see you again,' said K., furious with disappointment, and he gave the student a punch in the back that made him stumble for a moment, only to spring off more nimbly than ever out of relief that he had not fallen. K. slowly walked after them, he recognized that this was the first unequivocal defeat that he had received from these people. There was no reason, of course, for him to worry about that, he had received the defeat only because he had insisted on giving battle. While he stayed quietly at home and went about his ordinary vocations he remained superior to all these people and could clear any of them out of his path with a hearty kick. And he pictured to himself the highly comic situation which would arise if, for instance, this wretched student, this puffed-up hobbledehoy, this bandy-legged twiddle-beard, had to kneel by Elsa's bed some day wringing his hands and begging for favours. This picture pleased K. so much that he decided, if ever the opportunity came, to take the student along to visit Elsa.

Out of curiosity K. hurried to the door, he wanted to see where the woman was being carried off to, for the student could scarcely bear her in his arms across the street. But the journey was much shorter than that. Immediately opposite the door a flight of narrow wooden stairs led, as it seemed, to a garret, it had a turning so that one could not see the other end. The student was now carrying the woman up this stairway, very slowly, puffing and groaning, for he was beginning to be exhausted. The woman waved her hand to K. as he stood below, and shrugged her shoulders to suggest that she was not to blame for this abduction, but very little reluctance could be read into that dumb show. K. looked at her expressionlessly, as if she were a stranger, he was resolved not to betray to her either that he was disappointed or even that he could not easily get over any disappointment he might feel.

The two had already vanished, yet K. still stood in the doorway. He was forced to the conclusion that the woman not only had betrayed him, but had also lied in saying that she was being carried to the Examining Magistrate. The Examining Magistrate surely could not be sitting waiting in a garret. The little wooden stairway did not reveal anything, no matter how long one regarded it. But K. noticed a small card pinned up beside it, and crossing over he read in childish, unpractised handwriting: 'Law-Court Offices upstairs.' So the Law-Court offices were up in the attics of this tenement? That was not an arrangement likely to inspire much respect, and for an accused man it was reassuring to reckon how little money this Court could have at its disposal when it housed its offices in a part of the building where the tenants, who themselves belonged to the poorest of the poor, flung their useless lumber. Though, of course, the possibility was not to be ignored that the money was abundant enough, but that the officials pocketed it before it could be used for the purposes of justice. To judge from K.'s experience hitherto, that was indeed extremely probable, yet if it were so, such disreputable practices, while certainly humiliating to an accused man, suggested more hope for him than a merely pauperized condition of the Law Courts. Now K. could understand too why in the beginning they had been ashamed to summon him into their attics and had chosen instead to molest him in his lodgings. And how well-off K. was compared with the Magistrate, who had to sit in a garret, while K. had a large room in the Bank with a waiting-room attached to it and could watch the busy life of the city through his enormous plate-glass window. True, he drew no secondary income from bribes or peculation and could not order his attendant to pick up a woman and carry her to his room. But K. was perfectly willing to renounce these advantages, at least in this life.

K. was still standing beside the card when a man came up from below, looked into the room through the open door, from which he could also see the court-room, and then asked K. if he had seen a woman about anywhere. 'You are the Law-Court Attendant, aren't you?' asked K. 'Yes,' said the man. 'Oh, you're the defendant K., now I recognize you, you're welcome.' And he held out his hand to K., who had not expected that. 'But no sitting was announced for to-day,' the Law-Court Attendant went on, as K. remained silent. 'I know,' said K., gazing at the Attendant's civilian clothes, which displayed on the jacket, as the sole emblem of his office, two gilt buttons in addition to the ordinary ones, gilt buttons that looked as if they had been stripped from an old army coat. 'I was speaking to your wife a moment ago. She's not here now. The student has carried her up to the Examining Magistrate.' 'There you are,' said the Attendant, 'they're always carrying her away from me. To-day is Sunday too, I'm not supposed to do any work, but simply to get me away from the place they sent me out on a useless errand. And they took care not to send me too far away, so that I had some hopes of being able to get back in time if I hurried. And there was I running as fast as I could, shouting the message through the half-open door of the office I was sent to, nearly breathless so that they could hardly make me out, and back again at top speed, and yet the student was here before me, he hadn't so far to come, of course, he had only to cut down that short wooden staircase from the attics. If my job didn't depend on it, I would have squashed that student flat against the wall here long ago. Just beside this card. It's a daily dream of mine. I see him squashed flat here, just a little above the floor, his arms wide, his fingers spread, his bandy legs writhing in a circle, and splashes of blood all round. But so far it's only been a dream.' 'Is there no other remedy?' asked K., smiling. 'Not that I know of,' said the Law-Court Attendant. 'And now it's getting worse than ever, up till now he has been carrying her off for his own pleasure, but now, as I've been expecting for a long time, I may say, he's carrying her to the Examining Magistrate as well.' 'But isn't your wife to blame too?' asked K.; he had to keep a grip of himself while asking this, he still felt so jealous. 'But of course,' said the Law-Court Attendant, 'she's actually most to blame of all. She simply flung herself at him. As for him, he runs after every woman he sees. In this building alone he's already been thrown out of five flats he managed to insinuate himself into. And my wife is the best-looking woman in the whole tenement, and I'm in a position where I can't defend myself.' 'If that's how things stand, then there's no help, it seems,' said K. 'And why not?' asked the Law-Court Attendant. 'If he only got a good thrashing some time when he was after my wife – he's a coward, anyway – he would never dare to do it again. But I can't thrash him, and nobody else will oblige me by doing it, for they're all afraid of him, he's too influential. Only a man like you could do it.' 'But why a man like me?' asked K. in astonishment. 'You're under arrest, aren't you?' said the Law-Court Attendant. 'Yes,' said K., 'and that means I have all the more reason to fear him, for though he may not be able to influence the outcome of the case, he can probably influence the preliminary interrogations.' 'Yes, that's so,' said the Law-Court Attendant, as if K.'s view of the matter were as self-evident as his own. 'Yet as a rule none of our cases can be looked on as prejudiced.' 'I am not of that opinion,' said K., 'but that needn't prevent me from taking the student in hand.' 'I should be very thankful to you,' said the Law-Court Attendant rather formally; he did not appear really to believe that his heart's desire could be fulfilled. 'It may be,' K. went on, 'that some more of your officials, probably all of them, deserve the same treatment.' 'Oh yes,' said the Law-Court Attendant, as if he were assenting to a commonplace. Then he gave K. a confidential look, such as he had not yet ventured in spite of all his friendliness, and added: 'A man can't help being rebellious.' But the conversation seemed to have made him uneasy, all the same, for he broke it off by saying: 'I must report upstairs now. Would you like to come too?' 'I have no business there,' said K. 'You can have a look at the offices. Nobody will pay any attention to you.' 'Why, are they worth seeing?' asked K. hesitatingly, but suddenly feeling a great desire to go. 'Well,' said the Law-Court Attendant, 'I thought it might interest you.' 'Good,' said K. at last, 'I'll come with you.' And he ran up the stairs even more quickly than the Attendant.

On entering he almost stumbled, for behind the door there was an extra step. 'They don't show much consideration for the public,' he said. 'They show no consideration of any kind,' replied the Law-Court Attendant. 'Just look at this waiting-room.' It was a long passage, a lobby communicating by roughly hewn doors with the different offices on the floor. Although there was no window to admit light, it was not entirely dark, for some of the offices were not properly boarded off from the passage but had an open frontage of wooden rails, reaching, however, to the roof, through which a little light penetrated and through which one could see a few clerks as well, some writing at their desks, and some standing close to the rails peering through the interstices at the people in the lobby. There were only a few people in the lobby, probably because it was Sunday. They made a very modest showing. At almost regular intervals they were sitting singly along a row of wooden benches fixed to either side of the passage. All of them were shabbily dressed, though to judge from the expression of their faces, their bearing, the cut of their beards, and many almost imperceptible little details, they obviously belonged to the upper classes. As there was no hat-rack in the passage, they had placed their hats under the benches, in this probably following each other's example. When those who were sitting nearest the door caught sight of K. and the Law-Court Attendant, they rose in acknowledgement, followed in turn by their neighbours, who also seemed to think it necessary to rise, so that everyone stood as the two men passed. They did not stand quite erect, their backs remained bowed, their knees bent, they stood like street beggars. K. waited for the Law-Court Attendant, who kept slightly behind him, and said: 'How humbled they must be!' 'Yes,' said the Law-

Court Attendant, 'these are the accused men, all of them are accused of guilt.' 'Indeed!' said K. 'Then they're colleagues of mine.' And he turned to the nearest, a tall, slender, almost grey-haired man. 'What are you waiting here for?' asked K. courteously. But this unexpected question confused the man, which was the more deeply embarrassing as he was obviously a man of the world who would have known how to comport himself anywhere else and would not lightly have renounced his natural superiority. Yet in this place he did not know even how to reply to a simple question and gazed at the other clients as if it were their duty to help him, as if no one could expect him to answer should help not be forthcoming. Then the Law-Court Attendant stepped up and said, to reassure the man and encourage him: 'This gentleman merely asked what you are waiting for. Come, give him an answer.' The familiar voice of the Law-Court Attendant had its effect: 'I'm waiting —' the man started to say, but could get out no more. He had obviously begun by intending to make an exact reply to the question but did not know how to go on. Some of the other clients had drifted up and now clustered round, and the Law-Court Attendant said to them: 'Off with you, keep the passage clear.' They drew back a little, but not to their former places. Meanwhile the man had collected himself and actually replied with a faint smile: 'A month ago I handed in several affidavits concerning my case and I am waiting for the result.' 'You seem to put yourself to a great deal of trouble,' said K. 'Yes,' said the man, 'for it is my case.' 'Everyone doesn't think as you do,' said K. 'For example, I am under arrest too, but as sure as I stand here I have neither put in any affidavit nor attempted anything whatever of the kind. Do you consider such things necessary, then?' 'I can't exactly say,' replied the man, once more deprived of all assurance; he evidently thought that K. was making fun of him, and appeared to be on the point of repeating his first answer all over again for fear of making a new mistake, but under K.'s impatient eye he merely said: 'Anyhow, I have handed in my affidavits.' 'Perhaps you don't believe that I am under arrest?' asked K. 'Oh yes, certainly,' said the man, stepping somewhat aside, but there was no belief in his answer, merely apprehension. 'So you don't really believe me?' asked K. and, provoked without knowing it by the man's humility, he seized him by the arm as if to compel him to believe. He had no wish to hurt him, and besides had grasped him quite loosely, yet the man cried out as if K. had gripped him with glowing pincers instead of with two fingers. That ridiculous outcry was too much for K.; if the man would not believe that he was under arrest, so much the better; perhaps he actually took him for a Judge. As a parting gesture he gripped the man with real force, flung him back on the bench, and went on his way. 'Most of these accused men are so sensitive,' said the Law-Court Attendant. Behind them almost all the clients were now gathered round the man, whose cries had already ceased, and they seemed to be eagerly asking him about the incident. A warder came up to K., he was mainly recognizable by his sword, whose sheath, at least to judge from its colour, was of aluminium. K. gaped at it and actually put out his hand to feel it. The warder, who had come to inquire into the commotion, asked what had happened. The Law-Court Attendant tried to put him off with a few words, but the warder declared that he must look into this matter himself, saluted, and strutted on with hasty but very short steps, probably resulting from gout.

75

K. did not trouble his head for long over him and the people in the lobby, particularly as, when he had walked half-way down the lobby, he saw a turning leading to the right through an opening which had no door. He inquired of the Law-Court Attendant if this was the right way, the Law-Court Attendant nodded, and K. then turned into it. It troubled him that he had always to walk one or two paces ahead of the Law-Court Attendant, in a place like this it might look as if he were a prisoner under escort. Accordingly he paused several times to wait for the Law-Court Attendant, but the man always dropped behind again. At last K. said, to put an end to his discomfort: 'I've seen the place now, and I think I'll go.' 'You haven't seen everything yet,' said the Law-Court Attendant innocently. 'I don't want to see everything,' said K., who by now felt really tired. 'I want to get away, how does one reach the outside door?' 'You surely haven't lost your way already?' asked the Law-Court Attendant in surprise. 'You just go along here to the corner and then turn to the right along the lobby straight to the door.' 'You come too,' said K. 'Show me the way, there are so many lobbies here, I'll never find the way.' 'There's only the one way,' said the Law-Court Attendant reproachfully. 'I can't go back with you, I must deliver my message and I've lost a great deal of time through you already.' 'Come with me,' said K. still more sharply, as if he had at last caught the Law-Court Attendant in a falsehood. 'Don't shout like that,' whispered the Law-Court Attendant, 'there are offices everywhere hereabouts. If you don't want to go back by yourself, then come a little farther with me, or wait here until I've delivered my message, then I'll be glad to take you back.' 'No, no,' said K., 'I won't wait and you must come with me now.' K. had not yet even glanced round the place where he was, and only when one of the many wooden doors opened did he turn his head. A girl whose attention must have been caught by K.'s raised voice appeared and asked: 'What does the gentleman want?' A good way behind her he could also see a male figure approaching in the half-light. K. looked at the Law-Court Attendant. The man had said that nobody would pay any attention to him, and now two people were already after him, it wouldn't take much to bring all the officials down on him, demanding an explanation of his presence. The only comprehensible and acceptable one was that he was an accused man and wished to know the date of his next interrogation, but that explanation he did not wish to give, especially as it was not even in accordance with the truth, for he had come only out of curiosity or, what was still more impossible as an explanation of his presence, out of a desire to assure himself that the inside of this legal system was just as loathsome as its external aspect. And it seemed, indeed, that he had been right in that assumption, he did not want to make any further investigation, he was dejected enough by what he had already seen, he was not at that moment in a fit state to confront any higher official such as might appear from behind one of these doors, he wanted to quit the place with the Attendant, or, if need be, alone.

But his dumb immobility must make him conspicuous, and the girl and the Law-Court Attendant were actually gazing at him as if they expected some immense transformation to happen to him the next moment, a transformation which they did not want to miss. And at the end of the passage now stood the man whom K. had noticed before in the distance; he was holding on to the lintel of the low doorway and rocking lightly on his toes, like an eager spectator. But the girl was the first to see that K.'s behaviour was really caused by a slight feeling of faintness; she produced a chair and asked: 'Won't you sit down?' K. sat down at once and leaned his elbows on the arms of the chair so as to support himself still more securely. 'You feel a little dizzy, don't you?' she asked. Her face was close to him now, it had that severe look which the faces of many women have in the first flower of their youth. 'Don't worry,' she said. 'That's nothing out of the common here, almost everybody has an attack of that kind the first time they come here. This is your first visit? Well, then, it's nothing to be surprised at. The sun beats on the roof here and the hot roof-beams make the air dull and heavy. That makes this place not particularly suitable for offices, in spite of the other great advantages it has. But the air, well, on days when there's a great number of clients to be attended to, and that's almost every day, it's hardly breathable. When you consider, too, that all sorts of washing are hung up here to dry – you can't wholly prohibit the tenants from washing their dirty linen – you won't find it surprising that you should feel a little faint. But in the end one gets quite used to it. By the time you've come twice or thrice you'll hardly notice how oppressive it is here. Do you really feel better now?' K. did not answer, he realized too painfully the shame of being delivered into the hands of these people by his sudden weakness; besides, even now that he knew the cause of the faintness, it did not get any better but grew somewhat worse instead. The girl noticed this at once, and to help K. seized a bar with a hook at the end that leaned against the wall and opened with it a little skylight just above K. to let in the fresh air. Yet so much soot fell in that she had to close the skylight again at once and wipe

K.'s hands clean with her handkerchief, since K. was too far gone to attend to himself. He would have preferred to sit quietly there until he recovered enough strength to walk away, yet the less he was bothered by these people the sooner he would recover. But now the girl said: 'You can't stay here, we're causing an obstruction here' – K. glanced round inquiringly to see what he could be obstructing – 'if you like, I'll take you to the sick-room. Please give me a hand,' she said to the man standing in the door, who at once came over. But K. had no wish to go to the sick-room, he particularly wanted to avoid being taken any farther, the farther he went the worse it must be for him. 'I'm quite able to go away now,' he said and got up from his comfortable seat, which had relaxed him so that he trembled as he stood. But he could not hold himself upright. 'I can't manage it after all,' he said, shaking his head, and with a sigh sat down again. He thought of the Law-Court Attendant, who could easily get him out of the place in spite of his weakness, but he seemed to have vanished long ago. K. peered between the girl and the man standing before him, but could see no sign of the Law-Court Attendant.

'I fancy,' said the man, who was stylishly dressed and was wearing a conspicuously smart grey waistcoat ending in two long sharp points, 'that the gentleman's faintness is due to the atmosphere here, and the best thing to do – and what he would like best – is not to take him to the sick-room at all, but out of these offices altogether.' 'That's it!' cried K., in his excessive joy almost breaking into the man's words, 'I should feel better at once, I'm sure of it, I'm not so terribly weak either, I only need a little support under my arms, I won't give you much trouble, it isn't very far after all, just take me to the door, then I'll sit for a little on the stairs and recover in no time, for I don't usually suffer from these attacks, I was surprised myself by this one. I am an official too and accustomed to office air, but this is really more than one can bear, you said so yourselves. Will you have the goodness, then, to let me lean upon you a little, for I feel dizzy and my head goes round when I try to stand up by myself.' And he lifted his shoulders to make it easier for the two of them to take him under the arms.

Yet the man did not respond to his request but kept his hands quietly in his pockets and laughed. 'You see,' he said to the girl. 'I hit the nail on the head. It's only here that this gentleman feels upset, not in other places.' The girl smiled too, but tapped the man lightly on the arm with her finger-tips, as if he had gone too far in jesting like that with K. 'But dear me,' said the man, still laughing, 'I'll show the gentleman to the door, of course I will!' 'Then that's all right,' said the girl, drooping her pretty head for a moment. 'Don't take his laughter too much to heart,' she said to K., who had sunk again into vacant melancholy and apparently expected no explanation. 'This gentleman – may I introduce you?' (the gentleman waved his hand to indicate permission) – 'this gentleman, then, represents our Inquiries Department. He gives clients all the information they need, and as our procedure is not very well known among the populace, a great deal of information is asked for. He has an answer to every question, if you ever feel like it you can try him out. But that isn't his only claim to distinction, he has another, the smartness of his clothes. We – that's to say the staff – made up our minds that the Clerk of Inquiries, since he's always dealing with clients and is the first to see them, must be smartly dressed so as to create a good first impression. The rest of us, as you must have noticed at once from myself, are very badly and old-fashionedly dressed, I'm sorry to say; there isn't much sense anyhow in spending money on clothes, for we're hardly ever out of these offices, we even sleep here. But, as I say, we considered that in his case good clothes were needed. And as the management, which in this respect is somewhat peculiar, refused to provide these clothes, we took up a collection – some of the clients contributed too – and we bought him this fine suit and some others as well. Nothing more would be needed now to produce a good impression, but he spoils it all again by his laughter which puts people off.' 'That's how it is,' said the gentleman ironically, 'yet I don't understand, Fräulein, why you should tell this gentleman all our intimate secrets, or rather thrust them on him, for he doesn't want to hear them at all. Just look at him, he's obviously much too busy with his own thoughts.' K. felt no inclination even to make a retort, the girl's intentions were no doubt good, probably she merely wanted to distract him or give him a chance to pull himself together, but she had not gone the right way about it. 'Well, I needed to explain your laughter to him,' the girl said. 'It sounded insulting.' 'I fancy he would overlook much worse insults if I would only take him out of here.' K. said nothing, he did not even look up, he suffered the two of them to discuss him as if he were an inanimate object, indeed he actually preferred that. Then suddenly he felt the man's hand under one arm and the girl's hand under the other. 'Up you get, you feeble fellow,' said the man. 'Many thanks to both of you,' said K., joyfully surprised, and he got up slowly and himself moved these strangers' hands to the places where he felt most in need of support. 'It must seem to you,' said the girl softly in K.'s ear as they neared the passage, 'as if I were greatly concerned to show the Clerk of Inquiries in a good light, but you can believe me, I only wanted to speak the truth about him. He isn't a hard-hearted man. He isn't obliged to help sick people out of here, and yet he does so, as you can see. Perhaps none of us are hard-hearted, we should be glad to help everybody, yet as Law-Court officials we easily take on the appearance of being hard-hearted and of not wishing to help. That really worries me.' 'Wouldn't you like to sit down here for a little?' asked the Clerk of Inquiries; they were out in the main lobby now and just opposite the client to whom K. had first spoken. K. felt almost ashamed before the man, he had stood so erect before him the first time; now it took a couple of people to hold him up, the Clerk of Inquiries was balancing his hat on the tips of his fingers, his hair was in disorder and hung down over his sweat-drenched forehead. But the client seemed to see nothing of all this, he stood up humbly before the Clerk of Inquiries (who stared through him) and merely sought to excuse his presence. 'I know,' he said, 'that the decision on my affidavits cannot be expected to-day. But I came all the same, I thought that I might as well wait here, it is Sunday, I have lots of time and here I disturb nobody.' 'You needn't be so apologetic,' replied the Clerk of Inquiries. 'Your solicitude is entirely to be commended; you're taking up extra room here, I admit, but so long as you don't inconvenience me, I shan't hinder you at all from following the progress of your case as closely as you please. When one sees so many people who scandalously neglect their duty, one learns to have patience with men like you. You may sit down.' 'How well he knows how to talk to clients!' whispered the girl. K. nodded but immediately gave a violent start when the Clerk of Inquiries asked again: 'Wouldn't you like to sit down here?' 'No,' said K. 'I don't want a rest.' He said this with the utmost possible decision, though in reality he would have been very glad to sit down. He felt as if he were seasick. He felt he was on a ship rolling in heavy seas. It was as if the waters were dashing against the wooden walls, as if the roaring of breaking waves came from the end of the passage, as if the passage itself pitched and rolled and the waiting clients on either side rose and fell with it. All the more incomprehensible, therefore, was the composure of the girl and the man who were escorting him. He was delivered into their hands, if they let him go he must fall like a block of wood. They kept glancing around with their sharp little eyes. K. was aware of their regular advance without himself taking part in it, for he was now being almost carried from step to step. At last he noticed that they were talking to him, but he could not make out what they were saying, he heard nothing but the din that filled the whole place, through which a shrill unchanging note like that of a siren seemed to ring. 'Louder,' he whispered with bowed head, and he was ashamed, for he knew that they were speaking loudly enough, though he could not make out what they said. Then, as if the wall in front of him had been split in two, a current of fresh air was at last wafted towards him, and he heard a voice near him saying: 'First he wants to go, then you tell him a hundred times that the door is in front of him and he makes no move to go.' K. saw that he was standing before the outside door, which the girl had opened. It was as if all his energies returned at one bound; to get a foretaste of freedom he set his feet at once on a step of the staircase and from there said good-bye to his conductors, who bent their heads down to hear him. 'Many thanks,' he said several times, then shook hands with them again and again and only left off when he thought he saw that they, accustomed as they were to the office air, felt ill in the relatively fresh air that came up the stairway. They could scarcely answer him and the girl might have fallen if K. had not shut the door with the utmost haste. K. stood still for a moment, put his hair to rights with the help of his pocket mirror, lifted up his hat, which lay on the step below him – the Clerk of Inquiries must have thrown it there – and then leapt down the stairs so buoyantly and with such long strides that he became almost afraid of his own reaction. His usually sound constitution had never provided him with such surprises before. Could his body possibly be meditating a revolution and preparing to spring something new on him, since he had borne with the old state of affairs so effortlessly? He did not entirely reject the idea of going to consult a doctor at the first opportunity, in any case he had made up his mind – and there he could consult himself – to spend all his Sunday mornings in future to better purpose.

IV

Fräulein Bürstner's Friend

IN the next few days K. found it impossible to exchange even a word with Fräulein Bürstner. He tried to get hold of her by every means he could think of, but she always managed to elude him. He went straight home from his office and sat on the sofa in his room, with the light out and the door open, concentrating his attention on the entrance hall. If the maid on her way past shut the door of his apparently empty room, he would get up after a while and open it again. He rose every morning an hour earlier than usual on the chance of catching Fräulein Bürstner alone, before she went to her work. But none of these stratagems succeeded. Then he wrote a letter to her, sending it both to her office and to her house address, in which he once more tried to justify his behaviour, offered to make any reparation required, promised never to overstep the bounds that she should prescribe for him, and begged her to give him an opportunity of merely speaking to her, more especially as he could arrange nothing with Frau Grubach until he had first consulted with her, concluding with the information that next Sunday he would wait in his room all day for some sign that she was prepared either to grant his request or at least to explain why, even although he was pledging his word to defer to her in everything, she would not grant it. His letters were not returned, but neither were they answered. On Sunday, however, he was given a sign whose meaning was sufficiently clear. In the early morning K. observed through the keyhole of his door an unusual commotion in the entrance hall, which soon explained itself. A teacher of French, she was a German girl called Montag, a sickly, pale girl with a slight limp who till now had occupied a room of her own, was apparently moving into Fräulein Bürstner's room. For hours she kept on trailing through the entrance hall. She seemed to be always forgetting some article of underwear or a scrap of drapery or a book that necessitated a special journey to carry it into the new apartment.

When Frau Grubach brought in his breakfast – since K. had flown out at her she had devoted herself to performing even the most trifling services for him – K. could not help breaking the silence between them for the first time. 'Why is there such a row in the entrance hall to-day?' he asked as he poured out his coffee. 'Couldn't it be put off to some other time? Must the place be spring-cleaned on a Sunday?' Although K. did not glance up at Frau Grubach, he could observe that she heaved a sigh of relief. These questions, though harsh, she construed as forgiveness or as an approach towards forgiveness. 'The place is not being spring-cleaned, Herr K.,' she said. 'Fräulein Montag is moving in with Fräulein Bürstner and shifting her things across.' She said no more, waiting first to see how K. would take it and if he would allow her to go on. But K. kept her on the rack, reflectively stirring his coffee and remaining silent. Then he looked up at her and said: 'Have you given up your previous suspicions of Fräulein Bürstner?' 'Herr K.,' cried Frau Grubach, who had been merely waiting for this question and now stretched out her clasped hands towards him, 'you took a casual remark of mine far too seriously. It never entered my head to offend you or anyone else.

You have surely known me long enough, Herr K., to be certain of that. You have no idea how I have suffered during these last few days! I to speak ill of my boarders! And you, Herr K., believed it! And said I should give you notice! Give you notice!' The last ejaculation was already stifled in her sobs, she raised her apron to her face and wept aloud.

'Please don't cry, Frau Grubach,' said K., looking out through the window, he was really thinking of Fräulein Bürstner and of the fact that she had taken a strange girl into her room. 'Please don't cry,' he said again as he turned back to the room and found Frau Grubach still weeping. 'I didn't mean what I said so terribly seriously either. We misunderstood each other. That can happen occasionally even between old friends.' Frau Grubach took her apron from her eyes to see whether K. was really appeased. 'Come now, that's all there was to it,' said K., and then ventured to add, since to judge from Frau Grubach's expression her nephew the Captain could not have divulged anything: 'Do you really believe that I would turn against you because of a strange girl?' 'That's just it, Herr K.,' said Frau Grubach, it was her misfortune that as soon as she felt relieved in her mind she immediately said something tactless, 'I kept asking myself: Why should Herr K. bother himself so much about Fräulein Bürstner? Why should he quarrel with me because of her, though he knows that every cross word from him makes me lose my sleep? And I said nothing about the girl that I hadn't seen with my own eyes.' K. made no reply to this, he should have driven her from the room at the very first word, and he did not want to do that. He contented himself with drinking his coffee and leaving Frau Grubach to feel that her presence was burdensome.

Outside he could hear again the trailing step of Fräulein Montag as she limped from end to end of the entrance hall. 'Do you hear that?' asked K., indicating the door. 'Yes,' said Frau Grubach, sighing, 'I offered to help her and to order the maid to help too, but she's self-willed, she insists on moving everything herself. I'm surprised at Fräulein Bürstner. I often regret having Fräulein Montag as a boarder, but now Fräulein Bürstner is actually taking her into her own room.' 'You mustn't worry about that,' said K., crushing with the spoon the sugar left at the bottom of his cup. 'Does it mean any loss to you?' 'No,' said Frau Grubach, 'in itself it's quite welcome to me, I am left with an extra room, and I can put my nephew, the Captain, there. I've been bothered in case he might have disturbed you these last few days, for I had to let him occupy the living-room next door. He's not very careful.' 'What an idea!' said K., getting up. 'There's no question of that. You really seem to think I'm hypersensitive because I can't stand Fräulein Montag's trailings to and fro – there she goes again, coming back this time.' Frau Grubach felt quite helpless. 'Shall I tell her, Herr K., to put off moving the rest of her things until later? If you like I'll do so at once.' 'But she's got to move into Fräulein Bürstner's room!' cried K. 'Yes,' said Frau Grubach, she could not quite make out what K. meant. 'Well then,' said K., 'she must surely be allowed to shift her things there.' Frau Grubach simply nodded. Her dumb helplessness, which outwardly had the look of simple obstinacy, exasperated K. still more. He began to walk up and down from the window to the door and back again, and by doing that he hindered Frau Grubach from being able to slip out of the room, which she would probably have done.

K. had just reached the door again when there was a
knock. It was the maid, who announced that Fräulein
Montag would like a word or two with Herr K. and that
she accordingly begged him to come to the dining-room,
where she was waiting for him. K. listened grimly to the
message, then he turned an almost sarcastic eye on the
horrified Frau Grubach. His look seemed to say that he
had long foreseen this invitation of Fräulein Montag's,
and that it accorded very well with all the persecution he
had had to endure that Sunday morning from Frau Grubach's boarders. He sent the maid back with the information that he would come at once, then went to his wardrobe to change his coat, and in answer to Frau Grubach,
who was softly lamenting over the behaviour of the im-
portunate Fräulein Montag, had nothing to say but to
request her to remove his breakfast tray. 'Why, you've
scarcely touched anything,' said Frau Grubach. 'Oh, take
it away, all the same,' cried K. It seemed to him as if
Fräulein Montag were mixed up with everything, it was
too sickening.

As he crossed the entrance hall he glanced at the closed
door of Fräulein Bürstner's room. Still, he had not been
invited there, but to the dining-room, where he flung
open the door without knocking.

It was a very long narrow room with one large window.
There was only enough space in it to wedge two cupboards at an angle on either side of the door, the rest of
the room was completely taken up by the long dining-
table, which began near the door and reached to the very
window, making it almost inaccessible. The table was
already laid, and for many people too, since on Sunday
almost all the boarders had their midday dinner in the
house.

When K. entered, Fräulein Montag advanced from the window along one side of the table to meet him. They greeted each other in silence. Then Fräulein Montag said, holding her head very erect as usual: 'I don't know if you know who I am.' K. stared at her with contracted brows. 'Of course I do,' he said, 'you've been staying quite a long time with Frau Grubach, haven't you?' 'But you don't take much interest in the boarders, I fancy,' said Fräulein Montag. 'No,' said K. 'Won't you take a seat?' asked Fräulein Montag. In silence they pulled out two chairs at the very end of the table and sat down opposite each other. But Fräulein Montag immediately stood up again, for she had left her little handbag lying on the window-sill and now went to fetch it; she trailed for it along the whole length of the room. As she came back, swinging the bag lightly in her hand, she said: 'I've been asked by my friend to say something to you, that's all. She wanted to come herself, but she is feeling a little unwell to-day. She asks you to excuse her and listen to me instead. She would not have said anything more to you, in any case, than I am going to say. On the contrary, I fancy that I can actually tell you more, as I am relatively impartial. Don't you think so too?'

'Well, what is there to say?' replied K., who was weary of seeing Fräulein Montag staring so fixedly at his lips. Her stare was already trying to dominate any words he might utter. 'Fräulein Bürstner evidently refuses to grant me the personal interview I asked for.' 'That is so,' said Fräulein Montag, 'or rather that isn't it at all, you put it much too harshly. Surely, in general, interviews are neither deliberately accepted nor refused. But it may happen that one sees no point in an interview, and that is the case here. After that last remark of yours I can speak frankly, I take it. You have begged my friend to communicate with you by letter or by word of mouth. Now, my friend, at least that is what I must assume, knows what this conversation would be about, and is therefore convinced, for reasons of which I am ignorant, that it would be to nobody's benefit if it actually took place. To tell the truth, she did not mention the matter to me until yesterday and only in passing, she said among other things that you could not attach very much importance to this interview either, for it could only have been by accident that you hit on the idea, and that even without a specific explanation you would soon come to see how silly the whole affair was, if indeed you didn't see that already. I told her that that might be quite true, but that I considered it advisable, if the matter were to be completely cleared up, that you should receive an explicit answer. I offered myself as an intermediary, and after some hesitation my friend yielded to my persuasions. But I hope that I have served your interests, too, for the slightest uncertainty even in the most trifling matter is always a worry, and when, as in this case, it can be easily dispelled, it is better that that should be done at once.' 'Thank you,' said K., and he slowly rose to his feet, glanced at Fräulein Montag, then at the table, then out through the window – the sun was shining on the house opposite – and walked to the door. Fräulein Montag followed him for a few steps, as if she did not quite trust him. But at the door they had both to draw back, for it opened and Captain Lanz entered. This was the first time that K. had seen him close at hand. He was a tall man in the early forties with a tanned, fleshy face. He made a slight bow which included K. as well as Fräulein Montag, then went up to her and respectfully kissed her hand. His movements were easy. His politeness towards Fräulein Montag was in striking contrast to the treatment which she had received from K. All the same, Fräulein Montag did not seem to be offended with K., for she actually purposed, K. fancied, to introduce him to the Captain. But K. did not wish to be introduced, he was not in the mind to be polite either to the Captain or to Fräulein Montag, the hand-kissing had in his eyes turned the pair of them into accomplices who, under a cloak of the utmost amiability and altruism, were seeking to bar his way to Fräulein Bürstner. Yet he fancied that he could see even more than that, he recognized that Fräulein Montag had chosen a very good if somewhat two-edged weapon. She had exaggerated the importance of the connexion between Fräulein Bürstner and K., she had exaggerated above all the importance of the interview he had asked for, and she had tried at the same time so to manipulate things as to make it appear that it was K. who was exaggerating. She would find that she was deceived. K. wished to exaggerate nothing, he knew that Fräulein Bürstner was an ordinary little typist who could not resist him for long. In coming to this conclusion he deliberately left out of account what Frau Grubach had told him about Fräulein Bürstner. He was thinking all this as he quitted the room with a curt word of leave-taking. He made straight for his own room, but a slight titter from Fräulein Montag, coming from the dining-room behind him, put it into his head that perhaps he could provide a surprise for the pair of them, the Captain as well as Fräulein Montag. He glanced round and listened to make sure that no interruption was likely from any of the adjacent rooms, all was still, nothing was to be heard but a murmur of voices in the dining-room and the voice of Frau Grubach coming from the passage leading to the kitchen. The opportunity seemed excellent, and K. went over to Fräulein Bürstner's door and knocked softly. When nothing happened he knocked again, but again no answer came. Was she sleeping? Or was she really unwell? Or was she pretending she wasn't there, knowing that it could only be K. who was knocking so softly? K. assumed that she was pretending and knocked more loudly, and at last, as his knocking had no result, cautiously opened the door, not without a feeling that he was doing something wrong and even more useless than wrong. There was nobody in the room. Moreover it had scarcely any resemblance now to the room which K. had seen. Against the wall two beds stood next to each other, three chairs near the door were heaped with dresses and underclothes, a wardrobe was standing open. Fräulein Bürstner had apparently gone out while Fräulein Montag was saying her piece in the dining-room. K. was not very much taken aback, he had hardly expected at this stage to get hold of Fräulein Bürstner so easily, he had made this attempt, indeed, mainly to annoy Fräulein Montag. Yet the shock was all the greater when, as he was shutting the door again, he saw Fräulein Montag and the Captain standing talking together in the open door of the dining-room. They had perhaps been standing there all the time, they scrupulously avoided all appearance of having been observing him, they talked in low voices, following K.'s movements only with the abstracted gaze one has for people passing when one is deep in conversation. All the same, their glances weighed heavily upon K., and he made what haste he could to his room, keeping close against the wall.

V

The Whipper

A FEW evenings later K. was passing along the Bank corridor from his office to the main staircase – he was almost the last to leave, only two clerks in the dispatch department were still at work by the dim light of a glow lamp – when he heard convulsive sighs behind a door, which he had always taken to be the door of a lumber-room, although he had never opened it. He stopped in astonishment and listened to make sure that he had not been mistaken – all was still, yet in a little while the sighing began again. At first he thought of fetching one of the dispatch clerks, he might need a witness, but then he was seized by such uncontrollable curiosity that he literally tore the door open. It was, as he had correctly assumed, a lumber-room. Bundles of useless old papers and empty earthenware ink-bottles lay in a tumbled heap behind the threshold. But in the room itself stood three men, stooping because of the low ceiling, by the light of a candle stuck on a bookcase. 'What are you doing here?' asked K., in a voice broken with agitation but not loud. One of the men, who was clearly in authority over the other two and took the eye first, was sheathed in a sort of dark leather garment which left his throat and a good deal of his chest and the whole of his arms bare. He made no answer. But the other two cried: 'Sir! We're to be flogged because you complained about us to the Examining Magistrate.' And only then did K. realize that it was actually the warders Franz and Willem, and that the third man was holding a rod in his hand with which to beat them. 'Why,' said K., staring at them, 'I never complained, I only told what happened in my rooms. And, anyhow, your behaviour there was not exactly blameless.' 'Sir,' said Willem, while Franz openly tried to take cover behind him from the third man, 'if you only knew how badly we are paid, you wouldn't be so hard on us. I have a family to feed and Franz here wants to get married, a man tries to make whatever he can, and you don't get rich on hard work, not even if you work day and night. Your fine shirts were a temptation, of course that kind of thing is forbidden to warders, it was wrong, but it's a tradition that body-linen is the warders' perquisite, it has always been the case, believe me; and it's understandable too, for what importance can such things have for a man who is unlucky enough to be arrested? Yet if he insists on telling, punishment is bound to follow.' 'I had no idea of all this, nor did I ever demand that you should be punished, I was only defending a principle.' 'Franz,' Willem turned to the other warder, 'didn't I tell you that the gentleman never asked for us to be punished? Now you see that he didn't even know we should be punished.' 'Don't be taken in by what they say,' remarked the third man to K., 'the punishment is as just as it is inevitable.' 'Don't listen to him,' said Willem, interrupting himself to clap his hand to his mouth, over which he had got a stinging blow with the rod. 'We are only being punished because you accused us; if you hadn't, nothing would have happened, not even if they had discovered what we did. Do you call that justice? Both of us, and especially myself, have a long record of trustworthy service as warders – you must yourself admit that, officially speaking, we guarded you quite well – we had every prospect of advancement and would certainly have been promoted to be Whippers pretty soon, like this man here, who simply had the luck never to be complained of, for a complaint of that kind really happens very seldom indeed. And all is lost now, sir, our careers are done for, we'll be set to do much more menial work than a warder's, and, besides that, we're in for a whipping, and that's horribly painful.' 'Can that birch-rod cause such terrible pain?' asked K., studying the switch, which the man waved to and fro in front of him. 'We'll have to take off all our clothes first,' said Willem. 'Ah, I see,' said K., and he looked more attentively at the Whipper, who was tanned like a sailor and had a brutal, healthy face. 'Is there no way of getting these two off their whipping?' K. asked him. 'No,' said the man, smilingly shaking his head. 'Strip,' he ordered the warders. And he said to K.: 'You mustn't believe all they say, they're so terrified of the whipping that they've already lost what wits they had. For instance, all that this one here' – he pointed to Willem – 'says about his possible career is simply absurd. See how fat he is – the first cuts of the birch will be quite lost in fat. Do you know what made him so fat? He stuffs himself with the breakfasts of all the people he arrests. Didn't he eat up your breakfast too? There, you see, I told you so. But a man with a belly like that couldn't ever become a Whipper, it's quite out of the question.' 'There are Whippers just like me,' maintained Willem, loosening his trouser belt. 'No,' said the Whipper, drawing the switch across his back so that he winced, 'you aren't supposed to be listening, you're to take off your clothes.' 'I'll reward you well if you'll let them go,' said K., and without glancing at the Whipper again – such things should be done with averted eyes on both sides – he drew out his pocket-book.

'So you want to lay a complaint against me too,' said the Whipper, 'and get me a whipping as well? No, no!' 'Do be reasonable,' said K. 'If I had wanted these two men to be punished, I shouldn't be trying to buy them off now. I could simply leave, shut this door after me, close my eyes and ears, and go home; but I don't want to do that, I really want to see them set free; if I had known that they would be punished or even that they could be punished, I should never have mentioned their names. For I don't in the least blame them, it is the organization that is to blame, the high officials who are to blame.' 'That's so,' cried the warders and at once got a cut of the switch over their backs, which were bare now. 'If it was one of the high Judges you were flogging,' said K., and as he spoke he thrust down the rod which the Whipper was raising again, 'I certainly wouldn't try to keep you from laying on with a will, on the contrary I would pay you extra to encourage you in the good work.' 'What you say sounds reasonable enough,' said the man, 'but I refuse to be bribed. I am here to whip people, and whip them I shall.' The warder Franz, who, perhaps hoping that K.'s intervention might succeed, had thus far kept as much as possible in the background, now came forward to the door clad only in his trousers, fell on his knees, and clinging to K.'s arm whispered: 'If you can't get him to spare both of us, try to get me off at least. Willem is older than I am, and far less sensitive too; besides he's had a small whipping already, some years ago, but I've never been in disgrace yet, and I was only following Willem's lead in what I did, he's my teacher, for better or worse. My poor sweetheart is waiting for me at the door of the Bank. I'm so ashamed and miserable.' He dried his tear-wet face on K.'s jacket. 'I can't wait any longer,' said the Whipper,

grasping the rod with both hands and making a cut at
Franz, while Willem cowered in a corner and secretly
watched without daring to turn his head. Then the shriek
rose from Franz's throat, single and irrevocable, it did
not seem to come from a human being but from some
tortured instrument, the whole corridor rang with it, the
whole building must hear it. 'Don't,' cried K.; he was
beside himself, he stood staring in the direction from
which the clerks must presently come running, but he
gave Franz a push, not a violent one but violent enough
nevertheless to make the half-senseless man fall and con-
vulsively claw at the floor with his hands; but even then
Franz did not escape his punishment, the birch-rod found
him where he was lying, its point swished up and down
regularly as he writhed on the floor. And now a clerk
was already visible in the distance and a few paces behind
him another. K. quickly slammed the door, stepped over
to a window close by, which looked out on the courtyard,
and opened it. The shrieks had completely stopped. To
keep the clerks from approaching any nearer, K. cried:
'It's me.' 'Good evening, Herr Assessor,' they cried back.
'Has anything happened?' 'No, no,' replied K. 'It was
only a dog howling in the courtyard.' As the clerks still
did not budge, he added: 'You can go back to your work.'
And to keep himself from being involved in any conversation he leaned out of the window. When after a while
he glanced into the corridor again, they were gone. But
he stayed beside the window, he did not dare to go back
into the lumber-room, and he had no wish to go home
either. It was a little square courtyard into which he was
looking down, surrounded by offices, all the windows
were dark now, but the topmost panes cast back a faint
reflection of the moon. K. intently strove to pierce the

darkness of one corner of the courtyard, where several hand-barrows were jumbled close together. He was deeply disappointed that he had not been able to prevent the whipping, but it was not his fault that he had not succeeded; if Franz had not shrieked – it must have been very painful certainly, but in a crisis one must control oneself – if he had not shrieked, then K., in all probability at least, would have found some other means of persuading the Whipper. If the whole lower grade of this organization were scoundrels, why should the Whipper, who had the most inhuman office of all, turn out to be an exception? Besides, K. had noticed his eyes glittering at the sight of the banknote, obviously he had set about his job in earnest simply to raise his price a little higher. And K. would not have been stingy, he was really very anxious to get the warders off; since he had set himself to fight the whole corrupt administration of this Court, it was obviously his duty to intervene on this occasion. But at the moment when Franz began to shriek, any intervention became impossible. K. could not afford to let the dispatch clerks and possibly all sorts of other people arrive and surprise him in a scene with these creatures in the lumber-room. No one could really demand that sacrifice from him. If a sacrifice had been needed, it would almost have been simpler to take off his own clothes and offer himself to the Whipper as a substitute for the warders. In any case the Whipper certainly would not have accepted such a substitution, since without gaining any advantage he would have been involved in a grave dereliction of duty, for as long as this trial continued, K. must surely be immune from molestation by the servants of the Court. Though of course ordinary standards might not apply here either. At all events, he could have done nothing but slam the door, though even that action had not shut off all danger. It was a pity that he had given Franz a push at the last moment, the state of agitation he was in was his only excuse.

He still heard the steps of the clerks in the distance; so as not to attract their attention he shut the window and began to walk away in the direction of the main staircase. At the door of the lumber-room he stopped for a little and listened. All was as silent as the grave. The man might have beaten the warders till they had given up the ghost, they were entirely delivered into his power. K.'s hand was already stretched out to grasp the door-handle when he withdrew it again. They were past help by this time, and the clerks might appear at any moment; but he made a vow not to hush up the incident and to deal trenchantly, so far as lay in his power, with the real culprits, the high officials, none of whom had yet dared show his face. As he descended the outside steps of the Bank he carefully observed everyone he passed, but even in the surrounding streets he could perceive no sign of a girl waiting for anybody. So Franz's tale of a sweetheart waiting for him was simply a lie, venial enough, designed merely to procure more sympathy for him.

All the next day K. could not get the warders out of his head; he was absent-minded and to catch up on his work had to stay in his office even later than the day before. As he passed the lumber-room again on his way out he could not resist opening the door. And what confronted him, instead of the darkness he had expected, bewildered him completely. Everything was still the same, exactly as he had found it on opening the door the previous evening. The files of old papers and the ink-bottles were still tumbled behind the threshold, the Whipper with his rod and the warders with all their clothes on were still standing there, the candle was burning on the bookcase, and the warders immediately began to cry out: 'Sir!' At once K. slammed the door shut and then beat on it with his fists, as if that would shut it more securely. He ran almost weeping to the clerks, who were quietly working at the copying-presses and looked up at him in surprise. 'Clear that lumber-room out, can't you?' he shouted. 'We're being smothered in dirt!' The clerks promised to do so next day. K. nodded, he could hardly insist on their doing it now, so late in the evening, as he had originally intended. He sat down for a few moments, for the sake of their company, shuffled through some duplicates, hoping to give the impression that he was inspecting them, and then, seeing that the men would scarcely venture to leave the building along with him, went home, tired, his mind quite blank.

VI

K.'s Uncle – Leni

ONE afternoon – it was just before the day's letters went out and K. was very busy – two clerks bringing him some papers to sign were violently thrust aside and his Uncle Karl, a petty squire from the country, came striding into the room. K. was the less alarmed by the arrival of his uncle since for a long time he had been shrinking from it in anticipation. His uncle was bound to turn up, he had been convinced of that for about a month past. He had often pictured him just as he appeared now, his back slightly bent, his panama hat crushed in his left hand, stretching out his right hand from the very doorway, and then thrusting it recklessly across the desk, knocking over everything that came in its way. His uncle was always in a hurry, for he was harassed by the disastrous idea that whenever he came to town for the day he must get through all the programme he had drawn up for himself, besides missing not a single chance of a conversation or a piece of business or an entertainment. In all this K., who as his former ward was peculiarly obliged to him, had to help him as best he could and also sometimes put him up for the night. 'The family skeleton,' he was in the habit of calling him.

Immediately after his first greetings – he had no time to sit down in the chair which K. offered him – he begged K. to have a short talk with him in strict privacy. 'It is necessary,' he said, painfully gulping, 'it is necessary for my peace of mind.' K. at once sent his clerks out of the

room with instructions to admit no one. 'What is this I
hear, Joseph?' cried his uncle when they were alone, sitting down on the desk and making himself comfortable
by stuffing several papers under him without looking at
them. K. said nothing, he knew what was coming, but
being suddenly released from the strain of exacting work,
he resigned himself for the moment to a pleasant sense of
indolence and gazed out through the window at the opposite side of the street, of which only a small triangular
section could be seen from where he was sitting, a slice of
empty house-wall between two shop-windows. 'You sit
there staring out of the window!' cried his uncle, flinging
up his arms. 'For God's sake, Joseph, answer me. Is it
true? Can it be true?' 'Dear Uncle,' said K., tearing himself out of his reverie. 'I don't know in the least what you
mean.' 'Joseph,' said his uncle warningly, 'you've always
told the truth, as far as I know. Am I to take these words
of yours as a bad sign?' 'I can guess, certainly, what you're
after,' said K. accommodatingly. 'You've probably heard
something about my trial.' 'That is so,' replied his uncle,
nodding gravely. 'I have heard about your trial.' 'But
from whom?' asked K. 'Erna wrote to me about it,' said
his uncle. 'She doesn't see much of you, I know, you
don't pay much attention to her, I regret to say, and yet
she heard about it. I got the letter this morning and of
course took the first train here. I had no other reason for
coming, but it seems to be a sufficient one. I shall read
you the bit from her letter that mentions you.' He took
the letter from his pocket-book. 'Here it is. She writes: "I
haven't seen Joseph for a long time, last week I called at
the Bank, but Joseph was so busy that I couldn't see him;
I waited for almost an hour, but I had to leave then, for I
had a piano lesson. I should have liked very much to speak

to him, perhaps I shall soon have the chance. He sent me
a great big box of chocolates for my birthday, it was very
nice and thoughtful of him. I forgot to write and mention
it at the time, and it was only your asking that reminded
me. For I may tell you that chocolate vanishes on the spot
in this boarding-house, hardly do you realize that you've
been presented with a box when it's gone. But about
Joseph, there is something else that I feel I should tell
you. As I said, I was not able to see him at the Bank because he was engaged with a gentleman. After I had
waited meekly for a while I asked an attendant if the interview was likely to last much longer. He said that that
might very well be, for it had probably something to do
with the case which was being brought against the Herr
Assessor. I asked what case, and was he not mistaken, but
he said he was not mistaken, there was a case and a very
serious one too, but more than that he did not know. He
himself would like to help the Herr Assessor, for the Herr
Assessor was a good and just man, but he did not know
how he was to do it, and he only wished that some influential gentleman would take the Herr Assessor's part. To be
sure, that was certain to happen and everything would be
all right in the end, but for the time being, as he could see
from the Herr Assessor's state of mind, things looked far
from well. Naturally I did not take all this too seriously, I
tried to reassure the simple fellow and forbade him to talk
about it to anyone else, and I'm sure it's just idle gossip.
All the same it might be as well, if you, dearest Father,
were to inquire into it on your next visit to town, it will
be easy for you to find out the real state of things, and if
necessary to get some of your influential friends to intervene. Even if it shouldn't be necessary, and that is most
likely, at least it will give your daughter an early chance

of welcoming you with a kiss, which is a joyful thought."
A good child,' said K.'s uncle when he had finished reading, wiping a tear from his eye. K. nodded, he had completely forgotten Erna among the various troubles he had
had lately, and the story about the chocolates she had obviously invented simply to save his face before his uncle
and aunt. It was really touching, and the theatre tickets
which he now resolved to send her regularly would be a
very inadequate return, but he did not feel equal at
present to calling at her boarding-house and chattering to
an eighteen-year-old schoolgirl. 'And what have you got
to say now?' asked his uncle, who had temporarily forgotten all his haste and agitation over the letter, which he
seemed to be re-reading. 'Yes, Uncle,' said K., 'it's quite
true.' 'True?' cried his uncle. 'What is true? How on
earth can it be true? What case is this? Not a criminal
case, surely?' 'A criminal case,' answered K. 'And you sit
there coolly with a criminal case hanging round your
neck?' cried his uncle, his voice growing louder and
louder. 'The cooler I am, the better in the end,' said K.
wearily. 'Don't worry.' 'That's a fine thing to ask of me,'
cried his uncle. 'Joseph, my dear Joseph, think of yourself, think of your relatives, think of your good name.
You have been a credit to us until now, you can't become
a family disgrace. Your attitude,' he looked at K. with
his head slightly cocked, 'doesn't please me at all, that
isn't how an innocent man behaves if he's still in his
senses. Just tell me quickly what it is all about, so that I
can help you. It's something to do with the Bank, of
course?' 'No,' said K., getting up. 'But you're talking too
loudly, Uncle. I feel pretty certain the attendant is standing behind the door listening, and I dislike the idea.
We had better go out somewhere. I'll answer all your

questions then as far as I can. I know quite well that I owe the family an explanation.' 'Right,' cried his uncle, 'quite right, but hurry, Joseph, hurry!' 'I have only to leave some instructions,' said K., and he summoned his chief assistant by telephone, who appeared in a few minutes. In his agitation K.'s uncle indicated to the clerk by a sweep of the hand that K. had sent for him, which, of course, was already obvious enough. K., standing beside his desk, pointed to various papers and in a low voice explained to the young man, who listened coolly but attentively, what remained to be done in his absence. His uncle disturbed him by standing beside him round-eyed and biting his lips nervously; he was not actually listening, but the mere suggestion of listening was disturbing enough in itself. He next began to pace up and down the room, pausing every now and then by the window or before a picture, with sudden ejaculations, such as: 'It's completely incomprehensible to me' or 'Goodness knows what's to come of this.' The young man behaved as if he noticed nothing, quietly heard K.'s instructions to the end, took a few notes, and went, after having bowed both to K. and to his uncle, who, however, turned his back abruptly, gazed out of the window, flung out his arms, and clutched at the curtains. The door had scarcely closed when K.'s uncle cried: 'At last the creature's gone; now we can go too. At last!' Unluckily K. could find no means to make his uncle stop inquiring about the case in the main vestibule, where several clerks and attendants were standing about, while the Deputy Manager himself was crossing the floor. 'Come now, Joseph,' began his uncle, returning a brief nod to the bows of the waiting clerks, 'tell me frankly now what this case is all about.' K. made a few non-committal remarks, laughing a little, and only on the staircase

explained to his uncle that he had not wanted to speak
openly before the clerks. 'Right,' said his uncle, 'but get it
off your chest now.' He listened with bent head, puffing
hastily at a cigar. 'The first thing to grasp, Uncle,' said
K., 'is that this is not a case before an ordinary court.'
'That's bad,' said his uncle. 'How?' asked K., looking at
his uncle. 'I mean that it's bad,' repeated his uncle. They
were standing on the outside steps of the Bank; as the
doorkeeper seemed to be listening, K. dragged his uncle
away; they were swallowed up in the street traffic. The
uncle, who had taken K.'s arm, now no longer inquired
so urgently about the case, and for a while they actually
walked on in silence. 'But how did this happen?' his
uncle asked at last, stopping so suddenly that the people
walking behind him shied off in alarm. 'Things like this
don't come down on one suddenly, they roll up for a long
time beforehand, there must have been indications. Why
did you never write to me? You know I would do anything for you, I'm still your guardian in a sense and till
now I have been proud of it. Of course I'll do what I can
to help you, only it's rather difficult so late in the day,
when the case is already in full swing. The best thing, at
any rate, would be for you to take a short holiday and
come to stay with us in the country. You've got a bit
thinner, I notice that now. You'd get back your strength
in the country, that would be all to the good, for this trial
will certainly be a severe strain on you. But besides that,
in a sense you'd be getting away from the clutches of the
Court. Here they have all sorts of machinery which they
can set automatically in motion against you if they like,
but if you were in the country they would have to appoint
agents or get at you by letter or telegram or telephone.
That would naturally weaken the effect, not that you

would escape them altogether, but you'd have a breathing-space.' 'Still, they might forbid me to go away,' said K., who was beginning to follow his uncle's line of thought. 'I don't think they would do that,' said his uncle reflectively, 'after all, they wouldn't lose so much by your going away.' 'I thought,' said K., taking his uncle's arm to keep him from standing still, 'that you would attach even less importance to this business than I do, and now you are taking it so seriously.' 'Joseph!' cried his uncle, trying to get his arm free so as to hold up the traffic again, only K. would not let him, 'you're quite changed, you always used to have such a clear brain, and is it going to fail you now? Do you want to lose this case? And do you know what that would mean? It would mean that you would be simply ruined. And that all your relatives would be ruined too or at least dragged in the dust. Joseph, pull yourself together. Your indifference drives me mad. Looking at you, one would almost believe the old saying: "A litigant always loses." ' 'Dear Uncle,' said K., 'it's no use getting excited, it's as useless on your part as it would be on mine. No case is won by getting excited, you might let my practical experience count for something, look how I respect yours, as I have always done, even when you astonish me. Since you tell me that the family would be involved in any scandal arising from the case — I don't see myself how that could be so, but it doesn't really matter — I'll submit willingly to your judgement. Only I think going to the country would be inadvisable even from your point of view, for it would look like flight and therefore guilt. Besides, though I'm more closely pressed here, I can push the case on my own more energetically.' 'Quite right,' said his uncle in a tone of relief, as if he saw their minds converging at last, 'I only made the suggestion because I thought your indifference would endanger the case while you stayed here, and that it might be better if I took it up for you instead. But if you intend to push it energetically yourself, that of course would be far better.' 'We're agreed on that, then,' said K. 'And now can you suggest what my first step should be?' 'I'll have to do a bit of thinking about it, naturally,' said his uncle, 'you must consider that I have lived in the country for twenty years almost without a break, and my flair for such matters can't be so good as it was. Various connexions of mine with influential persons who would probably know how to tackle this affair have slackened in the course of time. I'm a bit isolated in the country, but you know that yourself. Actually it's only in emergencies like this that one becomes aware of it. Besides, this affair of yours has come on me more or less unexpectedly, though strangely enough, after Erna's letter, I guessed at something of the kind, and as soon as I saw you to-day I was almost sure of it. Still that doesn't matter, the important thing now is to lose no time.' Before he had finished speaking he was already on tiptoe waiting for a taxi, and now, shouting an address to the driver, he dragged K. into the car after him. 'We'll drive straight to Huld, the Advocate,' he said. 'He was at school with me. You know his name, of course? You don't? That is really extraordinary. He has quite a considerable reputation as a defending counsel and a poor man's lawyer. But it's as a human being that I'm prepared to pin my faith to him.' 'I'm willing to try anything you suggest,' said K., though the hasty headlong way in which his uncle was dealing with the matter caused him some perturbation. It was not very flattering to be driven to a poor man's lawyer as a petitioner. 'I don't know,' he said, 'that in a case like this one can employ an advocate.' 'But of course,' said his uncle. 'That's obvious. Why not? And now tell me everything that has happened up to now, so that I have some idea where we stand.' K. at once began his story and left out no single detail, for absolute frankness was the only protest he could make against his uncle's assumption that the case was a terrible disgrace. Fräulein Bürstner's name he mentioned only once and in passing, but that did not detract from his frankness, since Fräulein Bürstner had no connexion with the case. As he told his story he gazed out through the window and noted that they were approaching the very suburb where the Law Court had its attic offices; he drew his uncle's attention to this fact, but his uncle did not seem to be particularly struck by the coincidence. The taxi stopped before a dark house. His uncle rang the bell of the first door on the ground floor; while they were waiting he bared his great teeth in a smile and whispered: 'Eight o'clock, an unusual time for clients to call. But Huld won't take it ill of me.' Behind a grille in the door two great dark eyes appeared, gazed at the two visitors for a moment, and then vanished again; yet the door did not open. K. and his uncle assured each other that they had really seen a pair of eyes. 'A new maid, probably afraid of strangers,' said K.'s uncle and knocked again. Once more the eyes appeared and now they seemed almost sombre, yet that might have been an illusion created by the naked gas-jet which burned just over their heads and kept hissing shrilly but gave little light. 'Open the door!' shouted K.'s uncle, banging upon it with his fists, 'we're friends of the Herr Advocate's.' 'The Herr Advocate is ill,' came a whisper from behind them. A door had opened at the other end of the little passage and a man in a dressing-gown was standing there imparting this information in a hushed voice. K.'s uncle, already furious at having had to wait so long, whirled round shouting: 'Ill? You say he's ill?' and bore down almost threateningly on the man as if he were the alleged illness in person. 'The door has been opened,' said the man, indicated the Advocate's door, caught his dressing-gown about him, and disappeared. The door was really open, a young girl – K. recognized the dark, somewhat protuberant eyes – was standing in the entrance hall in a long white apron, holding a candle in her hand. 'Next time be a little smarter in opening the door,' K.'s uncle threw at her instead of a greeting, while she sketched a curtsy. 'Come on, Joseph,' he cried to K., who was slowly insinuating himself past the girl. 'The Herr Advocate is ill,' said the girl, as K.'s uncle, without any hesitation, made towards an inner door. K. was still gaping at the girl, who turned her back on him to bolt the house door; she had a doll-like rounded face; not only were her pale cheeks and her chin quite round in their modelling, but her temples and the line of her forehead as well. 'Joseph!' K.'s uncle shouted again, and he asked the girl: 'Is it his heart?' 'I think so,' said the girl, she had now found time to precede him with the candle and open the door of a room. In one corner, which the candlelight had not yet reached, a face with a long beard attached rose from a pillow. 'Leni, who is it?' asked the Advocate, blinded by the candlelight; he could not recognize his visitors. 'It's your old friend Albert,' said K.'s uncle. 'Oh, Albert,' said the Advocate, sinking back on his pillow again, as if there were no need to keep up appearances before this visitor. 'Are you really in a bad way?' asked K.'s uncle, sitting down on the edge of the bed. 'I can't believe it. It's one of your heart attacks and it'll pass over like all the others.'

'Maybe,' said the Advocate in a faint voice, 'but it's worse than it's ever been before. I find it difficult to breathe, can't sleep at all, and am losing strength daily.' 'I see,' said K.'s uncle, pressing his panama hat firmly against his knee with his huge hand. 'That's bad news. But are you being properly looked after? And it's so gloomy in here, so dark. It's a long time since I was here last, but it looked more cheerful then. And this little maid of yours doesn't seem to be very bright, or else she's concealing the fact.' The girl was still standing near the door with her candle; as far as one could make out from the vague flicker of her eyes, she seemed to be looking at K. rather than at his uncle, even while the latter was speaking about her. K. was leaning against a chair which he had pushed near her. 'When a man is as ill as I am,' said the Advocate, 'he must have quiet. I don't find it uncheerful.' After a slight pause he added: 'And Leni looks after me well, she's a good girl.' But this could not convince K.'s uncle, who was visibly prejudiced against the nurse, and though he made no reply to the sick man he followed her with a stern eye as she went over to the bed, set down the candle on the bedside table, bent far over her patient, and whispered to him while she rearranged the pillows. K.'s uncle, almost forgetting that he was in a sick-room, jumped to his feet and prowled up and down behind the girl; K. would not have been surprised if he had seized her by the skirts and dragged her away from the bed. K. himself looked on with detachment, the illness of the Advocate was not entirely unwelcome to him, he had not been able to stem his uncle's growing ardour for his cause, and he thankfully accepted the situation, which had deflected that ardour without any connivance from him. Then his uncle, perhaps only with the intention of annoying the nurse, cried out: 'Fräulein, please be so good as to leave us alone for a while; I must consult my friend on some personal business.' The girl, who was still bending far over the sick man smoothing the sheet beside the wall, merely turned her head and said quite calmly, in striking contrast to the furious stuttering and frothing of K.'s uncle: 'You see that my master is ill; you cannot consult him on any business.' Probably she reiterated the phrase out of simple good nature; all the same it could have been construed as ironical even by an unprejudiced observer, and K.'s uncle naturally flared up as if he had been stung. 'You damned –' he spluttered, but he was so furious that it was difficult to make out the language he used. K. started up in alarm, though he had expected some such outburst, and rushed over to his uncle with the firm intention of clapping both hands over his mouth and so silencing him. Fortunately the patient raised himself up in bed behind the girl. K.'s uncle made a wry grimace as if he were swallowing some nauseous draught and he said in a smoother voice: 'I assure you we aren't altogether out of our senses; if what I ask were impossible I should not ask it. Please go away now.' The girl straightened herself beside the bed, turning full towards K.'s uncle, but with one hand, at least so K. surmised, she was patting the hand of the Advocate. 'You can discuss anything before Leni,' said the Advocate in a voice of sheer entreaty. 'This does not concern myself,' said K.'s uncle, 'it is not my private affair.' And he turned away as if washing his hands of the matter, although willing to give the Advocate a moment for reconsideration. 'Then whom does it concern?' asked the Advocate in an exhausted voice, lying down again. 'My nephew,' said K.'s uncle, 'I have brought him here with me.' And he presented his nephew: Joseph K., Assessor. 'Oh,' said the sick man with much more animation, stretching out his hand to K., 'forgive me, I didn't notice you. Go now, Leni,' he said to the nurse, clasping her by the hand as if saying good-bye to her for a long time, and she went submissively enough. 'So you haven't come,' he said at last to K.'s uncle, who was now appeased and had gone up to the bed again, 'to pay me a sick visit; you've come on business.' It was as if the thought of a sick visit had paralysed him until now, so rejuvenated did he look as he supported himself on his elbow, which must itself have been something of a strain; and he kept combing with his fingers a strand of hair in the middle of his beard. 'You look much better already,' said K.'s uncle, 'since that witch went away.' He broke off, whispered: 'I bet she's listening,' and sprang to the door. But there was no one behind the door and he returned again, not so much disappointed, since her failure to listen seemed to him an act of sheer malice, as disgusted. 'You are unjust to her,' said the Advocate, without adding anything more in defence of his nurse; perhaps by this reticence he meant to convey that she stood in no need of defence. Then in a much more friendly tone he went on: 'As for this case of your nephew's, I should certainly consider myself very fortunate if my strength proved equal to such an arduous task; I'm very much afraid that it will not do so, but at any rate I shall make every effort; if I fail, you can always call in someone else to help me. To be quite honest, the case interests me too deeply for me to resist the opportunity of taking some part in it. If my heart does not hold out, here at least it will find a worthy obstacle to fail against.' K. could not fathom a single word of all this, he glanced at his uncle, hoping for some explanation, but

with the candle in his hand his uncle was sitting on the
bedside table, from which a medicine-bottle had already
rolled on to the carpet, nodding assent to everything that
the Advocate said, apparently agreeing with everything
and now and then casting a glance at K. which demanded
from him a like agreement. Could his uncle have told
the Advocate all about the case already? But that was impossible, the course of events ruled it out. 'I don't understand –' he therefore began. 'Oh, perhaps I have misunderstood you?' asked the Advocate, just as surprised
and embarrassed as K. 'Perhaps I have been too hasty.
Then what do you want to consult me about? I thought
it concerned your case?' 'Of course it does,' said K.'s
uncle, turning to K. with the question: 'What's bothering you?' 'Well, but how do you come to know about me
and my case?' asked K. 'Oh, that's it,' said the Advocate,
smiling. 'I'm an Advocate, you see, I move in circles
where all the various cases are discussed, and the more
striking ones are bound to stick in my mind, especially
one that concerns the nephew of an old friend of mine.
Surely that's not so extraordinary.' 'What's bothering
you?' K.'s uncle repeated. 'You're all nerves.' 'So you
move in these circles?' asked K. 'Yes,' replied the Advocate. 'You ask questions like a child,' said K.'s uncle.
'Whom should I associate with if not with men of my
own profession?' added the Advocate. It sounded incon-
trovertible and K. made no answer. 'But you're attached
to the Court in the Palace of Justice, not to the one with
the skylight,' he wanted to say, yet could not bring himself actually to say it. 'You must consider,' the Advocate
continued in the tone of one perfunctorily explaining
something that should be self-evident, 'you must consider
that this intercourse enables me to benefit my clients in

all sorts of ways, some of which won't even bear mentioning. Of course I'm somewhat handicapped now because of my illness, but in spite of that, good friends of
mine from the Law Courts visit me now and then and
I learn lots of things from them. Perhaps more than many
a man in the best of health who spends all his days in the
Courts. For example, there's a dear friend of mine visiting me at this very moment,' and he waved a hand towards a dark corner of the room. 'Where?' asked K.,
almost roughly, in his first shock of astonishment. He
looked round uncertainly; the light of the small candle
did not nearly reach the opposite wall. And then some
form or other in the dark corner actually began to stir.
By the light of the candle, which his uncle now held high
above his head, K. could see an elderly gentleman sitting
there at a little table. He must have been sitting without
even drawing breath, to have remained for so long un-
noticed. Now he got up ceremoniously, obviously dis-
pleased to have his presence made known. With his
hands, which he flapped like short wings, he seemed to
be deprecating all introductions or greetings, trying to
show that the last thing he desired was to disturb the
other gentlemen, and that he only wanted to be translated again to the darkness where his presence might be
forgotten. But that privilege could no longer be his. 'I
may say you took us by surprise,' said the Advocate in
explanation, and he waved his hand to encourage the
gentleman to approach, which he did very slowly and
hesitatingly, glancing around him all the time, but with
a certain dignity. 'The Chief Clerk of the Court – oh, I
beg your pardon, I have not introduced you – this is my
friend Albert K., this is his nephew the Assessor Joseph
K., and this is the Chief Clerk of the Court – the Herr

Clerk of the Court, to return to what I was saying, has been so good as to pay me a visit. The value of such a visit can really be appreciated only by the initiated who know how dreadfully our dear Clerk of the Court is overwhelmed with work. Yet he came to see me all the same, we were talking here peacefully, as far as my ill health permitted; we didn't actually forbid Leni to admit visitors, it was true, for we expected none, but we naturally thought that we should be left in peace, and then came your furious tattoo, Albert, and the Herr Clerk of the Court withdrew into the corner with his chair and his table, but now it seems we have the chance, that is, if you care to take it, of making the discussion general, since this case concerns us all, and we can reassemble our forces again. – Please, Herr Clerk of the Court,' he said with a bow and an obsequious smile, indicating an arm-chair near the bed. 'Unfortunately I can only stay for a few minutes longer,' said the Chief Clerk of the Court affably, seating himself in the chair and looking at his watch, 'my duties call me. But I don't want to miss this opportunity of becoming acquainted with a friend of my friend here.' He bowed slightly to K.'s uncle, who appeared very flattered to make this new acquaintance, yet, being by nature incapable of expressing obligation, requited the Clerk of the Court's words with a burst of embarrassed but raucous laughter. A hateful moment! K. could observe everything calmly, for nobody paid any attention to him. The Chief Clerk of the Court, now that he had been brought into prominence, seized the lead, as seemed to be his usual habit. The Advocate, whose first pretence of weakness had probably been intended simply to drive away his visitors, listened attentively, cupping his hand to his ear. K.'s uncle as candle-bearer – he was balancing the candle on his knee, the Advocate often glanced at it in apprehension – had soon rid himself of his embarrassment and was now delightedly absorbed in the Clerk of the Court's eloquence and the delicate wave-like gestures of the hand with which he accompanied it. K., leaning against the bedpost, was completely overlooked by the Clerk of the Court, perhaps by deliberate intention, and served merely as an audience to the other old gentleman. Besides, he could hardly follow the conversation and spent one minute thinking of the nurse and the rude treatment she had received from his uncle, and the next wondering if he had not seen the Clerk of the Court before, perhaps actually among the audience during his first interrogation. He might be mistaken, yet the Clerk of the Court would have fitted excellently into the first row of the audience, the elderly gentlemen with the brittle beards.

Then a sound from the entrance hall as of breaking crockery made them all prick up their ears. 'I'll go and see what has happened,' said K., and he went out, rather slowly, to give the others a last chance to call him back. Hardly had he reached the entrance hall and begun to think of groping his way in the darkness, when a hand much smaller than his own covered the hand with which he was still holding the door and gently drew the door shut. It was the nurse who had been waiting there. 'Nothing has happened,' she whispered. 'I simply flung a plate against the wall to bring you out.' K. said in his embarrassment: 'I was thinking of you too.' 'That's all the better,' said the nurse. 'Come this way.' A step or two brought them to a door panelled with thick glass, which opened. 'In here,' she said. It was evidently the Advocate's office; as far as one could see in the moonlight, which brilliantly lit up a small square section of the floor in front of each of the two large windows, it was fitted out with antique solid furniture. 'Here,' said the nurse, pointing to a dark chest with a high carved back. After he had sat down K. still kept looking round the room, it was a lofty, spacious room, the clients of this 'poor man's' lawyer must feel lost in it. K. pictured to himself the timid, short steps with which they would advance to the huge table. But then he forgot all this and had eyes only for the nurse, who was sitting very close to him, almost squeezing him against the opposite arm of the bench. 'I thought,' she said, 'you would come out of your own accord, without waiting till I had to call you out. A queer way to behave. You couldn't keep your eyes off me from the very moment you came in, and yet you leave me to wait. And you'd better just call me Leni,' she added quickly and abruptly, as if there were not a moment to waste. 'I'll be glad to,' said K. 'But as for my queer behaviour, Leni, that's easy to explain. In the first place I had to listen to these old men jabbering. I couldn't simply walk out and leave them without any excuse, and in the second place I'm not in the least a bold young man, but rather shy, to tell the truth, and you too, Leni, really didn't look as if you were to be had for the asking.' 'It isn't that,' said Leni, laying her arm along the back of the seat and looking at K. 'But you didn't like me at first and you probably don't like me even now.' 'Liking is a feeble word,' said K. evasively. 'Oh!' she said, with a smile, and K.'s remark and that little exclamation gave her a certain advantage over him. So K. said nothing more for a while. As he had grown used to the darkness in the room, he could now distinguish certain details of the furnishings. He was particularly struck by a large picture which hung to the right of the door, and bent forward to see it more clearly. It represented a man in a Judge's robe; he was sitting on a high throne-like seat, and the gilding of the seat stood out strongly in the picture. The strange thing was that the Judge did not seem to be sitting in dignified composure, for his left arm was braced along the back and the side-arm of his throne, while his right arm rested on nothing, except for the hand, which clutched the other arm of the chair; it was as if in a moment he must spring up with a violent and probably wrathful gesture to make some fateful observation or even to pronounce sentence. The accused might be imagined as standing on the lowest step leading up to the chair of justice; the top step, which was covered with a yellowish carpet, was shown in the picture. 'Perhaps that is my Judge,' said K., pointing with his finger at the picture. 'I know him,' said Leni, and she looked at the picture too. 'He often comes here. That picture was painted when he was young, but it could never have been in the least like him, for he's a small man, almost a dwarf. Yet in spite of that he had himself drawn out to that length in the portrait, for he's madly vain like everybody else here. But I'm a vain person, too, and it upsets me that you don't like me in the least.' To this last statement K. replied merely by putting his arm round her and drawing her to him; she leaned her head against his shoulder in silence. But to the rest of her remarks he answered: 'What's the man's rank?' 'He is an Examining Magistrate,' she said, seizing the hand with which K. held her and beginning to play with his fingers. 'Only an Examining Magistrate again,' said K. in disappointment. 'The higher officials keep themselves well hidden. But he's sitting on a high seat.' 'That's all invention,' said Leni, with her face bent over his hand. 'Actually he sits on a kitchen chair, with

an old horse-rug doubled under him. But must you etern-
ally be brooding over your case?' she queried slowly. 'No,
not at all,' said K. 'Probably I brood far too little over it.'
'That isn't the mistake you make,' said Leni. 'You're too
unyielding, that's what I've heard.' 'Who told you that?'
asked K.; he could feel her body against his breast and
gazed down at her rich, dark, firmly knotted hair. 'I
should give away too much if I told you that,' replied
Leni. 'Please don't ask me for names, take my warning
to heart instead, and don't be so unyielding in future, you
can't put up a resistance against this Court, you must admit your fault. Make your confession at the first chance
you get. Until you do that, there's no possibility of getting
out of their clutches, none at all. Yet even then you won't
manage it without help from outside, but you needn't
trouble your head about that, I'll see to it myself.' 'You
know a great deal about this Court and the intrigues that
prevail in it!' said K., lifting her on to his knee, for she
was leaning too heavily against him. 'That's better,' she
said, making herself at home on his knee by smoothing
her skirt and pulling her blouse straight. Then she clasped
both her hands round his neck, leaned back, and looked
at him for a long time. 'And if I don't make a confession
of guilt, then you can't help me?' K. asked experiment-
ally. 'I seem to recruit women helpers,' he thought almost
in surprise; 'first Fräulein Bürstner, then the wife of the
Law-Court Attendant, and now this cherishing little creature who appears to have some incomprehensible passion
for me. She sits there on my knee as if it were the only
right place for her!' 'No,' said Leni, shaking her head
slowly, 'then I can't help you. But you don't in the least
want my help, it doesn't matter to you, you're stiff-necked
and never will be convinced.' After a while she asked:

'Do you have a sweetheart?' 'No,' said K. 'Oh, yes, you do,' she said. 'Well, yes I have,' said K. 'Just imagine it, I have told you she didn't exist and yet I am carrying her photograph in my pocket.' At her entreaty he showed her Elsa's photograph; she studied it, curled up on his knee. It was a snapshot taken of Elsa as she was finishing a skirt dance such as she often gave at the cabaret, her skirt was still flying round her like a fan, her hands were planted on her firm hips, and with her chin thrown up she was laughing over her shoulder at someone who did not appear in the photograph. 'She's very tightly laced,' said Leni, indicating the place where in her opinion the tight-lacing was evident. 'I don't like her, she's rough and clumsy. But perhaps she's soft and kind to you, one might guess that from the photograph. Big strong girls like that often can't help being soft and kind. But would she be capable of sacrificing herself for you?' 'No,' said K. 'She is neither soft nor kind, nor would she be capable of sacrificing herself for me. And up till now I have demanded neither the one thing nor the other from her. In fact I've never even examined this photograph as carefully as you have.' 'So she doesn't mean so very much to you,' said Leni. 'She isn't your sweetheart after all.' 'Oh, yes,' replied K. 'I refuse to take back my words.' 'Well, granted that she's your sweetheart,' said Leni, 'you wouldn't miss her very much, all the same, if you were to lose her or exchange her for someone else – me, for instance?' 'Certainly,' said K., smiling, 'that's conceivable, but she has one great advantage over you, she knows nothing about my case, and even if she knew she wouldn't bother her head about it. She wouldn't try to get me to be less unyielding.' 'That's no advantage,' said Leni. 'If that's all the advantage she has over me I shan't lose courage. Has she any physical defect?' 'Any physical defect?' asked K. 'Yes,' said Leni. 'For I have a slight one. Look.' She held up her right hand and stretched out the two middle fingers, between which the connecting web of skin reached almost to the top joint, short as the fingers were. In the darkness K. could not make out at once what she wanted to show him, so she took his hand and made him feel it. 'What a freak of nature!' said K. and he added, when he had examined the whole hand: 'What a pretty little paw!' Leni looked on with a kind of pride while K. in astonishment kept pulling the two fingers apart and then putting them side by side again, until at last he kissed them lightly and let them go. 'Oh!' she cried at once. 'You have kissed me!' She hastily scrambled up until she was kneeling open-mouthed on his knees. K. looked up at her almost in dumfounderment; now that she was so close to him she gave out a bitter exciting odour as of pepper; she clasped his head to her, bent over him, and bit and kissed him on the neck, biting into the very hairs of his head. 'You have exchanged her for me,' she cried over and over again. 'Look, you have exchanged her for me after all!' Then her knees slipped, with a faint cry she almost fell on the carpet, K. put his arms round her to hold her up and was pulled down with her. 'You belong to me now,' she said.

'Here's the key of the door, come whenever you like,' were her last words, and as he took his leave a final aimless kiss landed on his shoulder. When he stepped out on to the pavement a light rain was falling; he was making for the middle of the street so as perhaps to catch a last glimpse of Leni at her window, but a car which was waiting before the house and which in his distraction he had never noticed suddenly emitted his uncle, who seized him

by the arms and banged him against the house door as if
he wanted to nail him there. 'Boy!' he cried, 'how could
you do it! You have terribly damaged your case, which
was beginning to go quite well. You hide yourself away
with a filthy little trollop, who is obviously the Advocate's
mistress into the bargain, and stay away for hours. You
don't even seek any pretext, you conceal nothing, no,
you're quite open, you simply run off to her and stay beside her. And all this time we three sit there, your uncle,
who is doing his best for you, the Advocate, who has to
be won over to your side, above all the Chief Clerk of the
Court, a man of importance, who is actually in charge of
your case at its present stage. There we sit, consulting
how to help you, I have to handle the Advocate circum-
spectly, and the Advocate in turn the Clerk of the Court,
and one might think you had every reason to give me at
least some support. Instead of which you absent yourself.
You were away so long that there was no concealing it;
of course the two gentlemen, being men of the world,
didn't talk about it, they spared my feelings, but finally
even they couldn't get over it, and as they couldn't mention it they said nothing at all. We sat there for several
minutes in complete silence, listening for you to come
back. And all in vain. At last the Chief Clerk of the
Court, who had stayed much longer than he intended,
got up and said good night, evidently very sorry for me
without being able to help me, his kindness was really
extraordinary, he stood waiting for a while longer at the
door before he left. And I was glad when he went, let me
tell you; by that time I felt hardly able to breathe. And
the poor Advocate felt it even worse, the good man
couldn't utter a word as I took leave of him. In all probability you have helped to bring him to the verge of col-

lapse and so hastened the death of a man on whose good offices you are dependent. And you leave me, your uncle, to wait here in the rain for hours; just feel, I'm wet through and through!'

VII

Advocate – Manufacturer – Painter

ONE winter morning – snow was falling outside the window in a foggy dimness – K. was sitting in his office, already exhausted in spite of the early hour. To save his face before his subordinates at least, he had given his clerk instructions to admit no one, on the plea that he was occupied with an important piece of work. But instead of working he twisted in his chair, idly rearranged the things lying on his writing-table, and then, without being aware of it, let his outstretched arm rest on the table and sat on with bowed head, immobile.

The thought of his case never left him now. He had often considered whether it would not be better to draw up a written defence and hand it in to the Court. In this defence he would give a short account of his life, and when he came to an event of any importance explain for what reasons he had acted as he did, intimate whether he approved or condemned his way of action in retrospect, and adduce grounds for the condemnation or approval. The advantages of such a written defence, as compared with the mere advocacy of an expert in the Law who himself was not impeccable, were undoubted. K. had no idea what the Advocate was doing about the case; at any rate it did not amount to much, it was more than a month since Huld had sent for him, and even during the first few consultations K. had formed the impression that the man could not do much for him. To begin with, he had hardly cross-questioned him at all. And there were so

126

many questions to put. To ask questions was surely the main thing. Indeed K. felt that he himself could draw up all the necessary questions. But the Advocate, instead of asking questions, either did all the talking or sat quite dumb opposite him, bent slightly forward over his writing-table, probably because of his hardness of hearing, stroking a strand of hair in the middle of his beard and gazing at the carpet, perhaps at the very spot where K. had lain with Leni. Now and then he would give K. some empty admonitions such as people hand out to children. Admonitions as useless as they were wearisome, for which K. did not intend to pay a penny at the final reckoning. After the Advocate thought he had humbled him sufficiently, he usually set himself to encourage him again. He had already, so he would relate, won many similar cases either outright or partially. Cases which, though at bottom not quite so difficult, perhaps, as this one, had been outwardly still more hopeless. He had a summary of these cases in a drawer of his desk – at this he tapped one of them – but he regretted he couldn't show it, as it dealt with official secrets. Nevertheless the vast experience he had gained through all these cases would now redound to K.'s benefit. He had started on K.'s case at once, of course, and the first plea was almost ready for presentation. That was very important, for the first impression made by the defence often determined the whole course of subsequent proceedings. Though, unfortunately, it was his duty to warn K., it sometimes happened that the first plea was not read by the Court at all. They simply filed it among the other papers and pointed out that for the time being the observation and interrogation of the accused were more important than any formal petition. If the petitioner pressed them, they generally added that before the verdict was pronounced all the material accumulated, including, of course, every document relating to the case, the first plea as well, would be carefully examined. But unluckily even that was not quite true in most cases, the first plea was often mislaid or lost altogether and, even if it were kept intact till the end, was hardly ever read; that was of course, the Advocate admitted, merely a rumour. It was all very regrettable, but not wholly without justification. K. must remember that the proceedings were not public; they could certainly, if the Court considered it necessary, become public, but the Law did not prescribe that they must be made public. Naturally, therefore, the legal records of the case, and above all the actual charge-sheets, were inaccessible to the accused and his counsel, consequently one did not know in general, or at least did not know with any precision, what charges to meet in the first plea; accordingly it could be only by pure chance that it contained really relevant matter. One could draw up genuinely effective and convincing pleas only later on, when the separate charges and the evidence on which they were based emerged more definitely or could be guessed at from the interrogations. In such circumstances the Defence was naturally in a very ticklish and difficult position. Yet that, too, was intentional. For the Defence was not actually countenanced by the Law, but only tolerated, and there were differences of opinion even on that point, whether the Law could be interpreted to admit such tolerance at all. Strictly speaking, therefore, none of the Advocates was recognized by the Court, all who appeared before the Court as Advocates being in reality merely in the position of hole-and-corner Advocates. That naturally had a very humiliating effect on the whole profession, and the next time K.

visited the Law-Court offices he should take a look at the
Advocates' room, just for the sake of having seen it once
in his life. He would probably be horrified by the kind
of people he found assembled there. The very room, itself
small and cramped, showed the contempt in which the
Court held them. It was lit only by a small skylight,
which was so high up that if you wanted to look out, you
had to get some colleague to hoist you on his back, and
even then the smoke from the chimney close by choked
you and blackened your face. To give only one example
of the state the place was in – there had been for more
than a year now a hole in the floor, not so big that you
could fall through the floor, but big enough to let a man's
leg slip through. The Advocates' room was in the very
top attic, so that if you stumbled through the hole your
leg hung down into the lower attic, into the very corridor
where the clients had to wait. It wasn't saying too much
if the Advocates called these conditions scandalous. Complaints to the authorities had not the slightest effect, and
it was also strictly forbidden for the Advocates to make
any structural repairs or alterations at their own expense.
Still, there was some justification for this attitude on the
part of the authorities. They wanted to discourage defending counsel as much as possible, the whole onus of
the Defence must be laid on the accused himself. A
reasonable enough point of view, yet nothing could be
more erroneous than to deduce from this that accused persons had no need of Advocates when appearing before
this Court. On the contrary, in no other Court was legal
assistance so necessary. For the proceedings were not only
kept secret from the general public, but from the accused
as well. Of course only within possible limits, but it
proved possible to a very great extent. For even the

accused had no access to the Court records, and to guess from the course of an interrogation what documents the Court had up its sleeve was very difficult, particularly for an accused person, who was himself implicated and had all sorts of worries to distract him. Now here was where defending counsel stepped in. Generally speaking, an Advocate was not allowed to be present during the examination, consequently he had to cross-question the accused immediately after an interrogation, if possible at the very door of the Court of Inquiry, and piece together from the usually confused reports he got anything that might be of use for the Defence. But even that was not the most important thing, for one could not elicit very much in that way, though of course here as elsewhere a capable man could elicit more than others. The most important thing was the Advocate's personal connexion with officials of the Court; in that lay the chief value of the Defence. Now K. must have discovered from experience that the very lowest grade of the Court organization was by no means perfect and contained venal and corrupt elements, whereby to some extent a breach was made in the watertight system of justice. This was where most of the petty Advocates tried to push their way in, by bribing and listening to gossip, in fact there had actually been cases of purloining documents, at least in former times. It was not to be gainsaid that these methods could achieve for the moment surprisingly favourable results, on which the free-lance Advocates prided themselves, spreading them out as a lure for new clients, but they had no effect on the further progress of the case, or only a bad effect. Nothing was of any real value but respectable personal connexions with the higher officials, that was to say higher officials of subordinate rank, naturally. Only through these could the

course of the proceedings be influenced, imperceptibly at
first, perhaps, but more and more strongly as the case
went on. Of course very few Advocates had such connexions, and here K.'s choice had been a very fortunate one.
Perhaps only one or two other Advocates could boast of
the same connexions as Dr Huld. These did not worry
their heads about the mob in the Advocates' room and
had nothing whatever to do with them. But their relations
with the Court officials were all the more intimate. It was
not even necessary that Dr Huld should always attend the
Court, wait in the ante-room of the Examining Magistrates till they chose to appear, and be dependent on their
moods for earning perhaps a delusive success or a definite
snub. No, as K. had himself seen, the officials, and very
high ones among them, visited Dr Huld of their own accord, voluntarily providing information with great frankness or at least in broad enough hints, discussing the next
turn of the various cases; more, even sometimes letting
themselves be persuaded to a new point of view. Certainly
one should not rely too much on their readiness to be persuaded, for definitely as they might declare themselves for
a new standpoint favourable to the Defence, they might
well go straight to their offices and issue a statement in
the directly contrary sense, a verdict far more severe on
the accused than the original intention which they claimed
to have renounced. Against that, of course, there was no
remedy, for what they said to you in private was simply
said to you in private and could not be followed up in
public, even if the Defence were not obliged for other
reasons to do its utmost to retain the favour of these gentlemen. On the other hand it had also to be considered
that these gentlemen were not moved by mere human
benevolence or friendly feeling in paying visits to defend-

ing counsel — only to experienced counsel, of course; they were in a certain sense actually dependent on the Defence. They could not help feeling the disadvantages of a judiciary system which insisted on secrecy from the start. Their remoteness kept the officials from being in touch with contemporary life; for the average case they were excellently equipped, such a case proceeded almost mechanically and only needed a push now and then; yet confronted with quite simple cases, or particularly difficult cases, they were often utterly at a loss, they did not have any right understanding of human relations, since they were confined day and night to the workings of their judicial system, while in such cases a knowledge of human nature itself was indispensable. Then it was that they came to the Advocates for advice, with a servant behind them carrying the papers that were usually kept so secret. In that window over there many a gentleman one would never have expected to encounter had sat gazing out hopelessly into the street, while the Advocate at his desk examined his papers in order to give him good counsel. And it was on such occasions as these that one could perceive how seriously these gentlemen took their vocation and how deeply they were plunged into despair when they came upon obstacles which the nature of things kept them from overcoming. Their position was not easy, and one must not do them an injustice by regarding it as easy. The ranks of officials in this judiciary system mounted endlessly, so that not even adepts could survey the hierarchy as a whole. And the proceedings of the Courts were generally kept secret from subordinate officials, consequently they could hardly ever quite follow in their further progress the cases on which they had worked; any particular case thus appeared in their circle of jurisdiction often without their knowing whence it came, and passed from it they knew not whither. Thus the knowledge was only to be derived from a study of the various single stages of the case: the final verdict and the reasons for that verdict lay beyond the reach of these officials. They were forced to restrict themselves to that stage of the case which was prescribed for them by their Law, and as for what followed, in other words the results of their own work, they generally knew less about it than the Defence, which as a rule remained in touch with the accused almost to the end of the case. So in that respect, too, they could learn much that was worth knowing from the Defence. Would it surprise K., then, keeping all this in mind, to find that the officials lived in a state of irritability which sometimes expressed itself in offensive ways when they dealt with their clients? That was the universal experience. All the officials were in a constant state of touchiness, even when they appeared calm. Naturally the petty hedge-lawyers were most liable to suffer from it. The following story, for example, was current, and it had all the appearance of truth. An old official, a well-meaning, quiet man, had a difficult case in hand which had been greatly complicated by the Advocate's petitions, and he had studied it continuously for a whole day and night – the officials were really more conscientious than one would believe. Well, towards morning, after twenty-four hours of work with probably very little result, he went to the entrance door, hid himself behind it, and flung down the stairs every Advocate who tried to enter. The Advocates gathered down below on the stair-head and took counsel what they should do; on the one hand they had no real claim to be admitted and consequently could hardly take any legal action against the official, and also, as already mentioned, they had to guard against antagonizing the body of officials. But on the other hand every day they spent away from the Court was a day lost to them, and so a great deal depended on their getting in. At last they all agreed that the best thing to do was to tire out the old gentleman. One Advocate after another was sent rushing upstairs to offer the greatest possible show of passive resistance and let himself be thrown down again into the arms of his colleagues. That lasted for about an hour, then the old gentleman – who was exhausted in any case by his work overnight – really grew tired and went back to his office. The Advocates down below would not believe it at first and sent one of their number up to peep behind the door and assure himself that the room was actually vacant. Only then were they able to enter, and from all accounts they did not dare even to grumble. For although the pettiest Advocate might be to some extent capable of analysing the state of things in the Court, it never occurred to the Advocates that they should suggest or insist on any improvements in the system, while – and this was very characteristic – almost every accused man, even quite ordinary people among them, discovered from the earliest stages a passion for suggesting reforms which often wasted time and energy that could have been better employed in other directions. The only sensible thing was to adapt oneself to existing conditions. Even if it were possible to alter a detail for the better here or there – but it was simple madness to think of it – any benefit arising from that would profit clients in the future only, while one's own interests would be immeasurably injured by attracting the attention of the ever-vengeful officials. Anything but draw attention to oneself from above! One must lie low, no matter how much it went against the grain. Must try to understand that this great organization remained, so to speak, in a state of delicate balance, and that if someone took it upon himself to alter the disposition of things around him, he ran the risk of losing his footing and falling to destruction, while the organization would simply right itself by some compensating reaction in another part of its machinery — since everything interlocked — and remain unchanged, unless, indeed, which was very probable, it became still more rigid, more vigilant, more severe, and more ruthless. One must really leave the Advocates to do their work, instead of interfering with them. Reproaches were not of much use, particularly when the offender was unable to perceive the full scope of the grounds for them; all the same, he must say that K. had very greatly damaged his case by his discourtesy to the Chief Clerk of the Court. That influential man could already almost be eliminated from the list of those who might be got to do something for K. He now ignored with unmistakable coldness even the slightest reference to the case. In many ways the functionaries were like children. Often they could be so deeply offended by the merest trifle — unfortunately, K.'s behaviour could not be classed as a trifle — that they would stop speaking even to old friends, give them the cold shoulder, and work against them in all imaginable ways. But then, suddenly, in the most surprising fashion and without any particular reason, they would be moved to laughter by some small jest which you only dared to make because you felt you had nothing to lose, and then they were your friends again. It was both easy and difficult to handle them, you could hardly lay down any fixed principles for dealing with them. Sometimes you felt astonished to think that one single ordinary lifetime sufficed to gather all the knowledge needed for a fair degree of success in such a profession. There were dark hours, of course, such as came to everybody, in which you thought you had achieved nothing at all, in which it seemed to you that only the cases predestined from the start to succeed came to a good end, which they would have reached in any event without an Advocate's help, while every one of the others was doomed to fail in spite of all your running about, all your exertions, all the illusory little victories on which you plumed yourself. That was a frame of mind, of course, in which nothing at all seemed certain, and so you could not positively deny the suggestion that your intervention might have side-tracked some cases which would have run quite well on the right lines had they been left alone. A desperate kind of self-assurance, to be sure, yet it was the only kind available at such times. These moods – for of course they were only moods, nothing more – afflicted Advocates more especially when a case which they had conducted with all satisfaction to the desired point was suddenly taken out of their hands. That was beyond all doubt the worst thing that could happen to an Advocate. Not that a client ever dismissed his Advocate from a case, such a thing was not done, an accused man, once having briefed an Advocate, must stick to him whatever happened. For how could he keep going by himself, once he had called in someone to help him? So that never happened, but it did sometimes happen that the case took a turn where the Advocate could no longer follow it. The case and the accused and everything were simply withdrawn from the Advocate; then even the best connexions with officials could no longer achieve any result, for even they knew nothing. The case had simply reached the stage where further as-sistance was ruled out, it had vanished into remote, inaccessible Courts, where even the accused was beyond the reach of an Advocate. Then you might come home some day and find on your table all the countless pleas relating to the case, which you had drawn up with such pains and such flattering hopes; they had been returned to you because in the new stage of the process they were not admitted as relevant; they were mere waste paper. It did not follow that the case was lost, by no means, at least there was no evidence for such an assumption; you simply knew nothing more about the case and would never know anything more about it. Now, very luckily, such occurrences were exceptional, and even if K.'s case were a case of that nature, it still had a long way to go before reaching that stage. For the time being, there were abundant opportunities for an Advocate's labour, and K. might rest assured that they would be exploited to the uttermost. The first plea, as before mentioned, was not yet handed in, but there was no hurry; far more important were the preliminary consultations with the relevant officials, and they had already taken place. With only partial success, as must be frankly admitted. It would be better for the time being not to divulge details which might have a bad influence on K. by elating or depressing him unduly, yet this much could be asserted, that certain officials had expressed themselves very graciously and had also shown great readiness to help, while others had expressed themselves less favourably, but in spite of that had by no means refused their collaboration. The result on the whole was therefore very gratifying, though one must not seek to draw any definite conclusion from that, since all preliminary negotiations began in the same way and only in the course of further developments did it appear whether they had real value or not. At any rate nothing was yet lost, and if they could manage to win over the Chief Clerk of the Court in spite of all that had happened – various moves had already been initiated towards that end – then, to use a surgeon's expression, this could be regarded as a clean wound and one could await further developments with an easy mind.

In such and similar harangues the Advocate was inexhaustible. He reiterated them every time K. called on him. Progress had always been made, but the nature of the progress could never be divulged. The Advocate was always working away at the first plea, but it had never reached a conclusion, which at the next visit turned out to be an advantage, since the last few days would have been very inauspicious for handing it in, a fact which no one could have foreseen. If K., as sometimes happened, wearied out by the Advocate's volubility, remarked that, even taking into account all the difficulties, the plea seemed to be getting on very slowly, he was greeted with the retort that it was not getting on slowly at all, although they would have been much further on by now had K. come to the Advocate in time. Unfortunately he had neglected to do so and that omission was likely to keep him at a disadvantage, and not merely a temporal disadvantage, either.

The one welcome interruption to these visits was Leni, who always so arranged things that she brought in the Advocate's tea while K. was present. She would stand behind K.'s chair, apparently looking on, while the Advocate stooped with a kind of miserly greed over his cup and poured out and sipped his tea, but all the time she was letting K. surreptitiously hold her hand. There was total silence. The Advocate sipped, K. squeezed Leni's hand, and sometimes Leni ventured to caress his hair.

'Are you here still?' the Advocate would ask, after he had finished. 'I wanted to take the tea-tray away again,' Leni would answer, there would follow a last hand-clasp, the Advocate would wipe his mouth and begin again with new energy to harangue K.

Was the Advocate seeking to comfort him or to drive him to despair? K. could not tell, but he soon held it for an established fact that his defence was not in good hands. It might be all true, of course, what the Advocate said, though his attempts to magnify his own importance were transparent enough and it was likely that he had never till now conducted such an important case as he made K.'s out to be. But his continual bragging of his personal connexions with the officials was suspicious. Was it so certain that he was exploiting these connexions for K.'s benefit? The Advocate never forgot to mention that these officials were subordinate officials, therefore officials in a dependent position, for whose advancement certain turns in the various cases might in all probability be of some importance. Could they possibly employ the Advocate to bring about such turns in the case, turns which were bound, of course, to be unfavourable to the accused? Perhaps they did not always do that, it was hardly likely, there must be occasions on which they arranged that the Advocate should score a point or two as a reward for his services, since it was to their own interest for him to keep up his professional reputation. But if that were really the position, into which category were they likely to put K.'s case, which, as the Advocate maintained, was a very difficult, therefore important case, and had roused great interest in the Court from the very beginning? There could not be very much doubt what they would do. A clue was already provided in the fact that the first plea had not yet been handed in, though the case had lasted for months, and that according to the Advocate all the proceedings were still in their early stages, words which were obviously well calculated to lull the accused and keep him in a helpless state, in order suddenly to overpower him with the verdict or at least with the announcement that the preliminary examination had been concluded in his disfavour and the case handed over to higher authorities.

It was absolutely necessary for K. to intervene personally. In states of intense exhaustion, such as he experienced this winter morning, when all these thoughts kept running at random through his head, he was particularly incapable of resisting this conviction. The contempt which he had once felt for the case was no longer justified. Had he stood alone in the world he could easily have ridiculed the whole affair, though it was also certain that in that event it could never have arisen at all. But now his uncle had dragged him to this Advocate, family considerations had come in; his position was no longer quite independent of the course the case took, he himself, with a certain inexplicable satisfaction, had imprudently mentioned it to some of his acquaintances, others had come to learn of it in ways unknown to him, his relations with Fräulein Bürstner seemed to fluctuate with the case itself – in short, he hardly had the choice now to keep up the case or let it drop, he was in the middle of it and must look to himself. For him to be so tired was a bad look-out.

Yet there was no need for exaggerated anxiety at the moment. In a relatively short time he had managed to work himself up to his present high position in the Bank and to maintain himself in that position and win recognition from everybody; surely if the abilities which had made this possible were to be applied in unravelling his own case, there was no doubt that it would go well. Above all, if he were to achieve anything, it was essential that he should eliminate from his mind the idea of possible guilt. There was no such guilt. This legal action was nothing more than a business deal such as he had often concluded to the advantage of the Bank, a deal within which, as always happened, lurked various dangers which were simply to be obviated. The right tactics were to avoid letting one's thoughts stray to one's own possible shortcomings, and to cling as firmly as one could to the thought of one's advantage. From this standpoint the conclusion was inevitable that the case must be withdrawn from the Advocate as soon as possible, preferably that very evening. According to the Advocate that was something unheard of, it was true, and very likely an insult, but K. could not endure that his efforts in the case should be thwarted by moves probably originating in the office of his own representative. Once the Advocate was shaken off, the plea must be sent in at once and the officials be urged daily, if possible, to give their attention to it. This would never be achieved by sitting meekly in the attic lobby like the others with one's hat under the seat. K. himself, or one of the women, or some other messenger must keep at the officials day after day and force them to sit down at their desks and study K.'s papers instead of gaping out into the lobby through the wooden rails. These tactics must be pursued unremittingly, everything must be organized and supervised; the Court would encounter for once an accused man who knew how to stick up for his rights.

Yet even though K. believed he could manage all this, the difficulty of drawing up the plea seemed overwhelming. At one time, not more than a week ago, he had regarded the possibility of having to draw up his own plea with merely a slight feeling of shame, it never even occurred to him that there might be difficulties in the way. He could remember that one of those mornings, when he was up to his ears in work, he had suddenly pushed everything aside and seized his jotting-pad with the idea of drafting the plan of such a plea and handing it to the Advocate by way of egging him on, but just at that moment the door of the Manager's room opened and the Deputy Manager came in guffawing uproariously. That had been a very painful moment for K., though, of course, the Deputy Manager had not been laughing at the plea, of which he knew nothing, but at a funny story from the Stock Exchange which he had just heard, a story which needed illustrating for the proper appreciation of the point, so that the Deputy Manager, bending over the desk, took K.'s pencil from his hand and drew the required picture on the page of the jotting-pad which had been intended for the plea.

To-day K. was no longer hampered by feelings of shame; the plea simply had to be drawn up. If he could find no time for it in his office, which seemed very probable, then he must draft it in his lodgings by night. And if his nights were not enough, then he must ask for furlough. Anything but stop half-way, that was the stupidest thing one could do in any affair, not only in business. No doubt it was a task that meant almost interminable labour. One did not need to have a timid and fearful nature to be easily persuaded that the completion of this plea was a sheer impossibility. Not because of laziness or obstructive malice, which could only affect the Advocate, but because to meet an unknown accusation, not to mention other possible charges arising out of it, the whole of one's life would have to be passed in review, down to the smallest actions and accidents, clearly formulated and examined from every angle. And how dreary such a task would be! It would do well enough, perhaps, as an occupation for one's second childhood in years of retirement, when the long days needed filling up. But at this time when K. should be devoting his mind entirely to work, when every hour was hurried and crowded – for he was still in full career and rapidly becoming a rival even to the Deputy Manager – when his evenings and nights were all too short for the pleasures of a bachelor life, this was the time when he must sit down to such a task! Once more his train of thought had led him into self-pity. Almost involuntarily, simply to make an end of it, he put his finger on the button which rang the bell in the waiting-room. While he pressed it he glanced at the clock. It was eleven o'clock, he had wasted two hours in dreaming, a long stretch of precious time, and he was, of course, still wearier than he had been before. Yet the time had not been quite lost, he had come to decisions which might prove valuable. The attendants brought in several letters and two cards from gentlemen who had been waiting for a considerable time. They were, in fact, extremely important clients of the Bank who should on no account have been kept waiting at all. Why had they come at such an unsuitable hour? – and why, they might well be asking in their turn behind the door, did the assiduous K. allow his private affairs to usurp the best time of the day? Weary of what had gone before and wearily awaiting what was to come, K. got up to receive the first of his clients.

This was a jovial little man, a manufacturer whom K. knew well. He regretted having disturbed K. in the middle of important work and K. on his side regretted that he had kept the manufacturer waiting for so long. But his very regret he expressed in such a mechanical way, with such a lack of sincerity in his assurances, that the manufacturer could not have helped noticing it, had he not been so engrossed by the business in hand. As it was, he tugged papers covered with statistics out of every pocket, spread them before K., explained various entries, corrected a trifling error which his eye had caught even in this hasty survey, reminded K. of a similar transaction which he had concluded with him about a year before, mentioned casually that this time another bank was offering better terms to secure the deal, and finally sat in eager silence waiting for K.'s comments. K. had actually followed the man's argument quite closely in its early stages, the thought of such an important piece of business had its attractions for him too, but unfortunately not for long, he had soon ceased to listen and merely nodded now and then as the manufacturer's claims waxed in enthusiasm, until in the end he lost even that interest and confined himself to staring at the other's bald head bent over the papers and asking himself when the fellow would begin to realize that all his eloquence was being wasted. When the manufacturer stopped speaking, K. actually thought for a moment that the pause was intended to give him the chance of confessing that he was not in a fit state to attend to business. And it was merely with regret that he perceived the intent look on the manufacturer's face, the alertness, as if prepared for every objection, which indicated that the interview was supposed to continue. So he bowed his head as at a word of command and began slowly to move his pencil point over the papers, pausing here and there to stare at some figure. The manufacturer suspected K. of looking for flaws in the scheme, perhaps the figures were not quite reliable after all, perhaps they were not the decisive factors in the deal, or at any rate he laid his hand over them and shifting closer to K. began to expound the general policy behind the transaction. 'It's difficult,' said K., pursing his lips, and now that the papers, the only things he had to hold on to, were covered up, he sank weakly against the arm of his chair. He glanced up slightly, but only slightly, when the door of the Manager's room opened, disclosed the Deputy Manager, a blurred figure who looked as if veiled in some kind of gauze. K. did not bother about this apparition, but merely registered its immediate effect, which was very gratifying to him. For the manufacturer at once bounded from his chair and rushed over to the Deputy Manager, though K. could have wished him to be ten times quicker, since he was afraid the apparition might vanish again. His fear was superfluous, the two gentlemen met each other, shook hands, and advanced together towards K.'s desk. The manufacturer lamented that his proposals were being cold-shouldered by the Assessor, indicating K., who under the Deputy Manager's eye had once more bent over the papers. Then as the two of them leaned against his desk, and the manufacturer set himself to win the newcomer's approval for his scheme, it seemed to K. as though two giants of enormous size were bargaining above his head for himself. Slowly, lifting his eyes as far as he dared, he peered up to see what they were about, then picked one of the documents from the desk at random, laid it flat on his open palm, and gradually raised it, rising himself with it, to their level. In doing so he had no definite purpose, but merely acted with the feeling that this was how he would have to act when he had finished the great task of drawing up the plea which was completely to acquit him. The Deputy Manager, who was giving his full attention to the conversation, merely glanced at the paper without even reading what was on it, for anything that seemed important to the Assessor was un-important to him, took it from K.'s hand, said: 'Thanks, I know all that already,' and quietly laid it back on the desk again. K. darted an angry look at him, but the De-puty Manager did not notice that, or, if he did, was only amused, he laughed loudly several times, visibly discon-certed the manufacturer by a quick thrust, at once saved him by countering it himself, and finally invited the man into his private office, where they could decide the tran-saction together. 'It is a very important proposal,' he said to the manufacturer, 'I entirely agree. And the Herr As-sessor,' – even in saying this he went on addressing him-self only to the manufacturer – 'will I am sure be relieved if we take it off his shoulders. This business needs think-ing over. And he seems to be overworked to-day; besides, there are some people who have been waiting for him in the ante-room for hours.' K. had still enough self-com-mand to turn away from the Deputy Manager and ad-dress his friendly but somewhat fixed smile solely to the manufacturer; except for this he made no response, sup-porting himself with both hands on the desk, bending forward a little like an obsequious clerk, and looked on while the two men, still talking away, gathered up the papers and disappeared into the Manager's room. In the very doorway, the manufacturer turned round to remark that he would not say good-bye yet, for of course he would report the result of the interview to the Herr Assessor; besides, there was another little matter he had to men-tion.

At last K. was alone. He had not the slightest intention of interviewing any more clients and vaguely realized how pleasant it was that the people waiting outside believed him to be still occupied with the manufacturer, so that nobody, not even the attendant, would disturb him. He went over to the window, perched on the sill, holding on to the latch with one hand, and looked down on the square below. The snow was still falling, the sky had not yet cleared.

For a long time he sat like this, without knowing what really troubled him, only turning his head from time to time with an alarmed glance towards the ante-room, where he fancied, mistakenly, that he heard a noise. But as no one came in he recovered his composure, went over to the wash-basin, washed his face in cold water, and returned to his place at the window with a clearer mind. The decision to take his defence into his own hands seemed now more grave to him than he had originally fancied. So long as the Advocate was responsible for the case it had not come really home to him, he had viewed it with a certain detachment and kept beyond reach of immediate contact with it, he had been able to intervene whenever he liked but could also withdraw whenever he liked. Now, on the other hand, if he were to conduct his own defence he would be putting himself completely at the defence of the Court, at least for the time being, a policy which would eventually bring about his absolute and definite acquittal, but would meanwhile, provisionally at least, involve him in far greater dangers than before. If he had ever doubted that, his state of mind to-day in his encounter with the Deputy Manager and the manufacturer would have been more than enough to convince him. What a stupor had overcome him, merely because he had decided to conduct his own defence! And what would develop later on? What days were lying in wait for him? Would he ever find the right path through all these difficulties? If he were to put up a thoroughgoing defence — and any other kind would be a waste of time — to put up a thoroughgoing defence, did that not involve cutting himself off from every other activity? Would he be able to survive that? And how was he to conduct his case from a Bank office? It was not merely the drawing up of a plea; that might be managed on a few weeks' furlough, though to ask for leave of absence just now would be decidedly risky; it was a matter of substantial action, whose duration it was impossible to foresee. What an obstacle had suddenly arisen to block K.'s career!

And this was the moment when he was supposed to do Bank work? He looked down at his desk. This the time to interview clients and bargain with them? While his case was unfolding itself, while up in the attics the Court clerks were poring over the charge papers, was he to devote his attention to the affairs of the Bank? It looked like a kind of torture sanctioned by the Court, arising from his case and concomitant with it. And would allowances be made for his peculiar position when his work in the Bank came to be judged? Never, and by nobody. The existence of his case was not exactly unknown in the Bank, though it was not quite clear who knew of it and how much they knew. But apparently the rumour had not yet reached the Deputy Manager, otherwise K. could hardly have failed to perceive it, since the man could have exploited his knowledge without any scruples as a colleague or as a human being. And the Manager himself? He was certainly well disposed to K. and as soon as he heard of the case would probably be willing enough to

lighten K.'s duties as far as lay in his power, but his good
intentions would be checkmated, for K.'s waning prestige
was no longer sufficient to counterbalance the influence
of the Deputy Manager, who was gaining a stronger hold
on the Manager and exploiting the latter's invalid condition to his own advantage. So what had K. to hope? It
might be that he was only sapping his powers of resistance by harbouring these thoughts; still, it was necessary
to have no illusions and to view the position as clearly as
the moment allowed.

Without any particular motive, merely to put off returning to his desk, he opened the window. It was difficult to open, he had to push the latch with both hands.
Then there came into the room through the great window
a blend of fog and smoke, filling it with a faint smell of
burning soot. Some snowflakes fluttered in too. 'An awful
autumn,' came the voice of the manufacturer from behind
K.; returning from his colloquy with the Deputy Manager he had entered the room unobserved. K. nodded and
shot an apprehensive glance at the man's attaché-case,
from which doubtless he would now extract all his papers
in order to inform K. how the negotiations had gone. But
the manufacturer, catching K.'s eye, merely tapped his
attaché-case without opening it and said: 'You would like
to know how it has turned out? The final settlement is as
good as in my pocket. A charming fellow, your Deputy
Manager, but dangerous to reckon with.' He laughed and
shook K. by the hand, trying to make him laugh too. But
now K.'s suspicions seized on the fact that the manufacturer had not offered to show him the papers, and he
found nothing to laugh at. 'Herr Assessor,' said the manufacturer, 'you're under the weather to-day. You look so
depressed.' 'Yes,' said K., puting his hand to his brow, 'a

headache, family troubles.' 'Ah, yes,' said the manufacturer, who was a hasty man and could never listen quietly
to anybody, 'we all have our troubles.' K. had involuntarily taken a step towards the door, as if to show the
manufacturer out, but the latter said: 'Herr Assessor,
there's another little matter I should mention to you. I'm
afraid this isn't exactly the moment to bother you with it,
but the last two times I've been here I forgot to mention
it. And if I put off mentioning it any longer it will probably lose its point altogether. And that would be a pity,
since my information may have some real value for you.'
Before K. had time to make any reply the man stepped
up close to him, tapped him with one finger on the chest,
and said in a low voice: 'You're involved in a case, aren't
you?' K. started back, crying out: 'The Deputy Manager
told you that.' 'Not at all,' said the manufacturer. 'How
should the Deputy Manager know anything about it?'
'How do you know about it?' asked K., pulling himself
together. 'I pick up scraps of information about the Court
now and then,' said the manufacturer, 'and that accounts
for what I have to mention.' 'So many people seem to be
connected with the Court!' said K. with a bowed head,
as he led the manufacturer back to the desk. They sat
down as before and the manufacturer began: 'Unfortunately it isn't much that I can tell you. But in these
affairs one shouldn't leave the smallest stone unturned.
Besides, I feel a strong desire to help you, no matter how
modest the help. We have always been good business
friends till now, haven't we? Well, then.' K. wanted to
excuse himself for his behaviour that morning, but the
manufacturer would not hear of it, pushed his attaché-
case firmly under his arm to show that he was in a hurry
to go, and continued: 'I heard of your case from a man

called Titorelli. He's a painter, Titorelli is only his pseudonym, I don't know at all what his real name is. For years he has been in the habit of calling at my office from time to time, bringing little paintings for which I give him a sort of alms – he's almost a beggar. And they're not bad pictures, moors and heaths and so on. These deals – we have got into the way of them – pass off quite smoothly. But there was a time when he turned up too frequently for my taste, I told him so, we fell into conversation, I was curious to know how he could keep himself going entirely by his painting, and I discovered to my astonishment that he really earned his living as a portrait-painter. He worked for the Court, he said. For what Court, I asked. And then he told me about this Court. With your experience you can well imagine how amazed I was at the tales he told me. Since then he brings me the latest news from the Court every time he arrives, and in this way I have gradually acquired a considerable insight into its workings. Of course Titorelli wags his tongue too freely, and I often have to put a stopper on him, not just because he's naturally a liar, but chiefly because a business man like myself has so many troubles of his own that he can't afford to bother much about other people's. That's only by the way. Perhaps – I thought to myself – Titorelli might be of some use to you, he knows many of the Judges, and even if he can hardly have much influence himself, he can at least advise you how to get in touch with influential men. And even if you can't take him as an oracle, still it seems to me that in your hands his information might become important. For you are as good as a lawyer yourself. I'm always saying: Assessor K. is almost a lawyer. Oh, I have no anxiety about your case. Well, would you care to go and see Titorelli? On my recommendation he will certainly do all he can for you, I really think you should go. It needn't be to-day, of course, some time, any time will do. Let me add that you needn't feel bound to go just because I advise you to, not in the least. No, if you think you can dispense with Titorelli, it's certainly better to leave him entirely out of it. Perhaps you've a detailed plan of your own already drawn up and Titorelli might spoil it. Well, in that case you'd much better not go to see him. It certainly means swallowing one's pride to go to such a fellow for advice. Anyhow, do just as you like. Here is my letter of recommendation and here is the address.'

K. took the letter, feeling dashed, and stuck it in his pocket. Even in the most favourable circumstances the advantages which his recommendation could bring him must be outweighed by the damage implied in the fact that the manufacturer knew about his case and that the painter was spreading news of it. He could hardly bring himself to utter the few obligatory words of thanks to the manufacturer, who was already on his way out. 'I'll go to see the man,' he said as he shook hands at the door, 'or write to him to call here, since I'm so busy.' 'I knew,' said the manufacturer, 'that you could be depended on to find the best solution. Though I must say I should have thought you would rather avoid receiving people like this Titorelli at the Bank, if you mean to discuss your case with him. Besides, it's not always advisable to let such people get their hands on letters of yours. But I'm sure you've thought it all over and know what you are doing.' K. nodded and accompanied the manufacturer a stage farther, through the waiting-room. In spite of his outward composure he was horrified at his own lack of sense. His suggestion of writing to Titorelli had been made merely to show the manufacturer that he appreciated the recommendation and meant to lose no time in making contact with the painter, but, left to himself, he would not have hesitated to write to Titorelli had he regarded the man's assistance as important. Yet it needed the manufacturer to point out the dangers lurking in such an action. Had he really lost his powers of judgement to that extent already? If it was possible for him to think of explicitly inviting a questionable character to the Bank in order to stage a discussion of his case with only a door between him and the Deputy Manager, was it not also possible and even extremely probable that he was overlooking other dangers as well, or blindly running into them? There wasn't always someone at his side to warn him. And this was the moment, just when he intended to concentrate all his energies on the case, this was the moment for him to start doubting the alertness of his faculties! Must the difficulties he was faced with in carrying out his office work begin to affect the case as well? At all events he simply could not understand how he could ever have thought of writing to Titorelli and inviting him to come to the Bank.

He was still shaking his head over this when the attendant came up to him and indicated three gentlemen sitting on a bench in the waiting-room. They had already waited for a long time to see K. Now that the attendant accosted K. they sprang to their feet, each one of them eager to seize the first chance of monopolizing K.'s attention. If the Bank officials were inconsiderate enough to make them waste their time in the waiting-room, they felt entitled in their turn to behave with the same lack of consideration. 'Herr Assessor,' one of them began. But K. sent for his overcoat and said to all three of them while the attendant helped him into it: 'Forgive me, gentlemen, I'm sorry to tell you that I have no time to see you at present. I can't say how desolated I am, but I have to go out on urgent business and must leave the building at once. You have seen for yourselves how long I have been held up by my last caller. Would you be so good as to come back to-morrow or at some other time? Or could we talk the matter over on the telephone, perhaps? Or perhaps you could inform me now, briefly, what your business is, and I shall give you an explicit answer in writing. Though it would certainly be much better if you made an appointment for some other time.' These suggestions threw the three men, whose time had thus been wasted to no purpose at all, into such astonishment that they gazed at each other dumbly. 'That's settled, then?' asked K., turning to the attendant, who was bringing him his hat. Through the open door of his room he could see that the snow was now falling more thickly. Consequently he put up his coat-collar and buttoned it high round his neck.

At that very moment the Deputy Manager stepped out of the next room, glanced smilingly at K. in his overcoat talking to the clients, and asked: 'Are you going out, Herr Assessor?' 'Yes,' said K., straightening himself, 'I have to go out on business.' But the Deputy Manager had already turned to the three clients. 'And these gentlemen?' he asked. 'I believe they have already been waiting a long time.' 'We have settled what we are to do,' said K. But now the clients could no longer be held in check, they clustered round K. protesting that they would not have waited for hours unless their business had been important, not to say urgent, necessitating immediate discussion at length, and in private at that. The Deputy Manager listened to them for a moment or two, meanwhile observing K., who stood holding his hat and dusting it spasmodically, then he remarked: 'Gentlemen, there is a very simple solution. If you will be content with me, I put myself gladly at your disposal instead of the Herr Assessor. Your business must, of course, be attended to at once. We are business men like yourselves and know how valuable time is to a business man. Will you be so good as to come with me?' And he opened the door which led to the waiting-room of his own office.

How clever the Deputy Manager was at poaching on the preserves which K. was forced to abandon! But was not K. abandoning more than was absolutely needful? While with the vaguest and – he could not but admit it – the faintest of hopes, he was rushing away to see an unknown painter, his prestige in the Bank would suffer irreparable injury. It would probably be much better for him to take off his overcoat again and conciliate at least the two clients waiting next door for their turn to receive the Deputy Manager's attention. K. might actually have attempted this if he had not at that moment caught sight of the Deputy Manager himself in K.'s own room, searching through his files as if they belonged to him. In great agitation K. appeared in the doorway of the room and the Deputy Manager exclaimed: 'Oh, you're not away yet.' He turned his face towards K. – the deep lines scored upon it seemed to speak of power rather than old age – and immediately resumed his search. 'I'm looking for a copy of an agreement,' he said, 'which the firm's representative thinks should be among your papers. Won't you help me to look?' K. took a step forward, but the Deputy Manager said: 'Thanks, now I've found it,' and carrying a huge package of documents, which obviously contained not only the copy of the agreement but many other papers as well, he returned to his office.

'I'm not equal to him just now,' K. told himself, 'but once my personal difficulties are settled he'll be the first to feel it, and I'll make him suffer for it, too.' Somewhat soothed by this thought, K. instructed the attendant, who had been holding open the corridor door for a long time, to inform the Manager at any convenient time that he had gone out on a business call, and then, almost elated at the thought of being able to devote himself entirely to his case for a while, he left the Bank.

He drove at once to the address where the painter lived, in a suburb which was almost at the diametrically opposite end of the town from where the Court held its meetings. This was an even poorer neighbourhood, the houses were still darker, the streets filled with sludge oozing about slowly on top of the melting snow. In the tenement where the painter lived only one wing of the great double door stood open, and beneath the other wing, in the masonry near the ground, there was a gaping hole out of which, just as K. approached, issued a disgusting yellow fluid, steaming hot, from which a rat fled into the adjoining canal. At the foot of the stairs an infant lay belly down on the ground bawling, but one could scarcely hear its shrieks because of the deafening din that came from a tinsmith's workshop at the other side of the entry. The door of the workshop was open; three apprentices were standing in a half-circle round some object on which they were beating with their hammers. A great sheet of tin hanging on the wall cast a pallid light, which fell between two of the apprentices and lit up their faces and aprons. K. flung only a fleeting glance at all this, he wanted to get out of the neighbourhood as quickly as possible, he would merely ask the painter a few searching questions and return at once to the Bank. His work at the Bank for the rest of the day would benefit should he have any luck at all on this visit. When he reached the third floor he had to moderate his pace, he was quite out of breath, both the stairs and the storeys were disproportionately high, and the painter was supposed to live quite at the top, in an attic. The air was stifling; there was no well for these narrow stairs, which were enclosed on either side by blank walls, showing only at rare intervals a tiny window very high up. Just as K. paused to take breath, several young girls rushed out of one of the flats and laughingly raced past him up the stairs. K. slowly followed them, catching up with one who had apparently stumbled and been left behind, and as they ascended together he asked her: 'Does a painter called Titorelli live here?' The girl, who had a slight spinal deformity and seemed scarcely thirteen years old, nudged him with her elbow and peered up at him knowingly. Neither her youth nor her deformity had saved her from being prematurely debauched. She did not even smile, but stared unwinkingly at K. with shrewd, bold eyes. K. pretended not to have noticed her behaviour and asked: 'Do you know the painter Titorelli?' She nodded and asked in her turn: 'What do you want him for?' K. thought it a good chance to find out a little more about Titorelli while he still had time: 'I want him to paint my portrait,' he said. 'To paint your portrait?' she repeated, letting her jaw fall open, then she gave K. a little slap as if he had said something extraordinarily unexpected or stupid, lifted her abbreviated skirts with both hands, and raced as fast as she could after the other girls, whose shrieks were already dying away in the distance. Yet at the very next turn of the stair K. ran into all of them. Obviously the hunch-back had reported K.'s intention, and they were waiting there for him. They stood lined up on either side of the stairway, squeezing against the walls to leave room for K. to pass, and smoothing their skirts down with their hands. All their faces betrayed the same mixture of childishness and sophistication which had prompted this idea of making him run the gauntlet between them. At the top end of the row of girls, who now closed in behind K. with spurts of laughter, stood the hunch-back ready to lead the way. Thanks to her, he was able to make straight for the right door. He had intended to go on up the main stairs, but she indicated a side-stair that branched off towards Titorelli's dwelling. This stairway was extremely narrow, very long, without any turning, could thus be surveyed in all its length, and was abruptly terminated by nothing but Titorelli's door. In contrast to the rest of the stairway this door was relatively brightly lit by a little fanlight set at an angle above it, and was made of unpainted planks on which sprawled the name Titorelli in red, traced in sweeping brush-strokes. K. with his escort was hardly more than half-way up the stairs when someone above, obviously disturbed by the clatter of so many feet, opened the door a little way, and a man who seemed to be wearing nothing but a nightshirt appeared in the opening. 'Oh!' he cried when he saw the approaching mob, and promptly vanished. The hunch-back clapped her hands in joy, and the other girls crowded K. from behind to urge him on faster.

Yet they were still mounting towards the top when the painter flung the door wide open and with a deep bow invited K. to enter. As for the girls, he turned them off, he would not admit one of them, eagerly as they implored and hard as they tried to enter by force if not by permission. The hunch-back alone managed to slip under his outstretched arm, but he rushed after her, seized her by the skirts, whirled her once round his head, and then set her down before the door among the other girls, who had not dared meanwhile, although he had quitted his post, to cross the threshold. K. did not know what to make of all this, for they seemed to be on the friendliest terms together. The girls outside the door, craning their necks behind one another, shouted various jocular remarks at the painter which K. did not understand, and the painter was laughing too as he almost hurled the hunch-back through the air. Then he shut the door, bowed once more to K., held out his hand, and said in introduction: 'I'm the painter Titorelli.' K. pointed at the door, behind which the girls were whispering, and said: 'You seem to be a great favourite here.' 'Oh, these brats!' said the painter, trying unsuccessfully to button his nightshirt at the neck. He was barefooted and besides the nightshirt had on only a pair of wide-legged yellow linen trousers girt by a belt with a long end flapping to and fro. 'These brats are a real nuisance,' he went on, while he desisted from fiddling with his nightshirt, since the top button had just come off, fetched a chair and urged K. to sit down. 'I painted one of them once – not any of those you saw – and since then they've all persecuted me. When I'm here myself they can only get in if I let them, but whenever I go away there's always at least one of them here. They've had a key made for my door, and they lend it round. You can hardly imagine what a nuisance that is. For instance, if I bring a lady here whom I want to paint, I unlock the door with my own key and find, say, the hunch-back over there at the table, reddening her lips with my paint brushes, while her little sisters, who she's supposed to keep an eye on, are sprawling over the whole place and messing up every corner of the room. Or, and this actually happened last night, I come home very late – by the way, that's why I'm in this state of disrepair, and the room too, please excuse it – I come home late, then, and start climbing into bed and something catches me by the leg; I look under the bed and haul out another of these pests. Why they should make such a set at me I don't know, you must have noticed yourself that I don't exactly encourage them. And, of course, all this disturbs me in my work. If it hadn't been that I have free quarters in this studio I should have cleared out long ago.' Just then a small voice piped behind the door with anxious cajolery: 'Titorelli, can we come in now?' 'No,' replied the painter. 'Not even me?' the voice asked again. 'Not even you,' said the painter, and he went to the door and locked it.

Meanwhile K. had been looking round the room, it would never have occurred to him that anyone could call this wretched little hole a studio. You could scarcely take two strides in any direction. The whole room, floor, walls, and ceiling, was a box of bare wooden planks with cracks showing between them. Opposite K., against a wall, stood a bed with a variegated assortment of coverings. In the middle of the room an easel supported a canvas covered by a shirt whose sleeves dangled on the floor. Behind K. was the window, through which in the fog one could not see farther than the snow-covered roof of the next house.

The turning of the key in the lock reminded K. that he had not meant to stay long. Accordingly he fished the manufacturer's letter from his pocket, handed it to the painter, and said: 'I heard of you from this gentleman,

a friend of yours, and have come here at his suggestion.'
The painter hastily read the letter through and pitched it
on to the bed. If the manufacturer had not so explicitly
claimed acquaintance with Titorelli as a poor man dependent on his charity, one might actually have thought
that Titorelli did not know the manufacturer or at least
could not remember him. On top of this he now asked:
'Have you come to buy pictures or to have your portrait
painted?' K. stared at him in amazement. What could
have been in the letter? He had assumed as a matter of
course that the manufacturer would tell Titorelli that he
had come for no other purpose than to inquire about his
case. He had been altogether too rash and reckless in
rushing to this man. But he must make a relevant reply
of some kind, and so he said with a glance at the easel:
'You're working on a painting just now?' 'Yes,' said
Titorelli, stripping the shirt from the easel and throwing
it on the bed after the letter. 'It's a portrait. A good piece
of work, but not quite finished yet.' K. was apparently in
luck, the opportunity to mention the Court was being
literally thrown at his head, for this was obviously the
portrait of a Judge. Also it strikingly resembled the portrait hanging in the Advocate's office. True, this was
quite a different Judge, a stout man with a black bushy
beard which reached far up on his cheeks on either side;
moreover the other portrait was in oils, while this was
lightly and as yet indistinctly sketched in pastel. Yet
everything else showed a close resemblance, for here too
the Judge seemed to be on the point of starting menac-
ingly from his high seat, bracing himself firmly on the
arms of it. 'That must be a Judge,' K. felt like saying at
once, but he checked himself for the time being and approached the picture as if he wished to study the detail.

A large figure rising in the middle of the picture from the high back of the chair he could not identify, and he asked the painter whom it was intended to represent. It still needed a few more touches, the painter replied, and fetched a crayon from a table, armed with which he worked a little at the outline of the figure but without making it any more recognizable to K. 'It is Justice,' said the painter at last. 'Now I can recognize it,' said K. 'There's the bandage over the eyes, and here are the scales. But aren't there wings on the figure's heels, and isn't it flying?' 'Yes,' said the painter, 'my instructions were to paint it like that; actually it is Justice and the goddess of Victory in one.' 'Not a very good combination, surely,' said K., smiling. 'Justice must stand quite still, or else the scales will waver and a just verdict will become impossible.' 'I had to follow my client's instructions,' said the painter. 'Of course,' said K., who had not wished to give any offence by his remark. 'You have painted the figure as it actually stands above the high seat.' 'No,' said the painter, 'I have neither seen the figure nor the high seat, that is all invention, but I am told what to paint and I paint it.' 'How do you mean?' asked K., deliberately pretending that he did not understand. 'It's surely a Judge sitting on his seat of justice?' 'Yes,' said the painter, 'but it is by no means a high Judge and he has never sat on such a seat in his life.' 'And yet he has himself painted in that solemn posture? Why, he sits there as if he were the actual President of the Court.' 'Yes, they're very vain, these gentlemen,' said the painter. 'But their superiors give them permission to get themselves painted like that. Each one of them gets precise instructions how he may have his portrait painted. Only you can't judge the detail of the costume and the seat itself from this picture, unfortunately, pastel is really unsuited for this kind of thing.' 'Yes,' said K. 'it's curious that you should have used pastel.' 'My client wished it,' said the painter, 'he intends the picture for a lady.' The sight of the picture seemed to have roused his ardour, he rolled up his shirt-sleeves, took several crayons in his hand, and as K. watched the delicate crayon-strokes a reddish shadow began to grow round the head of the Judge, a shadow which tapered off in long rays as it approached the edge of the picture. This play of shadow bit by bit surrounded the head like a halo or a high mark of distinction. But the figure of Justice was left bright except for an almost imperceptible touch of shadow; that brightness brought the figure sweeping right into the foreground and it no longer suggested the goddess of Justice, or even the goddess of Victory, but looked exactly like a goddess of the Hunt in full cry. The painter's activities absorbed K. against his will, and in the end he began to reproach himself for having stayed so long without even touching on the business that brought him. 'What is the name of this Judge?' he asked suddenly. 'I'm not allowed to tell,' replied the painter, stooping over the picture and ostentatiously ignoring the guest whom at first he had greeted with such consideration. K. put this down to caprice and was annoyed that his time should be wasted in such a manner. 'You're in the confidence of the Court, I take it?' he asked. The painter laid down his crayons at once, straightened himself, rubbed his hands, and looked at K. with a smile. 'So the truth has come out at last,' he said. 'You want to find out something about the Court, as your letter of recommendation told me, I may say, and you started talking about my paintings only to win me over. But I don't take that ill, you could hardly know

that that wasn't the right way to tackle me. Oh, please
don't apologize!' he said sharply, as K. tried to make
some excuse. And then he continued: 'Besides, you were
quite right in what you said; I am in the confidence of
the Court.' He paused, as if he wanted to give K. time to
digest this fact. Now they could hear the girls behind the
door again. They seemed to be crowding round the keyhole, perhaps they could see into the room through the
cracks in the door as well. K. abandoned any attempt at
apology, for he did not want to deflect the conversation,
nor did he want the painter to feel too important, and so
become in a sense inaccessible, accordingly he asked: 'Is
your position an official appointment?' 'No,' said the
painter curtly, as if the question had cut him short. K.,
being anxious to keep him going, said: 'Well, such un-
recognized posts often carry more influence with them
than the official ones.' 'That is just how it is with me,'
said the painter, knitting his brow and nodding. 'The
manufacturer mentioned your case to me yesterday, he
asked me if I wouldn't help you, I said to him: "Let the
man come and see me some time," and I'm delighted to
see you here so soon. The case seems to lie very near your
heart, which, of course, is not in the least surprising.
Won't you take off your coat for a moment?' Although
K. had it in mind to stay only for a short time, this request was very welcome to him. He had begun to feel the
air in the room stifling, several times already he had eyed
with amazement a little iron stove in the corner which
did not seem even to be working, the sultry heat in the
place was inexplicable. He took off his overcoat, unbut-
toning his jacket as well, and the painter said apologetically: 'I must have warmth. It's very cosy in here, isn't
it? I'm well enough off in that respect.' K. said nothing

to this, for it was not the warmth that made him so uncomfortable, it was rather the stuffy, oppressive atmosphere; the room could not have been aired for a long time. His discomfort was still more intensified when the painter begged him to sit down on the bed, while he himself took the only chair in the room, which stood beside the easel. Titorelli also seemed to misunderstand K.'s reasons for sitting on the extreme edge of the bed, he urged him to make himself comfortable and actually pushed the reluctant K. deep down among the bedclothes and pillows. Then he returned to his chair again and at last put his first serious question, which made K. forget everything else. 'Are you innocent?' he asked. 'Yes,' said K. The answering of this question gave him a feeling of real happiness, particularly as he was addressing a private individual and therefore need fear no consequences. Nobody else had yet asked him such a frank question. To savour to the full his elation he added: 'I am completely innocent.' 'I see,' said the painter, bending his head as if in thought. Suddenly he raised it again and said: 'If you are innocent, then the matter is quite simple.' K.'s eyes darkened, this man who said he was in the confidence of the Court was talking like an ignorant child. 'My innocence doesn't make the matter any simpler,' said K. But after all he could not help smiling, and then he slowly shook his head. 'I have to fight against countless subtleties in which the Court is likely to lose itself. And in the end, out of nothing at all, an enormous fabric of guilt will be conjured up.' 'Yes, yes, of course,' said the painter, as if K. were needlessly interrupting the thread of his ideas. 'But you're innocent all the same?' 'Why, yes,' said K. 'That's the main thing,' said the painter. He was not to be moved by argument, yet in spite of his decisive-

ness it was not clear whether he spoke out of conviction
or out of mere indifference. K. wanted first to be sure of
this, so he said: 'You know the Court much better than
I do, I feel certain, I don't know much more about it than
what I've heard from all sorts and conditions of people.
But they all agree on one thing, that charges are never
made frivolously, and that the Court, once it has brought
a charge against someone, is firmly convinced of the guilt
of the accused and can be dislodged from that conviction
only with the greatest difficulty.' 'The greatest difficulty?'
cried the painter, flinging one hand in the air. 'Never in
any case can the Court be dislodged from that conviction. If I were to paint all the Judges in a row on one
canvas and you were to plead your case before it, you
would have more hope of success than before the actual
Court.' 'I see,' said K. to himself, forgetting that he
merely wished to probe the painter.

Again a girl's voice piped from behind the door:
'Titorelli, won't he be going away soon?' 'Quiet there!'
cried the painter over his shoulder. 'Can't you see that
I'm engaged with this gentleman?' But the girl, not to be
put off, asked: 'Are you going to paint him?' And when
the painter did not reply she went on: 'Please don't
paint him, such an ugly man as that.' The others yelled
agreement in a confused jabbering. The painter made a
leap for the door, opened it a little – K. could see the imploring, outstretched, clasped hands of the girls – and
said: 'If you don't stop that noise I'll fling you all down
the stairs. Sit down here on the steps and see that you
keep quiet.' Apparently they did not obey him at once,
for he had to shout in an imperious voice: 'Down with
you on the steps!' After that all was still.

'Excuse me,' said the painter, returning to K. again. K.

had scarcely glanced towards the door, he had left it to the painter to decide whether and in what manner he was to be protected. Even now he scarcely made a movement when the painter bent down to him and whispered in his ear, so that the girls outside might not hear: 'These girls belong to the Court too.' 'What?' cried K., screwing his head round to stare at the painter. But Titorelli sat down again on his chair and said half in jest, half in explanation: 'You see, everything belongs to the Court.' 'That's something I hadn't noticed,' said K. shortly; the painter's general statement stripped his remark about the girls of all its disturbing significance. Yet K. sat gazing for some time at the door, behind which the girls were now sitting quietly on the stairs. One of them had thrust a blade of straw through a crack between the planks and was moving it slowly up and down.

'You don't seem to have any general idea of the Court yet,' said the painter, stretching his legs wide in front of him and tapping with his shoes on the floor. 'But since you're innocent you won't need it anyhow. I shall get you off all by myself.' 'How can you do that?' asked K. 'For you told me yourself a few minutes ago that the Court was quite impervious to proof.' 'Impervious only to proof which one brings before the Court,' said the painter, raising one finger as if K. had failed to perceive a fine distinction. 'But it is quite a different matter with one's efforts behind the scenes; that is, in the consulting-rooms, in the lobbies or, for example, in this very studio.' What the painter now said no longer seemed incredible to K., indeed it agreed in the main with what he had heard from other people. More, it was actually hopeful in a high degree. If a Judge could really be so easily influenced by personal connexions as the Advocate insisted, then the painter's connexions with these vain functionaries were especially important and in any case not to be undervalued. That made the painter an excellent recruit to the ring of helpers which K. was gradually gathering round him. His talent for organization had once been the pride of the Bank, and now that he had to act entirely on his own responsibility this was his chance to prove it to the uttermost. Titorelli observed the effect his words had produced upon K. and then said with a slight uneasiness: 'Perhaps it strikes you that I talk almost like a jurist? It's my long association with the gentlemen of the Court that has made me grow like that. I have many advantages from it, of course, but I'm losing a great deal of my *élan* as an artist.' 'How did you come in contact with the Judges to begin with?' asked K.; he wanted to win the painter's confidence first, before actually enlisting him in his service. 'That was quite simple,' said the painter. 'I inherited the connexion. My father was the Court painter before me. It's the only post that is always hereditary. New people are of no use for it. There are so many complicated and various and above all secret rules laid down for the painting of the different grades of functionaries that a knowledge of them must be confined to certain families. Over there in that chest, for instance, I keep all my father's drawings, which I never show to anyone. And only a man who has studied them can possibly paint the Judges. Yet even if I were to lose them, I have enough private knowledge tucked away in my head to make my post secure against all comers. For every Judge insists on being painted as the great old Judges were painted, and nobody can do that but me.' 'Yours is an enviable situation,' said K., who was thinking of his own post in the Bank. 'So your position is unassailable?' 'Yes, unassailable,' replied the painter, proudly bracing his shoulders. 'And for that reason, too, I can venture to help a poor man with his case now and then.' 'And how do you do it?' asked K., as if it were not himself who had just been described as a poor man. But Titorelli refused to be drawn in and went on: 'In your case, for instance, as you are completely innocent, this is the line I shall take.' The repeated mention of his innocence was already making K. impatient. At moments it seemed to him as if these repetitions were based on a naïve assumption that his case was bound to turn out well, and on these terms the painter's help would be worth having. But in spite of his doubts K. held his tongue and did not interrupt the man. He was not prepared to renounce Titorelli's assistance, on that point he was decided; the painter was no more questionable as an ally than the Advocate. Indeed he very much preferred the painter's offer of assistance, since it was made so much more ingenuously and frankly.

Titorelli drew his chair closer to the bed and continued in a low voice: 'I forgot to ask you first what sort of acquittal you want. There are three possibilities, that is, definite acquittal, ostensible acquittal, and indefinite postponement. Definite acquittal is of course the best, but I haven't the slightest influence on that kind of verdict. As far as I know, there is no single person who could influence the verdict of definite acquittal. The only deciding factor seems to be the innocence of the accused. Since you're innocent, of course it would be possible for you to ground your case on your innocence alone. But then you would require neither my help nor help from anyone.'

This lucid explanation took K. aback at first, but he replied in the same subdued voice as the painter: 'It seems to me that you're contradicting yourself.' 'In what

way?' asked the painter patiently, leaning back with a
smile. The smile awoke in K. a suspicion that he was
now about to expose contradictions not so much in the
painter's statements as in the Court procedure itself. However, he was not abashed but went on: 'You made the
assertion earlier that the Court is impervious to proof,
later you qualified that assertion by confining it to the
public sessions of the Court, and now you actually say
that an innocent man requires no help before the Court.
That alone implies a contradiction. But, in addition, you
said at first that the Judges can be moved by personal
intervention, and now you deny that definite acquittal, as
you call it, can ever be achieved by personal intervention.
In that lies the second contradiction.' 'These contradictions are easy to explain,' said the painter. 'We must distinguish between two things: what is established by the
Law, and what I have discovered through personal experience; you must not confuse the two. In the code of
the Law, which I may say I have not read, it is of course
laid down on the one hand that the innocent shall be
acquitted, but it is not stated on the other hand that the
Judges are open to influence. Now, my experience is diametrically opposed to that. I have not met one case of
definite acquittal, and I have met many cases of influential intervention. It is possible, of course, that in all the
cases known to me there was none in which the accused
was really innocent. But is not that probable? Among so
many cases no single case of innocence? Even as a child
I used to listen carefully to my father when he spoke of
cases he had heard about; the Judges, too, who came to
his studio were always telling stories about the Court, in
our circle it is still the sole topic of discussion; no sooner
did I get the chance to attend the Court myself than I

took full advantage of it, I have listened to countless cases in their most crucial stages, and followed them as far as they could be followed, and yet – I must admit it – I have never encountered one case of definite acquittal.' 'Not one case of definite acquittal, then,' said K. as if he were speaking to himself and his hopes, 'but that merely confirms the opinion that I have already formed of this Court. It is an aimless institution from any point of view. A single executioner could do all that is needed.' 'You mustn't generalize,' said the painter in displeasure. 'I have only quoted my own experience.' 'That's quite enough,' said K. 'Or have you ever heard of acquittals in earlier times?' 'Such acquittals,' replied the painter, 'there must certainly have been. Only it is very difficult to prove the fact. The final decisions of the Court are never recorded, even the Judges can't get hold of them, consequently we have only legendary accounts of ancient cases. These legends certainly provide instances of acquittal; actually the majority of them are about acquittals, they can be believed, but they cannot be proved. All the same, they shouldn't be entirely left out of account, they must have an element of truth in them, and besides they are very beautiful. I myself have painted several pictures founded on such legends.' 'Mere legends cannot alter my opinion,' said K. 'and I fancy that one cannot appeal to such legends before the Court?' The painter laughed. 'No, one can't do that,' he said. 'Then there's no use talking about them,' said K., willing for the time being to fall in with the painter's views, even where they seemed improbable or contradicted other reports he had heard. He had no time now to inquire into the truth of all the painter said, much less disprove it, the utmost he could hope to do was to get the man to help him in some way, even should the help prove inconclusive. Accordingly he said: 'Let us leave definite acquittal out of account, then; you mentioned two other possibilities as well.' 'Ostensible acquittal and postponement. These are the only possibilities,' said the painter. 'But won't you take off your jacket before we go on to speak of them? You look very hot.' 'Yes,' said K., who had been paying no attention to anything but the painter's expositions, but now that he was reminded of the heat found his forehead drenched in sweat. 'It's almost unbearable.' The painter nodded as if he comprehended K.'s discomfort quite well. 'Couldn't we open the window?' asked K. 'No,' replied the painter. 'It's only a sheet of glass let into the roof, it can't be opened.' Now K. realized that he had been hoping all the time that either the painter or himself would suddenly go over to the window and fling it open. He was prepared to gulp down even mouthfuls of fog if he could only get air. The feeling of being desperately cut off from the fresh air made his head swim. He brought the flat of his hand down on the feather bed and said in a feeble voice: 'That's both uncomfortable and unhealthy.' 'Oh no,' said the painter in defence of his window. 'Because it's sealed down it keeps the warmth in much better than a double window, though it's only a simple pane of glass. And if I want to air the place, which isn't really necessary, for the air comes in everywhere through the chinks, I can always open one of the doors or even both of them.' Somewhat reassured by this explanation, K. glanced round to discover the second door. The painter saw what he was doing and said: 'It's behind you, I had to block it up by putting the bed in front of it.' Only now did K. see the little door in the wall. 'This is really too small for a studio,' said the painter, as if to forestall K.'s criticisms.

'I simply had to put my things where I could. Of course it's a bad place for a bed, just in front of that door. The Judge whom I'm painting just now, for instance, always comes in by that door, and I've had to give him a key for it so that he can wait for me in the studio if I happen to be out. Well, he usually arrives early in the morning, while I'm still asleep. And of course however fast asleep I am, it wakens me with a start when the door behind my bed suddenly opens. You would lose any respect you have for the Judges if you could hear the curses that welcome him when he climbs over my bed in the early morning. I could certainly take the key away from him again, but that would only make things worse. It would be easy enough to burst open any of the doors here.' All during these exchanges K. kept considering whether he should take off his jacket, but at last he realized that if he did not he would be incapable of staying any longer in the room, so he took it off, laying it, however, across his knee, to save time in putting it on again whenever the interview was finished. Scarcely had he taken off his jacket when one of the girls cried: 'He's taken off his jacket now,' and he could hear them all crowding to peer through the cracks and view the spectacle for themselves. 'The girls think,' said the painter, 'that I'm going to paint your portrait and that's why you are taking off your jacket.' 'I see,' said K., very little amused, for he did not feel much better than before, although he was now sitting in his shirt-sleeves. Almost morosely he asked: 'What did you say the other two possibilities were?' He had already forgotten even the names of them. 'Ostensible acquittal and indefinite postponement,' said the painter. 'It lies with you to choose between them. I can help you to either of them, though not without taking some trouble, and, as far as that is concerned, the difference between them is that ostensible acquittal demands intense concentration at long intervals, while postponement taxes your strength less but means a steady strain. First, then, let us take ostensible acquittal. If you decide on that, I shall write down on a sheet of paper an affidavit of your innocence. The text for such affidavits has been handed down to me by my father and allows of no quibbling. Then with this affidavit I shall make a round of the Judges I know, beginning, let us say, with the Judge I am painting now, when he comes for his sitting to-night. I shall lay the affidavit before him, explain to him that you are innocent, and myself guarantee your innocence. And that is not merely a formal guarantee but a real and binding one.' In the eyes of the painter there was a faint suggestion of reproach that K. should lay upon him the burden of such a responsibility. 'That would be very kind of you,' said K. 'And the Judge would believe you and yet not give me a definite acquittal?' 'As I have already explained,' replied the painter. 'Besides, it is not in the least certain that every Judge will believe me; some Judges, for instance, will ask to see you in person. And then I should have to take you with me to call on them. Though when that happens the battle is already half won, particularly as I should tell you beforehand, of course, exactly what line to take with each Judge. The real difficulty comes with the Judges who turn you down at the start — and that's sure to happen too. I should go on hammering at them, of course, but we might have to do without them, though one cannot afford to do that, since dissent by individual Judges cannot affect the result. Well then, if I get a sufficient number of Judges to subscribe to the affidavit, I shall then deliver it to the Judge who is actually conducting your trial. Possibly I may have secured his signature too, then everything will be settled fairly soon, a little sooner than usual. Generally speaking, there should be no difficulties worth mentioning after that, the accused at this stage can feel supremely confident. Indeed it's remarkable, but true, that people's confidence mounts higher at this stage than after their acquittal. There's no need for them to do much more. The Judge is covered by the guarantees of the other Judges subscribing to the affidavit, and so he can grant an acquittal with an easy mind, and though some formalities may remain to be settled, he will undoubtedly grant the acquittal to please me and his other friends. Then you can walk out of the Court a free man.' 'So then I'm free,' said K. doubtfully. 'Yes,' said the painter, 'but only ostensibly free, or more exactly, provisionally free. For the Judges of the lowest grade, to whom my acquaintances belong, haven't the power to grant a final acquittal, that power is reserved for the highest Court of all, which is quite inaccessible to you, to me, and to all of us. What the prospects are up there we do not know and, I may say in passing, do not even want to know. The great privilege, then, of absolving from guilt our Judges do not possess, but they do have the right to take the burden of the charge off your shoulders. That is to say, when you are acquitted in this fashion the charge is lifted from your shoulders for the time being, but it continues to hover above you and can, as soon as an order comes from on high, be laid upon you again. As my connexion with the Court is such a close one, I can also tell you how in the routine of the Law-Court offices the distinction between definite and ostensible acquittal takes formal effect. In definite acquittal the documents relating to the case are completely annulled, they simply vanish from sight, not only the charge but also the records of the case and even the acquittal are destroyed, everything is destroyed. That's not the case with ostensible acquittal. The documents remain as they were, except that the affidavit is added to them and a record of the acquittal and the grounds for granting it. The whole dossier continues to circulate, as the regular official routine demands, passing on to the higher Courts, being referred to the lower ones again, and thus swinging backwards and forwards with greater or smaller oscillations, longer or shorter delays. These peregrinations are incalculable. A detached observer might sometimes fancy that the whole case had been forgotten, the documents lost, and the acquittal made absolute. No one really acquainted with the Court could think such a thing. No document is ever lost, the Court never forgets anything. One day – quite unexpectedly – some Judge will take up the documents and look at them attentively, recognize that in this case the charge is still valid, and order an immediate arrest. I have been speaking on the assumption that a long time elapses between the ostensible acquittal and the new arrest; that is possible and I have known of such cases, but it is just as possible for the acquitted man to go straight home from the Court and find officers already waiting to arrest him again. Then, of course, all his freedom is at an end.' 'And the case begins all over again?' asked K. almost incredulously. 'Certainly,' said the painter. 'The case begins all over again, but again it is possible, just as before, to secure an ostensible acquittal. One must again apply all one's energies to the case and never give in.' These last words were probably uttered because he noticed that K. was looking somewhat faint. 'But,' said K., as if he wanted to forestall any more revelations, 'isn't the engineering of a second acquittal more difficult than the first?' 'On that point,' said the painter, 'one can say nothing with certainty. You mean, I take it, that the second arrest might influence the Judges against signing a new affidavit? That is not so. Even while they are pronouncing the first acquittal the Judges foresee the possibility of the new arrest. Such a consideration, therefore, hardly comes into question. But it may happen, for hundreds of reasons, that the Judges are in a different frame of mind about the case, even from a legal viewpoint, and one's efforts to obtain a second acquittal must consequently be adapted to the changed circumstances, and in general must be every whit as energetic as those that secured the first one.' 'But this second acquittal isn't final either,' said K., turning away his head in repudiation. 'Of course not,' said the painter. 'The second acquittal is followed by the third arrest, the third acquittal by the fourth arrest, and so on. That is implied in the very idea of ostensible acquittal.' K. said nothing. 'Ostensible acquittal doesn't seem to appeal to you,' said the painter. 'Perhaps postponement would suit you better. Shall I explain to you how postponement works?' K. nodded. The painter was lolling back in his chair, his nightshirt gaped open, he had thrust one hand inside it and was lightly fingering his breast. 'Postponement,' he said, gazing in front of him for a moment as if seeking a completely convincing explanation, 'postponement consists in preventing the case from ever getting any further than its first stages. To achieve that it is necessary for the accused and his agent, but more particularly his agent, to remain continuously in personal touch with the Court. Let me point out again that this does not demand such intense concentration of one's energies as an ostensible acquittal, yet on the other hand it does require far greater vigilance. You daren't let the case out of your sight, you visit the Judge at regular intervals as well as in emergencies and must do all that is in your power to keep him friendly; if you don't know the Judge personally, then you must try to influence him through other Judges whom you do know, but without giving up your efforts to secure a personal interview. If you neglect none of these things, then you can assume with fair certainty that the case will never pass beyond its first stages. Not that the proceedings are quashed, but the accused is almost as likely to escape sentence as if he were free. As against ostensible acquittal postponement has this advantage, that the future of the accused is less uncertain, he is secured from the terrors of sudden arrest and doesn't need to fear having to undergo – perhaps at a most inconvenient moment – the strain and agitation which are inevitable in the achievement of ostensible acquittal. Though postponement, too, has certain drawbacks for the accused, and these must not be minimized. In saying this I am not thinking of the fact that the accused is never free; he isn't free either, in any real sense, after the ostensible acquittal. There are other drawbacks. The case can't be held up indefinitely without at least some plausible grounds being provided. So as a matter of form a certain activity must be shown from time to time, various measures have to be taken, the accused is questioned, evidence is collected, and so on. For the case must be kept going all the time, although only in the small circle to which it has been artificially restricted. This naturally involves the accused in occasional unpleasantness, but you must not think of it as being very unpleasant. For it's all a formality, the interrogations, for instance, are only short ones; if you have neither the time nor the inclination to go, you can excuse yourself on occasion, with some Judges you can even plan your interviews a long time ahead, all that it amounts to is a formal recognition of your status as an accused man by regular appearances before your Judge.' Already while these last words were being spoken K. had taken his jacket across his arm and got up. 'He's getting up now,' came the cry at once from behind the door. 'Are you going already?' asked the painter, who had also got up. 'I'm sure it's the air here that is driving you away. I'm sorry about it. I had a great deal more to tell you. I have had to express myself very briefly. But I hope my state-ments were lucid enough.' 'Oh yes,' said K., whose head was aching with the strain of forcing himself to listen. In spite of K.'s confirmation, the painter went on to sum up the matter again, as if to give him a last word of com-fort: 'Both methods have this in common, that they save the accused from coming up for sentence.' 'But they also prevent an actual acquittal,' said K. in a low voice, as if embarrassed by his own perspicacity. 'You have grasped the kernel of the matter,' said the painter quickly. K. laid his hand on his overcoat, but could not even summon the resolution to put on his jacket. He would have liked best of all to bundle them both together and rush out with them into the fresh air. Even the thought of the girls could not move him to put on his garments, although their voices were already piping, in anticipation, the news that he was doing so. The painter was anxious to guess K.'s intentions, so he said: 'I take it that you haven't come to any decision yet on my suggestions. That's right. In fact, I should have advised you against it had you at-tempted an immediate decision. It's like splitting hairs to distinguish the advantages and disadvantages. You must weigh everything very carefully. On the other hand you mustn't lose too much time either.' 'I'll come back again soon,' said K., in a sudden fit of resolution putting on his jacket, flinging his overcoat across his shoulders and hastening to the door, behind which the girls at once began shrieking. K. felt he could almost see them through the door. 'But you must keep your word,' said the painter, who had not followed him, 'or else I'll have to come to the Bank myself to make inquiries.' 'Unlock this door, will you?' said K., tugging at the handle, which the girls, as he could tell from the resistance, were hanging on to from outside. 'You don't want to be bothered by the girls, do you?' asked the painter. 'You had better take this way out,' and he indicated the door behind the bed. K. was perfectly willing and rushed back to the bed. But instead of opening the bedside door the painter crawled right under the bed and said from down there: 'Wait just a minute. Wouldn't you like to see a picture or two that you might care to buy?' K. did not want to be discourteous, the painter had really taken an interest in him and promised to help him further, also it was entirely owing to K.'s distractedness that the matter of a fee for the painter's services had not been mentioned, consequently he could not turn aside his offer now, and so he consented to look at the pictures, though he was trembling with impatience to be out of the place. Titorelli dragged a pile of unframed canvases from under the bed, they were so thickly covered with dust that when he blew some of it from the topmost, K. was almost blinded and choked by the cloud that flew up. 'Wild Nature, a heathscape,' said the painter, handing K. the picture. It showed two stunted trees standing far apart from each other in darkish grass. In the background was a many-hued sunset. 'Fine,' said K., 'I'll buy it.' K.'s curtness had been unthinking and so he was glad when the painter, instead of being offended, lifted another canvas from the floor. 'Here's the companion picture,' he said. It might be intended as a companion picture, but there was not the slightest difference that one could see between it and the other, here were the two trees, here the grass, and there the sunset. But K. did not bother about that. 'They're fine prospects,' he said. 'I'll buy both of them and hang them up in my office.' 'You seem to like the subject,' said the painter, fishing out a third canvas. 'By a lucky chance I have another of these studies here.' But it was not merely a similar study, it was simply the same wild heathscape again. The painter was apparently exploiting to the full this opportunity to sell off his old pictures. 'I'll take that one as well,' said K. 'How much for the three pictures?' 'We'll settle that next time,' said the painter. 'You're in a hurry to-day and we're going to keep in touch with each other, anyhow. I may say I'm very glad you like these pictures and I'll throw in all the others under the bed as well. They're heathscapes every one of them, I've painted dozens of them in my time. Some people won't have anything to do with these subjects because they're too depressing, but there are always people like yourself who prefer depressing pictures.' But by now K. had no mind to listen to the professional pronouncements of the peddling painter. 'Wrap the pictures up,' he cried, interrupting Titorelli's garrulity, 'my attendant will call to-morrow and fetch them.' 'That isn't necessary,' said the painter. 'I think I can manage to get you a porter to take them along with you now.' And at last he reached over the bed and unlocked the door. 'Don't be afraid to step on the bed,' he said. 'Everybody who comes here does that.' K. would not have hesitated to do it even without his invitation, he had actually set one foot plump on the middle of the feather bed, but when he looked out through the open door he drew his foot back again. 'What's this?' he asked the painter. 'What are you surprised at?' returned the painter, surprised in his turn. 'These are the Law-Court offices. Didn't you know that there were Law-Court offices here? There are Law-Court offices in almost every attic, why should this be an exception? My studio really belongs to the Law-Court offices, but the Court has put it at my disposal.' It was not so much the discovery of the Law-Court offices that startled K.; he was much more startled at himself, at his complete ignorance of all things concerning the Court. He accepted it as a fundamental principle for an accused man to be always forearmed, never to let himself be caught napping, never to let his eyes stray unthinkingly to the right when his judge was looming up on the left—and against that very principle he kept offending again and again. Before him stretched a long passage, from which was wafted an air compared to which the air in the studio was refreshing. Benches stood on either side of the passage, just as in the lobby of the offices that were handling K.'s case. There seemed, then, to be exact regulations for the interior disposition of these offices. At the moment there was no great coming and going of clients. A man was half sitting, half reclining on a bench, his face was buried in his arms and he seemed to be asleep; another man was standing in the dusk at the end of the passage. K. now stepped over the bed, the painter following him with the pictures. They soon found a Law-Court Attendant – by this time K. recognized these men from the gold buttons added to their ordinary civilian clothing – and the painter gave him instructions to accompany K. with the pictures. K. tottered rather than walked, keeping his handkerchief pressed to his mouth. They had almost reached the exit when the girls came rushing to meet them, so K. had not been spared even that encounter. The girls had obviously seen the second door of the studio opening and had made a detour at full speed, coming round by another stairway. 'I can't escort you any farther,' cried the painter laughingly, as the girls surrounded him. 'Till our next meeting. And don't take too long to think it over!' K. did not even look back. When he reached the street he hailed the first cab that came along. He must get rid of the Attendant, whose gold buttons offended his eyes, even though, likely enough, they escaped everyone else's attention. The Attendant, zealously dutiful, got up beside the coachman on the box, but K. made him get down again. Midday was long past when K. reached the Bank. He would have liked to leave the pictures in the cab, but was afraid that some day he might be required to give an account of them to the painter. So he had them carried into his office and locked them in the bottom drawer of his desk, to save them for the next few days at least from the eyes of the Deputy Manager.

VIII

The Commercial Traveller – Dismissal of the Advocate

AT long last K. had made up his mind to take his case out of the Advocate's hands. He could not quite rid himself of doubts about the wisdom of this step, but his conviction of its necessity prevailed. To screw himself to the decision cost him a lot of energy, on the day when he resolved to visit the Advocate his work lagged behind, he had to stay very late in the office, and so he did not reach the Advocate's door until well past ten o'clock. Before actually ringing the bell he thought it over once again, it might be better to dismiss the Advocate by telephone or by letter, a personal interview was bound to prove painful. Still, he did not want to lose the advantage of a personal interview, any other mode of dismissal would be accepted in silence or with a few formal words of acknowledgement, and unless he were to extract information from Leni he would never learn how the Advocate had reacted to the dismissal and what consequences for himself were likely to ensue according to the Advocate's opinion, which was not without its importance. Face to face with the Advocate, one could spring the dismissal on him as a surprise, and however guarded the man might be, K. would be easily able to learn from his demeanour all that he wanted to know. It was even possible that he might perceive the wisdom of leaving the case in the Advocate's hands after all and might withdraw his ultimatum.

The first ring at the Advocate's door produced, as usual, no result. 'Leni could be a little quicker,' thought K. But it was enough to be thankful for that no third party had come nosing in, as usually happened, the man in the dressing-gown, for instance, or some other interfering creature. K. glanced at the farther door as he pressed the button a second time, but on this occasion both doors remained firmly shut. At last a pair of eyes appeared at the grille in the Advocate's door, but they were not Leni's eyes. Someone shot back the bolt, but still blocked the way, calling down the lobby: 'It's him,' and only then flinging the door open. K. had been pushing against the door, for he could already hear a key being hastily turned in the neighbouring lock, and when it suddenly opened he was literally precipitated into the hall and caught a glimpse of Leni, for whom the warning cry must have been intended, rushing down the lobby in her nightgown. He peered after her for a moment and then turned to see who had opened the door. It was a dried-up little man with a long beard, he was holding a candle in one hand. 'Are you employed here?' asked K. 'No,' said the man, 'I don't belong to the house, I'm only a client, I've come here on business.' 'In your shirt-sleeves?' asked K., indicating the man's unceremonious attire. 'Oh, excuse me,' said the man, peering at himself by the light of the candle as if he had been unaware of his condition. 'Is Leni your mistress?' inquired K. curtly. He was straddling his legs slightly, his hands, in which he was holding his hat, clasped behind his back. The mere possession of a thick greatcoat gave him a feeling of superiority over the meagre little fellow. 'Oh God,' said the other, raising one hand before his face in horrified repudiation, 'no, no, what are you thinking of?' 'You look an honest man,' said K., smiling, 'but all the same – come along.' He waved him on with his hat, urging him to go first. 'What's your name?' K. asked as they were proceeding. 'Block, a commercial traveller,' said the little man, turning round to introduce himself, but K. would not suffer him to remain standing. 'Is that your real name?' went on K. 'Of course,' came the answer, 'why should you doubt it?' 'I thought you might have some reason for concealing your name,' said K. He was feeling at ease now, at ease as one is when speaking to an inferior in some foreign country, keeping one's own affairs to oneself and discussing with equanimity the other man's interests, which gain consequence for the attention one bestows on them yet can be dismissed at will. As they came to the Advocate's study K. halted, opened the door, and called to the fellow, who was meekly advancing along the lobby: 'Not so fast, show a light here.' K. fancied that Leni might have hidden herself in the study, he made the commercial traveller shine the candle into all the corners, but the room was empty. In front of the Judge's portrait K. caught the fellow from behind by the braces and pulled him back. 'Do you know who that is?' he asked, pointing upward at the picture. The man raised the candle, blinked up at the picture, and said: 'It's a Judge.' 'A high Judge?' asked K., stationing himself beside the other to observe what impression the portrait made on him. The man gazed up with reverence. 'It is a high Judge,' he said. 'You haven't much insight,' said K., 'that's the lowest of the low among the Judges.' 'Now, I remember,' said the man, letting the candle sink. 'I've been told that before.' 'But of course,' cried K., 'how could I forget, of course you must have heard it before.' 'But why, why must I?' asked the man, moving towards the door, for K. was propelling him from behind. When they were out in the lobby K. said: 'I suppose you know where Leni's hiding?' 'Hiding?' said he. 'No, she should be in the kitchen making soup for the Advocate.' 'Why didn't you tell me that at first?' asked K. 'I was going to take you there but you called me back,' answered the man, as if bewildered by these contradictory demands. 'You fancy you're being very sly,' said K., 'lead the way then!' K. had never yet been in the kitchen, and it was surprisingly large and well furnished. The cooking-stove alone was three times the size of an ordinary stove; the rest of the fittings could not be seen in detail since the sole light came from a small lamp hanging near the door. Leni was standing by the stove in a white apron, as usual, emptying eggs into a pan that simmered on an alcohol flame. 'Good evening, Joseph,' she said, glancing over her shoulder. 'Good evening,' said K., waving the commercial traveller to a chair some distance away, on which the man obediently sat down. Then K. went quite close up behind Leni, leaned over her shoulder, and asked: 'Who's this man?' Leni put her disengaged arm round K., stirring the soup with the other, and pulled him forward. 'He's a miserable creature,' she said, 'a poor commercial traveller called Block. Just look at him.' They both glanced round. The commercial traveller was sitting in the chair K. had indicated for him; having blown out the candle, which was no longer needed, he was snuffing the wick with his fingers. 'You were in your nightgown,' said K., turning Leni's head forcibly to the stove. She made no answer. 'Is he your lover?' asked K. She reached for a soup-bowl but K. imprisoned both her hands and said: 'Give me an answer!' She said: 'Come into the study and I'll tell you all about it.' 'No,' said K., 'I want you to tell me here.' She slipped her arm into his and tried to give him a kiss but K. fended her off, saying: 'I don't want you to kiss me now.' 'Joseph,' said Leni, gazing at him imploringly and yet frankly, 'surely you're not jealous of Herr Block?' Then she turned to the commercial traveller and said: 'Rudi, come to the rescue, you can see that I'm under suspicion, put that candle down.' One might have thought that he had been paying no attention, but he knew at once what she meant. 'I can't think what you have to be jealous about either,' he said, with no great acumen. 'Nor can I, really,' replied K., regarding him with a smile. Leni laughed outright and profited by K.'s momentary distraction to hook herself on to his arm, whispering: 'Leave him alone now, you can see the kind of creature he is. I've paid him a little attention because he's one of the Advocate's best clients, but that was the only reason. What about yourself? Do you want to see the Advocate tonight? He's far from well to-day; all the same, if you like I'll tell him you're here. But you're certainly going to spend the night with me. It's such a long time since you were here last, even the Advocate has been asking after you. It won't do to neglect your case! And I've got some information for you, too, things I've found out. But the first thing is to get your coat off.' She helped him out of his coat, took his hat from him, ran into the hall to hang them up, and then ran back to keep an eye on the soup. 'Shall I announce you first or give him his soup first?' 'Announce me first,' said K. He felt irritated, for he had originally intended to discuss the whole case thoroughly with Leni, especially the question of dismissing the Advocate, and the commercial traveller's being there spoiled the situation. But again it struck him that his affairs were too important to allow of decisive interference by a petty commercial traveller, and so he called back Leni, who was already out in the lobby. 'No, let him have his soup first,' he said, 'it'll strengthen him for his interview with me, and he'll need it.' 'So you're one of the Advocate's clients too,' said the commercial traveller quietly from his corner, as if confirming a statement. His comment was but ill received. 'What's that got to do with you?' said K., and Leni put in: 'You be quiet.' To K. Leni said: 'Well, then, I'll take him his soup first,' and she poured the soup into a bowl. 'Only there's a risk that he might go to sleep immediately, he always falls asleep after food.' 'What I have to say to him will keep him awake all right,' said K., who took every chance of letting it be known that his interview with the Advocate promised to be momentous; he wanted Leni to question him about it and only then would he ask her advice. But Leni merely followed out to the letter the orders he gave her. As she passed him with the bowl of soup she deliberately nudged him and whispered: 'I'll announce you the minute he's finished his soup, so that I can have you back as soon as possible.' 'Get along,' said K., 'get along with you.' 'Don't be so rude,' she said, turning right round in the doorway, soup-bowl and all.

K. stood gazing after her; now it was definitely settled that he would dismiss the Advocate, and it was just as well that he should have no chance of discussing it beforehand with Leni; the whole affair was rather beyond her scope and she would certainly have tried to dissuade him, possibly she might even have prevailed on him to put it off this time, and he would have continued to be a prey to doubts and fears until in the long run he carried out his resolve, since it was too imperative a resolve to be dropped. But the sooner it was carried out the less he would suffer. Perhaps, after all, the commercial traveller might be able to throw some light on the subject.

K: turned towards the man, who immediately gave a start as if to jump to his feet. 'Keep your seat,' said K., drawing a chair up beside him. 'You're an old client of the Advocate's, aren't you?' 'Yes,' said the traveller, 'a very old client.' 'How long has he been in charge of your affairs?' asked K. 'I don't quite know what affairs you mean,' said the traveller; 'in my business affairs – I'm a corn-dealer – the Advocate has been my representative since the very beginning, that must be for the past twenty years, and in my private case, which is probably what you are thinking of, he has been my Advocate also from the beginning, which is more than five years ago. Yes, well over five years now,' he confirmed, drawing out an old pocket-book. 'I have it all written down here. I can give you the exact dates if you like. It's difficult to keep them in one's head. My case probably goes back further than I said, it began just after my wife's death, certainly more than five and a half years ago.' K. moved his chair closer to the man. 'So the Advocate has an ordinary practice as well?' he asked. This alliance between business and equity seemed to him uncommonly touching. 'Of course,' said the traveller, adding in a whisper: 'They even say that he's a better Advocate for business rights than for the other kind.' Then apparently he regretted having ventured so far, for he laid a hand on K.'s shoulder and said: 'Don't give me away, I implore you.' K. patted him soothingly on the knee and said: 'No, I'm not an informer.' 'He's a revengeful man, you see,' said the traveller. 'Surely he wouldn't harm a faithful client like you?' said K. 'Oh, yes,' said the traveller, 'once he's roused he draws no distinctions; besides, I'm not really faithful to him.' 'How is that?' asked K. 'Perhaps I oughtn't to tell you,' said the traveller doubtfully. 'I think you can risk it,' said K. 'Well,' said the traveller, 'I'll tell you a certain amount, but in your turn you must tell me one of your secrets, so that we stand surety for each other with the Advocate.' 'You're very cautious,' said K., 'but I'll entrust you with a secret that will allay all your suspicions. In what way, then, are you unfaithful to the Advocate?' 'Well,' said the traveller hesitatingly, as if confessing something dishonourable, 'I have other Advocates as well as him.' 'That's nothing very dreadful,' said K., somewhat disappointed. 'It's supposed to be,' said the traveller, who had not breathed freely since making his confession but now gained a little confidence from K.'s rejoinder. 'It's not allowed. And least of all is it allowed to consult hedge-advocates when one is a client of an official Advocate. And that's exactly what I've been doing, I have five hedge-advocates besides him.' 'Five!' cried K., amazed at the mere number, 'five Advocates besides this one?' The traveller nodded: 'I'm even trying out a sixth one.' 'But what do you need so many for?' asked K. 'I need every one of them,' said the traveller. 'Tell me why, will you?' asked K. 'With pleasure,' said the traveller. 'To begin with I don't want to lose my case, as you can well understand. And so I daren't ignore anything that might help me! if there's even the faintest hope of an advantage for myself I daren't reject it. That's how I've spent every penny I possess on this case of mine. For instance, I've drawn all the money out of my business; my business offices once filled nearly a whole floor of the building where now I need only a small back room and an assistant clerk. Of course it's not only the withdrawal of my money that has brought the business down, but the withdrawal of my energies. When you're trying to do anything you can to help your case along you haven't much energy to spare for other things.' 'So you've been working on your own behalf as well,' interrupted K., 'that's precisely what I wanted to ask you about.' 'There's not much to tell you,' said the traveller. 'I did try my hand at it in the beginning, but I soon had to give it up. It's too exhausting, and the results are disappointing. Merely attending the Court to keep an eye on things proved too much, for me, at least. It makes you feel limp even to sit about and wait your turn. But you know yourself what the air's like.' 'How do you know I was ever up there?' asked K. 'I happened to be in the lobby when you were passing through.' 'What a coincidence!' cried K., quite carried away and completely forgetting the ridiculous figure the traveller had cut in his estimation. 'So you saw me! You were in the lobby when I passed through. Yes, I did pass through the lobby once.' 'It's not such a coincidence as all that,' said the traveller, 'I'm up there nearly every day.' 'I'm likely to be up there, too, often enough after this,' said K., 'only I can hardly expect to be received with such honour as on that occasion. Everyone stood up. I suppose they took me for a Judge.' 'No,' said the traveller, 'it was the Attendant we stood up for. We knew you were an accused man. News of that kind spreads rapidly.' 'So you knew that already,' commented K., 'then perhaps you thought me somewhat high and mighty. Did no one say anything?' 'No,' said the traveller, 'people got quite a different impression. But it's a lot of nonsense.' 'What's a lot of nonsense?' asked K. 'Why do you insist on asking?' said the traveller, irritably. 'Apparently you don't know the people there and you might take it up wrongly. You must remember that in these Courts things are always coming up for discussion that are simply beyond reason, people are too tired and distracted to think and so they take refuge in superstition. I'm as bad as anyone myself. And one of the superstitions is that you're supposed to tell from a man's face, especially the line of his lips, how his case is going to turn out. Well, people declared that judging from the expression of your lips you would be found guilty, and in the near future too. I tell you, it's a silly superstition and in most cases completely at variance with the facts, but if you live among these people it's difficult to escape the prevailing opinion. You can't imagine what a strong effect such superstitions have. You spoke to a man up there, didn't you? And he could hardly utter a word in answer. Of course there's many a reason for being bewildered up there, but one of the reasons why he couldn't bring out an answer was the shock he got from looking at your lips. He said afterwards that he saw on your lips the sign of his own condemnation.' 'On my lips?' asked K., taking out a pocket-mirror and studying them. 'I can't see anything peculiar about my lips. Do you?' 'I don't either,' said the traveller, 'not in the least.' 'How superstitious these people are!' cried K. 'Didn't I tell you so?' asked the traveller. 'Do they meet each other so frequently, then, and exchange all these ideas?' queried K., 'I've never had anything to do with them myself.' 'As a rule they don't meet much,' said the traveller, 'it would be hardly possible, there are too many of them. Besides, they have few interests in common. Occasionally a group believes it has found a common interest, but it soon finds out its mistake. Combined action against the Court is impossible. Each case is judged on its own merits, the Court is very conscientious about that, and so common action is out of the question. An individual here and there may score a point in secret, but no one hears it until afterwards, no one knows how it has been done. So there's no real community, people drift in and out of the lobbies together, but there's not much conversation. The superstitious beliefs are an old tradition and simply hand themselves down.' 'I saw all the people in the lobby,' remarked K., 'and thought how pointless it was for them to be hanging about.' 'It's not pointless at all,' said the traveller, 'the only pointless thing is to try taking independent action. As I told you, I have five Advocates besides this one. You might think – as I did once – that I could safely wash my hands of the case. But you would be wrong. I have to watch it more carefully than if I had only one Advocate. I suppose you don't understand that?' 'No,' said K., laying his hand appealingly on the other's to keep him from talking so fast, 'I would only like to beg you to speak more slowly, all these things are extremely important to me and I can't follow so quickly.' 'I'm glad you reminded me,' said the traveller; 'of course you're a new-comer, you're young in the matter. Your case is six months old, isn't it? Yes, that's what I heard. An infant of a case! But I've had to think these things out I don't know how many times, they've become a second nature to me.' 'I suppose you're thankful to think that your case is so far advanced,' asked K., not liking to make a direct inquiry how the traveller's case stood. But he received no direct answer either. 'Yes, I've carried my burden for five long years,' said the traveller, drooping his head, 'it's no small achievement, that.' Then he sat silent for a little. K. listened to hear if Leni were coming back. On the one hand he did not want her to come in just then, for he had many questions still to ask, nor did he want her to find him so deep in intimate conversation with the traveller, but on the other hand he was annoyed because she was spending so much time with the Advocate while he was in the house, much more time than was needed for handing over a bowl of soup. 'I can still remember exactly,' began the traveller again, and K. was at once all attention, 'the days when my case was at much the same stage as yours is now. I had only this Advocate then, and I wasn't particularly satisfied with him.' 'Now I'm going to find out things,' thought K., nodding his head eagerly, as if that would encourage the traveller to bring out all the right information. 'My case,' went on the traveller, 'wasn't making any progress; there were of course interrogations, and I attended every one of them, I collected evidence, I even laid all my account-books before the Court, which wasn't necessary at all, as I discovered later. I kept running to the Advocate, he presented various petitions —' 'Various petitions?' asked K. 'Yes, certainly,' said the traveller. 'That's an important point for me,' said K., 'for in my case he's still boggling over the first petition. He's done nothing at all yet. Now I see how scandalously he's neglecting me.' 'There might be several excellent reasons why the petition isn't ready yet,' said the traveller. 'Let me tell you that my petitions turned out later to be quite worthless. I even had a look at one of them, thanks to the kindness of a Court official. It was very learned but it said nothing of any consequence. Crammed with Latin in the first place, which I don't understand, and then whole pages of general appeals to the Court, then flattering references to particular officials, who weren't actually named but were easy enough for anyone versed in these matters to recognize, then some self-praise of the Advocate himself, in the course of which he addressed the Court with a crawling humility, ending up with an analysis of various cases from ancient times that were supposed to resemble mine. I must say that this analysis, in so far as I could follow it, was very careful and thorough. You're not to think that I'm passing judgement on the Advocate's work; that petition, after all, was only one of many; but at any rate, and this is what I'm coming to, I couldn't see that my case was making any progress.' 'What kind of progress did you expect to see?' asked K. 'A good question,' said the traveller with a smile, 'it's very rarely that progress in these cases is visible at all. But I didn't know that then. I'm a business man, and I was much more of a business man then than now, I wanted to see palpable results, the whole negotiation should be either on the up-grade, I thought, or on the down-grade and coming to a finish. Instead of that there were only ceremonial interviews, one after another, mostly of the same tenor, where I could reel off the responses like a litany; several times a week messengers came to my place of business or to my house or wherever I was to be found, and that, of course, was a nuisance (to-day I'm much better off in that respect, for telephone calls bother me less); and besides all that, rumours about my case began to spread among my business friends, but especially among my relatives, so that I was being harassed on all sides without the slightest sign of any intention on the part of the Court to bring my case up for judgement in the near future. So I went to the Advocate and made my complaint. He treated me to a lengthy explanation but refused utterly to take action in my sense of the word, saying that nobody could influence the Court to appoint a day for hearing a case, and that to urge anything of the kind in a petition – as I wanted him to do – was simply unheard of and would only ruin myself and him. I thought: what this Advocate won't or

can't do, another will and can. So I looked round for
other Advocates. I may as well tell you now that not one
of them ever prayed the Court to fix a day for the settlement of my case, or managed to obtain such a settlement;
it is really an impossibility – with one qualification that I
shall explain later – and the Advocate had not misled me
there, although I found no cause for regretting having
called in the other Advocates. I suppose Dr Huld has told
you plenty of things about the hedge-advocates, he has
probably described them as contemptible creatures, and
so they are, in a sense. All the same, in speaking of them
and contrasting himself and his colleagues with them he
always makes a small mistake, which I may as well call
your attention to in passing. He always refers to the Advocates of his own circle as the "great Advocates", by way
of contrast. Now that's untrue; any man can call himself
"great", of course, if he pleases, but in this matter the
Court tradition must decide. And according to the Court
tradition, which recognizes both small and great Advocates outside the hole-and-corner Advocates, our Advocate and his colleagues rank only among the small Advocates, while the really great Advocates, whom I have
merely heard of and never seen, stand as high above the
small Advocates as these above the despised hedge-advocates.' 'The really great Advocates?' asked K. 'Who are
they, then? How does one get at them?' 'So you've never
heard of them,' said the traveller. 'There's hardly an accused man who doesn't spend some time dreaming of
them after hearing about them. Don't you give way to
that temptation. I have no idea who the great Advocates
are and I don't believe they can be got at. I know of no
single instance in which it could be definitely asserted
that they had intervened. They do defend certain cases,

but only when they want to, and they never take action,
I should think, until the case is already beyond the province of the lower Court. Generally speaking, it's better
to put them out of one's mind altogether, or else one finds
interviews with ordinary Advocates so stale and stupid,
with their niggling counsels and proposals – I have experienced it myself – that one feels like throwing the
whole thing up and taking to bed with one's face to the
wall. And of course that would be stupider still, for even
in bed one wouldn't find peace.' 'So you didn't entertain
the thought of going to the great Advocates?' asked K.
'Not for long,' said the traveller, smiling again; 'unfortunately one can never quite forget about them, especially during the night. But at that time I was looking
for immediate results, and so I went to the hedge-advocates.'

'How you're putting your heads together!' cried Leni,
who had come back with the soup-bowl and was standing
in the doorway. They were indeed sitting so close to each
other that they must have bumped their heads together at
the slightest movement; the traveller, who was not only a
small man but stooped forward as he sat, spoke so low
that K. was forced to bend down to hear every word he
said. 'Give us a moment or two,' cried K., warning Leni
off, the hand which he still kept on the traveller's hand
twitched with irritation. 'He wanted me to tell him about
my case,' said the traveller to Leni. 'Well, go on telling
him,' said she. Her tone in speaking to the traveller was
kindly but a little contemptuous. That annoyed K.; the
man, after all, as he had discovered, possessed a certain
value, he had had experiences and knew how to communicate them. Leni apparently misjudged him. To K.'s
further annoyance Leni removed the traveller's candle,

which he had been grasping all this time, wiped his hand with her apron, and knelt down to scratch off some tallow which had dripped on his trousers. 'You were going to tell me about your hedge-advocates,' said K., pushing Leni's hand away without comment. 'What do you think you're doing?' she asked, giving K. a small slap and resuming her task. 'Yes, the hedge-advocates,' said the traveller, passing his hand over his brow as if in reflection. K. wanted to help him out and added: 'You were looking for immediate results and so you went to the hedge-advocates.' 'That's right,' said the traveller, but he did not continue. 'Perhaps he doesn't want to talk of it before Leni,' thought K., suppressing his impatience to hear the rest of the story and not urging the man any more.

'Did you announce me?' he asked Leni instead. 'Of course,' she said, 'and the Advocate's waiting for you. Leave Block alone now, you can talk to him later, for he's staying here.' K. still hesitated. 'Are you staying here?' he asked the traveller; he wanted the man to speak for himself, he disliked the way Leni discussed him as if he were absent, he was filled with obscure irritation to-day against Leni. And again it was Leni who did the speaking: 'He often sleeps here.' 'Sleeps here?' cried K., he had thought that the traveller would wait only till the interview with the Advocate was brought to a speedy conclusion, and that then they would go off together to discuss the whole business thoroughly in private. 'Yes,' said Leni, 'everyone isn't like you, Joseph, getting an interview with the Advocate at any hour they choose. It doesn't even seem to strike you as surprising that a sick man like the Advocate should agree to see you at eleven o'clock at night. You take all that your friends do for you far too much as a matter of course. Well, your friends, or I at least, like doing things for you. I don't ask for thanks and I don't need any thanks, except that I want you to be fond of me.' 'Fond of you?' thought K., and only after framing the words did it occur to him: 'But I am fond of her.' Yet he said, ignoring the rest of her remarks: 'He agrees to see me because I'm his client. If I needed others' help even to get an interview with my lawyer, I'd have to be bowing and scraping at every turn.' 'How difficult he is to-day, isn't he?' said Leni to the traveller. 'Now it's my turn to be treated as if I were absent,' thought K., and his irritation extended to the traveller too when the latter, copying Leni's discourtesy, remarked: 'But the Advocate has other reasons for agreeing to see him. His is a much more interesting case than mine. Besides, it's only beginning, probably still at a hopeful stage, and so the Advocate likes handling it. You'll see a difference later on.' 'Yes, yes,' said Leni, regarding the traveller laughingly, 'what a tongue-wagger!' Here she turned to K. and went on: 'You mustn't believe a word he says. He's a nice fellow but his tongue wags far too much. Perhaps that's why the Advocate can't bear him. Anyhow, he never consents to see him unless he's in the mood. I've tried my best to change that, but it can't be done. Only fancy, sometimes I tell the Advocate Block is here and he puts off seeing him for three days together. And then if Block isn't on the spot when he's called for, his chance is gone and I have to announce him all over again. That's why I let Block sleep here, for it has happened before now that the Advocate has rung for him in the middle of the night. So Block has to be ready night and day. It sometimes happens, too, that the Advocate changes his mind, once he has discovered that Block actually is on the spot, and refuses the interview.' K. threw a questioning glance at the traveller, who nodded and said, with the same frankness as before, or perhaps merely discomposed by a feeling of shame: 'Yes, one becomes very dependent on one's Advocate in the course of time.' 'He's just pretending to complain,' said Leni, 'for he likes sleeping here, as he has often told me.' She went over to a small door and pushed it open. 'Would you like to see his bedroom?' she asked. K. followed her and gazed from the threshold into a low-roofed chamber which had room only for a narrow bed. One had to climb over the bedposts to get into the bed. At the head of it, in a recess in the wall, stood a candle, an ink-well, and a pen, carefully arranged beside a bundle of papers, probably documents concerning the traveller's case. 'So you sleep in the maid's room?' asked K., turning to the traveller. 'Leni lets me have it,' said he, 'it's very convenient.' K. gave him a long look; the first impression he had had of the man was perhaps, after all, the right one; the traveller was a man of experience, certainly, since his case had lasted for years, yet he had paid dearly for his experience. Suddenly K. could no longer bear the sight of him. 'Put him to bed,' he cried to Leni, who seemed not to comprehend what he meant. Yet what he wanted was to get away to the Advocate and dismiss from his life not only him but Leni and the commercial traveller too. Before he could reach the room, however, the traveller spoke to him in a low voice: 'Herr Assessor.' K. turned round angrily. 'You've forgotten your promise,' said the traveller, reaching out imploringly towards K. 'You were going to tell me one of your secrets.' 'True,' said K., casting a glance also at Leni, who was regarding him attentively, 'well, listen then, though it's almost an open secret by this time. I'm going to the Advocate now to dismiss him from my case.' 'Dismiss him!' exclaimed

the traveller; he sprang from his seat and rushed round
the kitchen with upraised arms, crying as he ran: 'He's
dismissing the Advocate!' Leni made a grab for K. but
the traveller got in her way, an awkwardness which she
requited with her fists. Still clenching her fists she chased
after K., who was well ahead of her. He got inside the
Advocate's room before she caught up with him; he tried
to close the door behind him, but Leni put one foot in the
crack and reached through it to grab his arm and haul
him back. K. caught her wrist and squeezed it so hard
that she had to loose her hold with a whimper. She would
not dare to force her way right in, but K. made certain
by turning the key in the lock.

'I've been waiting a long time for you,' said the Advocate from his bed, laying on the table a document which
he had been reading by the light of a candle, and putting
on a pair of spectacles through which he scrutinized K.
sharply. Instead of apologizing K. said: 'I shan't detain
you long.' This remark, as it was no apology, the Advocate ignored, saying: 'I shall not see you again at such a
late hour.' 'That agrees with my intentions,' retorted K.
The Advocate gave him a questioning look and said: 'Sit
down.' 'Since you ask me to,' said K., pulling up a chair
to the night-table and seating himself. 'I fancied I heard
you locking the door,' said the Advocate. 'Yes,' said K.,
'that was because of Leni.' He was not thinking of shielding anyone, but the Advocate went on: 'Has she been
pestering you again?' 'Pestering me?' asked K. 'Yes,'
said the Advocate, chuckling until he took a fit of coughing, after which he began to chuckle once more. 'I suppose you can't have helped noticing that she pesters you?'
he asked, patting K.'s hand, which in his nervous distraction he had laid on the night-table and now hastily with-

drew. 'You don't attach much importance to it,' went on the Advocate as K. remained silent. 'So much the better. Or else I might have had to apologize for her. It's a peculiarity of hers, which I have long forgiven her and which I wouldn't mention now had it not been for your locking the door. This peculiarity of hers, well, you're the last person I should explain it to, but you're looking so bewildered that I feel I must, this peculiarity of hers consists in her finding nearly all accused men attractive. She makes up to all of them, loves them all, and is loved in return; she often tells me about these affairs to amuse me, when I allow her. It doesn't surprise me so much as it seems to surprise you. If you have the right eye for these things, you can see that accused men are often attractive. It's a remarkable phenomenon, almost a natural law. For of course the fact of being accused makes no alteration in a man's appearance that is immediately obvious and recognizable. These cases are not like ordinary criminal cases, most of the defendants continue in their usual vocations, and if they are in the hands of a good Advocate their interests don't suffer much. And yet those who are experienced in such matters can pick out one after another all the accused men in the largest of crowds. How do they know them? you will ask. I'm afraid my answers won't seem satisfactory. They know them because accused men are always the most attractive. It can't be a sense of guilt that makes them attractive, for – it behoves me to say this as an Advocate, at least – they aren't all guilty, and it can't be the justice of the penance laid on them that makes them attractive in anticipation, for they aren't all going to be punished, so it must be the mere charge preferred against them that in some way enhances their attraction. Of course some are much more attractive than others. But they are all attractive, even that wretched creature Block.'

By the time the Advocate finished this harangue K. had completely regained his composure, he had even frankly nodded as if in agreement with the last words, whereas he was really confirming his own long-cherished opinion that the Advocate invariably attempted, as now, to bring in irrelevant generalizations in order to distract his attention from the main question, which was: how much actual work had been achieved in furthering the case? Presumably the Advocate felt that K. was more hostile than usual, for now he paused to give him the chance of putting in a word, and then asked, since K. remained silent: 'Did you come here this evening for some specific reason?' 'Yes,' said K., shading the light of the candle a little with one hand so as to see the Advocate better. 'I came to tell you that I dispense with your services as from to-day.' 'Do I understand you rightly?' asked the Advocate, half propping himself up in bed with one hand on the pillows. 'I expect so,' said K., sitting bolt upright as if on guard. 'Well, that's a plan we can at least discuss,' said the Advocate after a pause. 'It's no plan, it's a fact,' said K. 'Maybe,' said the Advocate, 'but we mustn't be in too much of a hurry.' He used the word 'we' as if he had no intention of letting K. detach himself, as if he meant to remain at least K.'s adviser if not his official agent. 'It's not a hurried decision,' said K., slowly getting up and retreating behind his chair, 'I have thought it well over, perhaps even for too long. It is my final decision.' 'Then you might allow me a few comments,' said the Advocate, throwing off his coverings and sitting on the edge of the bed. His bare legs, sprinkled with white hairs, trembled with cold. He asked K. to hand him a rug from the sofa.

K. fetched the rug and said: 'It's quite unnecessary for you to expose yourself to a chill.' 'I have grave enough reasons for it,' said the Advocate, wrapping the bed-quilt round his shoulders and tucking the rug round his legs. 'Your uncle is a friend of mine, and I've grown fond of you, too, in the course of time. I admit it freely. It's nothing to be ashamed of.' This outburst of sentiment from the old man was most unwelcome to K., for it compelled him to be more explicit in his statements, which he would have liked to avoid, and disconcerted him too, as he admitted to himself, although without in the least affecting his decision. 'I am grateful for your friendly attitude,' he said, 'and I appreciate that you have done all you could do for what you thought to be my advantage. But for some time now I have been growing convinced that your efforts are not enough. I shall not, of course, attempt to thrust my opinions on a man so much older and more experienced than myself; if I have unwittingly seemed to do so, please forgive me, but I have grave enough reasons for it, to use your own phrase, and I am convinced that it is necessary to take much more energetic steps in this case of mine than have been taken so far.' 'I understand you,' said the Advocate, 'you are feeling impatient.' 'I'm not impatient,' said K., a little irritated and therefore less careful in his choice of words, 'you must have noticed on my very first visit here, when I came with my uncle, that I did not take my case very seriously; if I wasn't forcibly reminded of it, so to speak, I forgot it completely. Still my uncle insisted on my engaging you as my representative, and I did so to please him. One would naturally have expected the case to weigh even less on my conscience after that, since one engages an Advocate to shift the burden a little on to his shoulders. But the very opposite of that resulted. I was never so plagued by my case in earlier days as since engaging you to be my Advocate. When I stood alone I did nothing at all, yet it hardly bothered me; after acquiring an Advocate, on the other hand, I felt that the stage was set for something to happen, I waited with unceasing and growing expectancy for something to happen, and you did nothing whatever. I admit that you gave me information about the Court which I probably could not have obtained elsewhere. But that is hardly adequate assistance for a man who feels this thing secretly encroaching upon him and literally touching him to the quick.' K. had pushed the chair away and now stood upright, his hands in his jacket pockets. 'After a certain stage in one's practice,' said the Advocate quietly in a low voice, 'nothing really new ever happens. How many of my clients have reached the same point in their cases and stood before me in exactly the same frame of mind as you and said the same things!' 'Well,' said K., 'then they were all as much in the right as I am. That doesn't counter my arguments.' 'I wasn't trying to counter them,' said the Advocate, 'but I should like to add that I expected you to show more judgement than the others, especially as I have given you far more insight into the workings of the Court and my own procedure than I usually give my clients. And now I cannot help seeing that in spite of everything you haven't enough confidence in me. You don't make things very easy for me.' How the Advocate was humbling himself before K.! And without any regard for his professional dignity, which was surely most sensitive on this very point. Why was he doing it? If appearances spoke true he was in great demand as an Advocate and wealthy as well, the loss of K.'s business or the loss of his fees could not mean much to such a man.

Besides, he was an invalid and should himself have contemplated the possibility of losing clients. Yet he was clinging to K. with insistence! Why? Was it personal affection for K.'s uncle, or did he really regard the case as so extraordinary that he hoped to win prestige either from defending K. or – a possibility not to be excluded – from pandering to his friends in the Court? His face provided no clue, searchingly as K. scrutinized it. One could almost suppose that he was deliberately assuming a blank expression, while waiting for the effect of his words. But he was obviously putting too favourable an interpretation on K.'s silence when he went on to say: 'You will have noticed that although my office is large enough I don't employ any assistants. That wasn't so in former years, there was a time when several young students of the Law worked for me, but to-day I work alone. This change corresponds in part to the change in my practice, for I have been confining myself more and more to cases like yours, and in part to a growing conviction that has been borne in upon me. I found that I could not delegate the responsibility for these cases to anyone else without wronging my clients and imperilling the tasks I have undertaken. But the decision to cover all the work myself entailed the natural consequences: I had to refuse most of the cases brought to me and apply myself only to those which touched me nearly – and I can tell you there's no lack of wretched creatures even in this very neighbourhood, ready to fling themselves on any crumb I choose to throw them. And then I broke down under stress of overwork. All the same, I don't regret my decision, perhaps I ought to have taken a firmer stand and refused more cases, but the policy of devoting myself single-mindedly to the cases I did accept has proved both necessary and successful judging from the results. I once read a very finely worded description of the difference between an Advocate for ordinary legal rights and an Advocate for cases like these. It ran like this: the one Advocate leads his client by a slender thread until the verdict is reached, but the other lifts his client on his shoulders from the start and carries him bodily without once letting him down until the verdict is reached, and even beyond it. That is true. But it is not quite true to say that I do not at all regret devoting myself to this great task. When, as in your case, my labours are as completely misunderstood, then, yes, then and only then, I come near to regretting it.' This speech, instead of convincing K., only made him impatient. He fancied that the very tone of the Advocate's voice suggested what was in store for him should he prove complaisant; the same old exhortations would begin again, the same references to the progress of the petition, to the more gracious mood of this or that official, while not forgetting the enormous difficulties that stood in the way — in short, the same stale platitudes would be brought out again either to delude him with vague false hopes or to torment him with equally vague menaces. That must be stopped once and for all, so he said: 'What steps do you propose to take in my case if I retain you as my representative?' The Advocate meekly accepted even this insulting question and replied: 'I should continue with those measures that I have already begun.' 'I knew it,' said K., 'well, it's a waste of time to go on talking.' 'I'll make one more attempt,' said the Advocate, as if it were K. who was at fault and not himself. 'I have an idea that what makes you so wrong-headed not only in your judgement of my capacities but also in your general behaviour is the fact that you have been treated too well, although you are an accused man, or rather, more precisely, that you have been treated with negligence, with apparent negligence. There's a reason for the negligence, of course; it's often safer to be in chains than to be free. But I'd like to show you how other accused men are treated, and perhaps you may learn a thing or two. I shall now send for Block; you'd better unlock the door and sit here beside the bed-table.' 'With pleasure,' said K., fulfilling these injunctions; he was always ready to learn. As a precaution, however, he asked once more: 'You realize that I am dispensing with your services?' 'Yes,' said the Advocate, 'but you may change your mind about it yet.' He lay back in bed again, drew the quilt over his knees, and turned his face to the wall. Then he rang the bell.

Almost at the same moment Leni was on the spot, darting quick glances to learn what was happening; she seemed to find it reassuring that K. was sitting so quietly beside the Advocate's bed. She nodded to him with a smile, but he gazed at her blankly. 'Fetch Block,' said the Advocate. Instead of fetching Block, however, she merely went to the door, called out: 'Block! The Advocate wants you!' and then, probably because the Advocate had his face turned to the wall and was paying no attention to her, insinuated herself behind K., where she distracted him during all the rest of the proceedings by leaning over the back of his chair or running her fingers, gently and tenderly enough, through his hair and over his temples. In the end K. sought to prevent her by holding on to her hand, which after a little resistance she surrendered to him.

Block had answered the summons by coming immediately, yet he hesitated outside the door, apparently wondering whether he was to come in or not. He raised his eyebrows and cocked his head as if listening for the summons to be repeated. K. could have encouraged the man to come in, but he was determined to make a final break not only with the Advocate but with all the persons in the house, and so he remained immobile. Leni too was silent. Block noticed that at least no one was turning him away, and he tiptoed into the room with anxious face and hands clutched behind him, leaving the door open to secure his retreat. He did not once look at K., but kept his eyes fixed on the humped-up quilt beneath which the Advocate was not even visible, since he had shifted close up to the wall. A voice, however, came from the bed, saying: 'Is that Block?' This question acted like a blow upon Block, who had advanced a goodish way; he staggered, as if he had been hit on the chest and then beaten on the back, and, submissively drooping, stood still, answering: 'At your service.' 'What do you want?' asked the Advocate. 'You've come at the wrong time.' 'Wasn't I called for?' said Block, more to himself than to the Advocate, thrusting out his hands as if to guard himself, and preparing to back out. 'You were called for,' said the Advocate, 'and yet you've come at the wrong time.' After a pause he added: 'You always come at the wrong time.' From the moment when the Advocate's voice was heard Block averted his eyes from the bed and stood merely listening, gazing into a far corner, as if to meet a shaft from the Advocate's eyes were more than he could bear. But it was difficult for him even to listen, since the Advocate was speaking close to the wall and in a voice both low and quick. 'Do you want me to go away?' asked Block. 'Well, since you're here,' said the Advocate, 'stay!' One might have fancied that instead of granting Block his desire the Advocate had threatened to have him beaten, for the fellow now began to tremble in earnest. 'Yesterday,' said the Advocate, 'I saw my friend the Third Judge and gradually worked the conversation round to your case. Would you like to know what he said?' 'Oh, please,' said Block. Since the Advocate made no immediate reply, Block implored him again and seemed on the point of getting down on his knees. But K. intervened with a shout: 'What's that you're doing?' Leni had tried to stifle his shout and so he gripped her other hand as well. It was no loving clasp in which he held her; she sighed now and then and struggled to free herself. But it was Block who paid the penalty for K.'s outburst; the Advocate shot the question at him: 'Who is your Advocate?' 'You are,' said Block. 'And besides me?' asked the Advocate. 'No one besides you,' said Block. 'Then pay no heed to anyone else,' said the Advocate. Block took the full force of these words; he gave K. an angry glare and shook his head violently at him. If these gestures had been translated into speech they would have made a tirade of abuse. And this was the man with whom K. had wished to discuss his own case in all friendliness! 'I shan't interfere again,' said K., leaning back in his chair. 'Kneel on the floor or creep on all fours if you like, I shan't bother.' Yet Block had some self-respect left, at least where K. was concerned, for he advanced upon him flourishing his fists and shouting as loudly as he dared in the Advocate's presence: 'You're not to talk to me in that tone, it isn't allowed. What do you mean by insulting me? Before the Herr Advocate, too, who admits us here, both of us, you and me, only out of charity? You're no better than I am, you're an accused man too and have the same charges on your conscience. If you think you're a gentleman as well, let me tell you I'm as great a gentleman as you, if not a greater. And I'll have you address me as such, yes, you especially. For if you think you have the advantage of me because you're allowed to sit there at your ease and watch me creeping on all fours, as you put it, let me remind you of the old maxim: people under suspicion are better moving than at rest, since at rest they may be sitting in the balance without knowing it, being weighed together with their sins.' K. said not a word, he merely stared in unwinking astonishment at this madman. What a change had come over the fellow in the last hour! Was it his case that agitated him to such an extent that he could not distinguish friend from foe? Did he not see that the Advocate was deliberately humiliating him, for no other purpose on this occasion than to make a display of his power before K. and so perhaps cow K. into acquiescence as well? Yet if Block were incapable of perceiving this, or if he were so afraid of the Advocate that he could not allow himself to perceive it, how did it come about that he was sly enough or brave enough to deceive the Advocate and deny that he was having recourse to other Advocates? And how could he be so foolhardy as to attack K., knowing that K. might betray his secret? His foolhardiness went even further, he now approached the Advocate's bed and laid a complaint against K. 'Herr Advocate,' he said, 'did you hear what this man said to me? His case is only a few hours old compared with mine, and yet, though I have been five years involved in my case, he takes it on himself to give me advice. He even abuses me. Knows nothing at all and abuses me, me, who have studied as closely as my poor wits allow every precept of duty, piety, and tradition.' 'Pay no heed to anyone,' said the Advocate, 'and do what seems right to yourself.' 'Certainly,' said Block, as if to give himself confidence, and then with a hasty side-glance knelt down close beside the bed. 'I'm on my knees, my Advocate,' he said. But the Advocate made no reply. Block cautiously caressed the quilt with one hand. In the silence that now reigned Leni said, freeing herself from K.: 'You're hurting me. Let go. I want to be with Block.' She went over and sat on the edge of the bed. Block was greatly pleased by her arrival; he made impressive gestures, though in dumb show, imploring her to plead his cause with the Advocate. Obviously he was urgently in need of any information which the Advocate might give, but perhaps he only wanted to hand it on to his other Advocates for exploitation. Leni apparently knew exactly the right way to coax the Advocate; she pointed to his hand and pouted her lips as if giving a kiss. Block immediately kissed the hand, repeating the performance twice at Leni's instigation. But the Advocate remained persistently unresponsive. Then Leni, displaying the fine lines of her taut figure, bent over close to the old man's face and caressed his long white hair. That finally evoked an answer. 'I hesitate to tell him,' said the Advocate, and one could see him shaking his head, perhaps only the better to enjoy the pressure of Leni's hand. Block listened with downcast eyes, as if it were a duty laid upon him. 'Why do you hesitate, then?' asked Leni. K. had the feeling that he was listening to a well-rehearsed dialogue which had been often repeated and would be often repeated and only for Block would never lose its novelty. 'How has he been behaving to-day?' inquired the Advocate instead of answering. Before providing this information Leni looked down at Block and watched him for a moment as he raised his hands towards her and clasped them appealingly together. At length she nodded gravely, turned to the Advocate, and said: 'He has been quiet and industrious.' An elderly business man, a man with a long beard, begging a young girl to say a word in his favour! Let him make what private reservations he would, in the eyes of his fellow-men he could find no justification. It was humiliating even to an onlooker. So the Advocate's methods, to which K. fortunately had not been long enough exposed, amounted to this: that the client finally forgot the whole world and lived only in hope of toiling along this false path until the end of his case should come in sight. The client ceased to be a client and became the Advocate's dog. If the Advocate were to order this man to crawl under the bed as if into a kennel and bark there, he would obey the order. K. listened to everything with critical detachment, as if he had been commissioned to observe the proceedings closely, to report them to a higher authority, and to put down a record of them in writing. 'What has he been doing all day?' went on the Advocate. 'I locked him into the maid's room,' said Leni, 'to keep him from disturbing me at my work, that's where he usually stays, anyhow. And I could peep at him now and then through the ventilator to see what he was doing. He was kneeling all the time on the bed, reading the book you lent him, which was spread out on the window-sill. That made a good impression on me, since the window looks out on an air-shaft and doesn't give much light. So the way Block stuck to his reading showed me how faithfully he does what he is told.' 'I'm glad to hear that,' said the Advocate. 'But did he understand what he was reading?' All this time Block's lips were moving unceasingly, he was obviously formulating the answers he hoped Leni would make. 'Well, of course,' said Leni, 'that's something I don't know with certainty. At any rate, I could tell that he was thorough in his reading. He never got past the same page all day and he was following the lines with his fingers. Whenever I looked at him he was sighing to himself as if the reading cost him a great effort. Apparently the book you gave him to read is difficult to understand.' 'Yes,' said the Advocate, 'these scriptures are difficult enough. I don't believe he really understands them. They're meant only to give him an inkling how hard the struggle is that I have to carry on in his defence. And for whom do I carry on this hard struggle? It's almost ridiculous to put it into words – I do it for Block. He must learn to understand what that means. Did he read without stopping?' 'Almost without a stop,' answered Leni, 'he asked me only once for a drink of water, and I handed it to him through the ventilator. Then about eight o'clock I let him out and gave him something to eat.' Block gave a fleeting glance at K. as if expecting to see him impressed by this virtuous record. His hopes seemed to be mounting, his movements were less constrained, and he kept shifting his knees a little. It was all the more noticeable that the Advocate's next words struck him rigid. 'You are praising him up,' said the Advocate. 'But that only makes it more difficult for me to tell him. For the Judge's remarks were by no means favourable either to Block or to his case.' 'Not favourable?' asked Leni. 'How can that be possible?' Block was gazing at her as intently as if he believed her capable of giving a new and favourable turn to the words long pronounced by the Judge. 'Not favourable,' said the Advocate. 'He was even annoyed when I mentioned Block. "Don't speak about Block," he said. "But he's my client," I said. "You are wasting yourself on the man," he said. "I don't think his case is hopeless," said I. "Well, you're wasting yourself on him," he repeated. "I don't believe it," said I, "Block is sincerely concerned about his case and devotes himself to it. He almost lives in my house to keep in touch with the proceedings. One doesn't often find such zeal. Of course, he's personally rather repulsive, his manners are bad, and he is dirty, but as a client he is beyond reproach" – I said "beyond reproach", and it was a deliberate exaggeration. To that he replied: "Block is merely cunning. He has acquired a lot of experience and knows how to keep on manipulating the situation. But his ignorance is even greater than his cunning. What do you think he would say if he discovered that his case had actually not begun yet, if he were to be told that the bell marking the start of the proceedings hadn't even been rung?" – Quiet there, Block,' said the Advocate, for Block was just rising up on trembling legs, obviously to implore an explanation. This was the first time the Advocate had addressed a direct word to Block. With lack-lustre eyes he looked down, his glance was partly vague and partly turned upon Block, who slowly shrank back under it on his knees again. 'That remark of the Judge's has no possible significance for you,' said the Advocate. 'Don't get into a panic at every word. If you do it again I'll never tell you anything. I can't begin a statement without your gazing at me as if your final sentence had come. You should be ashamed to behave like that before my client. And you're destroying his confidence in me. What's the matter with you? You're still alive, you're still under my protection. Your panic is senseless. You've read somewhere or other that a man's condemnation often comes by a chance word from some chance person at some odd time. With many reservations that is certainly true, but it is equally true that your panic disgusts me and appears to betray a lack of the necessary confidence in me. All that I said was to report a remark made by a Judge. You know quite well that in these matters opinions differ so much that the confusion is impenetrable. This Judge, for instance, assumes that the proceedings begin at one point, and I assume that they begin at another point. A difference of opinion, nothing more. At a certain stage of the proceedings there is an old tradition that a bell must be rung. According to the Judge, that marks the beginning of the case, I can't tell you now all the arguments against him, you wouldn't understand them, let it be sufficient for you that there are many arguments against his view.' In embarrassment Block sat plucking at the hair of the skin rug lying before the bed, his terror of the Judge's utterance was so great that it ousted for a while his respectful fear of the Advocate and he was thinking only of himself, turning the Judge's words round and surveying them from all sides. 'Block,' said Leni in a tone of warning, catching him by the collar and jerking him upwards a little. 'Leave the rug alone and listen to the Advocate.'

K. did not understand how the Advocate could ever have imagined that this performance would win him over. If the Advocate had not already succeeded in alienating him, this scene would have finished him once and for all.

IX

In the Cathedral

An Italian colleague who was on his first visit to the town and had influential connexions that made him important to the Bank was to be taken in charge by K. and shown some of the town's art treasures and monuments. It was a commission that K. would once have felt to be an honour, but at the present juncture, now that all his energies were needed even to retain his prestige in the Bank, he was reluctant in his acceptance of it. Every hour that he spent away from the Bank was a trial to him; true, he was by no means able to make the best use of his office hours as once he had done, he wasted much time in the merest pretence of doing real work, but that only made him worry the more when he was not at his desk. In his mind he saw the Deputy Manager, who had always spied upon him, prowling every now and then into his office, sitting down at his desk, running through his papers, receiving clients who had become almost old friends of K.'s in the course of many years, and turning them against him, perhaps even discovering mistakes that he had made, for K. now saw himself continually threatened by mistakes intruding into his work from all sides and was no longer able to circumvent them. Consequently if he were charged with a mission, however honourable, which involved his leaving the office on business or even taking a short journey – and missions of that kind by some chance had recently come his way fairly often – then he could not help suspecting that there was a plot to get him out of the way while his work was investigated, or at least that he was considered far from indispensable in the office. Most of these missions he could easily have refused. Yet he did not dare do so, since, if there were even the smallest ground for his suspicions, a refusal to go would only have been taken as an admission of anxiety. For that reason he accepted every one of them with apparent coolness, and on one occasion when he was expected to take an exhausting two days' journey said nothing even about a severe chill he had, to avoid the risk of having the prevailing wet autumnal weather advanced as an excuse for his not going. When he came back from this journey with a racking headache, he discovered that he had been selected to act as escort next day for the Italian visitor. The temptation simply to refuse, for once, was very great, especially since the charge laid upon him was not strictly a matter of business; still, it was a social duty towards a colleague and doubtless important enough, only it was of no importance to himself, knowing, as he did, that nothing could save him except work well done, in default of which it would not be of the slightest use to him were the Italian to find him the most enchanting companion; he shrank from being exiled from his work even for a single day, since he had too great a fear of not being allowed to return, a fear which he well knew to be exaggerated but which hampered him all the same. The difficulty on this occasion was to find a plausible excuse; his knowledge of Italian was certainly not very great but it was at least adequate, and there was a decisive argument in the fact that he had some knowledge of art, acquired in earlier days, which was absurdly overestimated in the Bank owing to his having been for some time, purely as a matter of business, a member of the Society for the Preservation of Ancient Monuments. Rumour had it that the Italian was also a connoisseur, and if so, the choice of K. to be his escort seemed inevitable.

It was a very wet and windy morning when K. arrived in his office at the early hour of seven o'clock, full of irritation at the programme before him, but determined to accomplish at least some work before being distracted from it by the visitor. He was very tired, for he had spent half the night studying an Italian grammar as some slight preparation; he was more tempted by the window, where he had recently been in the habit of spending much time, than by his desk, but he resisted the temptation and sat down to work. Unfortunately at that very moment the attendant appeared, reporting that he had been sent by the Manager to see if the Herr Assessor was in his office yet, and, if he was, to beg him to be so good as to come to the reception-room; the gentleman from Italy had already arrived. 'All right,' said K., stuffed a small dictionary into his pocket, tucked under his arm an album for sightseers, which he had procured in readiness for the stranger, and went through the Deputy Manager's office into the Manager's room. He was glad that he had turned up early enough to be on the spot immediately when required, probably no one had really expected him to do so. The Deputy Manager's office, of course, was as empty as in the dead of night, very likely the attendant had been told to summon the Deputy Manager too, and without result. When K. entered the reception-room the two gentlemen rose from their deep arm-chairs. The Manager smiled kindly on K., he was obviously delighted to see him, he performed the introduction at once, the Italian shook K. heartily by the hand and said laughingly that someone was an early riser from the bed. K. did not quite

catch what he meant, for it was an odd phrase the sense
of which did not dawn on him at once. He answered
with a few polite formalities which the Italian received
with another laugh, meanwhile nervously stroking his
bushy iron-grey moustache. This moustache was obviously perfumed; one was almost tempted to go close up
and have a sniff at it. When they all sat down again and
a preliminary conversation began, K. was greatly discon-
certed to find that he only partly understood what the
Italian was saying. He could understand him almost completely when he spoke slowly and quietly, but that happened very seldom, the words mostly came pouring out
in a flood, and he made lively gestures with his head as if
enjoying the rush of talk. Besides, when this happened,
he invariably relapsed into a dialect which K. did not
recognize as Italian but which the Manager could both
speak and understand, as indeed K. might have expected,
considering that this Italian came from the very south of
Italy, where the Manager had spent several years. At any
rate, it became clear to K. that little chance remained of
his coming to an understanding with the Italian, for the
man's French was just as difficult to follow and it was no
use watching his lips for clues, since their movements
were covered by the bushy moustache. K. began to foresee vexations and for the moment gave up trying to follow the talk – while the Manager was present to understand all that was said it was an unnecessary effort to
make – confining himself to peevish observation of the
Italian lounging so comfortably and yet lightly in his arm-
chair, tugging every now and then at the sharply peaked
corners of his short little jacket, and once raising his arms
with loosely fluttering hands to explain something which
K. found it impossible to understand, although he was

leaning forward to watch every gesture. In the end, as K. sat there taking no part in the conversation, only mechanically following with his eyes the see-saw of the dialogue, his earlier weariness made itself felt again, and to his horror, although fortunately just in time, he caught himself absent-mindedly rising to turn his back on the others and walk away. At long last the Italian looked at his watch and sprang to his feet. After taking leave of the Manager he pressed up to K. so close that K. had to push his chair back in order to have any freedom of movement. The Manager, doubtless seeing in K.'s eye that he was in desperate straits with this unintelligible Italian, intervened so cleverly and delicately that it appeared as if he were merely contributing little scraps of advice, while in reality he was briefly conveying to K. the sense of all the remarks with which the Italian unweariedly interrupted him. In this way K. learned that the Italian had some immediate business to attend to, that unfortunately he was likely to be pressed for time, that he had no intention of rushing round to see all the sights in a hurry, that he would much rather – of course only if K. were agreed, the decision lay with K. alone – confine himself to inspecting the Cathedral, but thoroughly. He was extremely delighted to have the chance of doing so in the company of such a learned and amiable gentleman – this was how he referred to K. who was trying hard to turn a deaf ear to his words and grasp as quickly as possible what the Manager was saying – and he begged him, if it were convenient, to meet him there in a couple of hours, say at about ten o'clock. He had certain hopes of being able to arrive there about that time. K. made a suitable rejoinder, the Italian pressed the Manager's hand, then K.'s hand, then the Manager's hand again, and, followed by both of them, turning only half towards them by this time but still maintaining a flow of words, departed towards the door. K. stayed a moment or two with the Manager, who was looking particularly unwell that day. He felt that he owed K. an apology and said – they were standing intimately together – that he had at first intended to escort the Italian himself, but on second thoughts – he gave no definite reason – he had decided that K. had better go. If K. found that he could not understand the man to begin with he mustn't let that upset him, for he wouldn't take long to catch the sense of what was said, and even if he didn't understand very much it hardly mattered, since the Italian cared little whether he was understood or not. Besides, K.'s knowledge of Italian was surprisingly good and he would certainly acquit himself well. With that K. was dismissed to his room. The time still at his disposal he devoted to copying from the dictionary various unfamiliar words which he would need in his tour of the Cathedral. It was an unusually exasperating task; attendants came in with letters, clerks arrived with inquiries, standing awkwardly in the doorway when they saw that K. was busy, yet not removing themselves until he answered, the Deputy Manager did not miss the chance of making himself a nuisance and appeared several times, taking the dictionary out of K.'s hand and with obvious indifference turning the pages over; even clients were dimly visible in the antechamber whenever the door opened, making deprecating bows to call attention to themselves but uncertain whether they had been remarked or not – all this activity rotated around K. as if he were the centre of it, while he himself was occupied in collecting the words he might need, looking them up in the dictionary, copying them out, practising their pronunciation, and finally trying to learn them by heart. His once excellent memory seemed to have deserted him, and every now and then he grew so furious with the Italian who was causing him all this trouble that he stuffed the dictionary beneath a pile of papers with the firm intention of preparing himself no further, yet he could not help seeing that it would not do to march the Italian round the art treasures of the Cathedral in dumb silence, and so with even greater rage he took the dictionary out again.

Just at half-past nine, as he was rising to go, the telephone rang; Leni bade him good morning and asked how he was; K. thanked her hastily and said he had no time to talk to her, since he must go to the Cathedral. 'To the Cathedral?' asked Leni. 'Yes, to the Cathedral.' 'But why the Cathedral?' cried Leni. K. tried to explain briefly to her, but hardly had he begun when Leni suddenly said: 'They're driving you hard.' Pity which he had not asked for and did not expect was more than K. could bear, he said two words of farewell, but even as he hung up the receiver he murmured half to himself and half to the faraway girl who could no longer hear him: 'Yes, they're driving me hard.'

By now it was growing late, he was already in danger of not being in time for the appointment. He drove off in a taxi-cab; at the last moment he remembered the album which he had found no opportunity of handing over earlier, and so took it with him now. He laid it on his knees and drummed on it impatiently with his fingers during the whole of the journey. The rain had slackened, but it was a raw, wet, murky day, one would not be able to see much in the Cathedral, and there was no doubt that standing about on the cold stone flags would make K.'s chill considerably worse.

The Cathedral Square was quite deserted, and K. recollected how even as a child he had been struck by the fact that in the houses of this narrow square nearly all the window-blinds were invariably drawn down. On a day like this, of course, it was more understandable. The Cathedral seemed deserted too, there was naturally no reason why anyone should visit it at such a time. K. went through both of the side aisles and saw no one but an old woman muffled in a shawl who was kneeling before a Madonna with adoring eyes. Then in the distance he caught sight of a limping verger vanishing through a door in the wall. K. had been punctual, ten o'clock was striking just as he entered, but the Italian had not yet arrived. He went back to the main entrance, stood there undecidedly for a while, and then circled round the building in the rain, to make sure that the Italian was perhaps not waiting at some side door. He was nowhere to be seen. Could the Manager have made some mistake about the hour? How could anyone be quite sure of understanding such a man? Whatever the circumstances, K. would at any rate have to wait half an hour for him. Since he was tired he felt like sitting down, went into the Cathedral again, found on a step a remnant of carpet-like stuff, twitched it with his toe towards a near-by bench, wrapped himself more closely in his greatcoat, turned up his collar, and settled himself. By way of filling in time he opened the album and ran idly through it, but he soon had to stop, for it was growing so dark that when he looked up he could distinguish scarcely a single detail in the neighbouring aisle.

Away in the distance a large triangle of candle-flames flickered on the high altar; K. could not have told with any certainty whether he had noticed them before or not.

Perhaps they had been newly kindled. Vergers are by profession stealthy-footed, one never remarks them. K. happened to turn round and saw not far behind him the gleam of another candle, a tall thick candle fixed to a pillar. It was lovely to look at, but quite inadequate for illuminating the altar-pieces, which mostly hung in the darkness of the side chapels; it rather heightened the darkness. So the Italian was as sensible as he was discourteous in not coming, for he would have seen nothing, he would have had to content himself with scrutinizing a few pictures inch-meal by the light of K.'s pocket-torch. Curious to see what effect it would have, K. went up to a small side chapel near by, mounted a few steps to a low balustrade, and bending over it shone his torch on the altar-piece. The errant light hovered over it like an intruder. The first thing K. perceived, partly by guess, was a huge armoured knight on the outermost verge of the picture. He was leaning on his sword, which was stuck into the bare ground, bare except for a stray blade of grass or two. He seemed to be watching attentively some event unfolding itself before his eyes. It was surprising that he should stand so still without approaching nearer to it. Perhaps he had been set there to stand guard. K., who had not seen any pictures for a long time, studied this knight for a good while, although the greenish light of the torch made his eyes blink. When he played the torch over the rest of the altar-piece he discovered that it was a portrayal of Christ being laid in the tomb, quite conventional in style although a fairly recent painting. He pocketed the torch and returned again to his seat.

In all likelihood it was now needless to wait any longer for the Italian, but the rain was probably pouring down outside, and since it was not so cold in the Cathedral as

K. had expected, he decided to linger there for the present. Quite near him rose the great pulpit, on its small vaulted canopy two plain golden crucifixes were slanted so that their shafts crossed at the tip. The outer balustrade and the stonework connecting it with the supporting columns were wrought all over with foliage in which little angels were entangled, now vivacious and now serene. K. went up to the pulpit and examined it from all sides, the carving of the stonework was delicate and thorough, the deep caverns of darkness among and behind the foliage looked as if caught and imprisoned there; K. put his hand into one of them and lightly felt the contour of the stone, he had never known that this pulpit existed. By pure chance he noticed a verger standing behind the nearest row of benches, a man in a loose-hanging black garment with a snuff-box in his left hand; he was gazing at K. 'What's the man after?' thought K. 'Do I look a suspicious character? Does he want a tip?' But when he saw that K. had become aware of him, the verger started pointing with his right hand, still holding a pinch of snuff in his fingers, in some vaguely indicated direction. His antics seemed to have little meaning. K. hesitated for a while, but the verger did not cease pointing at something or other and emphasizing the gesture with nods of his head. 'What does the man want?' said K. in a low tone, he did not dare to raise his voice in this place; then he pulled out his purse and made his way along the benches towards him. But the verger at once made a gesture of refusal, shrugged his shoulders, and limped away. With something of the same gait, a quick, limping motion, K. had often as a child imitated a man riding on horseback. 'A childish ancient,' thought K., 'with only wits enough to be a verger. How he stops when I stop and peers to see if I am following him!' Smiling to himself, K. went on following him through the side aisle almost as far as the high altar; the old man kept pointing in another direction, but K. deliberately refrained from looking round to see what he was pointing at, the gesture could have no other purpose than to shake K. off. At last he desisted from the pursuit, he did not want to alarm the old man too much; besides, in case the Italian were to turn up after all, it might be better not to scare away the only verger.

As he returned to the nave to find the seat on which he had left the album lying, K. caught sight of a small side pulpit attached to a pillar almost immediately adjoining the choir, a simple pulpit of plain, bleak stone. It was so small that from a distance it looked like an empty niche intended for a statue. There was certainly no room for the preacher to take a full step backwards from the balustrade. The vaulting of the stone canopy, too, began very low down and curved forward, although without ornamentation, in such a way that a medium-sized man could not stand upright beneath it but would have to keep leaning over the balustrade. The whole structure was designed to harass the preacher; there seemed no comprehensible reason why it should be there at all while the other pulpit, so large and finely decorated, was available.

And K. certainly would not have noticed it had not a lighted lamp been fixed above it, the usual sign that a sermon was going to be preached. Was a service going to be held now? In the empty church? K. peered down at the small flight of steps which led upwards to the pulpit, hugging the pillar as it went, so narrow that it looked like an ornamental addition to the pillar rather than a stairway for human beings. But at the foot of it, K. smiled in astonishment, there actually stood a clerical figure ready to ascend, with his hand on the balustrade and his eyes fixed on K. The priest gave a little nod and K. crossed himself and bowed, as he ought to have done earlier. The priest swung himself lightly on to the stairway and mounted into the pulpit with short, quick steps. Was he really going to preach a sermon? Perhaps the verger was not such an imbecile after all and had been trying to urge K. towards the preacher, a highly necessary action in that deserted building. But somewhere or other there was an old woman before an image of the Madonna; she ought to attend the service too. And if it were going to be a service, why was it not introduced by the organ? But the organ remained silent, its tall pipes looming faintly in the darkness.

K. wondered whether this was not the time to remove himself quickly; if he did not go now he would have no chance of doing so during the service, he would have to stay as long as that lasted, he was already behindhand in the office and was no longer obliged to wait for the Italian; he looked at his watch, it was eleven o'clock. But could it really be a sermon? Could K. represent the congregation all by himself? What if he had been a stranger merely visiting the church? That was more or less his position. It was absurd to think that a sermon was going to be preached at eleven in the morning on a week-day, in such dreadful weather. The priest – he was beyond doubt a priest, a young man with a smooth, dark face – was obviously mounting the pulpit simply to turn out the lamp, which had been lit by mistake.

It was not so, however, the priest after examining the lamp screwed it higher instead, then turned slowly towards the balustrade and gripped the angular edge of it with both hands. He stood like that for a while, looking around him without moving his head. K. had retreated a good distance and was leaning his elbows on the foremost pew. Without knowing exactly where the verger was stationed, he was vaguely aware of the old man's bent back, peacefully at rest as if his task had been fulfilled. What stillness there was now in the Cathedral! Yet K. had to violate it, for he was not minded to stay; if it were this priest's duty to preach a sermon at such and such an hour regardless of circumstances, let him do it, he could manage it without K.'s support, just as K.'s presence would certainly not contribute to its effectiveness. So he began slowly to move off, feeling his way along the pew on tiptoe until he was in the broad centre aisle, where he advanced undisturbed except for the ringing noise that his lightest footstep made on the stone flags and the echoes that sounded from the vaulted roof faintly but continuously, in manifold and regular progression. K. felt a little forlorn as he advanced, a solitary figure between the rows of empty seats, perhaps with the priest's eyes following him; and the size of the Cathedral struck him as bordering on the limit of what human beings could bear. When he came to the seat where he had left the album he simply snatched the book up without stopping and took it with him. He had almost passed the last of the pews and was emerging into the open space between himself and the doorway when he heard the priest lifting up his voice. A resonant, well-trained voice. How it rolled through the expectant Cathedral! But it was no congregation the priest was addressing, the words were unambiguous and inescapable, he was calling out: 'Joseph K.!'

K. started and stared at the ground before him. For the moment he was still free, he could continue on his way and vanish through one of the small, dark, wooden doors that faced him at no great distance. It would simply indicate that he had not understood the call, or that he had understood it and did not care. But if he were to turn round he would be caught, for that would amount to an admission that he had understood it very well, that he was really the person addressed, and that he was ready to obey. Had the priest called his name a second time K. would certainly have gone on, but since there was a persistent silence, though he stood waiting a long time, he could not help turning his head a little just to see what the priest was doing. The priest was standing calmly in the pulpit as before, yet it was obvious that he had observed K.'s turn of the head. It would have been like a childish game of hide-and-seek if K. had not turned right round to face him. He did so, and the priest beckoned him to come nearer. Since there was now no need for evasion, K. hurried back – he was both curious and eager to shorten the interview – with long flying strides towards the pulpit. At the first rows of seats he halted, but the priest seemed to think the distance still too great, he stretched out an arm and pointed with sharply bent forefinger to a spot immediately before the pulpit. K. followed this direction too; when he stood on the spot indicated he had to bend his head far back to see the priest at all. 'You are Joseph K.?' said the priest, lifting one hand from the balustrade in a vague gesture. 'Yes,' said K., thinking how frankly he used to give his name and what a burden it had recently become to him; nowadays people he had never seen before seemed to know his name. How pleasant it was to have to introduce oneself before being recognized! 'You are an accused man,' said the priest in a very low voice. 'Yes,' said K., 'so I have been informed.' 'Then you are the man I seek,' said the priest. 'I am the prison chaplain.' 'Indeed,' said K. 'I had you summoned here,' said the priest, 'to have a talk with you.' 'I didn't know that,' said K. 'I came here to show an Italian round the Cathedral.' 'A mere detail,' said the priest. 'What is that in your hand? Is it a prayer-book?' 'No,' replied K., 'it is an album of sights worth seeing in the town.' 'Lay it down,' said the priest. K. pitched it away so violently that it flew open and slid some way along the floor with dishevelled leaves. 'Do you know that your case is going badly?' asked the priest. 'I have that idea myself,' said K. 'I've done what I could, but without any success so far. Of course, my first petition hasn't been presented yet.' 'How do you think it will end?' asked the priest. 'At first I thought it must turn out well,' said K., 'but now I frequently have my doubts. I don't know how it will end. Do you?' 'No,' said the priest, 'but I fear it will end badly. You are held to be guilty. Your case will perhaps never get beyond a lower Court. Your guilt is supposed, for the present, at least, to have been proved.' 'But I am not guilty,' said K.; 'it's a misunderstanding. And if it comes to that, how can any man be called guilty? We are all simply men here, one as much as the other.' 'That is true,' said the priest, 'but that's how all guilty men talk.' 'Are you prejudiced against me too?' asked K. 'I have no prejudices against you,' said the priest. 'I thank you,' said K.; 'but all the others who are concerned in these proceedings are prejudiced against me. They are influencing even outsiders. My position is becoming more and more difficult.' 'You are misinterpreting the facts of the case,' said the priest. 'The verdict is not so suddenly arrived at, the proceedings only gradually merge into the verdict.' 'So that's how it is,' said K., letting his head sink. 'What is the next step you propose to take in the matter?' asked the priest. 'I'm going to get more help,' said K., looking up again to see how the priest took his statement. 'There are several possibilities I haven't explored yet.' 'You cast about too much for outside help,' said the priest disapprovingly, 'especially from women. Don't you see that it isn't the right kind of help?' 'In some cases, even in many I could agree with you,' said K., 'but not always. Women have great influence. If I could move some women I know to join forces in working for me, I couldn't help winning through. Especially before this Court, which consists almost entirely of petticoat-hunters. Let the Examining Magistrate see a woman in the distance and he almost knocks down his desk and the defendant in his eagerness to get at her.' The priest drooped over the balustrade, apparently feeling for the first time the oppressiveness of the canopy above his head. What could have happened to the weather outside? There was no longer even a murky daylight; black night had set in. All the stained glass in the great window could not illumine the darkness of the wall with one solitary glimmer of light. And at this very moment the verger began to put out the candles on the high altar, one after another. 'Are you angry with me?' asked K. of the priest. 'It may be that you don't know the nature of the Court you are serving.' He got no answer. 'These are only personal experiences,' said K. There was still no answer from above. 'I wasn't trying to insult you,' said K. And at that the priest shrieked from the pulpit: 'Can't you see anything at all?' It was an angry cry, but at the same time sounded like the involuntary shriek of one who sees another fall and is startled out of himself.

Both were now silent for a long time. In the prevailing

darkness the priest certainly could not make out K.'s features, while K. saw him distinctly by the light of the small lamp. Why did he not come down from the pulpit? He had not preached a sermon, he had only given K. some information which would be likely to harm him rather than help him when he came to consider it. Yet the priest's good intentions seemed to K. beyond question, it was not impossible that they could come to some agreement if the man would only quit his pulpit, it was not impossible that K. could obtain decisive and acceptable counsel from him which might, for instance, point the way, not towards some influential manipulation of the case, but towards a circumvention of it, a getting rid of it altogether, a mode of living completely outside the jurisdiction of the Court. This possibility must exist, K. had of late given much thought to it. And should the priest know of such a possibility, he might perhaps impart his knowledge if he were appealed to, although he himself belonged to the Court and as soon as he heard the Court impugned had forgotten his own gentle nature so far as to shout K. down.

'Won't you come down here?' said K. 'You haven't got to preach a sermon. Come down beside me.' 'I can come down now,' said the priest, perhaps repenting of his outburst. While he detached the lamp from its hook he said: 'I had to speak to you first from a distance. Otherwise I am too easily influenced and tend to forget my duty.'

K. waited for him at the foot of the steps. The priest stretched out his hand to K. while he was still on the way down from a higher level. 'Have you a little time for me?' asked K. 'As much time as you need,' said the priest, giving K. the small lamp to carry. Even close at hand he still wore a certain air of solemnity. 'You are very good to me,' said K. They paced side by side up and down the dusky aisle. 'But you are an exception among those who belong to the Court. I have more trust in you than in any of the others, though I know many of them. With you I can speak openly.' 'Don't be deluded,' said the priest. 'How am I being deluded?' asked K. 'You are deluding yourself about the Court,' said the priest. 'In the writings which preface the Law that particular delusion is described thus: before the Law stands a door-keeper on guard. To this door-keeper there comes a man from the country who begs for admittance to the Law. But the door-keeper says that he cannot admit the man at the moment. The man, on reflection, asks if he will be allowed, then, to enter later. "It is possible," answers the door-keeper, "but not at this moment." Since the door leading into the Law stands open as usual and the door-keeper steps to one side, the man bends down to peer through the entrance. When the door-keeper sees that, he laughs and says: "If you are so strongly tempted, try to get in without my permission. But note that I am powerful. And I am only the lowest door-keeper. From hall to hall, keepers stand at every door, one more powerful than the other. Even the third of these has an aspect that even I cannot bear to look at." These are difficulties which the man from the country has not expected to meet, the Law, he thinks, should be accessible to every man and at all times, and when he looks more closely at the door-keeper in his furred robe, with his huge pointed nose and long thin, Tartar beard, he decides that he had better wait until he gets permission to enter. The door-keeper gives him a stool and lets him sit down at the side of the door. There he sits waiting for days and years. He makes many attempts to be allowed in and wearies the door-keeper with his importunity. The door-keeper often engages him in brief conversation, asking him about his home and about other matters, but the questions are put quite impersonally, as great men put questions, and always conclude with the statement that the man cannot be allowed to enter yet. The man, who has equipped himself with many things for his journey, parts with all he has, however valuable, in the hope of bribing the door-keeper. The door-keeper accepts it all, saying, however, as he takes each gift: "I take this only to keep you from feeling that you have left something undone." During all these long years the man watches the door-keeper almost incessantly. He forgets about the other door-keepers, and this one seems to him the only barrier between himself and the Law. In the first years he curses his evil fate aloud; later, as he grows old, he only mutters to himself. He grows childish, and since in his prolonged watch he has learned to know even the fleas in the door-keeper's fur collar, he begs the very fleas to help him and to persuade the door-keeper to change his mind. Finally his eyes grow dim and he does not know whether the world is really darkening around him or whether his eyes are only deceiving him. But in the darkness he can now perceive a radiance that streams immortally from the door of the Law. Now his life is drawing to a close. Before he dies, all that he has experienced during the whole time of his sojourn condenses in his mind into one question, which he has never yet put to the door-keeper. He beckons the door-keeper, since he can no longer raise his stiffening body. The door-keeper has to bend far down to hear him, for the difference in size between them has increased very much to the man's disadvantage. "What do you want to know now?" asks the door-keeper, "you are insatiable." "Everyone strives to attain the Law," answers the man, "how does it come about, then, that in all these years no one has come seeking admittance but me?" The door-keeper perceives that the man is at the end of his strength and his hearing is failing, so he bellows in his ear: "No one but you could gain admittance through this door, since this door was intended only for you. I am now going to shut it."'

'So the door-keeper deluded the man,' said K. immediately, strongly attracted by the story. 'Don't be too hasty,' said the priest, 'don't take over an opinion without testing it. I have told you the story in the very words of the scriptures. There's no mention of delusion in it.' 'But it's clear enough,' said K., 'and your first interpretation of it was quite right. The door-keeper gave the message of salvation to the man only when it could no longer help him.' 'He was not asked the question any earlier,' said the priest, 'and you must consider, too, that he was only a door-keeper, and as such fulfilled his duty.' 'What makes you think he fulfilled his duty?' asked K. 'He didn't fulfil it. His duty might have been to keep all strangers away, but this man, for whom the door was intended, should have been let in.' 'You have not enough respect for the written word and you are altering the story,' said the priest. 'The story contains two important statements made by the door-keeper about admission to the Law, one at the beginning, the other at the end. The first statement is: that he cannot admit the man at the moment, and the other is: that this door was intended only for the man. If there were a contradiction between the two, you would be right and the door-keeper would have deluded the man. But there is no contradiction. The first statement, on the contrary, even implies the second. One could almost say that in suggesting to the man the possibility of future admittance the door-keeper is exceeding his duty. At that moment his apparent duty is to refuse admittance and indeed many commentators are surprised that the suggestion should be made at all, since the door-keeper appears to be a precisian with a stern regard for duty. He does not once leave his post during these many years, and he does not shut the door until the very last minute; he is conscious of the importance of his office, for he says: "I am powerful"; he is respectful to his superiors, for he says: "I am only the lowest door-keeper"; he is not garrulous, for during all these years he puts only what are called "impersonal questions"; he is not to be bribed, for he says in accepting a gift: "I take this only to keep you from feeling that you have left something undone"; where his duty is concerned he is to be moved neither by pity nor rage, for we are told that the man "wearied the door-keeper with his importunity"; and finally even his external appearance hints at a pedantic character, the large, pointed nose and the long, thin, black, Tartar beard. Could one imagine a more faithful door-keeper? Yet the door-keeper has other elements in his character which are likely to advantage anyone seeking admittance and which make it comprehensible enough that he should somewhat exceed his duty in suggesting the possibility of future admittance. For it cannot be denied that he is a little simpleminded and consequently a little conceited. Take the statements he makes about his power and the power of the other door-keepers and their dreadful aspect which even he cannot bear to see — I hold that these statements may be true enough, but that the way in which he brings them out shows that his perceptions are confused by simpleness of mind and conceit. The commentators note in this connexion: "The right perception of any matter and

a misunderstanding of the same matter do not wholly ex-
clude each other." One must at any rate assume that such
simpleness and conceit, however sparingly indicated, are
likely to weaken his defence of the door; they are breaches
in the character of the door-keeper. To this must be added
the fact that the door-keeper seems to be a friendly creature by nature, he is by no means always on his official
dignity. In the very first moments he allows himself the
jest of inviting the man to enter in spite of the strictly
maintained veto against entry; then he does not, for instance, send the man away, but gives him, as we are told,
a stool and lets him sit down beside the door. The patience with which he endures the man's appeals during so
many years, the brief conversations, the acceptance of the
gifts, the politeness with which he allows the man to curse
loudly in his presence the fate for which he himself is responsible – all this lets us deduce certain motions of sympathy. Not every door-keeper would have acted thus. And
finally, in answer to a gesture of the man's he stoops low
down to give him the chance of putting a last question.
Nothing but mild impatience – the door-keeper knows
that this is the end of it all – is discernible in the words:
"You are insatiable." Some push this mode of interpretation even further and hold that these words express a
kind of friendly admiration, though not without a hint of
condescension. At any rate the figure of the door-keeper
can be said to come out very differently from what you
fancied.' 'You have studied the story more exactly and for
a longer time than I have,' said K. They were both silent
for a little while. Then K. said: 'So you think the man
was not deluded?' 'Don't misunderstand me,' said the
priest, 'I am only showing you the various opinions concerning that point. You must not pay too much attention

to them. The scriptures are unalterable and the comments often enough merely express the commentator's bewilderment. In this case there even exists an interpretation which claims that the deluded person is really the door-keeper.' 'That's a far-fetched interpretation,' said K. 'On what is it based?' 'It is based,' answered the priest, 'on the simple-mindedness of the door-keeper. The argument is that he does not know the Law from inside, he knows only the way that leads to it, where he patrols up and down. His ideas of the interior are assumed to be childish, and it is supposed that he himself is afraid of the other guardians whom he holds up as bogies before the man. Indeed, he fears them more than the man does, since the man is determined to enter after hearing about the dreadful guardians of the interior, while the door-keeper has no desire to enter, at least not so far as we are told. Others again say that he must have been in the interior already, since he is after all engaged in the service of the Law and can only have been appointed from inside. This is countered by arguing that he may have been appointed by a voice calling from the interior, and that anyhow he cannot have been far inside, since the aspect of the third door-keeper is more than he can endure. Moreover, no indication is given that during all these years he ever made any remarks showing a knowledge of the interior, except for the one remark about the door-keepers. He may have been forbidden to do so, but there is no mention of that either. On these grounds the conclusion is reached that he knows nothing about the aspect and significance of the interior, so that he is in a state of delusion. But he is deceived also about his relation to the man from the country, for he is subject to the man and does not know it. He treats the man instead as his own subordinate, as can be recognized from many details that must be still fresh in your mind. But, according to this view of the story, it is just as clearly indicated that he is really subordinated to the man. In the first place, a bondman is always subject to a free man. Now the man from the country is really free, he can go where he likes, it is only the Law that is closed to him, and access to the Law is forbidden him only by one individual, the door-keeper. When he sits down on the stool by the side of the door and stays there for the rest of his life, he does it of his own free will; in the story there is no mention of any compulsion. But the door-keeper is bound to his post by his very office, he does not dare strike out into the country, nor apparently may he go into the interior of the Law, even should he wish to. Besides, although he is in the service of the Law, his service is confined to this one entrance; that is to say, he serves only this man for whom alone the entrance is intended. On that ground too he is subject to the man. One must assume that for many years, for as long as it takes a man to grow up to the prime of life, his service was in a sense an empty formality, since he had to wait for a man to come, that is to say someone in the prime of life, and so had to wait a long time before the purpose of his service could be fulfilled, and, moreover, had to wait on the man's pleasure, for the man came of his own free will. But the termination of his service also depends on the man's term of life, so that to the very end he is subject to the man. And it is emphasized throughout that the door-keeper apparently realizes nothing of all this. That is not in itself remarkable, since according to this interpretation the door-keeper is deceived in a much more important issue, affecting his very office. At the end, for example, he says regarding the entrance to the Law: "I am now going to shut it," but at the beginning of the story we are told that the door leading into the Law stands always open, and if it stands open always, that is to say at all times, without reference to the life or death of the man, then the door-keeper is incapable of closing it. There is some difference of opinion about the motive behind the door-keeper's statement, whether he said he was going to close the door merely for the sake of giving an answer, or to emphasize his devotion to duty, or to bring the man into a state of grief and regret in his last moments. But there is no lack of agreement that the door-keeper will not be able to shut the door. Many indeed profess to find that he is subordinate to the man even in wisdom, towards the end, at least, for the man sees the radiance that issues from the door of the Law while the door-keeper in his official position must stand with his back to the door, nor does he say anything to show that he has perceived the change.' 'That is well argued,' said K., after repeating to himself in a low voice several passages from the priest's exposition. 'It is well argued, and I am inclined to agree that the door-keeper is deluded. But that has not made me abandon my former opinion, since both conclusions are to some extent compatible. Whether the door-keeper is clear-sighted or deluded does not dispose of the matter. I said the man is deluded. If the door-keeper is clear-sighted, one might have doubts about that, but if the door-keeper himself is deluded, then his delusion must of necessity be communicated to the man. That makes the door-keeper not, indeed, a swindler, but a creature so simple-minded that he ought to be dismissed at once from his office. You mustn't forget that the door-keeper's delusions do himself no harm but do infinite harm to the man.' 'There are objections to that,' said the priest. 'Many aver that the story confers no right on anyone to pass judgement on the door-keeper. Whatever he may seem to us, he is yet a servant of the Law; that is, he belongs to the Law and as such is set beyond human judgement. In that case one dare not believe that the door-keeper is subordinate to the man. Bound as he is by his service, even at the door of the Law, he is incomparably freer than anyone at large in the world. The man is only seeking the Law, the door-keeper is already attached to it. It is the Law that has placed him at his post; to doubt his integrity is to doubt the Law itself.' 'I don't agree with that point of view,' said K. shaking his head, 'for if one accepts it, one must accept as true everything the door-keeper says. But you yourself have sufficiently proved how impossible it is to do that.' 'No,' said the priest, 'it is not necessary to accept everything as true, one must only accept it as necessary.' 'A melancholy conclusion,' said K. 'It turns lying into a universal principle.'

K. said that with finality, but it was not his final judgement. He was too tired to survey all the conclusions arising from the story, and the trains of thought into which it was leading him were unfamiliar, dealing with impalpabilities better suited to a theme for discussion among Court officials than for him. The simple story had lost its clear outline, he wanted to put it out of his mind, and the priest, who now showed great delicacy of feeling, suffered him to do so and accepted his comment in silence, although undoubtedly he did not agree with it.

They paced up and down for a while in silence, K. walking close beside the priest without being able to orient himself in the darkness. The lamp in his hand had long since gone out. The silver image of some saint once glimmered into sight immediately before him, by the sheen of its own silver, and was instantaneously lost in the darkness again. To keep himself from being utterly dependent on the priest, K. asked: 'Aren't we near the main doorway now?' 'No,' said the priest, 'we're a long way from it. Do you want to leave already?' Although at that moment K. had not been thinking of leaving, he answered at once: 'Of course, I must go. I'm the assistant manager of a Bank, they're waiting for me, I only came here to show a business friend from abroad round the Cathedral.' 'Well,' said the priest, reaching out his hand to K., 'then go.' 'But I can't find my way out alone in this darkness,' said K. 'Turn left to the wall,' said the priest, 'then follow the wall without leaving it and you'll come to a door.' The priest had already taken a step or two away from him, but K. cried out in a loud voice. 'Please wait a moment.' 'I am waiting,' said the priest. 'Don't you want anything more to do with me?' asked K. 'No,' said the priest. 'You were so friendly to me for a time,' said K., 'and explained so much to me, and now you let me go as if you cared nothing about me.' 'But you have to leave now,' said the priest. 'Well, yes,' said K., 'you must see that I can't help it.' 'You must first see that I can't help being what I am,' said the priest. 'You are the prison chaplain,' said K., groping his way nearer to the priest again; his immediate return to the Bank was not so necessary as he had made out, he could quite well stay longer. 'That means I belong to the Court,' said the priest. 'So why should I make any claims upon you? The Court makes no claims upon you. It receives you when you come and it relinquishes you when you go.'

X

The End

ON the evening before K.'s thirty-first birthday – it was
about nine o'clock, the time when a hush falls on the
streets – two men came to his lodging. In frock-coats,
pallid and plump, with top-hats that were apparently un-
collapsible. After some exchange of formalities regarding
precedence at the front door, they repeated the same ceremony more exhaustively before K.'s door. Without having
been informed of their visit, K. was sitting also dressed in
black in an arm-chair near the door, slowly pulling on a
pair of new gloves that fitted tightly over the fingers,
looking as if he were expecting guests. He stood up at
once and scrutinized the gentlemen with curiosity. 'So
you are appointed for me?' he asked. The gentlemen
bowed, each indicating the other with the hand that held
the top-hat. K. admitted to himself that he had been expecting different visitors. He went to the window and
took another look at the dark street. Nearly all the windows at the other side of the street were also in darkness;
in many of them the curtains were drawn. At one lighted
tenement window some babies were playing behind bars,
reaching with their little hands towards each other although not able to move themselves from the spot. 'Tenth-
rate old actors they send for me,' said K. to himself,
glancing round again to confirm the impression. 'They
want to finish me off cheaply.' He turned abruptly towards the men and asked: 'What theatre are you playing
at?' 'Theatre?' said one, the corners of his mouth twitch-

ing as he looked for advice to the other, who acted as if he were a dumb man struggling to overcome an unnatural disability. 'They're not prepared to answer questions,' said K. to himself and went to fetch his hat.

While still on the stairs the two of them tried to take K. by the arms, and he said: 'Wait till we're in the street, I'm not an invalid.' But just outside the street door they fastened on him in a fashion he had never before seen or experienced. They kept their shoulders close behind his and instead of crooking their elbows, wound their arms round his at full length, holding his hands in a method-ical, practised, irresistible grip. K. walked rigidly between them, the three of them were interlocked in a unity which would have brought all three down together had one of them been knocked over. It was a unity such as can be formed almost by lifeless elements alone.

Under the street lamps K. attempted time and time again, difficult though it was at such very close quarters, to see his companions more clearly than had been possible in the dusk of his room. 'Perhaps they are tenors,' he thought, as he studied their fat double chins. He was re-pelled by the painful cleanliness of their faces. One could literally see that the cleansing hand had been at work in the corners of the eyes, rubbing the upper lip, scrubbing out the furrows at the chin.

When that occurred to K. he halted, and in conse-quence the others halted too; they stood on the verge of an open, deserted square adorned with flower-beds. 'Why did they send you, of all people!' he said, it was more a cry than a question. The gentlemen obviously had no answer to make, they stood waiting with their free arms hanging, like sickroom attendants waiting while their patient takes a rest. 'I won't go any farther,' said K. ex-

perimentally. No answer was needed to that, it was sufficient that the two men did not loosen their grip and tried
to propel K. from the spot; but he resisted them. 'I shan't
need my strength much longer, I'll expend all the strength
I have,' he thought. Into his mind came a recollection of
flies struggling away from the fly-paper till their little legs
were torn off. 'The gentlemen won't find it easy.'

And then before them Fräulein Bürstner appeared,
mounting a small flight of steps leading into the square
from a low-lying side-street. It was not quite certain
that it was she, but the resemblance was close enough.
Whether it was really Fräulein Bürstner or not, however,
did not matter to K.; the important thing was that he
suddenly realized the futility of resistance. There would
be nothing heroic in it were he to resist, to make difficulties for his companions, to snatch at the last appearance of
life in the exertion of struggle. He set himself in motion,
and the relief his warders felt was transmitted to some
extent even to himself. They suffered him now to lead the
way, and he followed the direction taken by the Fräulein
ahead of him, not that he wanted to overtake her or to
keep her in sight as long as possible, but only that he
might not forget the lesson she had brought into his
mind. 'The only thing I can do now,' he told himself, and
the regular correspondence between his steps and the
steps of the other two confirmed his thought, 'the only
thing for me to go on doing is to keep my intelligence
calm and discriminating to the end. I always wanted to
snatch at the world with twenty hands, and not for a very
laudable motive, either. That was wrong, and am I to
show now that not even a whole year's struggling with
my case has taught me anything? Am I to leave this
world as a man who shies away from all conclusions? Are

people to say of me after I am gone that at the beginning of my case I wanted it to finish, and at the end of it wanted it to begin again? I don't want that to be said. I am grateful for the fact that these half-dumb, stupid creatures have been sent to accompany me on this journey, and that I have been left to say to myself all that is needed.'

The Fräulein meanwhile had bent into a side-street, but by this time K. could do without her and submitted himself to the guidance of his escort. In complete harmony all three now made their way across a bridge in the moonlight, the two men readily yielded to K.'s slightest movement, and when he turned slightly towards the parapet they turned, too, in a solid front. The water, glittering and trembling in the moonlight, divided on either side of a small island, on which the foliage of trees and bushes rose in thick masses, as if bunched together. Beneath the trees ran gravel paths, now invisible, with convenient benches on which K. had stretched himself at ease many a summer. 'I didn't mean to stop altogether,' he said to his companions, shamed by their obliging compliance. Behind K.'s back the one seemed to reproach the other gently for the mistaken stop they had made, and then all three went on again.

They passed through several steeply-rising streets, in which policemen stood or patrolled at intervals; sometimes a good way off, sometimes quite near. One with a bushy moustache, his hand on the hilt of his sabre, came up as of set purpose close to the not quite harmless-looking group. The two gentlemen halted, the policeman seemed to be already opening his mouth, but K. forcibly pulled his companions forward. He kept looking round cautiously to see if the policeman was following; as soon as he had put a corner between himself and the policeman he started to run, and his two companions, scant of breath as they were, had to run beside him.

So they came quickly out of the town, which at this point merged almost without transition into the open fields. A small stone quarry, deserted and bleak, lay quite near to a still completely urban house. Here the two men came to a standstill, whether because this place had been their goal from the very beginning or because they were too exhausted to go farther. Now they loosened their hold of K., who stood waiting dumbly, took off the top-hats and wiped the sweat from their brows with pocket hand-kerchiefs, meanwhile surveying the quarry. The moon shone down on everything with that simplicity and seren-ity which no other light possesses.

After an exchange of courteous formalities regarding which of them was to take preference in the next task — these emissaries seemed to have been given no specific as-signments in the charge laid jointly upon them — one of them came up to K. and removed his coat, his waistcoat, and finally his shirt. K. shivered involuntarily, where-upon the man gave him a light, reassuring pat on the back. Then he folded the clothes carefully together, as if they were likely to be used again at some time, although perhaps not immediately. Not to leave K. standing mo-tionless, exposed to the night breeze, which was chilly enough, he took him by the arm and walked him up and down a little, while his partner investigated the quarry to find a suitable spot. When he found it he beckoned, and K.'s companion led him over there. It was a spot near the cliff-side where a loose boulder was lying. The two of them laid K. down on the ground, propped him against the boulder, and settled his head upon it. But in spite of the pains they took and all the willingness K. showed, his posture remained contorted and unnatural-looking. So one of the men begged the other to let him dispose K. all by himself, yet even that did not improve matters. Finally they left K. in a position which was not even the best of the positions they had already rehearsed. Then one of them opened his frock-coat and out of a sheath that hung from a belt girt round his waistcoat drew a long, thin, double-edged butcher's knife, held it up, and tested the cutting edges in the moonlight. Once more the odious ceremonial of courtesy began, the first handed the knife across K. to the second, who handed it across K. back again to the first. K. now perceived clearly that he was supposed to seize the knife himself, as it travelled from hand to hand above him, and plunge it into his own breast. But he did not do so, he merely turned his head, which was still free to move, and gazed around him. He could not completely rise to the occasion, he could not relieve the officials of all their tasks; the responsibility for this last failure of his lay with him who had not left him the remnant of strength necessary for the deed. His glance fell on the top story of the house adjoining the quarry. With a flicker as of a light going up, the casements of a window there suddenly flew open; a human figure, faint and insubstantial at that distance and that height, leaned abruptly far forward and stretched both arms still farther. Who was it? A friend? A good man? Someone who sympathized? Someone who wanted to help? Was it one person only? Or were they all there? Was help at hand? Were there some arguments in his favour that had been overlooked? Of course there must be. Logic is doubtless unshakable, but it cannot withstand a man who wants to go on living. Where was the

Judge whom he had never seen? Where was the High
Court, to which he had never penetrated? He raised his
hands and spread out all his fingers.

But the hands of one of the partners were already at
K.'s throat, while the other thrust the knife into his heart
and turned it there twice. With failing eyes K. could still
see the two of them, cheek leaning against cheek, immediately before his face, watching the final act. 'Like a
dog!' he said: it was as if he meant the shame of it to
outlive him.

Epilogue

NEARLY everything of Kafka's that was published in his lifetime was rescued from him by dint of persuasion and guile on my part. That does not mean that he took no pleasure in his work; often enough and for long periods he showed great pleasure in his writings, although he always referred to them as 'scribblings'. Anyone who had the privilege of hearing him read his own prose to a small circle, with a rhythmic sweep, a dramatic fire, a spontaneity such as no actor ever achieves, got an immediate impression of the delight in creation and the passion that informed his work. His unwillingness to publish it arose in the first place from certain unhappy experiences that drove him to a kind of self-sabotage, and therefore to an attitude of Nihilism regarding his own work; in the second place, however, it arose independently from the fact that he applied the highest religious standards to all work of his (although he never actually said so), and, of course, it always fell short of these standards, wrung as it was from his own perplexities. He would not admit the argument that his work might help other seekers for faith, naturalness, and spiritual wholeness, being himself too earnestly and implacably a seeker for the right way of living to feel that he could advise others when his first need was to advise himself.

That is how I interpret Kafka's negative attitude towards his work. He spoke often of the 'false hands that reach out to one while one is writing'; he also said that what he had already written, not to say published, led him astray in his further work. There were many resistances to overcome before a book of his could be published. None the less, the handsome volumes gave him real delight, and sometimes he relished even the effect they had; there were times when he

252

regarded both himself and his work with a benevolent eye, never quite without irony, but with a friendly irony.

Among Franz Kafka's papers no will was ever found. In his writing-table, beneath a pile of other papers, lay a folded note written in ink and addressed to me. This is what it said:

DEAREST MAX, my last request: Everything I leave behind me (that is, in the bookcases, chest of drawers, writing-table, both at home and in the office, or wherever anything may have got to, whatever you happen to find), in the way of note-books, manuscripts, letters, my own and other people's, sketches and so on, is to be burned unread and to the last page, as well as all writings of mine or notes which either you may have or other people, from whom you are to beg them in my name. Letters which are not handed over to you should at least be faithfully burned by those who have them.

Yours,
FRANZ KAFKA

A closer search brought to light a yellowed and obviously more ancient piece of paper on which was written in pencil:

DEAR MAX, perhaps this time I shan't recover, pneumonia is likely enough after the month of pulmonary fever I have had, and not even my setting it down in writing will keep it off, although there's some power even in that.

Just in case, then, this is my last will concerning all I have written:

Of all my writings the only books that count are these: *The Judgement, The Stoker, Metamorphosis, Penal Colony, Country Doctor*, and the short story: *Hunger-Artists*. (The few copies that exist of the *Meditation* can be left; I don't want to give anyone the trouble of pulping them, but there's to be no reprinting.) When I say that these five books and the short story count, I don't mean that I want them to be printed again and handed down to posterity; on the contrary, should they disappear altogether that would be what I want. Only, since they do exist, I don't mind anyone's keeping them if he wants to.

But everything else of mine that I have written (printed in magazines or newspapers, written in manuscripts or letters) without exception, so far as it can be got hold of, or begged from the addressees (the most of these you know, the main ones are . . . and be sure not to forget the note-books . . . has) – all this, without exception and preferably unread (though I don't mind you looking into it, but I would much prefer that you didn't, and in any case no one else is to look at it) – all this, without exception, is to be burned, and that you should do it as soon as possible is what I beg of you.

Franz

If in spite of these categorical instructions I refuse to commit the incendiary act my friend demanded of me, I have good reasons for it.

Some of these are private, but there are others which can be made public and which in my opinion justify my decision.

The chief reason is this: when I took up a new profession in 1921 I told my friend that I had made a will begging him to destroy various papers of mine, to edit others, and so forth. Kafka said in reply, showing me the outside of the note written in ink which was later found in his writing-table: 'My will is going to be quite simple – a request to you to burn everything.' I can still remember the exact wording of my answer: 'In case you ever seriously think of doing such a thing, let me tell you now that I would not fulfil any such request.' The whole conversation was carried on in the jesting tone habitual to us, but there was always a background of seriousness assumed by each of us in what we said to each other. Franz knew that my refusal was in earnest, and at the end, if he had still intended these wishes to be carried out, he would have appointed another executor.

Other reasons are: the instructions in the pencilled note were not followed by Franz himself, since he gave specific permission later on for parts of the *Meditation* to be printed in a newspaper, and for three other stories of his to be published, which he himself made up into a volume together with *Hunger-Artists* and gave to a publishing firm. Besides, both these notes were written at a time when my friend's self-critical tendencies had reached their peak. But during his last years his whole life took an unforeseen turn for the better, a new, happy, and positive turn which cancelled out his self-hatred and Nihilism. Also, my decision to publish now is made easier for me by the recollections of the struggles I waged to get out of Kafka, sometimes by sheer importunity, every single publication of his; and yet afterwards he was reconciled to these publications and relatively pleased with them. Finally, in a posthumous edition many personal arguments cease to apply, such as, for instance, Kafka's objection that the publication of work he had done would lead him astray in his future work, or that it would call up the shadows of painful past experience. That Kafka's dislike of publication was intimately bound up with his personal problems could be gathered from much that he said, and from the following letter to me: '... I am not going to include the novels. Why rake up these old attempts? Only because they happen not to have been burned yet? ... Next time I come I hope they will be burned. What sense would there be in reviving such ... bungled pieces of work? Only if one hoped to create a whole out of the fragments, some complete work to which one could make a final appeal, a breast on which I could beat in my hour of need. But I know that is impossible here, there is no help for me in these. So what am I to do with the things? Since they can't help me am I to let them harm me, as must be the case, given my knowledge about them?'

The manuscript of this novel, *The Trial,* I took home with me in June 1920 and set in order soon after. The manuscript has no title. But in speaking of it Kafka always referred to it as *The Trial*. For the division into chapters as well as the chapter headings Kafka is responsible, but for the arrangement of the chapters I have had to depend on my own judgement. Since, however, my friend had read me a great part of the manuscript, my judgement has been supported by actual recollection.

Franz Kafka regarded the novel as unfinished. Before the final chapter, which is here included, various further stages of the mysterious trial should have been described. But since the trial, according to the author himself, was never to get as far as the highest Court, in a certain sense the novel was interminable; that is to say, it could be prolonged into infinity. And the finished chapters, taken in conjunction with the conclusive last chapter, in any case suffice to let the meaning and form of the work appear with the utmost clarity; anyone who was not informed that the author had proposed to do further work on it – he never did so, because his life entered an entirely new atmosphere – would scarcely notice its deficiencies.

My labours with the huge bundle of papers were confined to separating the finished from the unfinished chapters. The unfinished chapters I am keeping back for the final volume of the posthumous edition of Kafka's works; they contain nothing that is essential to the action. One of these fragments, called 'A Dream', was included by the author himself in the volume entitled *A Country Doctor*. The finished chapters have been here combined and arranged. Of the unfinished chapters I have used only one, which is obviously very nearly finished; with a small rearrangement of four lines it appears in this book as Chapter VIII.

In the text I have naturally altered nothing. I have only transcribed in full the innumerable contractions (for instance, instead of F. B., Fräulein Bürstner; instead of T., Titorelli) and corrected one or two slips that remained in the manuscript obviously only because the author had never subjected it to a definite revision.

MAX BROD

The " Teaching of English " Series

General Editor—Dr. Richard Wilson

EIGHT MODERN PLAYS

No. 102

A. A. MILNE

*From a pen-drawing by E. Heber
Thompson, after a photograph by
"Coster—Photographer of Men."*
(*Copyright.*)

EIGHT
MODERN PLAYS

Selected and Edited by

JOHN HAMPDEN

THOMAS NELSON & SONS, LTD.
LONDON, EDINBURGH, AND NEW YORK

First published September 1927
  Reprinted December 1927; July 1928; December 1928;
  August 1929; November 1930; November 1931; March 1933;
  February, November 1934; November 1935; January 1937;
  October 1937

CONTENTS

THE PRINCESS AND THE WOODCUTTER. *A. A. Milne* 9

ROBIN HOOD. *Alfred Noyes* 31

THE SLIPPERS OF CINDERELLA. *W. Graham Robertson* 49

THE DISCOVERY. *Hermon Ould* 81

ELDORADO. *Bernard Gilbert* 97

CAMPBELL OF KILMOHR. *J. A. Ferguson* . . 125

CATHERINE PARR. *Maurice Baring* . . . 145

MICHAEL. *Miles Malleson* 157

COMMENTARY :
  ON THINKING IT OVER 177
  ON WRITING LITTLE PLAYS 197

ACTING NOTES 201

APPENDIX :
  PROCEDURE FOR A MOCK TRIAL . . . 228
  A CHRISTMAS EPILOGUE 235

EIGHT MODERN PLAYS

PREFACE

IF this little volume of one-act plays may claim any
originality of plan, it is that though primarily intended
for junior readers and actors, it does not consist of "plays
for children" or of adaptations from novels. With one
excellent exception, all the plays in the book were written
for performance by adult actors in the professional
theatre, but as they have been chosen for their appeal to
junior forms as well as their quality, it is hoped that they
will be found worth reading, studying, and acting for
their own sake—and as an introduction to Shakespeare.

For all their instinctive appreciation of the dramatic
form, the small boy and girl are too often baffled and
bewildered by being plunged straight into *The Merchant
of Venice* or *A Midsummer Night's Dream*. A Fourth
Form boy, who had just been introduced to Shakespeare,
spoke for many of his peers when he approached the
master's desk with the dismayed question : " Please, sir,
is ALL this book *Julius Cæsar* ? " To meet this difficulty,
to provide an introduction to the treasures of our dramatic
literature, the modern one-act play may be used to very
good effect, for it is free from archaism in thought and
speech, arresting, quickly understood, and short enough
to be acted or read in one lesson.

This book can be used simply as a reader ; but if any
suggestion as to method may be ventured, it is that
the plays should be treated as plays—to be acted rather
than to be read. Parts should be carefully assigned in
advance, and the players encouraged to study them, and

sometimes to learn them by heart, as they will frequently offer to do. It is of great help if the most important entrances, exits, and stage-movements are settled by the teacher or by a " producer " chosen from the form, and a " stage-manager " may be appointed to look after any simple furniture and properties which are used. The important point is that each " performance " should be an attempt at interpretation. However crude form-room conditions may be, the youthful imagination transforms them, rejoicing in the simplest equipment ; and acting so quickens interest and appreciation that immediately there are opportunities to give training in speech and movement and " team-work," and to develop a rudimentary understanding of dramatic structure and characterization.

J. H.

ACKNOWLEDGMENTS

The editor wishes to express his thanks to the following authors and publishers for permission to include their plays in this book :
Mr. Alfred Noyes and Messrs. Blackwood for *Robin Hood ;* Mr. W. Graham Robertson and Messrs. Heinemann for *The Slippers of Cinderella ;* Mr. Hermon Ould and Messrs. Samuel French for *The Discovery ;* Mr. Bernard Gilbert and Messrs. Samuel French for *Eldorado ;* The Honourable Maurice Baring and Messrs. Heinemann for *Catherine Parr ;* Mr. A. A. Milne and Messrs. Samuel French for *The Princess and the Woodcutter ;* Mr. Miles Malleson and Messrs. Allen and Unwin for *Michael ;* and especially Mr. J. A. Ferguson, for revising *Campbell of Kilmohr* (published by Messrs. Gowans and Gray) for this edition, and adding his Acting Notes.
The editor also desires to acknowledge once again his great indebtedness to Dr. Richard Wilson ; to the lending libraries of the British Drama League and the Village Drama Society; to the British Drama League's Librarian, Miss Violet Clayton ; and to his wife.

THE PRINCESS AND THE WOODCUTTER

BY A. A. MILNE

CHARACTERS

The Woodcutter.
The Princess.
The King.
The Queen.
The Red Prince.
The Blue Prince.
The Yellow Prince.
Attendants.

The music for the play is published by Messrs. Samuel French, Ltd.

THE PRINCESS AND THE WOODCUTTER

THE WOODCUTTER'S SONG

Woodcutter—
> A humble woodman I,
> A plain hard-working peasant,
> A simple soul, who on the whole
> Finds life extremely pleasant.
> I envy none to-day
> His lofty rank or station,
> Enough for me to have a free
> And healthy occupation.

Refrain : Singing and swinging my axe
> On the monarch uprearing,
> Stroke upon stroke, till the oak
> Crashes down in the clearing.
> So shall I vanquish, perchance,
> Both the haughty and splendid,
> Love shall have brought them to naught
> When the tale shall be ended.

> In realms of faery lore
> I need no guide or tutor,
> And there, I learn, princesses yearn
> To wed the humble suitor.

11

The truly noble mind
All outward show despises ;
It is not rank, or wealth, or swank
That takes the highest prizes !

Refrain (As before).

The Woodcutter is discovered singing at his work, in a glade of the forest outside his hut. He is tall and strong, and brave and handsome ; all that a woodcutter ought to be. Now it happened that the Princess was passing, and as soon as his song is finished, sure enough, on she comes.

Princess. Good-morning, Woodcutter.
Woodcutter. Good-morning.
                    [*But he goes on with his work.*]
Princess [*after a pause*]. Good-morning, Woodcutter.
Woodcutter. Good-morning.
Princess. Don't you ever say anything except good-morning ?
Woodcutter. Sometimes I say good-bye.
Princess. You *are* a cross woodcutter to-day.
Woodcutter. I have work to do.
Princess. You are still cutting wood ? Don't you ever do anything else ?
Woodcutter. Well, you are still a Princess ; don't *you* ever do anything else ?
Princess [*reproachfully*]. Now, that's not fair, Woodcutter. You can't say I was a Princess yesterday, when I came and helped you stack your wood. Or the day before, when I tied up your hand where you had cut it. Or the day before that, when we had our meal together on the grass. Was I a Princess then ?
Woodcutter. Somehow I think you were. Somehow I think you were saying to yourself, " Isn't it sweet of a Princess to treat a mere woodcutter like this ? "

Princess. I think you are perfectly horrid. I've a good mind never to speak to you again. [*Turns* R.] And—and I would, if only I could be sure that you would notice I wasn't speaking to you.

Woodcutter. After all, I'm just as bad as you. Only yesterday I was thinking to myself how unselfish I was to interrupt my work in order to talk to a mere Princess.

Princess. Yes, but the trouble is that you *don't* interrupt your work.

Woodcutter [*interrupting it and going up to her with a smile*]. Madam, I am at your service.

Princess. I wish I thought you were.

Woodcutter. Surely you have enough people at your service already. Princes and chancellors and chamberlains and waiting-maids.

Princess. Yes, that's just it. That's why I want your help. Particularly in the matter of Princes.

Woodcutter. Why, has a suitor come for the hand of Her Royal Highness ?

Princess. Three suitors. And I hate them all.

Woodcutter. And which are you going to marry ?

Princess. I don't know. Father hasn't made up his mind yet.

Woodcutter. And this is a matter which father— which His Majesty decides for himself ?

Princess. Why, of course ! You should read the history books, Woodcutter. The suitors to the hand of a Princess are always set some trial of strength or test of quality by the King, and the winner marries his daughter.

Woodcutter. Well, I don't live in a palace, and I think my own thoughts about these things. I'd better get back to my work.

[*He goes on with his chopping.*]

Princess [*gently, after a pause*]. Woodcutter !

Woodcutter [*looking up*]. Oh, are you there ? I thought you were married by this time.

Princess [*meekly*]. I don't want to be married. [*Hastily*] I mean, not to any of those three.

Woodcutter. You can't help yourself.

Princess. I know.   That's why I wanted *you* to help me.

Woodcutter [*going up to her*]. Can a simple wood-cutter help a Princess ?

Princess. Well, perhaps a simple one couldn't, but a clever one might.

Woodcutter. What would his reward be ?

Princess. His reward would be that the Princess, not being married to any of her three suitors, would still be able to help him chop his wood in the mornings. . . . I *am* helping you, aren't I ?

Woodcutter [*smiling*]. Oh, decidedly.

Princess [*nodding*]. I thought I was.

Woodcutter. It is kind of a great lady like yourself to help so humble a fellow as I.

Princess [*meekly*]. I'm not *very* great.

[*And she isn't.   She is the smallest, daintiest little Princess that ever you saw.*]

Woodcutter. There's enough of you to make a hundred men unhappy.

Princess. And one man happy ?

Woodcutter. And one man very, very happy.

Princess [*innocently*]. I wonder who he'll be. . . . Woodcutter, if *you* were a Prince, would you be my suitor ?

Woodcutter [*scornfully*]. One of three ?

Princess [*excitedly*]. Oh, would you kill the others ? With that axe ?

Woodcutter. I would not kill them in order to help His Majesty make up his mind about his son-in-law. But if the Princess had made up her mind—and wanted me——

Princess. Yes ?

Woodcutter. Then I would marry her, however many suitors she had.

Princess. Well, she's only got three at present.

Woodcutter. What is that to me ?

Princess. Oh, I just thought you might want to be doing something to your axe.

Woodcutter. My axe ?

Princess. Yes. You see, she *has* made up her mind.

Woodcutter [*amazed*]. You mean—— But—but I'm only a woodcutter.

Princess. That's where you'll have the advantage of them when it comes to axes.

Woodcutter. Princess ! [*He takes her in his arms.*] My Princess !

Princess. Woodcutter ! My Woodcutter ! My, oh so very slow and uncomprehending, but entirely adorable Woodcutter !

[*They sing together. They just happen to feel like that.*]

OUR FAIRY STORY

Duet : Woodcutter and Princess

Princess. My dear, brown man,
With your strength and grace,
And your most attractive face,
Do you wonder how my love for you began ?
Well, I don't quite know,
But with those dear arms around me
I know my fate has found me.

Woodcutter. My own, fair maid,
With all heaven in your eyes,
Are we mad or truly wise
When the laws of courts and kings are disobeyed ?
Let the world go by,
With its pride and pomp and glory,
We have made our fairy story.

Both. This is just our fairy story,
Every word of which is true,
Older than the hills around us,
Yet so wonderfully new.
All the stories worth the telling
Surely must be told by two,
Each must have the self-same ending,
" You love me and I love you."

Princess. My dear, brown man !
Just because I love you blindly
You must rule me very kindly,
For I mean to be obedient—if I can !
I'm a poor spoiled child,
And my future education
Will afford you occupation,
But I recognize my master underneath the toiler's tan.

Woodcutter. My own, fair maid,
I declare your very meekness
Is the measure of my weakness,
And my mastery will seldom be displayed.
For at one shy glance
From beneath those drooping lashes
All my airy kingship crashes.

Both. (As before).

Woodcutter [*the song finished*]. But what will His Majesty say ?

Princess. All sorts of things. . . . Do you really love me, Woodcutter, or have I proposed to you under a misapprehension ?

Woodcutter. I adore you !

Princess [*nodding*]. I thought you did. But I wanted to hear you say it. If I had been a simple peasant, I suppose you would have said it a long time ago ?

(2,907)

Woodcutter. I expect so.

Princess [*nodding*]. Yes. . . . Well, now we must think of a plan for making mother like you.

Woodcutter. Might I just kiss you again before we begin ?

Princess. Well, I don't quite see how I am to stop you.

[*The Woodcutter picks her up in his arms and kisses her.*]

Woodcutter. There !

Princess [*in his arms*]. Oh, Woodcutter, Wood-cutter, why didn't you do that the first day I saw you ? Then I needn't have had the bother of pro-posing to you. [*He puts her down suddenly.*] What is it ?

Woodcutter [*listening*]. Somebody coming. [*He peers through the trees and then says in surprise,*] The King !

Princess. Oh ! I must fly !

Woodcutter. But you'll come back ?

Princess. Perhaps.

[*She disappears quickly through the trees.*]

[*The Woodcutter goes on with his work, and is dis-covered at it a minute later by the King and Queen. The music of " Tête à Tête " is played for the entrance. There enter first one red and one black attendant, walking backwards and bowing to the King and Queen. They are followed by two other attendants.*]

King [*puffing*]. Ah ! and a seat all ready for us. How satisfying.

[*They sit down, a distinguished couple—reading from left to right, " King, Queen "—on a bench outside the Woodcutter's hut.*]

Queen [*crossly—she was like that*]. I don't know why you dragged me here.

King. As I told you, my love, to be alone.

[*All attendants go off.*]

2

Queen. Well, you aren't alone.

> [*She indicates the Woodcutter.*]

King. Pooh, he doesn't matter. . . . Well now, about these three Princes. They are getting on my mind rather. It is time we decided which one of them is to marry our beloved child. The trouble is to choose between them.

Queen. As regards appetite, there is nothing to choose between them. They are three of the heartiest eaters I have met for some time.

King. You are right. The sooner we choose one of them, and send the other two about their business, the better. [*Reflectively*] There were six peaches on the breakfast-table this morning. Did I get one ? No.

Queen. Did *I* get one ? No.

King. Did our darling get one—not that it matters ? No.

Queen. It is a pity that the seven-headed bull died last year.

King [*with a sigh*]. Those days are over. We must think of a new test. Somehow I think that, in a son-in-law, moral worth is even more to be desired than mere brute strength. Now my suggestion is this : that you should disguise yourself as a beggar woman and approach each of the three Princes in turn, supplicating their charity. In this way we shall discover which of the three has the kindest heart. What do you say, my dear ?

Queen. An excellent plan. If you remember, I suggested it myself yesterday.

King [*annoyed*]. Well, of course, it had been in my mind for some time. I don't claim that the idea is original ; it has often been done in our family. [*Getting up*] Well then, if you will get ready, my dear, I will go and find our three friends and see that they come this way.

> [*They go out together. The music of " Tête à Tête "*

       is played again. As soon as they are out of
       sight the Princess comes back.]

Princess. Well, Woodcutter, what did I tell you ?

Woodcutter. What *did* you tell me ?

Princess. Didn't you listen to what they said ?

Woodcutter. I didn't listen, but I couldn't help hearing.

Princess. Well, *I* couldn't help listening.　And unless you stop it somehow, I shall be married to one of them to-night.

Woodcutter. Which one ?

Princess. The one with the kindest heart—whichever that is.

Woodcutter. Supposing they all have kind hearts ?

Princess [*confidently*]. They won't.　They never have.　In our circles when three Princes come together, one of them has a kind heart and the other two haven't.　[*Surprised*] Haven't you read any history at all ?

Woodcutter. I have no time for reading.　But I think it's time history was altered a little.　We'll alter it this afternoon.

Princess. What do you mean ?

Woodcutter. Leave this to me.　I've got an idea.

Princess [*clapping her hands*]. Oh, how clever of you ! But what do you want me to do ?

Woodcutter [*pointing*]. You know the glade over there where the brook runs through it ?　Wait for me there.

Princess. I obey my lord's commands.

       [*She blows him a kiss and runs off.*]

[*The Woodcutter resumes his work.　By-and-by the*
     Red Prince comes along.　He is a—well, you will
     see for yourself what he is like.]

Red Prince. Ah, fellow . . . Fellow ! . . . I said fellow !　[*Yes, that sort of man.*]

Woodcutter [*looking up*]. Were you speaking to me, my lord ?

Red Prince. There is no other fellow here that I can see.

[*The Woodcutter looks round to make sure, peers behind a tree or two, and comes back to the Prince.*]

Woodcutter. Yes, you must have meant me.

Red Prince. Yes, of course I meant you, fellow. Have you seen the Princess come past this way? I was told she was waiting for me here.

Woodcutter. She is not here, my lord. [*Looking round to see that they are alone*] My lord, are you one of the Princes who is seeking the hand of the Princess?

Red Prince [*complacently*]. I am, fellow.

Woodcutter. His Majesty the King was here awhile ago. He is to make his decision between you this afternoon. [*Meaningly*] I think I can help you to be the lucky one, my lord.

Red Prince. You suggest that I take an unfair advantage over my fellow-competitors?

Woodcutter. I suggest nothing, my lord. I only say that I can help you.

Red Prince [*magnanimously*]. Well, I will allow you to help me.

Woodcutter. Thank you. Then I will give you this advice. If a beggar woman asks you for a crust of bread this afternoon, remember—it is the test!

Red Prince [*staggered*]. The test! But I haven't *got* a crust of bread!

Woodcutter. Wait here and I will get you one.

[*He goes into the hut.*]

Red Prince [*speaking after him as he goes*]. My good fellow, I am extremely obliged to you, and if ever I can do anything for you, such as returning a crust to you of similar size, or even lending you another slightly smaller one, or—— [*The Woodcutter comes back with the crust*] Ah, thank you, my man, thank you.

Woodcutter. I would suggest, my lord, that you

should take a short walk in this direction [*pointing in the opposite direction to that which the Princess has taken*], and stroll back casually in a few minutes' time when the Queen is here.

Red Prince. Thank you, my man, thank you.

[*He puts the crust in his pocket and goes off.*]

[*The Woodcutter goes on with his work. The Blue Prince comes in and stands watching him in silence for some moments.*]

Woodcutter [*looking up*]. Hullo !

Blue Prince. Hullo !

Woodcutter. What do you want ?

Blue Prince. The Princess.

Woodcutter. She's not here.

Blue Prince. Oh !

[*The Woodcutter goes on with his work and the Prince goes on looking at him.*]

Woodcutter [*struck with an idea*]. Are you one of the Princes who is wooing the Princess ?

Blue Prince. Yes.

Woodcutter [*coming towards him*]. I believe I could help your Royal Highness.

Blue Prince. Do.

Woodcutter [*doubtfully*]. It would perhaps be not quite fair to the others.

Blue Prince. Don't mind.

Woodcutter. Well then, listen.

[*He pauses a moment and looks round to see that they are alone.*]

Blue Prince. I'm listening.

Woodcutter. If you come back in five minutes, you will see a beggar woman sitting here. She will ask you for a crust of bread. You must give it to her, for it is the way His Majesty has chosen of testing your kindness of heart.

Blue Prince [*feeling in his pocket*]. No bread.

Woodcutter. I will give you some.

Blue Prince. Do.

Woodcutter [*taking a piece from his pocket*]. Here you are.

Blue Prince. Thanks.

Woodcutter. Not at all, I'm very glad to have been able to help you.

[*He goes on with his work.   The Blue Prince remains looking at him.*]

Blue Prince [*with a great effort*]. Thanks.

[*He goes slowly away.   A moment later the Yellow Prince makes a graceful and languid entry.*]

Yellow Prince. Ah, come hither, my man, come hither.

Woodcutter [*stopping his work and looking up*]. You want me, sir ?

Yellow Prince. Come hither, my man.   Tell me, has Her Royal Highness the Princess passed this way lately ?

Woodcutter. The Princess ?

Yellow Prince [*slaps Woodcutter's shoulder*]. Yes, the Princess, my bumpkin.   But perhaps you have been too much concerned in your own earthly affairs to have noticed her.   You—ah—cut wood, I see.

Woodcutter. Yes, sir, I am a woodcutter.

Yellow Prince. A most absorbing life.   Some day we must have a long talk about it.   But just now I have other business waiting for me.   With your permission, good friend, I will leave you to your fagots.

[*He starts to go.*]

Woodcutter. Beg your pardon, sir, but are you one of those Princes that want to marry our Princess ?

Yellow Prince. I had hoped, good friend, to obtain your permission to do so.   I beg you not to refuse it.

Woodcutter. You are making fun of me, sir.

Yellow Prince. Discerning creature.

Woodcutter. All the same, I *can* help you.

Yellow Prince. Then pray do so, log-chopper, and earn my everlasting gratitude.

Woodcutter. The King has decided that whichever of

you three Princes has the kindest heart shall marry
his daughter.

Yellow Prince. Then you will be able to bear witness
to him that I have already wasted several minutes of
my valuable time in condescending to a mere fagot-
splitter. Tell him this and the prize is mine. [*Kiss-
ing the tips of his fingers*] Princess, I embrace you.

Woodcutter. The King will not listen to me. But if
you return here in five minutes, you will find an old
woman begging for bread. It is the test which their
Majesties have arranged for you. If you share your
last crust with her——

Yellow Prince. Yes, but do I look as if I carried a
last crust about with me ?

Woodcutter. But see, I will give you one.

Yellow Prince [*taking it between the tips of his
fingers*]. Yes, but——

Woodcutter. Put it in your pocket, and when——

Yellow Prince. But, my dear bark-scraper, have
you no feeling for clothes at all ? How can I put a
thing like this in my pocket ? [*Handing it back to
him*] I beg you to wrap it up. Here, take this [*gives
him a scarf*]. Neatly, I pray you. [*Taking an orange
ribbon out of his pocket*] Perhaps a little of this round
it would make it more tolerable. You think so ? I
leave it to you. I trust your taste entirely. . . .
Leaving a loop for the little finger, I entreat you . . .
so. [*He hangs it on his little finger.*] In about five
minutes, you said ? We will be there. [*With a bow*]
We thank you.

[*He departs delicately. The Woodcutter smiles to
himself, puts down his axe and goes off to the
Princess. And just in time. For behold ! the
King and Queen return. The same music as
before. At least we think it is the Queen, but she
is so heavily disguised by a cloak which she
wears over her Court dress, that for a moment we
are not quite sure.*]

King. Now then, my love, if you will sit down on that log there—[*placing her*]—excellent—I think perhaps you should remove the crown. [*Removes it.*] There! Now the disguise is perfect.

Queen. You're sure they are coming? It's a very uncomfortable seat. [*Takes out long nail.*]

King. I told them that the Princess was waiting for them here. Their natural disappointment at finding I was mistaken will make the test of their good-nature an even more exacting one. My own impression is that the Yellow Prince will be the victor.

Queen. Oh, I hate that man.

King [*soothingly*]. Well, well, perhaps it will be the Blue one.

Queen. If anything, I dislike him *more* intensely.

King. Or even the Red.

Queen. Ugh! I can't bear him.

King. Fortunately, dear, you are not called upon to marry any of them. It is for our darling that we are making the great decision. Listen! I hear one coming. I will hide in the cottage and take note of what happens.

[*He disappears into the cottage as the Blue Prince comes in.*]

Queen. Oh, sir, can you kindly spare a crust of bread for a poor old woman! Please, pretty gentleman!

Blue Prince [*standing stolidly in front of her and feeling in his pocket*]. Bread . . . Bread . . . Ah! Bread! [*He offers it.*]

Queen. Oh, thank you, sir. May you be rewarded for your gentle heart.

Blue Prince. Thank you.

[*He stands gazing at her. There is an awkward pause.*]

Queen. A blessing on you, sir.

Blue Prince. Thank you. [*He indicates the crust.*] Bread.

Queen. Ah, you have saved the life of a poor old woman——

Blue Prince. Eat it.

Queen [*embarrassed*]. I—er—you—er——

[*She takes a bite and mumbles something.*]

Blue Prince. What ?

Queen [*swallowing with great difficulty*]. I'm almost too happy to eat, sir. Leave a poor old woman alone with her happiness, and——

Blue Prince. Not too happy. Too weak. Help you eat. [*He breaks off a piece and holds it to her mouth. With a great effort the Queen disposes of it.*] Good ! . . . Again ! [*She does it again.*] Now ! [*She swallows another piece.*] Last piece ! [*She takes it in. He pats her kindly on the back, and she nearly chokes.*] Good. . . . Better now ?

Queen [*weakly*]. Much.

Blue Prince. Good-day.

Queen [*with an effort*]. Good-day, kind gentleman.

[*He goes out.*]

[*The King is just coming from the cottage, when he returns suddenly. The King slips back again.*]

Blue Prince. Small piece left over. [*He gives it to her. She looks hopelessly at him.*] Good-bye.

[*He goes.*]

Queen [*throwing the piece down violently*]. Ugh ! What a man !

King [*coming out*]. Well, well, my dear, we have discovered the winner.

Queen [*from the heart*]. Detestable person !

King. The rest of the competition is of course more in the nature of a formality——

Queen. Thank goodness.

King. However, I think that it will prevent unnecessary discussion afterwards if we—— Take care, here is another one. [*He hurries back.*]

[*Enter the Red Prince.*]

Queen [*with not nearly so much conviction*]. Could

you spare a crust of bread, sir, for a poor hungry old woman ?

Red Prince. A crust of bread, madam ? Certainly. As luck will have it, I have a crust on me. My last one, but—your need is greater than mine. Eat, I pray.

Queen. Th-thank you, sir.

Red Prince. Not at all. Come, eat. Let me have the pleasure of seeing you eating.

Queen. M-might I take it home with me, pretty gentleman ?

Red Prince [*firmly*]. No, no. I must see you eating. Come ! I will take no denial.

Queen. Th-thank you, sir. [*Hopefully*] Won't you share it with me ?

Red Prince. No, I insist on your having it all. I am in the mood to be generous. Oblige me by eating it now, for I am in a hurry ; yet I will not go until you have eaten. [*She does her best.*] You eat but slowly. [*Sternly.*] Did you deceive me when you said you were hungry ?

Queen. N-no. I'm very hungry.   [*She eats.*]

Red Prince. That's better. Now understand—however poor I am, I can always find a crust of bread for an old woman. Always ! Remember this when next you are hungry. . . . You spoke ? [*She shakes her head and goes on eating.*] Finished ?

Queen [*with great difficulty*]. Yes, thank you, pretty gentleman.

Red Prince. There's a piece on the ground there that you dropped. [*She eats it in dumb agony.*] Finished ?

Queen [*huskily*]. Yes, thank you, pretty gentleman.

Red Prince. Then I will leave you, madam. Good-morning.   [*He goes out.*]

[*The Queen rises in fury. The King is about to come out of the cottage, when the Yellow Prince enters. The Queen sits down again and mumbles some-*

> *thing. It is certainly not an appeal for bread,*
> *but the Yellow Prince is not to be denied.*]

Yellow Prince [*gallantly*]. My poor woman, you are in distress. It pains me to see it, madam, it pains me terribly. Can it be that you are hungry? I thought so, I thought so. Give me the great pleasure, madam, of relieving your hunger. See [*holding up his finger*], my own poor meal. Take it! It is yours.

Queen [*with difficulty*]. I am not hungry.

Yellow Prince. Ah, madam, I see what it is. You do not wish to deprive me. You tell yourself, perchance, that it is not fitting that one in your station of life should partake of the meals of the highly born. You are not used, you say, to the food of Princes. Your rougher palate——

Queen [*hopefully*]. Did you say the food of Princes?

Yellow Prince. Where was I, madam. You interrupted me. No matter—eat. [*She takes the scarf and unties the ribbon.*] Ah, now I remember. I was saying that your rougher palate——

Queen [*discovering the worst*]. No! no! not bread!

Yellow Prince. Bread, madam, the staff of life. Come, madam, will you not eat? [*She tries desperately.*] What can be more delightful than a crust of bread by the wayside?

[*The Queen shrieks and falls back in a swoon. The King rushes out to her.*]

King [*to Yellow Prince*]. Quick, quick, find the Princess.

Yellow Prince. The Princess—find the Princess!

[*He goes vaguely off and we shall not see him again. But the Woodcutter and the Princess do not need to be found. They are here.*]

Woodcutter [*to Princess*]. Go to her, but don't show that you know me.

[*He goes into the cottage, and the Princess hastens to her father.*]

Princess. Father!

King. Ah, my dear, you're just in time. Your mother——

Princess. My mother?

King. Yes, yes. A little plan of mine—of hers—your poor mother. Dear, dear!

Princess. But what's the matter?

King. She is suffering from a surfeit of bread, and——

[*The Woodcutter comes up with a flagon of wine.*]

Woodcutter. Poor old woman! She has fainted from exhaustion. Let me give her some——

Queen [*shrieking*]. No, no, not bread! I will *not* have any more bread.

Woodcutter. Drink this, my poor woman.

Queen [*opening her eyes*]. Did you say drink?

[*She seizes the flagon and drinks.*]

Princess. Oh, sir, you have saved my mother's life!

Woodcutter. Not at all.

King. I thank you, my man, I thank you.

Queen [*goes to Woodcutter and flings her arms round him*]. My deliverer! Tell me who you are!

Princess. It is my mother, the Queen, who asks you.

Woodcutter [*amazed, as well he may be*]. The Queen!

[*Kneels and covers his face.*]

King. Yes, yes. Certainly, the Queen.

Woodcutter [*taking off his hat*]. Pardon, your Majesty. I am a woodcutter, who lives alone here, far away from courts.

Queen. Well, you've got more sense in your head than any of the Princes that *I've* seen lately. You'd better come to court.

Princess [*shyly*]. You will be very welcome, sir.

Queen. And you'd better marry the Princess.

King. Isn't that perhaps going a *little* too far, dear?

Queen. Well, you wanted kindness of heart in your son-in-law, and you've got it. And he's got common sense too. [*To Woodcutter*] Tell me, what do you think of bread as—as a form of nourishment?

Woodcutter [*cautiously*]. One can have too much of it.

Queen. Exactly my view. [*To King*] There you are, you see.

King. Well, if you insist. The great thing, of course, is that our darling child should be happy.

Princess. I will do my best, father.

[*She takes the Woodcutter's hand.*]

King. Then the marriage will take place this evening. [*With a wave of his wand*] Let the revels begin.

[*They begin. Children dance, the refrain of the " Fairy Story" being used. The King and Queen go off, and the Curtain falls.*]

ROBIN HOOD

By Alfred Noyes

CHARACTERS

SCENE I

FIRST RUSTIC.
SECOND RUSTIC.
ROBIN HOOD.
THIRD RUSTIC.
THE SHERIFF.
WILL SCARLET.
THE KNIGHT.
Rustics and Outlaws.
The Sheriff's Guards.

SCENE II

JENNY, *Marian's maid*.
MAID MARIAN.
WIDOW SCARLET, *Will's mother*.
PRINCE JOHN.
WARMAN, *his man*.
ROBIN HOOD.
THE KNIGHT.
FRIAR TUCK.
WILL SCARLET.
SHADOW-OF-A-LEAF, *a Fool*.
Two servants of Prince John's.
Outlaws.

Sherwood in the twilight, is Robin Hood awake?
Grey and ghostly shadows are gliding through the brake,
Shadows of the dappled deer, dreaming of the morn,
Dreaming of a shadowy man that winds a shadowy horn.

Robin Hood is here again : all his merry thieves
Hear a ghostly bugle-note shivering through the leaves,
Calling as he used to call, faint and far away,
In Sherwood, in Sherwood, about the break of day.

Merry, merry England has kissed the lips of June :
All the wings of fairyland were here beneath the moon,
Like a flight of rose-leaves fluttering in a mist
Of opal and ruby and pearl and amethyst.

Merry, merry England is waking as of old
With eyes of blither hazel and hair of brighter gold :
For Robin Hood is here again beneath the bursting spray
In Sherwood, in Sherwood, about the break of day.

From " Sherwood."

Quoted from *Collected Poems of Alfred Noyes*, by kind permission of the author and of the publishers, Messrs. Blackwood and Sons.

ROBIN HOOD

SCENE I

May-day. An open place (near Nottingham). A crowd of rustics and townsfolk assembling to see the execution of Will Scarlet.

First Rustic. A sad May-day! Where yonder
    gallows glowers,
We should have raised the May-pole.
Second Rustic.   Ay, no songs,
No dancing on the green.
    [*Enter Robin Hood, disguised as an old beggar, with
    a green patch on one eye.*]
Robin.   Is this the place,
Masters, where they're agoin' to hang Will Scarlet?
First Rustic. Ay, father, more's the pity.
Robin.   Eh, don't ye think
There may be scuffling, masters?
First Rustic. There's many here would swing a
    cudgel and help
To trip the Sheriff up. If Robin Hood
Were only here!
Third Rustic.   They say Prince John is out
This very day, scouring thro' Sherwood Forest,
In quest of Lady Marian!
Robin [*sharply*].   You heard that?
Third Rustic. Ay, for they say she's flown to
    Sherwood Forest.

35

Second Rustic. She'd best beware then ; for I saw
    Prince John !
With these same eyes I saw him riding out
To Sherwood, not an hour ago.
    Robin.   You saw him ?
    Second Rustic. Ay, and he only took three men-at-
    arms.
    First Rustic. Three men-at-arms ! Why, then, he
    must ha' known
That Robin's men would all be busy here !
I think there'll be some scuffling after all.
    Robin. Ay, tell 'em so—go, spread it thro' the
    crowd !   [*He mutters to himself.*]
He'd take some time to find her, but 'fore God
We must be quick ; 'fore God we must be quick !
    Second Rustic. Why, father, one would never think
    to see thee
Thou hadst so sound a heart.
    First Rustic.   Ah, here they come !
The Sheriff and his men ; and, in the midst,
There's poor Will Scarlet bound.
    The Crowd.   Ah, here they come !
    First Rustic. There, there he is. His face is white ;
    but, Lord,
He takes it bravely.
    Second Rustic.   He's a brave man is Will.
    Sheriff. Back with the crowd there, guards ; delay
    no time !
    Some Women in the Crowd. Ah, ah, poor lad !
    Robin [*eagerly*].   What are they doing now ?
I cannot see !
    First Rustic. The Sheriff's angered now !
    Second Rustic. Ay, for they say the hangman has
    not come.
    Third Rustic. The Sheriff says he will not be delayed.
But who will do the hanging then ?
    Robin. I have a thought ; make way ; let me
    bespeak

The Sheriff !

Rustics. How now, father, what's to do ?

Robin. Make way, I tell you. I'm the man they want !

Sheriff. What's this ?

Robin. Good master Sheriff, I've a grudge
Against Will Scarlet. Let me have the task
Of sending him to heaven !

Crowd. Ah-h-h, the old devil !

Sheriff. Come on, then, and be brief !

Robin. I'm not a hangman ;
But I can cleave your thinnest hazel wand
At sixty yards.

Sheriff. Shoot, then, and make an end.
Make way there, clear the way !

[*An opening is made in the crowd. Robin stands in
the gap.*]

Crowd. Ah-h-h, the old devil !

Robin. I'll shoot him one on either side, just graze
him,
To show you how I love him ; then the third
Slick in his heart.

[*He shoots. A murmur goes up from the crowd.*]

Sheriff [*angrily*]. Take care ! You've cut the cord
That bound him on that side !

Robin. Then here's the second.
I will be careful. [*He takes a steady aim.*]

A Rustic to his Neighbours. I'faith, lads, he can
shoot.

[*Robin shoots. A louder murmur goes up from the
crowd.*]

Sheriff. You have cut the rope again !

A Cry. He has cut him free !

Robin. All right ! All right ! It's only to tease
the dog.
Here's for the third now.

[*He aims and shoots quickly. There is a loud cry of a
wounded man ; then a shout from the crowd.*]

First Rustic.   What has he done ?

Second Rustic.   He has killed
One of the Sheriff's men !

Sheriff.   There's treachery here !
I'll cleave the first man's heart that moves !

Robin.   Will Scarlet,
Pick up that dead man's dagger !

Sheriff.   Treachery ! Help !
Down with the villain !

Robin [*throws off his beggar's crouch and hurls the Sheriff and several of his men back amongst the crowd. His cloak drops off.*] Sherwood !   A merry Sherwood !

Rustics. Ah, ha !   The Lincoln green !   A Robin Hood !

[*A bugle rings out and immediately some of the yokels throw off their disguise, and the Lincoln green appears as by magic amongst the crowd.   The guards are rushed and hustled by them.   Robin and several of his men make a ring round Will Scarlet.*]

Sheriff. It is the outlawed Earl of Huntingdon :
There is a great reward upon his head.
Down with him !

[*The Sheriff's men make a rush at the little band.   A knight in jet-black armour, with a red-cross shield, suddenly appears and forces his way through the mob, sword in hand.*]

Knight.   What, so many against so few !
Back, you damned wolves.   Now, foresters, follow me,
Up, cudgels, for our Saint George, and drive them all
Home to the devil !

[*The foresters make a rush with him, and the Sheriff and his men take to flight.*]

Robin.   Now back to Sherwood, swiftly !

[*He sees the Knight in armour standing by his horse.*]
Your pardon, sir ; our debt to you is great,
Too great almost for thanks ; but if you be

Bound by the vows of chivalry, I pray you
Lend me your charger; and my men will bring you
To my poor home in Sherwood. There you'll find
A most abundant gratitude.
    Knight.   Your name?
    Robin. Was Huntingdon; but now is Robin Hood.
    Knight. If I refuse?
    Robin.   Then, sir, I must perforce
Take him. I am an outlaw, but the law
Of manhood still constrains me. It is a matter
Of life or death.
    Knight.   Take him and God be with you.
I'll follow you to Sherwood with your men.
    [*Robin seizes the horse, leaps to the saddle, and gallops
         away.*]

SCENE II

    *Sherwood Forest.   Outside the cave, Jenny, Marian,
and Widow Scarlet.*

    Marian. This dreadful waiting! Oh, I am selfish,
         mother;
You need not be afraid. Robin will bring
Will Scarlet safely back. Jenny, how long
D'you think they've been away. The sun is high,
And all the dew is gone.
    Jenny. Now don't you keep a-fretting. They'll be
         back,
Quite soon enough.   [*To Widow Scarlet.*]
                Come, widow, come with me.
I'll give you my own corner in the hut
And make you cosy. If you take a nap,
Will Scarlet will be here betimes you wake.
            [*Takes her to the hut and shuts her in.*]
There, drat her, for a mumping mumble-crust!
What's that?   [*She pauses and stares at the bracken.*]

Marian. Why, Jenny, how you startled me !

Jenny. I thought I saw a face there in the ferns
Yonder—there—see, they are shaking still.

[*She screams.*]

Ah ! Ah !

[*Prince John and another man appear advancing
across the glade.*]

John. So here's my dainty tigress in her den.

[*At a sign from Marian, Jenny goes quickly inside the
cave.*]

That's well ! Dismiss your maid !

Warman, remove a little. [*His man retires.*]

I see you think
A little better of me. Out in the wood
There waits a palfrey for you, and the stirrup
Longs, as I long, to clasp your dainty foot.

[*He draws nearer.*]

Marian. Wait—I must think, must think.

John. Give me your hand !
Why do you shrink from me ? If you could know
The fire that burns me night and day.

Marian. You are mad !

John. Ay, mad for you.

[*Jenny comes out of the cave and hands Marian a bow.
She leaps back and aims it at John.*]

Marian. Back, you wild beast, or by the heaven
above us,
I'll kill you ! Now, don't doubt me. I can shoot
Truly as any forester. I swear,
Prince or no prince, king or no king, I'll kill you
If you should stir one step from where you stand.

John. I was beside myself, was carried away.
I cannot help my love for——

Marian. I'll not hear
Another sickening word : throw down your arms,
That dagger at your side.

John. Marian, I swear—

Marian. You see that rusty stain

Upon the silver birch down yonder ? Watch.

[*She shoots. Then swiftly aims at him again.*]

Now, throw your weapon down.

[*He pulls out the dagger and throws it down, with a
shrug of his shoulders. One of his men steals up
behind Marian.*]

Jenny. There's one behind you ! Look !

[*The man springs forward and seizes Marian's arms.*]

John [*coming forward and taking hold of her also*]. So,
my sweet tigress,

You're trapped then, are you ? Well, we'll waste no
time !

We'll talk this over when we reach the castle.

Keep off the maid, there, Warman ; I can manage

This turbulent beauty. Ah, by God, you shall

Come ! Ah ! God's blood, what's this ?

[*Marian has succeeded in drawing her dagger and
slightly wounding him. She wrests herself free.*]

Marian.　　　　　　　　Keep back, I warn you !

John [*advancing slowly*]. Strike, now strike if you
will. You will not like

To see the red blood spurting up your hand.

That's not maid's work. Come, strike !

[*Robin Hood appears at the edge of the glade behind
him.*]

　　　　　　　　　　　You see, you cannot !

Your heart is tenderer than you think.

Robin [*quietly*].　　　　　　　Prince John !

John [*turns round and confronts Robin*]. Out with
your blade, Warman.

[*Robin draws his sword and sets his back to an oak.
The other two followers of Prince John come out
of the wood.*]

Robin.　　　　　　　　Come on, all four !

You must be tired of fighting women-folk.

Come on ! By God, sir, you must guard your head

Better than that,　　　　　[*He disarms Warman.*]

　　　　　　　Or you're just food for worms

Already ; come, you dogs !

John.   Work round, you three,
Behind him !   Drive him out from that damned
    oak !

    Robin. Oh, that's a princely speech !   Have at you,
      sir !

    [*He strikes Prince John's sword out of his hand,
      and turns suddenly to confront the others.   John
      picks up a dagger and makes as if to stab Robin
      in the back.   At the same instant bugles are heard
      in the distance.   The red-cross knight flashes
      between the trees, and seizing John's arm in his
      gauntleted hand, disarms him, then turns to help
      Robin.*

    Knight. What, four on one !   Down with your
      blades, you curs,
Or, by Mahound !—

    [*The three men take to flight.   John stands staring at
      the new-comer.   The foresters appear, surround-
      ing the glade.*]

    John [*muttering*]. What ?   Thou ?   Thou ?   Or his
      ghost ?
No—no—it cannot be.

    Robin.   Let them yelp home.
All's well ; but take this villain into the cave
And guard him there.

        [*The foresters lead Prince John into the cave.*]

    John [*to the foresters*]. Answer me one thing ; who
Is yonder red-cross knight ?

    A Forester.   No friend of thine,
Whoever he be !

    Knight [*to Robin*]. I need not ask *his* name.
I grieve to know it !

    Robin.   Sir, I am much beholden
To your good chivalry.   What thanks is mine
To give is all your own.

    Knight.   Then I ask this !
Give me that prisoner !   I think his life is mine !

Robin. You saved my own, and more, you saved
    much more
Than my poor life is worth. But, sir, think well
This man is dangerous, not to me alone,
But to the King of England.
    Knight. I have more reasons than you know.
    Robin.   So be it.
Bring back the prisoner !
    [*The foresters bring Prince John back. He stares at
    the knight as if in fear.*]
                Sir, you shall judge him.
This prisoner is your own.
    Knight.   Then—let him go !
    Foresters. What ! Set him free ?
    Robin.   Obey !
           [*They release Prince John.*]
    Knight.   Out of my sight ;
Go !
    Prince John. What man is this ?
    Knight.   Quickly, get thee gone !
    [*Prince John goes out, shaken and white.*]
    Robin. We'll think no more of him ! It is our rule
That every friend we meet in merry greenwood
Should dine with us. Will you not be our guest ?
    Knight. That's a most happy thought ! I have not
    heard
A merrier word than dinner all this day.
    Robin.   Will you not raise your visor,
And let us know to whose good knightly hand
We are so beholden ?
    Knight.   Sir, you will pardon me
If, for a little, I remain unknown.
But, tell me, are you not that Robin Hood
Who breaks the forest's laws ?
    Robin.   That is my name.
We hold this earth as naturally our own
As the glad common air we breathe. We think
No man, no king, can so usurp the world

As not to give us room to live free lives,
But, if you shrink from eating the King's deer——
   Knight. Shrink ? Ha ! ha ! ha ! I count it as my
      own !
   [*The foresters appear, preparing the dinner on a table
      of green turfs beneath a spreading oak. Marian
      and Jenny appear at the door of the hut. Jenny
      goes across to help at the preparations for dinner.*]
   Robin. Ah, there's my Lady Marian ! Will you not
      come
And speak with her ?
   [*He and the Knight go and talk to Marian in the back-
      ground.*]
   Little John [*at the table*]. The trenchers all are set ;
Manchets of wheat, cream, curds, and honey-cakes,
Venison pasties, roasted pigeons ! Much,
Run to the cave ; we'll broach our rarest wine
To-day.
   [*Enter Friar Tuck with several more foresters and Will
      Scarlet.*]
   Robin. Will Scarlet ! And all in time for dinner !
Go into the hut. Thy mother is waiting there.
Put thy big arm around her.
        [*Will Scarlet goes into the hut with a cry.*]
   Scarlet.   Mother !
   Friar Tuck.   You see,
My sons, you couldn't expect the lad to run !
There is a certain looseness in the limbs,
A quaking of the flesh that overcomes
The bravest who has felt a hangman's rope
Cuddling his neck.
   Robin.   You judge him by the rope
That cuddles your slim waist ! Oh, you sweet armful,
Sit down and pant ! I warrant you were glad
To bear him company.
   Friar Tuck.   I'll not deny it !
I am a man of solids. Like the Church,
I am founded on a rock.   [*He sits down.*]

Robin. Solids, i' faith !
Sir, it is true he is partly based on beef ;
He grapples with it squarely ; but fluids, too,
Have played their part in that cathedral choir
He calls his throat. One godless virtue, sir,
They seem to have given him. Never a nightingale
Gurgles jug ! jug ! in mellower tones than he
When jugs are flowing. Never a thrush can pipe
Sweet, sweet, so rarely as, when a pipe of wine
Summers his throttle, we'll make him sing to us
One of his heathen ditties—*The Malmsey Butt*,
Or *Down the Merry Red Lane !*

Jenny [*approaching*]. Please you, sirs, all is ready !

Friar Tuck. Ah, Jenny, Jenny, Jenny, that's good
news !

[*Will Scarlet comes out of the hut with his arm round his
mother. They all sit down at the table of turfs.*]
[*Enter Shadow-of-a-Leaf timidly.*]

Shadow-of-a-Leaf. Is there a place for me ?

A Forester. Ay, come along !

Friar Tuck. Now, Robin, don't forget the grace, my
son.

Robin [*standing up*]. It is our custom, sir, since our
repast
Is borrowed from the King, to drain one cup
To him, and his return from the Crusade,
Before we dine. That same wine-bibbing friar
Calls it our " grace " ; and constitutes himself
Remembrancer—without a cause, for never
Have we forgotten, never while bugles ring
Thro' Sherwood, shall forget—Outlaws, the King !

[*All stand up except the Knight.*]

Cries. The King and his return from the Crusade !

[*They drink and resume their seats.*]

Robin. You did not drink the health, sir Knight.
I hope
You hold with Lion-heart.

Knight. Yes ; I hold with him.

You were too quick for me.   I had not drawn
These gauntlets off.

                        But tell me, Lady Marian,
When is your bridal day with Robin Hood ?

    Marian. We shall be wedded when the King comes
        home
From the Crusade.

    Knight.   Ah, when the King comes home !
That's music—all the birds of April sing
In those four words for me—the King comes home.

    Marian. I am glad you love him, sir.

    Robin.   But you're not eating !
Your helmet's locked and barred.   Will you not raise
Your visor ?

    Knight. Or lose my dinner !   Hunger and thirst
Break down all masks and all disguises, Robin.

    [*He rises and removes his helmet, revealing the face of
        Richard Cœur de Lion.*]

    Robin. The King !   [*They all leap to their feet.*]

    Outlaws.   The King !   The King !

    Robin.   But oh, my liege,
I should have known, at the rescue of Will Scarlet,
When we were so outnumbered and hard beset,
And you came riding out of the Eastern sky,
I should have known, either it was Saint George
Or else the King come home from the Crusade.

    Richard. A lover's instinct might have told you,
        Robin,
If, as I understand, it means so much
To you and Lady Marian.   Huntingdon,
Your earldom we restore to you this day.
You and my Lady Marian shall return
To court with us, where your true bridal troth
Shall be fulfilled with golden marriage bells.
Now, friends, the venison pasty.   We must hear
The Malmsey Butt and *Down the Merry Red Lane.*

    Shadow-of-a-Leaf. Don't leave the forest.   There's
        darker things to come.

Robin. Pardon him, sire.   Poor Shadow-of-a-Leaf
      has lost
His mortal wits.
    Shadow-of-a-Leaf. Sire, you will pardon me,
For I am only a fool, and yet, methinks,
You know not half the meaning of those words—
The King, the King comes home from the Crusade !
Thrust up your swords, hilt uppermost, my lads,
And shout—the King comes home from the Crusade.
    [*He leaps on a seat, and thrusts up the King's sword,
      hilt uppermost, as if it were a cross.*]

CURTAIN

THE SLIPPERS OF CINDERELLA

By W. Graham Robertson

CHARACTERS

MYRA TREMAINE.
POLLY TREMAINE, } *Twins.*
DOLLY TREMAINE, }
JIMMY TREMAINE.
BELINDA TREMAINE.
AGATHA-NEXT-DOOR.
JANE.
ELIZA.
THE FAIRY GODMOTHER.

THE SLIPPERS OF CINDERELLA

SCENE.—*A very shabby parlour. At back is a curtained window on one side of which stands a bookcase, on the other a grandfather clock stopped at twenty minutes past eleven. A fireplace R. with mirror over mantelpiece. Doors R. and L. Myra, a tall girl of fourteen, sits at a table mending Jimmy's coat while he stands in his shirt-sleeves watching the operation. Belinda sits on a stool by the fire absorbed in a book. The curtains are drawn and the room lit. It is about five o'clock on the 31st of October.*

Myra. There. That's the best I can do with it. Really, Jimmy, any one would think that you walked on your elbows.

Jimmy [*putting on coat*]. Thanks awfully. Does it look very patchy?

Myra. Not so bad. You must try and keep full face when there's company, and sit with your back to the wall.

Jimmy. I don't do much sitting in these knickers; they're at their last gasp.

Myra. I suppose we're a very discontented family. When we had all the nice things we didn't particularly notice them; now we haven't got them we miss them dreadfully.

Jimmy. It's not so much having no nice things as having nasty ones that I object to.

Belinda [*holding out her frock*]. I know. I never cared for this when it was Myra's, and when it was

51

cut up for Dolly I hated it. Now it's mine I simply
loathe it.

Jimmy. At any rate you don't run the risk of going
off with a bang whenever you sit down.

[*Walks drearily to the window, draws aside curtain
and stares into the darkness.*]

What time will the Old Dears be back, Myra ?

Myra. I don't quite know ; mother said she would
telegraph. O Jimmy, I do hope to goodness that
father gets this appointment.

Jimmy. Estate agent to Lord What's-his-name,
isn't it ?

Myra. Yes. What exactly are the duties of an
estate agent, Jimmy ?

Jimmy. Oh—you wear riding breeches, you know,
and—well, you tell the other fellows to do the rest.

Belinda. I'm sure father could do that beautifully.

Myra. And it would show off his nice legs. I've
always recommended the ballet or a bishopric.

Jimmy. I suppose it wouldn't exactly restore the
fallen fortunes of our house ?

Myra. Not quite, of course, but we should be in the
country again, and poor Jane would be able to remember whether she's nurse or parlourmaid or cook.
[*Enter* R. *Polly and Dolly in hats and coats. They carry
satchels, which they throw down.*] Hullo, Tweenies—
late, aren't you ?

Polly. Not particularly. It's so dark ; there's a
fog coming on, I think.

Dolly. A good, thick, yellow one. Ugh. [*Shivers.*]
[*The twins take off hats and coats and throw them down.*]
And lots of the girls have got parties. It's Hallow-
e'en, you know.

Belinda. O Dolly—Hallowe'en, when all the fairies
are abroad ?

Polly. Little silly, with your fairies.

Dolly. What are you stodging over ? [*Looking over
Belinda's shoulder*] Cinderella, of course.

Myra. Fairies won't come our way, I'm afraid. Now, children, you must clear away all that litter [*pointing to coats*] and then try to get yourselves decently clean.

Twins [*open-mouthed*]. Clean ? Whatever for ?

Myra. Have you forgotten high tea and Aunt Maria ?

Jimmy. I say, Myra—it isn't *this* evening ?

Polly. And the Old Dears away, and just us—we, I mean ?

Myra. It is—worse luck. She's going to take me to a lecture.

Jimmy. Oughtn't we to have run to dinner for aunt ? She's one of the idle rich, you know.

Myra. The lecture's early : besides, I thought high tea rather a good touch ; hospitable, yet without the opulence of dinner.

Jimmy. Filling, but not fashionable, eh ?

Polly. What's the lecture about ?

Myra. Economy.

Dolly. What is economy ?

Myra. I believe it teaches you how to spend very little money.

Jimmy. We don't find much difficulty in doing *that*. Now, if it taught you how to spend a great deal of money when you haven't got any, then there'd be sense in it.

Myra. I'm not sure, but I can't help fancying that father looks to Aunt Maria to do that.

Twins. Aunt Maria ?

Myra. She's tremendously rich, you know. Simply frightfully. And you see, if she took a fancy to one of us——

Jimmy. Or even two—we could offer the pair of twins at a reduction.

Dolly. Oh, do chuck it, Jimmy. I don't know why there should be anything absurd about being a twin— but there *is*.

Polly. Yes. You needn't rub it in.

Jimmy. Well, unless I'm much mistaken she'll go in for quality, not quantity. A stalwart nephew to support her tottering steps will about fill her bill, I should say.

Myra. Or a sensible, elderly niece who would be a companion to her.

Belinda. Or a dear little girl to brighten her declining—oh, don't, Jimmy.

[*Jimmy shies a cushion at her.*]

Polly. But why Aunt Maria *now*? She has hardly ever come near us.

Jimmy. She doesn't like us; and she's only a half aunt really, you know.

Belinda. O Jimmy, how dreadful. Which half?

Jimmy. Shut up.

Myra. She saw Jimmy and me when we were little and loathed us; now, I suppose, she's coming back with a fresh eye to see if she likes us any better.

Jimmy [*gloomily*]. She won't.

Myra. No, I don't suppose she will. Of course, from the pathetic point of view, we should have made a better show as orphans.

Dolly. We can't very well work that.

Myra. Hardly, with a brace of parents in robust health on the premises. If we only knew her tastes we could play up better.

Polly. If we each take a different line she may find one of us sympathetic.

Myra. Good idea, Polly. Now—who shall be what? How about the Tweenies?

Jimmy. One can be pretty and the other good.

Polly. Bags I being pretty.

Dolly. No, Polly, you're ever so much better than I am. *I'll* be pretty.

Jimmy. Toss up—your call, Polly.

Polly. Heads.

Jimmy [*tossing a penny*]. Tails. Dolly's pretty,

you're good. Then there must be a clever one who swots over lessons—auntie may like that sort—and we ought to have an angel child.

Myra. I'm the clever one, I suppose : that leaves Belinda for the angel child.

Jimmy. Belinda, forward please.

Belinda [*advancing bashfully*]. O Jimmy——

Jimmy [*sternly*]. No back answers. You'll be sitting at the window, your wistful gaze fixed upon the distant hills.

Belinda. You can't see anything but chimney pots from this window—and it's pitch dark.

Jimmy. S-sh. And when she comes in you'll look up with a sad smile.

Myra. Let's try it once over and see how it works out. [*Group formed. Belinda at window, Myra sitting at table, and the twins gracefully posed at her feet.*] I ought to be reading aloud something improving.

Jimmy [*at bookcase*]. Try *Flowering Plants of Great Britain ;* some of the words in that are a fair treat. Catch. [*Myra fields a heavy volume with difficulty*] Now—picture ; the Poor but Virtuous Family. H'm-m. Not bad. Why are you making those silly faces, Dolly ?

Dolly. I'm looking pretty ; you told me to.

Jimmy. Better cut out the prettiness—it would put any aunt off. That's better. Don't grin, Belinda.

Belinda. You told me to. That's the sad smile.

Jimmy. Cut out the sad smile. What utter poops you girls are. You've no more notion of—I say, here *is* somebody ! Now then, Myra—and don't look up, any one, when the door opens. Let it all soak in.

Myra [*reading*]. ' In plants of the Umbelliferous Tribe the floral leaves, grown in a whorl and forming what is termed an Involucre, often grow at the base of the general and partial umbels——"

[*Jane appears at door.*]

Jane. If you please, Miss Myra, could I speak to you for a minute ?

Myra. Jane ! *Not* the kitchen flue ?

Jane. No, miss.

Myra. Then I can bear it. What's the matter ?

Jane. Nothing, miss, leastways no more than usual ; but was you wishful that I should be dressed for the door seeing I'm to dish up the minute your aunt comes and everything so to speak trembling in the balance ?

Myra. O Jane, I'm afraid so. Mother made such a point of it.

Jane. Then 'Eaven 'elp the lemon soles, miss, that's all I can say. No, Miss Myra, I can open a door with any one in the land, and I can cook you a sole as wouldn't have disgraced your Pa's table in the Dogwood Park days, but I can't do 'em both at once and keep my reason, and so I tell you.

Myra [*rising, and taking Jane's hand*]. Jane, dear, we must forget the Dogwood Park days. We've all come down in the world now, and you were a dear old silly to come with us.

Jane [*tearfully*]. And do I ever complain, Miss Myra ? Do I mind being engaged as a General and doing the work of a Commander-in-Chief ? Do I mind sleeping in what you may well call the pantry, for pant you do with a window the size of a sixpence, and arm-in-arm with the boiler—but dress for the door and leave them blessed soles, lemon though they be, and never would Mrs. Silverside have allowed such things to breathe the air of Dogwood Park while *she* was housekeeper. Well, Miss Myra, we lives and we learns, and I *may* learn to be in two places at once and do a dozen things at the same time—I may or I may *not*, but—— [*Myra looks anxiously at Jane and sniffs suspiciously. Jane sniffs.*] Something burning ? There ! If I turn my back half a minute— though I suppose we should reckon it as one of the blessings of living in a rabbit hutch ; what's done in the kitchen you smell in the attic.

[She dashes from the room.]

Myra [*laughing*]. Poor, dear Jane. I always smell burning when she gets a little long-winded ; it sends her off like a shot. But now, seriously, children, this is *my* evening, and the important question is—what *am* I to wear ? Mother particularly said that it was to be " quiet and appropriate." What would be appropriate for an Economy Lecture ?

Jimmy. Your oldest frock, or none at all, I should say.

Myra. But you couldn't call that quiet. As a fact, I haven't got anything. Agatha-next-Door offered me the loan of a purple velvet trimmed with swansdown, but I thought *not*.

Dolly. What on earth made you tell *her* about it ?

Jimmy. If there is one thing beastlier than the general beastliness of everything it's the continued patronage of Agatha-next-Door.

Polly. And her habit of " dropping in to play with us," as she puts it.

Dolly. At all hours.

Myra. She's really quite a good sort, and it's nice of her to offer her frocks. The mere fact that one wouldn't be found dead in them ought not to weigh with us. But I *do* wish that I had something decent.

Dolly. What we want is a little woman to come in.

Belinda [*suddenly*]. What we want is a fairy godmother.

All [*in scorn*]. A fairy godmother !

Belinda. Yes, and the Old Dears ought to have seen about it long ago.

Myra. Belinda, you are not to call father and mother the Old Dears. I've told you over and over again.

Belinda. But you and Jimmy—oh !

Jimmy [*shying another cushion*]. Shut it, Belinda.

Myra. All the same there's something in the idea. The fairy godmother would merely wave her wand and there should I be, " quiet and appropriate."

Polly. And a lovely motor to take you to the lecture.

Myra. And a splendid person to open the door in a gold-laced coat and canary-coloured knee-breeches.

Dolly. My dear Myra, Jane would die first.

Myra [*laughing*]. So she would : I forgot Jane. Well, then, a beautiful Greek maiden in flowing raiment and wreathed with roses.

Jimmy. And the high tea. Peacock pasties, haunches of venison, grapes, pineapples—my eye !

Myra. Ah, Jimmy, I'm afraid that fairy days are over. It is not for us poor moderns to stand in the slippers of Cinderella.   [*A knock at the door.*]

Polly [*in horror*]. Not aunt ? Not yet ?

A Voice [*without*]. May I come in ?

Jimmy. Worse. Agatha. [*Shouting.*] Oh, come in.

[*Enter Agatha, a very pretty girl, but showily and badly dressed.*]

Agatha. Jane had the door open, so I thought I would just drop in to——

Jimmy. I know. To play with us. We are feeling particularly sportive this evening. Let me introduce Miss Myra Tremaine, the champion Kiss-in-the-Ring player, and Miss Belinda Tremaine, who holds the cup for Hop Scotch.

Myra [*taking Agatha's hand and looking her up and down*]. Dear me, Agatha, another smart frock. You look like a bridesmaid.

Polly. Sorry to disappoint you, but Belinda's engagement to the Archbishop of Canterbury is off.

Dolly. Because she objects to his smoking all over the house.

Agatha [*sinking into a chair and holding out her frock*]. *This* smart ? My dear, my maid ran this up for me ages ago : it's as old as the hills and washes like a rag. By the bye, I came upon something that might be useful to you for to-night. I know you're such a one for the quiet shades. It's that very soft tone of pink ; frazy crazy the French call it.

Myra [*puzzled*]. What ? Oh, I see. Fraise écrasée —crushed strawberry. It's ever so kind of you, Agatha dear, but you really mustn't trouble.

Agatha. Trouble's a pleasure, I'm sure. My little maid shall run for it—she's waiting outside. [*Calling*] Faites monter le carton, Elise—tut—stupid of me. It seems so natural to speak to one's fum de chambre in French. [*Calling*] Bring up the box I left in our hall, Elise.

Jimmy. What's your—er—fum de chambre doing here ?

Agatha. She came round with me, of course ; mamma would not dream of letting me go out un-attended. So you are entertaining this evening ?

Myra. Only Lady Errington.

Agatha [*eagerly*]. Lady Errington ?

Polly. That's Aunt Maria.

Agatha. Lady Errington. Oh—but oughtn't you to smarten up a bit ? With a yard or two of art muslin and a few pins I could make this a different room. Mamma always says I am such a one for the delicate touches. Have you got the right cards to the top in the card plate ?

Dolly. We haven't a card plate.

Polly. And only the sweep's card to put in it if we had.

Agatha. Ah, well, you're new-comers, you see, and perhaps we *are* a little exclusive. How would it be if *I* stayed to dinner so as to give a tone and to show her ladyship that you visit with the *better* houses in the neighbourhood ?

Jimmy. But next door is just like this house.

Agatha [*gently*]. We come at the end of the row, you see, dear. That makes us Semi-detached, doesn't it ?

Myra [*smiling*]. And is that very distinguished?
We're dreadfully ignorant.

Agatha. Well, after the Semi you come to the
Detached—in gardens—and there you practically
touch the County.

Myra. Do you?

Agatha. At any rate the Landed Gentry. [*A knock.
Enter a very small child in cap and apron, carrying a
large dress box.*] There. Now we'll just have a peep
and then you must let Elise get you into it. So much
depends upon the way a thing's worn.

Myra. Oh, but—please, Agatha, I couldn't think of
troubling—er—Elise.

Agatha. My dear, what has she to do? A little
light fancy work——

Eliza [*anxiously*]. Please, miss——

Agatha. A little lace to mend—what is it, Elise?

Eliza. If you please, miss, I was to get back to
the potatoes the very minute you'd finished with
me.

Agatha [*hastily*]. Open the box at once, Elise.
There! [*An appalling garment is disclosed.*] Now,
won't that be just the thing? Dressy, you know,
and yet only a simple little demi-toilette.

[*Myra gazes in stricken silence, then kisses Agatha.*]

Myra. Thank you, Agatha. It's wonderful. It's
—it's wonderful. Isn't it, girls?

Awed Chorus. Quite—quite wonderful.

Myra. And I'm sure it would be *just* right for *some*
occasions——

Jimmy [*very politely*]. The Fifth of November, for
instance.

Myra. Jimmy! But I'm afraid it's a little too
smart for me.

Agatha. Ah, but wait till you see it on. Take the
box upstairs, Elise.

[*Agatha opens door* L. *for Eliza, who staggers out
with box.*]

Jimmy [*softly*]. Myra, you can't.   You'd look like a sweep on May-day.

Myra. Of course I can't, but we mustn't hurt her feelings.

Agatha [*at door*]. Come along, Myra.

Myra [*to Jimmy*]. You come too, and we'll work it somehow.

Agatha [*archly*]. Yes, Mr. Jimmy, you come too and give your opinion.   We all know how particular the gentlemen are.

[*Exeunt Myra, Agatha, and Jimmy,* L.]

Polly [*giggling*]. " The gentlemen."   Why not " gents " ?

Dolly. " There you touch the County."

Belinda [*looking up suddenly from her book*]. Brutes, both of you.

Polly. Brutes ?

Belinda. She's nice and kind and pretty, and you're always horrid to her.   And Myra told you to clear up the room and wash yourselves.

Polly. Well—I—never.

Dolly. For the first time I realize the feelings of Balaam.

Polly [*severely*]. Belinda clears up the room for sheer, unprovoked cheek.

Dolly [*twitching away Belinda's book*]. Step lively, Belinda.

Belinda [*rising*]. All right.   I don't mind.   I may as well fag for you as for Jimmy.   [*She takes up Polly's coat.   Three small objects fall from the pocket.*]   Hullo. Chestnuts.   [*Picking them up.*]   Only three ?

Dolly. Hand them over.   We'll roast them now— there'll be one each.   [*She arranges the three chestnuts on the bars of the grate.*]   That's mine, that's Polly's, and that's Belinda's—if she behaves herself.

Polly. One of the girls gave them to me because it's Hallowe'en.   I forget why.

Dolly [*kneeling on the rug*]. I know.   If your chestnut pops and jumps off the bar you get a wish—your "heart's desire," as some silly book calls it. What's your heart's desire, Polly.

Polly [*with a sigh*]. I couldn't possibly stuff 'em into one chestnut ; I've got so many.

Dolly [*clearing the fire with the poker*]. So have I. And of course it *is* all nonsense : Jane might just as well expect to get her heart's desire from a lemon sole.

Belinda. Dolly, you mustn't talk like that on Hallowe'en. It's the great fairy night, and I'm sure we *ought* to wish.

Polly. Well, there's your chestnut. Wish away and see what your fairies can do for you.

Belinda [*with closed eyes and tightly clenched hands*]. Then I wish—oh, I *do* wish—that a fairy godmother would appear and give us *all* our wishes. Why shouldn't she come to us as well as to Cinderella ? *She* only wanted to go to a silly ball ; *we* want such lots of things. [*The room darkens and a loud pop is heard.*]

Polly. There goes a chestnut. Whose is it ?

Dolly [*raking among the ashes*]. Belinda's, I think. What's wrong with the light ? I can hardly see.

Belinda. It *is* mine. O Polly, you—you don't *really* think that anything's going to happen, do you ? I almost wish that we *hadn't* wished.

[*The room darkens still more, leaving only the dull glow of the fire.*]

Dolly [*looking nervously round*]. Don't be absurd, child. It's—it's some stupid trick of Jimmy's, I expect.

[*A sound of music is heard ; soft, rippling arpeggios which seem to come from immense distance.*]

Polly [*loudly*]. Stop it, Jimmy. We're not a bit frightened. [*Clinging to Dolly.*] O—oh, Dolly.

[*The music sounds nearer and now voices can be heard, faint but shrill, blent in a wild, wordless chant. The three children huddle together on the hearth-rug.*]

Dolly. O—oh—look there.

[*Out of the darkness grows a pale silvery light. The window curtains wave as if in a strong gale, then sweep aside disclosing the tiny, shining figure of the Fairy. She wears a long red robe and a steeple-crowned hat ; her little face is that of a child, but long grey hair flows over her shoulders, and she leans upon a crutch of ebony. She peers into the room with drowsy eyes while the music sinks to a whisper, then ceases.*]

Fairy [*in a faint, far-away voice*]. Who calls upon the Name Forgotten ? Who wakes the Faerie from their dream ?

Belinda. We—we didn't know you were asleep. We're *so* sorry.

Fairy. What should we do but sleep in a world which knows us no longer ? My eyes are grown dim. [*She draws from her robe and puts on a huge pair of horn spectacles.*] Are you not my little Cinderella ?

Belinda. Please—I'm Belinda, please.

Fairy [*peering at her*]. I know not Belinda. But [*passing her hand over her brows*] I have slumbered long. [*Her eyes fall upon the prostrate twins.*] And these—these should be your sisters. [*Shaking her crutch with a menacing gesture.*] Ugly and cruel, doubtless.

Belinda [*hastily*]. Yes, they're my sisters, but they aren't ugly—at least, not particularly—and they're quite nice.

Twins [*piteously*]. Oh, we *are*—we really *are*, dear Fairy : quite.

Fairy. Then what ails the child ? Has the king, your father, brought you home a cruel stepmother ?

Polly. Mother is quite well, thank you.

Dolly. And father isn't a king.

Fairy. Strange. Strange. Then perchance he is a poor woodcutter ?

Belinda. He's poor, but he isn't a woodcutter.

Polly. He wants to be an estate agent.

Fairy. I know not the estate agent. Is it a noble calling ?

Dolly. They look after land, I think.

Fairy. Ah, the Governor of a Province. A modest ambition truly, and he shall attain it. [*She waves her crutch.*] He is an estate agent from henceforth. [*To Belinda.*] And now for you, my child. What boon would you ask of the Faerie ?

Belinda [*overcoming her nervousness and advancing a few steps*]. Oh, dear Fairy, it isn't for me—it's for Myra.

Fairy. Myra ?

Belinda. She's my eldest sister, you know.

Fairy. The Princess Royal ? Yes.

Belinda. She's going out to-night with Aunt Maria, and she hasn't a single decent frock.

Fairy. Is she good and true, this Myra ?

Belinda. She's a perfect dear.

Dolly. Everybody likes Myra.

Fairy. Then to-night she shall be fairest of the fair. Shall hers be the robe that blazes like the sun, that shines like the moon, or that glitters like the stars ?

Polly. I think—if you wouldn't mind—something a little quieter.

Dolly. Yes, she said " quiet and appropriate."

Fairy. Modest and wise Myra. White shall be her raiment ; white as the Dawn before the Sun has kissed her. What more ?

Belinda. Well—if she *could* have something to take her to the hall.

Polly. A taxi, you know——

Dolly. Or even the station fly——

Fairy. A suitable equipage. Good.

Belinda. Then—what was it she wanted for poor Jane ?

Polly. A neat gown to open the door in.

Fairy. A bower maiden in fair apparel. Yes.

But you have then bidden guests hither ?   I will transform this hovel to halls of splendour.

[*Raises her crutch.*]

Dolly [*hastily*]. No, no, please.   You mustn't. This is a furnished house—and we mayn't transform anything.

Polly. They won't even let us shift the bookcase.

Fairy. Then at least I will provide a banquet.

Belinda [*doubtfully*]. We've got lemon soles.

Polly. Of course, a cold chicken *would* be nice.

Fairy [*sharply*]. Tut, tut.   Leave that to me, child.

Polly. I beg your pardon, dear Fairy—and we're ever so much obliged.   Now Agatha-Next-Door won't be able to wave her frightful frocks at Myra any more.

Fairy. What is this malapert Agatha that she should taunt the Lady Myra ?   Shall I cause toads to fall from her lips with her every word ?

Belinda. Oh no, *please* don't.

Polly [*regretfully*]. Perhaps it would be better not. She never leaves off talking, so the place would be *full* of toads.

Dolly. And she doesn't exactly taunt, you know, only she has such heaps of frocks and there's Myra without one to her back.

Fairy. This at least shall be remedied.

[*She describes a circle round herself in the air with her crutch, then with arms uplifted, she chants.*]

> This to That and That to This,
> One shall find what one shall miss :
> Black to white and white to black,
> This shall gain what That shall lack ;
> This shall lose what That shall hold
> Till the strokes of twelve be told—a—ah !

[*As she speaks the last line she totters as if faint.*]
Children. Oh, what is it ?   Aren't you well ?
[*The Fairy recovers herself and stands leaning on her crutch, but her speech is faint and breathless.*]

Fairy. I have spoken no Spell this many a day. Now the Great Words come slowly to my lips and my feet falter on the Ancient Way. I am weary, my children : let me go.

[*The brightness about her begins to fade.*]

Polly. We are so sorry that you should have tired yourself for us.

Dolly. But, dear Fairy, why are you so old and weak ? I thought that Fairies were always young and dancing in the moonbeams.

[*The far-away music sounds again as the Fairy answers slowly.*]

Fairy. We are the world's first babies, dear ; the children of its youth and innocence : now it grows grim and overwise and cares to play with us no longer. It is falling—falling, the twilight of the fairies : soon the midsummer moon will look on us no more.

[*There is now only a pale glimmer of light round the little figure.*]

Polly. Oh—she's going.

Dolly. She's putting herself out.

Belinda [*darting forward*]. One minute, please, Fairy ! Must Myra be careful about twelve o'clock— like Cinderella, you know ?

[*Through the shadows the last words of the Fairy fall faintly.*]

Fairy. This shall lose what That shall hold
          Till the strokes of twelve be told.

[*Complete darkness. The music once more swells to a chorus of wild voices, then dies away to a mere breath—the sigh of an Æolian harp. Suddenly the room flashes again into brightness : the normal atmosphere has again returned, the window curtains are closed, and the Fairy has vanished.*]

Belinda. " Till the strokes of twelve be told." That means till twelve o'clock, doesn't it ?

Polly [*dreamily*]. I—suppose so.

Belinda. They'll be home long before that, but I'm

glad I remembered to ask. Aunt Maria would be dreadfully annoyed to find herself bouncing down High Street in a pumpkin.

Polly [*suddenly*]. Dolly—pinch me. Harder. I *can't* be awake.

Dolly. Polly—then it really did happen ? It's true ?

Polly. The—the Fairy ? I—suppose so.

Belinda [*clapping her hands and skipping*]. Of course it's true, and we've got all these nice things for Myra. A fly to take her to the lecture——

Polly. A cold chicken—that was *my* idea.

Belinda. A new frock.

Dolly. I suppose the—[*looking nervously over her shoulder*] the old lady knows the sort of thing that girls wear now ?

Polly. She said " white " : you can't go far wrong with plain white. When will this Spell affair begin to work ?

Dolly. Don't talk as if it were a mustard poultice. Almost at once, I should think. I wonder that we haven't heard cries of joy already.

Polly. S'sh. Listen.

[*A distant commotion is heard, voices raised in alarm, the upsetting of chairs, a door violently slammed. Hurried footsteps draw near, and Eliza bursts in* L. *and dashes across to the opposite door. She is pale and breathless.*]

Dolly and Belinda. What is it ?

Polly [*between Eliza and the door* R.]. What's the matter ?

Eliza [*wildly*]. Don't you stop me !—I wouldn't stay another minute in this house, not—not if it was *ever* so. Don't you stop me, Miss Polly !

[*She slips past Polly and out* R. *As the children stare at each other the front door is heard to bang.*]

Dolly. Can anything be wrong upstairs ?

Polly. Perhaps I'd better go and see.

Dolly. Wait—here comes some one else. Agatha !

[*Agatha runs in* L., *a terrified and dishevelled Agatha, dressed only in her bodice and petticoat. Her hair, freed from ribbons and combs, falls over her shoulders; all her affectations have vanished; she is a pretty and pathetic little figure.*]

Agatha [*in a choked voice*]. Girls—I—I didn't leave my clothes down here, did I ?

Polly. Clothes ?   Of course not.

Dolly. What on earth has happened ?

Agatha. I—I don't know.   Oh, poor Myra ! [*Covering her face with her hands.*]   I believe I'm going out of my mind.

Dolly [*severely*]. You've gone out of quite enough already, seems to me.   Where's your frock ?

Agatha. I—I don't know.

Polly. Don't *know* ?

Agatha [*wildly.*] Oh, don't ask questions or I shall scream !   Who's that ?   [*The door* L. *bursts open and Jimmy runs in.   Agatha rushes to him.*]   Jimmy.   Is she any better ?

Jimmy [*panting*]. Worse.   It's awful.   Why did you cut away ?

Agatha. I couldn't stand it—when she began to sprout.

Children. Sprout ?   Myra ?   What's she sprouting ?

Jimmy. It looks like feathers.

Children. Feathers ?

Jimmy. And now her tail's growing—there are yards and yards of it on the floor.

Children. Her *tail* ?

Agatha [*faintly*]. Oh, don't !   Jimmy—couldn't you run for the doctor ?

Jimmy. I suppose I'd better : Dr. Raynor at the corner ?

Agatha. No, no, he's homœopathic: I'm sure she wants violent treatment.   Dr. Bargrave in Milford Street.

Jimmy. Right-o.   [*Turning to twins.*]   And you

girls standing there like gaping geese, why don't you *do* something ?   Take her up a cup of tea—or a hot water bottle—or *something*.

Myra [*without*]. Jimmy.   Jimmy.

Polly. Hush.   I believe she's coming.

[*Belinda runs to door* L. *and flings it open.*]

Belinda [*staring in ecstacy*]. O Myra !   How lovely !

Jimmy. O Myra !   How awful !

All. O my good gracious goodness, Myra ! !

[*Myra totters in, supporting herself from chair to chair, until she reaches the table, against which she leans trembling.   A beam of fairy radiance falls upon her, emphasizing the glories of her toilette.   She is in full evening dress of white satin with a heavy court train falling from the shoulders, and embroidered with pearl and diamond flowers.   Diamonds blaze at her throat and on her corsage, ropes of pearls hang from her neck, and her arms and fingers are loaded with bracelets and rings.   On her head is a diamond tiara, from which waves a forest of white ostrich plumes.*]

Myra. Jimmy—how could you leave me, Jimmy ?

Jimmy. I'm going for the doctor.

Myra [*clutching him*]. No, no.   Let's all keep together.   I don't know what may be going to happen next.

Agatha. I don't know what has happened *now*.   I can't understand.

Myra. Well—you *saw*.   I was just trying on that frock of yours when all of a sudden it—it went.

Twins. Went ?

Myra. It wasn't there.   And then *her* frock went —and then I began to break out like this.   Don't come near me, children ;   it's probably catching.

Agatha. O Myra, the jewels !   I shouldn't mind catching some of them.   *Look* at the diamonds—and aren't those pearls—pearls as big as marbles ?

Jimmy. And they're stuck all over her.   My word,

if we could spout her as she stands she'd fetch pounds and pounds.

Agatha. Pounds ?   That dress is worth hundreds—thousands !

Myra. But it won't come off—I've tried.   Not a thing will come off.

Jimmy [*aghast*]. Won't come off ?   But it *must.* You can't go about like that.   I'll tell you plainly you don't come tagging after me down town in white satin and feathers.

Belinda [*solemnly*]. It will all vanish at twelve o'clock, just like Cinderella's ball dress.

Jimmy. Oh, shut your head, Belinda.

Myra. Look here, Belinda, we've got enough to worry us without *your* twaddle.   Don't talk of what you know nothing about.

Polly. But she *does* know.

Dolly. She's trying to tell you.   It's true.

Myra. One at a time, children.   *What's* true ?

Jimmy. Come on, cough it up, Belinda.

Belinda. True that a Fairy came and——

Myra. A *what* ?

Polly. A Fairy.

Dolly. Yes, really a Fairy.   We saw her too.

Belinda. It's Hallowe'en, you know.   She gave us all wishes, and I wanted you to have a nice new frock for the Economy Lecture.

Myra. And—is this it ?

Jimmy [*going into guffaws of laughter*]. Oh, my eye, the Economy Lecture !   Quiet and appropriate—eh, Myra ?

Belinda. We said it was to be quiet and appropriate, didn't we ?

Twins. Yes, yes, we did.

Myra [*with the calm of despair*]. I should like to see the Fairy's notion of something a little dressy. But what about poor Agatha ?   Is your Fairy responsible for *her* present—er—costume ?

Agatha [*ruefully*]. It seems to be all or nothing with her.

Belinda. That was Polly.

Polly. Sneak. I may have hinted that Agatha had too many frocks, but I never asked the old lady to take away every stitch the girl stands up in.

Dolly. How were we to know that fairies are so beastly literal ?

Jimmy [*taking off his coat*]. I call it a shame. Here, Agatha, put this on. It won't look quite so—so evening dress. [*Helps Agatha into the coat.*]

Myra. Well, there's only one thing to be done. Polly must go to the lecture, Agatha must go to bed, and I must shut myself into the boot cupboard until twelve o'clock. Now I hope this is all, Belinda—no more wishes.

Belinda. No.

Dolly [*feebly*]. N-no—except Jane.

Polly. And the cold chicken.

[*A loud crash is heard as of breaking crockery.*]

Myra. Belinda—that wretched Fairy isn't starting on *Jane* now—when you know as well as I do how the least thing upsets her ?

Children. But we only asked——

Jane [*without*]. If you please, miss—— [*The door* R. *is kicked violently open and Jane staggers in bearing upon a silver dish a monstrous gilded pasty from which emerge the head and tail of a well-grown peacock. Jane is attired in flowing robes of pale almond pink, and decked with gold bracelets and a necklet of gold coins ; on her head is a wreath of pink roses entwined with golden leaves.*] If you please, Miss Myra, was it by your orders that *this* was sent in ? [*She slams down the pasty on the table and stands gazing at it as though fascinated.*] When I see the creature staring at me it give me such a turn I dropped a pile o' plates—and never would your Ma approve of any such French fallals and kickshaws from the pastrycook, Miss Myra ;

" If you please, miss, was it by your orders that
this was sent in ? "

plain roast and boiled was good enough for Dogwood Park and—— [*Her glance falls upon Agatha.*] Lor, Miss Agatha! [*Realizing Myra.*] Sakes alive, Miss Myra!

Chorus. Jane!

Jane. Ah, Jane indeed. No, Miss Myra, it's not my place to pass remarks, and none shall be passed: I merely ask you whether *this* is what your Ma would have ordered for high tea for six, let alone the hares and pheasants, shot in like coals they were, and there's a whole stag in the passage and two swans in the sink.

Myra [*hopelessly*]. It's quite useless to explain. A—a friend has sent us a little present of game, Jane.

Jane. Then there's been some mistake in delivery, you mark my words; it's the Lord Mayor's Banquet we've got, Miss Myra, and our brace o' rabbits has gone to the Mansion House.

Belinda. O Jane, you do look lovely.

Jimmy [*struggling with laughter*]. I say, Jane, have you seen yourself lately?

Jane. Seen myself, Master Jimmy?. Ah, some of us *ought* to see ourselves—you standing there a disgrace in your shirt-sleeves and Miss Agatha dressed—well, I won't say how—and as to Miss Myra, it's not for me to pass remarks, but her Ma wouldn't like it, no more her aunt won't neither. *My* tastes was always quiet, thanks be; plain washin' print for week days and a nice bit o' black for Sunday——

Myra. Jane, dear—I think you had better take a look at yourself.

Jane. Me, Miss Myra? Is my cap crooked? [*Raising her hands to her wreath.*] Why—what's all this? [*Seeing her gold clasped arms.*] Oh! [*She cautiously approaches the mirror above the mantelpiece and takes one glance at it.*] Oh! [*She sinks into a chair by the table.*] What is it, Miss Myra? What's done it? Oh—oh, it's crool. Dressed for the door I was by your Ma's wish, and now [*extending her bare arms*] I might be going to do the week's washing.

[*Flings her arms along the table, buries her face in them and sobs.*]

Myra. Now she's going into hysterics. I hope you're satisfied, Belinda.

Jimmy. Yes, Belinda, you and your footling Fairy have got us into a rotten mess between you.

Polly. Don't speak of her like that, Jimmy.

Dolly. You might remember that she could turn us all into white rats or guinea pigs.

Myra [*wildly*]. I'd *rather* be a guinea pig. I shouldn't feel nearly such a f-fool as a guinea pig.

[*Drops into chair opposite Jane and hides her face on the table. A fanfare of trumpets. Myra and Jane simultaneously raise their heads.*]

Myra and Jane. What's that?

Jimmy. It sounded just outside.

Agatha [*running to the window and peeping out*]. Good gracious, look!

[*She draws the curtains, the street is seen to be brilliantly lit up. Shouts are heard and a distant hum of voices.*]

Jimmy [*running to the window*]. I say! Look at those chaps with torches—linkmen don't they call them? [*The three children run to the window.*]

Agatha. And here come outriders in crimson and silver and—O Myra, do look—[*A louder flourish of trumpets. The shouts and uproar increase*]—look at this coming round the corner—[*Jane jumps up and runs to the window*]—six milk-white horses with postilions in cloth of silver and—oh, my goodness—[*Trumpets and an outburst of cheering*]—such a coach, all gold and crystal, and as big as a haystack.

Jane. It's the Free Foresters' Feet.

Jimmy. It's the King and Queen.

Belinda [*dancing with excitement*]. No, it isn't. It's the suitable equipage. Wait a minute—there. [*A *thunderous knock at the front door.*] It's the carriage come for Myra.

Myra [*faintly*]. I knew it. The Fairy has done things thoroughly.

Dolly. And we only asked for the station fly.

A Tremendous Voice [*from the street*]. THE PRINCESS MYRA'S CARRIAGE STOPS THE WAY.

Jimmy. Stops the way—I should think it *did :* it's the size of a brewer's van.

The Voice. THE PRINCESS MYRA'S CARRIAGE.

Myra. If that creature keeps on bawling out my name I shall go silly.

A Man's Voice [*in the crowd*]. Cheers for the Princess Myra. Hip-hip-hip—— [*A burst of cheering.*]

Agatha. Myra—you'll have to come to the window and bow. Royalties always do.

Myra. No, no. I can't—I won't.

Jimmy [*at window*]. Myra, you jolly well *must.* They're packed like sardines in the street. Come on.

Twins. Yes, come on, Myra.

[*They drag the reluctant Myra to the window.*]

Jimmy. Coat, Agatha, quick. [*Agatha snatches off coat and helps Jimmy into it. Jimmy flings up the sash of window. Loud cheers.*] Ladies and Gentlemen, [*dead silence*] Her Royal Highness the Princess Myra has graciously consented to appear.

[*Bows elaborately. Trumpets. Roars of applause, amidst which Myra steps to the window and bows gravely right and left. She then slams down the sash and draws the curtains quickly. The hubbub sinks to a continuous murmur.*]

Myra [*leaning exhausted against the curtains*]. Will any one kindly tell me what we're going to do *now* ?

Jimmy [*scratching his head*]. *I* don't know. And aunt may blow in at any minute.

Polly. Perhaps she won't notice anything.

Jimmy. Perhaps not—with a full-fledged circus at

the door and Jane looking like the " Last Days of Pompeii."

[*Enter Eliza* R. *hastily. At sight of Myra she hesitates and makes for the door again.*]

Eliza. Please, miss——

Myra. What's the matter, Eliza ? Don't be frightened.

Eliza. Oh, if you please, miss—missus's compliments, and Miss Agatha's to come home this very minute.

Agatha. I can't, Eliza, you must see that I can't.

Eliza [*with increasing nervousness*]. And please, miss, Number Fifteen desires '*is* compliments and—and——

Myra [*coming towards her*]. Yes ? And what ?

Eliza [*desperately*]. And 'e's gone for the P'LICE.

[*Dashes from the room.*]

Children. The police.

Jane. The *police* !

Jimmy. That about puts the lid on.

Myra [*calmly*]. Yes. I think we may regard the police as the finishing touch.

Jimmy. Let's see. Five minutes to the station, five minutes back—— [*Agatha glances at the clock.*] That clock's no good : it has been at twenty past eleven ever since we came here. We've got about ten minutes. What's to be done ?

Myra [*advancing with tragic dignity*]. I have quite decided what is to be done. I am the eldest and therefore responsible ; if the police arrive I shall give myself up—" go quiet " I believe is the expression. You, Polly, will take my place as hostess. Jane, it is too late for the soles ; you had better serve that dreadful bird [*pointing to peacock*], but for goodness' sake let it be carved off the table. And you, children, at the height of your high tea, think of your unhappy sister sitting in white satin and diamonds in the police station, and [*almost breaking down*] don't make

greater fools of yourselves than is absolutely necessary.   [*She passes slowly out* L. *with hanging head.*]

Jimmy. She's handing out the sob stuff pretty
thick, isn't she ?

Agatha. I think it is very affecting: it's like Mary
Queen of Scots going to execution.

Jimmy. Of course we can't let her get jugged.
Now—what price medal for distinguished service ?
Jane, will you lead the forlorn hope—run down and
tell those chaps with the coach to go away ?

Agatha. Yes. Say it's the wrong house—they've
mistaken the day—anything.

Jane. What ! *me*, Master Jimmy ?. Not like this ?

Jimmy. Slip on mother's mackintosh.

Agatha. Put up an umbrella. And if the police
come——

Jimmy [*wildly*]. If the police come, just give the
whole bally show in charge. That ought to keep
them busy for a bit.

Jane [*picking up the great dish*]. If the police come
I shall give 'em *this* : that's the way to keep 'em
busy. Don't you worry, Master Jimmy : I'll see
what I can do.

Twins. And we'll come with you, Jane.

[*Exeunt* R. *Jane with the pasty, Polly and Dolly.*]

Jimmy [*stopping Belinda*]. Not you, Belinda ; I
want a word with you. [*Slaps Agatha on the back.*]
Good old Agatha.   Still sticking to the ship, eh ?

Agatha. Of course ; but when the policemen come
I shall nip behind those curtains ; I'm not—er—
dressed to receive.

Jimmy. Then you'd better nip : they'll be here
directly. [*Agatha hides behind the window curtains.*]
Now, Belinda.

[*Belinda advances timidly, her hands behind her.*]

Belinda. Yes, Jimmy.

Jimmy [*sternly*]. You're at the bottom of all this,
you know.

Belinda. Jimmy, I will not be bullied. I've got any amount of people their heart's desire, and if they don't like it, it's not my fault.

Jimmy. But d'you mean to say that this variety entertainment of yours is going to last till midnight ?

Belinda. Yes, till twelve o'clock. The Fairy told me so.

Jimmy. Are you sure ?

Agatha [*poking her head out between the curtains*]. Repeat what she said.

Belinda. It was all in poetry ; I can't remember.

Jimmy [*catching her by the shoulders and shaking her*]. But you must. Think, you little ass, think.

Belinda [*in gasps*]. I—can only—remember—the last two lines. She said them twice.

Jimmy [*releasing her*]. Well—let's have 'em.

Belinda. " This shall—shall——" Oh yes. " This shall lose what That shall hold——"

Jimmy. This shall lose——

Agatha. That's me. That's all right. Goodness knows I've lost enough.

Jimmy. —what That shall hold. That's Myra, I suppose : she's got away with the goods. Go on, child.

Belinda. " Till the strokes of twelve be told."

Jimmy [*hopelessly*]. Till twelve o'clock. That's plain enough. That does us in.

Agatha [*eagerly*]. Well, but, Jimmy, *does* it ? She didn't exactly say till twelve o'clock ; she said, " Until the clock strikes twelve."

Jimmy [*staring at the clock*]. By Jove ! I believe you've hit upon the weak spot. [*The trumpets begin to sound again.*] Oh, shut your heads ! I'll make the clock strike twelve in half a jiff.

[*Jumps on a chair, opens the clock face and seizes the minute hand.*]

Agatha. No, no, Jimmy, not yet ! I'm frightened. It may start something else off—do wait a minute.

Jimmy. What for ?

Agatha. Let's think—let's consult——

Jimmy. If we don't look slippy we shall do our consulting in the station. [*A loud ring, followed by a knock at the front door.*] There ! The police. Agatha, it's now or never. Risk it ?

Agatha [*nodding*]. Risk it.

[*Her head disappears within the curtains. Jimmy whirls the minute hand round to the hour and the clock slowly strikes twelve. As the last stroke falls all sounds from the street cease.*]

Jimmy [*breathlessly*]. Well ?

Agatha. The street is all dark again, and—Jimmy —I can't see the coach : I believe it has gone away.

Jimmy. Let's have a look. [*Draws the curtains, showing Agatha dressed as at first.*] Why—yes. The whole show has done a bunk. The street's quite empty and—[*seeing Agatha*]—hullo !

Agatha. And here's my frock ! Jimmy—it worked. O Jimmy ! [*Embraces him violently.*]

Jimmy [*struggling*]. Here, I say—drop it.

[*The twins rush in* R.]

Dolly. Jimmy, Jimmy ! Jane has come right again.

Polly. And we couldn't find the coach—it's not there.

Jimmy. Good business. My word, what a narrow squeak. Now then for the police—let 'em all come !

Dolly. The police ?

Jimmy. They rang just now. Didn't you let them in ?

Polly. That wasn't the police : it was this telegram for Myra. [*Holds up a telegram.*]

Jimmy [*taking it*]. Give it here.

[*Myra bursts in* L. *Her fairy robes have disappeared, and she is dressed as before.*]

Myra. Look. Look at me ! I'm all right again ! What has happened ?

Jimmy [*solemnly*]. The clock has struck twelve.

All the Girls [*after a pause*]. Oh—oh—you clever boy!   [*They all rush at him.*]

Jimmy. Now, drop it, drop it. It was Agatha's idea. Myra, here's a telegram for you.

Myra [*tearing it open and reading.*] " All settled, home this evening. Dad, Mother." Children—he has got it. Dad has really got the appointment.

Jimmy. Well played, the governor.

Twins. Hip, hurray!

Belinda. Of course he has. The Fairy said most particularly——

Jimmy. Oh, *hop* it, Belinda.

Myra. Belinda—if you so much as mention that Fairy again I'll—I'll slap you.

Agatha. Listen. Isn't that a taxi stopping?

Jimmy. Aunt, you bet. Agatha, you must stay to tea. I say, Myra, don't you rather wish you hadn't been shorn of all your splendour?

Myra. Not a bit. I wouldn't stand in Cinderella's shoes again for anything you liked to offer. Yes, here comes aunt.

Jimmy. Now, girls, pull yourselves together. 'Tention! Fall in behind there.

[*Buttons his coat and shoots his cuffs. The girls arrange their frocks and pat their hair. Enter Jane in neat black dress, white cap, and apron.*]

Jane. Lady Errington.

All [*advancing with outstretched hands.*] How d'you do, Aunt Maria?

QUICK CURTAIN

THE DISCOVERY

By Hermon Ould

EDITOR'S PREFACE

The first voyage made by Christopher Columbus across the Atlantic Ocean was one of the most daring and romantic adventures ever undertaken by man. Strong in his faith that by sailing westward from the coast of Europe he would reach the coast of Asia, he overcame all difficulties, and on Friday, August 3, 1492, he set sail from Palos, in Spain, with three little ships. First he touched at the Canary Islands, and then he launched out into the unknown seas which for centuries had been regarded as the end of the world. We can hardly imagine him worse equipped. His own ship, the " Santa Maria," the largest of the three and the only one which was completely decked, was about thirty-two yards long and nine yards wide. Many of his men were criminals released to join the expedition because so few sailors would venture, and there was hardly a man on the three ships who did not dislike Columbus as a foreigner and despise or fear him as a madman. Day after day the easterly winds drove them steadily across the ocean, till they grew afraid that they would never be able to return, and discontent and superstition were on the verge of breaking out into mutiny. Still Columbus held to his westward course, but on October 11 he knew that if land were not sighted very soon, his crew would murder him, seize the ship, and turn back to Spain.

CHARACTERS

CHRISTOPHER COLUMBUS.
PEDRO GUTIERREZ, *an officer.*
PEPE, *a page-boy.*
JUAN PATIÑO,
DIEGO GARCIA,
FRANCISCO,
GUILLERMO IRES, } *other seamen.*

Note.—Christopher Columbus first saw the light of the New World on the night of October 11, 1492. He was often " at open defiance " with his crew. These two circumstances, at least, are historical. For the rest, this little play had better be regarded as a work of imagination—H.O.

APPROXIMATE PRONUNCIATIONS

PEDRO GUTIERREZ—*Páy-dro Goo-tee-érreth.*
PEPE—*Páy-pay.*
JUAN PATIÑO—*Hoo-áhn Pah-tée-nyo.*
DIEGO GARCIA—*Dee-áy-go Gar-thée-ah.*
FRANCISCO—*Frahn-thís-co.*
GUILLERMO IRES—*Gill-yáir-mo Ée-rays.*

None of the Spanish vowels is exactly the same as the English. The *e* is something between *ay* in *pay* and *e* in *egg*. The *r* is always rolled. *Th* as in *think*. *G* as in *good*.

Columbus's Spanish name is *Christobal Colon*, but as no one calls him by name in the play, this is not needed.

THE DISCOVERY

SCENE.—*On board the " Santa Maria."*
TIME.—*October* 11, 1492.

The ship is seen from an angle, which brings the poop somewhat to the left, the quarter-deck taking up the greater part of the stage. If it is visible, the midmast should bear a crucifix, in passing which everybody mechanically crosses himself. A large lantern, containing a lighted candle, is fixed at the extreme top of the poop. The night is still, and there is little movement in the sails.

Two seamen are visible, both well to the right. Juan is on his knees, adjusting rigging; Diego is helping. The actions of both of them are indeterminate, clearly designed to conceal their real purpose. They speak in loud whispers.

Diego. Within the next half an hour he will go to the poop-head as sure as God's alive. He can't keep away from it. His eyes are glued on the sky as if he expected his precious New World to burst out of it like a thunderbolt !   [*He laughs derisively.*]

Juan. Poor wretch !

Diego. Now, then, Juan—quaking again !

Juan. That's a lie ! Why should I quake ? What is there to fear ? [*After a brief pause*] But I am sorry for him.

Diego. Why waste your pity ? Shall it be one madman, his head stocked with visions, or forty honest seamen pining for their homes ?

Juan. *Santisima Maria*, but he's a *gracious* madman . . .

Diego [*impatiently*]. Gracious when all goes to his pleasure, but as irritable as a teething child when crossed !

[*The song of seamen is heard : it is a scarcely distinguishable murmur.*]

> Here's a keg o' rum
> To Kingdom Come !
> The Devil laughs,
> But God is dumb !

Juan [*sharply*]. They ought to stop that. The captain is always furious when he hears it.

Diego. Shan't we even *sing* to keep up our spirits ? 'Sh !

[*They attend with assumed assiduity to the rigging. Pedro Gutierrez comes in ; he is somewhat surprised when he sees the others.*]

Pedro. Who's that ?

Diego [*rising*]. Diego Garcia and Juan Patiño, sir.

Pedro [*inclined to be communicative*]. It's dark. I would welcome the moon. . . .

Diego. Aye, aye, Don Pedro. Some of us would welcome the coast of Spain still more.

Pedro [*pumping*]. Impatient, Diego ?

Diego [*surlily*]. There are limits to patience, sir.

Pedro [*humouring him*]. And you've reached them, eh ?

Diego. We're like bats trying to fly by day. It's time he gave way. Why should one man have the lives of fifty in his hands ?

Pedro [*with authority*]. I hope we are not entertaining mutinous thoughts, Diego.

Diego. Mutiny is an ugly word, sir.

Pedro. And an uglier deed.

[*Juan, finishing his job at the rigging, rises, and with a salute goes off. Columbus comes on. He is a tall, well-built man of forty-six. Hair prematurely white, complexion fair, almost ruddy. A man of quick temper and irritability which he controls only with an effort. His face, in repose, is melancholy. Seeing Don Pedro in conversation with Diego, he looks a trifle suspicious. He turns quickly to Diego.]*

Columbus. That candle on the foremast is guttering ; see that it is put right.

Diego [sullenly]. Aye, aye, sir.　　　*[He goes.]*

Columbus [recalling him]. And, Diego !

Diego [coming back]. Yes. sir.

Columbus. This is the quarter-deck.

Diego. Yes, sir.

Columbus. A good sailor knows his place.

Diego [with repressed fury]. Yes, sir.

[Columbus points off ; Diego, scarcely concealing a scowl, goes off.]

Columbus [to Pedro]. A surly dog !

Pedro. And a dangerous one. He does more than his share to inspire discontent.

Columbus. I have remarked it.

[Columbus is thoughtful for a moment and remains stationary. Presently he goes on to the poop and looks out to sea. Pedro follows him. Simultaneously, Pepe, the page-boy, emerges from the hatchway, against which he stands, out of sight of the others. When they begin to talk he listens eagerly.]

Columbus. Easterly, ever easterly. God is in the wind, Don Pedro.

Pedro [with a short laugh]. The crew would say that it is the Devil, rather, captain. All day, and every day, the wind blows easterly, blowing them away from their homes and their country, their wives and children, their friends and sweethearts.

Columbus [hastily]. You too, Don Pedro ? Do you, too, doubt ?

Pedro. Have I said so, captain? Am I not here by your side, prepared?

Columbus. Forgive me, friend. You are one of the few with faith, and it is not easy to hold fast to faith when nothing seems to warrant faith. Listen to that.

Seamen [*off, singing*] :

> Here's a keg o' rum
> To Kingdom Come!
> The Devil laughs,
> But God is dumb!

[*Columbus and Pedro descend to the quarter-deck.*]

Columbus. Madre de Dios, they drink too much.

Pedro. They are simple men and must have their relaxation. [*The next words break from him almost involuntarily.*] We have not all your vision, captain.

Columbus. You *are* beginning to doubt, Don Pedro. Give me the contents of your mind. I am an impatient man and prone to be unjust; but—[*whimsically*]—I mean well, Don Pedro. I mean well. Speak without fear.

Pedro [*at first with diffidence, but rapidly gaining confidence*]. To-day is the 11th of October—more than two months since we saw the shores of Spain receding. You held a glittering hope of discovery before us, and we had faith. Day followed day, and soon we found ourselves in uncharted seas, but still we had faith. . . . I, at least, had faith. [*With dignity*] I am a man of some little learning, not easily led to wonder at natural phenomena as the unlettered might be. But I confess that I knew some uneasiness when the needle of the compass, instead of pointing to the constant North, jumped as if the devil had laid hand on it, and pointed to the North-west. I am not a child, nor a simpleton, nor a superstitious seaman; but there is such a thing as being too clever, prying into mysteries which were not meant for our eyes. In all humility, captain, I ask if it is

God's will that we should pursue this voyage in the
face of every portent of ill-luck ?

Columbus [*impatiently*]. It is *my* will.   Is that not
enough ?

Pedro [*bowing his head*]. I am answered.

Columbus [*hastily*]. Forgive me, Don Pedro.   A
curb for my tongue—oh, a curb for my unbridled
tongue, my worst enemy !   [*More quietly*] *My* will,
friend, because God's will.   Shall that suffice ?

Pedro [*not appeased*]. I do not claim your confidence, sir.

Columbus [*thundering again*]. But I claim yours.
[*The sound of the seamen's song is again heard.*]   A
blight upon their singing !   Bid them stop.   [*Pedro
goes off, with an air of discontent.   When he is alone,
Columbus looks out at sea.   Muttering.*]   Mystery ?
Would God implant the desire to solve mysteries and
not provide the solution ?   [*Suddenly Pepe runs up
the steps to the poop.   Columbus is startled.*]   Pañeta !
Who is that ?

Pepe. Me, captain—Pepe !

Columbus [*frowning on him*]. Have you been there
all the time ?

Pepe. Please, sir, I am off duty.

Columbus. Then why aren't you down below ?

Pepe [*whimsically, knowing that he is privileged*]. I
prefer your company to theirs.   [*He points below.*]
Am I in the way here, sir ?

Columbus [*humouring him*]. What a boy !   And
what do *they* say of the preference ?

Pepe. I don't speak to them.   I hate them.

Columbus. 'Sh, Pepe !   And get you gone !   [*Pepe
turns reluctantly.*]   Quick !   [*The boy goes more
quickly.*]   Here !   You heard what Don Pedro said ?

Pepe. Yes, captain.   And *he* is the best . . .

Columbus. But even he doubts . . .

Pepe. Everybody doubts . . . except me.

Columbus [*bitterly*]. Everybody . . .

Pepe [*eagerly*]. Except me, captain, except me.

[*He goes to him impetuously.*]

Columbus [*laying a hand on the boy's head*]. You are young enough to have faith. Thank you, boy.

[*The seamen's song is heard again.*]

Pepe. They are horrible when they drink too much. They say it makes them forget.

Columbus. Poor fellows!

Pepe [*approaching nearer*]. Captain, be careful! Sometimes they are desperate.

[*The song surges up like a growl.*]

Columbus. That is ugly. I bade Don Pedro stop them. So you think they might become dangerous? [*Don Pedro returns.*] Go, boy. [*Pepe moves away, but does not go out.*] Well, Don Pedro? Their singing changes to a roar. The deepening of their discontent is ominous. [*The noise grows louder.*]

Pedro. Captain, they ignore my order.

Columbus [*furious*]. I'll make an example of one of them. [*Suddenly.*] Hallo, there! What sneaking mischief-maker is that crawling about the deck? Show yourself! [*Francisco appears from the right.*]

Columbus. Ho, Francisco—you, is it?

Francisco. Yes, sir. And I'm no sneaking mischief-maker.

Columbus. Then why behave as one? Why are you here? Did I send for you? Is discipline obsolete in the Ocean Sea? Is Jack as good as his master nowadays?

Francisco [*humbly*]. Your words sting, sir!

Columbus. And are meant to. I am tired of the mumbling and grumbling of the crew. I have been patient too long.

Francisco. I came to warn you, sir. The temper of the crew is dangerous.

Columbus. Danger is the breath of my life. I should doubt I lived if I lived outside danger.

Francisco [*the words springing from him spasmodi-*

cally]. Our power of endurance has gone. We refuse to go on. I warn you. I respect your person and do not wish to see violence used ; but it is more than mortal can bear, this endless sailing into unknown seas.

Columbus [*to Pedro*]. Don Pedro, the ship is in your hands. I will talk to our friend as man to man. [*Pedro goes on to the poop. Columbus, his voice gentler, almost ingratiating, turns to Francisco, who shifts from foot to foot, nervous by reason of the unaccustomed propinquity.*] Francisco, let me plead with you. There are men whom God has chosen for the working of His will. I am such a man. There is no more merit in me than in this ship : we are both instruments of God. Sometimes He chooses oddly : a stronger than I might have served His purpose better. But since God chose me, who shall withstand me ? The four corners of the earth are to be linked up in the knowledge of their Saviour. I have lifted the veils which obscured the prophecies of Holy Writ, and I have learned that it was ordained that I, chosen among all men, should discover that great world beyond the ocean which I know exists as surely as I know that Heaven exists.

Francisco. Must simple men suffer because of *your* knowledge ?

Columbus [*quickly*]. Simple men shall do their duty.

Francisco. There are limits to duty. Men will give up many things for duty and for gain, but you ask too much. Country, family, friends, perhaps even life itself—all these things you ask us to give up for *your* glory. *We* are not chosen of God to open up new ways : we are simple, humble men, sick for our homes and hungry for our wives.

Columbus. My Heaven, Francisco, you try me . . .

Francisco [*gaining courage*]. Not more than *you* try us, sir. I come to you as a friend, sir. The men are at the end of their patience and spoiling for a fight.   The stoutest rope breaks at last.   [*The song swells up again.   Spoken words mingle with the song, and the voice of Guillermo Ires is heard above the rest.*] Did you hear that, sir !

Columbus. I heard the snarling of angry beasts.

Francisco. You heard the just complaints of angry men, sir.   [*Again Guillermo's voice pierces the din. Columbus stands rigid, endeavouring to catch the words.*] Did you hear *that*, sir ?

Pepe [*who has been unobserved*]. They shan't ! They shan't !

Columbus. Boy, come here.   What were the words ?

Pepe [*almost weeping*]. He said : " The *Santa Maria* will be the lighter for his carcass."

Columbus [*bitterly*]. He said that, did he ?

[*He blinks—is moved more than he will show.*]

Francisco. I am sorry, sir. . . . I knew how high feeling had run.

Columbus [*authoritatively*]. Send Guillermo Ires to me !

Francisco [*not without diffidence*]. Sorry, sir, but . . .

Columbus. Discipline knows no buts.

Francisco [*angrily*]. Discipline is a thing of the past, sir.   It's you or us.

Columbus [*to Don Pedro*]. Don Pedro, let Guillermo Ires be sent to me.   He shall know what it is like in irons.

[*Pedro is half-way down the stairs to the quarter-deck when Guillermo Ires and other seamen rush in an angry mass towards Columbus, growling like infuriated animals.*]

Columbus [*in a thunderous voice*]. Stop !   What is the meaning of this wild uproar ?   [*The men stand transfixed.*]   The first man to move shall spend the rest of the night in irons !

[*There is a perceptible pause, during which nobody moves.   Then, with a wild cry, Guillermo Ires*

*breaks away from the others and advances
towards Columbus.*]

Guillermo. And who's to put him in irons ? We
are thirty to one.

Columbus [*calmly*]. If nobody else is available for
the office, I will perform it myself. Get below ! Let
me hear no more of this.

Guillermo [*in high excitement*]. We've stood too
much. We've been duped day in, day out. We're
men with the common feelings of men. We want our
homes and our women. I say the *Santa Maria* shall
turn her helm towards Spain at once, or we are not
men but sheep.

Columbus [*still calm*]. And who shall navigate her ?

Guillermo. There's plenty here who can do that.
The Devil's with *you*, we all know that, riding the
easterly wind ; but we are not men unused to the sea.
Once clear of this Devil's track to nowhere, we'll blow
our way back to home.

[*Signs of assent from the rest of the crew. Columbus
raises his hand, appealing for silence. He is
paler than his wont, but very calm.*]

Columbus. Don Guillermo, you are an excellent
sailor, a man of abundant resourcefulness. Some
day, if your tongue does not run away with your dis-
cretion, you will achieve prosperity in your calling.
To-day you are an able-bodied seaman and no more :
I am your captain. Your duty is to obey me as mine
is to obey the Royal Sovereigns of Spain who sent me.
Let that be clearly understood between us and we shall
not fall out. Now return to your duties.

[*Again a perceptible pause. Columbus's authoritative
manner holds them. Presently Diego breaks out.*]

Diego. Words for children ! Froth and scum !
We are men : reason with us !

Columbus. Silence !

[*The tone of authority calms the men, who remain,
however, in a huddled crowd, murmuring dis-*

*contentedly. Columbus turns and goes up the
stairs to the poop, where he stands and looks down
upon the men.*]

Diego [*snarling*]. I suppose you think you're on
holy ground now ?　　[*He bounds towards the stairs.*]

Voices [*tumultuously*]. Have him down ! Pitch
him overboard ! Put *him* in irons ! Devil's tool !
Italian renegade !

[*They are about to stampede up the poop gangway,
when Pepe runs to the foot of the stairs and stands
with his arms spread out.*]

Pepe. Cowards ! Cowards ! You will have to kill
me first !

Voices. Out of the way ! Devil's whelp ! Lick-
spittle !

Columbus. What ! Does that child stand between
me and death ? [*Silence follows the commencement
of his speech.*] Pepe ! Come here !

Pepe [*going to him quickly*]. My captain !

[*The men are somewhat sheepish.*]

Columbus. Pepe ! This is a voyage of discovery.
[*The men growl.*] I set out to discover a new world,
a radiant land beyond unknown seas ; to find new
wealth and dominion for our Sovereign King and
Queen, new souls for the sacrifice of our Saviour to
redeem. So far I have discovered but one thing.
[*He pauses and continues with slow deliberation.*] I
have discovered that when a man is given a vision he
must follow it alone. Loyalty passes like seaweed
on an outgoing tide. Friendship breaks as a mast
hollowed by worms breaks. Discipline, duty, and
honourable obedience are bubbles that burst at the
first contact. There remains but oneself. That is
my only discovery so far, Pepe.

Pepe [*his eyes gleaming with excitement*]. Captain,
I am loyal, I am still obedient, still your devoted
servant. . . .

Columbus [*with some emotion*]. I am not ungrateful.

Pedro [*scraping his throat, with dignity*]. I hope my loyalty has never been in question, sir ?

[*He salutes.*]

Columbus [*returning the salute*]. You have sometimes been silent, Don Pedro, when speech would have made your loyalty clear. But I thank you. . . .

[*Columbus turns and looks out at sea : for a moment his attention is fixed. He peers more earnestly into the darkness. There is a movement among the men. He turns.*]

Juan. We are simple men, sir. . . .

Columbus [*hastily*]. Shall simple men judge their betters ?

Guillermo [*surlily*]. We may as well wait till tomorrow, at any rate.

Columbus. Dark deeds are better done in the dark.

[*Guillermo, scowling, but sheepish, slinks off, followed by one or two of the seamen.*]

Francisco. Desperate men do not always act up to the best that is in them, sir.

Columbus [*with quiet irony*]. I thank you for reminding me, Francisco. Your best cannot be bettered. Good-night !

[*Francisco half-turns to speak again, but thinks better of it and goes, shamefaced. Several others go, too, sheepish. A brief silence. Columbus does not move ; he is struggling with overwrought emotion. When he speaks his voice is not steady.*]

Columbus. Go, boy !

[*Pepe seizes his hand, kisses it, and hastily descends to the quarter-deck and goes out.*]

Columbus [*turning to Pedro*]. Two minutes ago, Don Pedro, I saw . . . I thought I saw . . [*He peers into the darkness.*] It was . . . It is . . .

Pedro [*in excitement*]. What, sir ?

Columbus. A light, faintly flickering, rising up and down. Look !   [*He points.*]

Pedro. It *is*, sir !   Glory be to God !

[*At this moment there is a wild shout, off.*]

Voice [*off*]. A light !   A light !   Land !   Land !

[*A sailor comes running on, delirious with joy and excitement.*]

Sailor. Did you see it, sir ?   A light !   Blessed Mother of God !   A light !

Columbus [*with quiet authority*]. Give the order to heave to.

CURTAIN

ELDORADO

By Bernard Gilbert

EDITOR'S PREFACE

When Spanish and English seamen were sailing westward ho! in search of wealth and great adventure, Eldorado was a magical word. It was the Spanish name for a City of Gold, fabled to be hidden in the forests of South America, and so many men sought for it in vain that it has become proverbial for any dream of great wealth.

In this play, "Eldorado," robbed of its romance, is the name of a seed-potato, which was so much in demand at the height of an extraordinary potato-boom that farmers gave amazing prices for it, certain that it would make their fortunes—and found that it did not.

CHARACTERS

JAMES WATSON, *a farmer ; age* 59.
HENRY WATSON, *his son ; age* 20.
BETSY WATSON, *his daughter ; age* 18.
EMMA BURROWS, *a widow, and market gardener ; age* 52.

The play takes place in a disused windmill, occupied by the Watsons as a farmhouse, in the village of Carrington.

ELDORADO

EXTRACT FROM COUNTY DIRECTORY

CARRINGTON, a village at the foot of the Wolds (476 inhabitants) on the river Sow. The principal land-owners are Lord David Herries of Herries Hall, and James Watson, Esquire. Church—St. Peter. Vicar—Rev. W. Martin. Wesleyan Chapel. " The Case is Altered " Inn (James Garvey). " The Nelson Arms " (B. Snow). Railway Station—Belton Junction. Carrington Wood is noted for its primroses. Three great moors—Caxton, Carrington, and Worlby meet here.

The curtain rises one fine March morning on the combined sitting- and dining-room of Jim Watson's farmhouse in the village of Carrington. It doesn't look much like a farmhouse, because it happens to be the bottom story of a disused windmill. The mill is a very substantial circular brick building, quite sixty feet high. Its ground floor is raised above the yard outside to the height of a wagon bottom, and when the outer door (which is in the centre at the back) is opened, a fine view is obtained across Caxton Moor to where Keal Hill rears its head several miles away. The floor of the living-room is of boards, and so is the ceiling, which is supported by stout beams, from which hang an oil lamp, a fine ham, bunches of dried herbs, and strings of onions. The circular brick wall is whitewashed, presenting a rough appearance, and the only attempts at ornament are a couple of the highly coloured almanacs given away by country tradesmen. Light is obtained from two windows placed high up ; one on the extreme left, the other half-

*way round on the right. Their deep ledges draw atten-
tion to the great thickness of the wall. Between the front
door and the left-hand window is a smaller door, opening
into a shed (once a stable) which serves as kitchen and
scullery. Between the right-hand window and the front
door, a step-ladder, close to the wall, leads to a trap-door
in the ceiling. A stout rope hangs from a hook beside
this trap. A clumsy deal table stands in the centre of
the floor, with a chair drawn up on its left. Under the
windows two large wooden bins have been converted
into cupboards, and wooden shoots run from the top of
these to the ceiling. A mill-stone lying on the floor on
the extreme right serves as the base of an iron stove,
whose pipe passes through the wall just under the ceiling.
An armchair occupies a square of coco-nut matting by
the stove, and two plain wooden chairs stand on either
side of the scullery door. On one of these is a small
lidded egg-basket. A square piece of zinc is nailed to
the floor in front of the scullery door, and exactly over
this is a second trap-door with two flaps, through a hole
in the centre of which hangs an endless chain reaching
nearly to the floor. The front door is a very stout affair,
with long iron hinge-plates, an iron bar, and a latch.
On the extreme left, a shaft with pulley wheels is fixed to
the wall.*

*A melancholy whistling is heard outside, and a young
man, coming up the steps to the front door, enters the
room and goes to the stove. Henry Watson is a well-built
fellow of about twenty, wearing a Norfolk jacket, tweed
breeches, and cycling stockings. As he stands holding
his hands out over the top of the stove, a high-pitched
querulous voice comes from above.*

Voice. Is that you, Henry?
Henry. Yes, dad.
[*A creaking of hinges is heard, the right-hand trap-
door is raised, and James Watson, grasping the
rope, descends the ladder backwards. He is a*

small, thin man, in tight cloth trousers, with a tightly-fitting coat of snuff-coloured cloth which he wears buttoned up to his chin. His grizzled beard is short and straggly, and his scanty moustache reveals a mean upper lip. The half-top hat he is wearing may have been black when it was fashionable a generation earlier, but is now green with age. His eyes are small and close together, and his whole appearance is mean and withered.]

James. Well—did you tell 'em what I said ?

Henry. Yes.

James. And what did they say ?

Henry [*laughing shortly*]. Said as they never expected nothing else.

James. Oh, they did, did they ! The bone idle rackapelts ! Beer ! Beer ! Do they think I've got Jackstraw's brewery in the mill-yard ? Here I've found 'em a whole gallon—amongst six of 'em, mind you—nearly a quart apiece—only three days ago, and now they want more ! If they'd turn teetotal and wear blue ribbons, instead of deafening me with their yauping for beer, I should think something of 'em. Did you tell 'em they could fill their bottles with cold tea ?

Henry. Ay ! I said I'd take it to them !

James. Were they thankful ? What did they say ?

Henry [*grinning*]. I don't hardly like to repeat it.

James. Out with it.

Henry. They said you wasn't named " Cheap Jim " for nothing.

James. The shucky mawkins ! If they come and beg on their bended knees for cold tea, they shan't have it now—not a drop ! I'll dock their wages !

Henry. Then they'll go away and we shan't get our potatoes planted.

Mawkins, Used of ugly or unpleasant people. (All the dialect words are Lincolnshire.)

James. As soon as we're a bit slacker, I will !

Henry. You can't cut 'em down any more, dad. We've only got the oldest hands now—what nobody else won't have. It takes 'em most of their time to draw their breath, and they hoe that careful you can see the weeds grown up behind 'em almost as thick as they are in front.

James. Young chaps is no use. If you get a good 'un, he won't stop ; and if you get a bad 'un, you don't want him. In my young days we never had no trouble at all. They were pleased to earn fifteen pence a day, and would very near go down on their knees for it. Nowadays they want us to go down on our knees to get them.

Henry [*interrupting him*]. Tom Harrod came back with me from the field, to fetch another bag of super-phosphate. He knows where it is, in the shed—oh yes, and they want another fork !

James [*anxiously*]. They use that manure as if it was sand. What do they think I'm made of !

Henry. If we don't put manure *in* the ground, we shan't get any crop *out*. This isn't fen land.

James. They use too much. I'll tell him they must be more careful.   [*He makes towards the front door.*]

Henry [*stopping him*]. What about that fork ?

James. Fetch one from the top—the one with the cracked shaft.

[*Henry goes up the steps and disappears through the trap-door. Fainter bangs record his ascent to the fourth story. As James reaches the front door, the scullery door opens and his daughter Betsy hurries out and stops him.*]

Betsy. I haven't got any potatoes for dinner.

James [*trying to get away from her*]. Well, get some.

Betsy. I'm not going through that mucky yard any more. Why can't we have a bag of eaters kept up here, same as you promised.

James. All right ! I'll see to it.

[He breaks loose and runs down the steps into the mill yard.]

Betsy [calling from the top of the steps]. I'm waiting for them !

[She comes inside, shuts the door, and goes to the stove to make the fire up. Betsy Watson is an obstreperous lass of eighteen, with a keen (and constantly outraged) sense of justice. She wears black hand-knitted stockings, a very old and torn tartan skirt, a spotted blue and white blouse, and down-at-heel black walking shoes, whose broken laces are mended with twine. She has on a dirty white apron, and her sleeves are rolled up. Her mass of straight dark-brown hair is thrown on to the top of her head to be secured there by two or three hairpins. Under favourable circumstances Betsy would be a good-looking girl, but constant nagging by her father has made her sullen.

There is a knock on the door, and Betsy, wiping her hands on her apron, goes to open it. The Watsons' next-door neighbour, Widow Burrows, stands on the doorstep.]

Mrs. Burrows. Is your father at home, Betsy ?

Betsy [in a pleased tone]. Why, Mrs. Burrows ! Come inside.

[Emma Burrows carries on the market gardening business of her late husband Nathan, with the help of her two sons, Joe and Abel. She is a biggish woman of over fifty, with iron-grey hair, humorous hazel eyes, dark rather bushy eyebrows, and a moustache. She wears a black bonnet, trimmed with beads, a full black mantle, heavy with jet trimmings, and a very full black skirt which would sweep the floor but for the fact that she has pinned it up in several places with safety pins, thus displaying her stout elastic-sided boots. She has clearly put on her best clothes to pay a call.]

Mrs. Burrows [looking round with intense interest].

I've never been in since your dad made this into a house.

Betsy. I'm ashamed for anybody to come in, Mrs. Burrows—mind that chain! What mother would have said to us living in a broken-down windmill, when that great Manor House belongs to us, I don't know.

Mrs. Burrows. And your poor mother such a strict Methodist! It's enough to make her turn in her grave to have the *parson* living in *her* house. You'd think they'd build a decent vicarage.

Betsy. Dad's made a laughing-stock of us. The boys shout after me when I go into the village.

Mrs. Burrows. When the sails was blown down in that great storm, folks did reckon as your father would be too mean to put 'em up again, specially as there's another mill so near—but nobody dreamt as he'd come to *live* in it. After all, though, it's a deal more comfortable than I'd have thought. [*She puts her head into the outhouse.*] And this is your scullery, is it?

Betsy [*sulkily*]. And kitchen as well. I'm nearly blown away with the draughts in there.

Mrs. Burrows [*returning*]. I suppose you sleep in the room over this?

Betsy [*sarcastically*]. Oh no! That's the best and driest floor, and so it's packed with potatoes.

Mrs. Burrows. Potatoes! Good gracious! Well, I'm glad your dad's got some left, because that's what I came to see him about.

Betsy. We've any amount. They're stored up in bags and hampers and chitting-boxes: that's why we've got a fire. *I* might starve on the coldest day if it wasn't for *them*.

Mrs. Burrows. Where do you sleep, then?

Betsy. Dad and Henry have the room over the

Chitting-boxes, Boxes in which potatoes are put to sprout in a dark place.   **Starve**, Die (of cold).

potatoes, and I'm in the one over that, and then there's one full of apples, and tools, and such-like. The top's empty, 'coz the roof's all broken in.

Mrs. Burrows. You must get a good view up there.

Betsy. I can see Kyme Castle and Sildyke Church on a fine day. They say you can see Barkston, but I never have.

Mrs. Burrows. I should be afraid of rats in a place like this !

Betsy. Oh, bless you, we keep a dog on purpose to catch them. He has to earn his keep, does Jack.

[*The front door is opened, and James Watson returns. Betsy hastily retreats to the scullery and shuts her door.*]

Mrs. Burrows. Good-morning, Mr. Watson.

James. Good-morning, Mrs. Burrows. Sit you down. How are things going with you now ?

Mrs. Burrows. Middling ! You know what a struggle I've had since Nathan died. If it hadn't been for brother-in-law Japhet coming over from Kyme now and again, I don't know how I should have managed.

James. Anybody 'ud be pleased to help you, Mrs. Burrows.

Mrs. Burrows. Then why didn't you lend me a horse and cart last week, when I was stuck fast ?

James [*earnestly*]. I would have done in a minute, only we couldn't manage it. I haven't nearly enough horses.

Mrs. Burrows. You should get more, then.

James. They eat so much. When it rains, they stand in the stable eating and eating, without ever stopping to take breath. I can't bear to see 'em. Every champ costs me a ha'penny.

Mrs. Burrows [*sarcastically*]. I wonder you don't give 'em less.

James. I do, as far as I dare, but the brutes only eat their bedding and nag the mangers.

Mrs. Burrows [*coming to business*]. What I came to see you about, Mr. Watson, was for a bag of your Early Rose potatoes. You've got some, haven't you?

James. Only a few. They're awful scarce this year.

Mrs. Burrows. I saw yours when they was growing. A rare nice patch they looked.

[*Henry comes down the steps with the fork, and hurries out, with a nod to Mrs. Burrows.*]

James. They're shy yielders, them Early Rose. Almost grown out, they are, like all potatoes as lives too long. Why! I can remember 'em when I was a lad only so high. [*He puts his hand near the floor.*] They're nearly all gone now—all them good old sorts —Magnum Bonum, Beauty of Hebron, Myatt's Ash-leaf—beautiful potatoes they was, floury and as sweet as butter.

Mrs. Burrows [*impatiently*]. Yes, yes. But can I have a bag of your Early Roses? They come before anything else in my garden.

James. I don't think you'll get any, anywhere.

Mrs. Burrows. Why?

James. They're so scarce. Tim Williamson of Fletton asked me at Bly Market last Saturday if I had any. He let out that there was very few about, and they're going to a famine price.

Mrs. Burrows. What! He told you that when he was trying to buy some?

James [*scornfully*]. Of course not! That was after I told him I hadn't any to spare.

Mrs. Burrows. Oh, I see! But I only want one bag. You'll let me have that.

James. I'm afraid I can't.

Mrs. Burrows. That's only a dodge to put the price up. Come on! What's the figure?

James. I really can't spare 'em.

Mrs. Burrows. Unless I pay three times what they're worth?

James. You'll not do that, Mrs. Burrows ; you're the closest buyer for miles round Carrington.

Mrs. Burrows. And you're the hardest seller this side the Gulland. How much ?

James [*suddenly turning serious and speaking slowly*]. Very well, then ! I'll let you have a bag as a great favour, being as you're a neighbour and a widow.

Mrs. Burrows. How much ?

James. That'll be all right. Leave the price to me. I shan't hurt you.

Mrs. Burrows. I shan't let you. What's the price ?

James. Twelve shillings.

Mrs. Burrows. Twelve shillings a bag ! Rubbish !

James. That's it, anyhow.

Mrs. Burrows. I shall never pay it.

James. Just as you like. Business is business. You want my potatoes—then you'll have to pay my price for 'em.

[*Henry enters from the yard, and stands by the scullery door, waiting until the old man is free. He plays idly with the endless chain.*]

Mrs. Burrows. I guessed what was up when you wanted me to leave the price. Heaven help anybody as did that ! [*Rising.*] Keep your Early Roses. I'll chit some of my Duke of Yorks instead.

James [*imperturbably*]. As you like, missis.

Mrs. Burrows. I'll get brother-in-law Japhet to send me a bag.

James. The carriage'll kill 'em.

Mrs. Burrows. I'd as leave pay the money to the railway as to you, you old skinflint.

Henry [*picking up his cue*]. We haven't many bags of Early Roses left, dad.

James. I thought not !

Mrs. Burrows. Then keep 'em.

James [*as she reaches the door*]. I'll knock you threepence off.

Chit, Sprout (so that they will grow more rapidly when planted).

Mrs. Burrows. Now you're getting rash! But I won't rob you. Brother-in-law Japhet will send me some. It isn't long since he sent a couple of pounds of some new-fangled sort for me to try.

Henry. What was they called, Mrs. Burrows?

Mrs. Burrows. Elderberry.

Henry. Elderberry?

Mrs. Burrows. It was Elder something—either bush or berry. I've got it! Fennell's Elderberry! Brother-in-law Japhet often sends me odd things down as he gets to try. Good-day, Mr. Watson!

James. Good-day to you, mum!

Mrs. Burrows [*closing and then reopening the door*]. I'll give you four and ninepence for a bag. [*James shakes his head.*] Five shillings, then.

James. Twelve shillings is my—no—I said three-pence off. I'll tell you what I'll do, Mrs. Burrows; I'll call it eleven and sixpence. [*Mrs. Burrows, in answer, bangs the door.*] She'll come back. She's bound to have 'em.

[*Ever since Mrs. Burrows mentioned the two pounds of potatoes " of some new-fangled sort " Henry had listened with the greatest attention, and when she gave the name of " Elderberry," he had gone to the nearest bin, unfolded a newspaper that lay on it, and studied it with care.*]

Henry [*looking up excitedly*]. Dad!

James. What?

Henry. When Widow Burrows said " Elder-some-thing," it came to me all of a sudden what she meant. And when she said Fennell's Elderberry, I was certain. I read about it this morning, here.

James. Who's been wasting their money buying papers? Have you?

Henry. It's to-day's *Bly Chronicle* that Bill Saunders lent me when I was out this morning. It's here, in black and white, all about the Potato Boom.

James. I'm sick of hearing all that cat-blash about

folks getting a pound apiece for potatoes. Now, is it likely? Who'd be fool enough to give it?

Henry [*reading*]. " The excitement in the potato trade continues. At Bly Market there was only one topic of conversation. The promise of the new varieties—Sutton's Discovery, Johnson's Diamond, Northern Star——"

James [*banging the table*]. The lies they tell makes my hair stand straight up.

Henry. It's not all lies, dad. Just listen! " Northern Star has proved a gold-mine to its lucky owners." [*James is about to protest against this waste of time, but these words cause him to relapse into his chair and listen carefully.*] " And every one is alert to secure the next favourite and make a rapid fortune. Mr. Findlay, who brought out the Up-to-Date, Evergood, Royal Kidney, and Northern Star, is reported to have a greater than all these up his sleeve. He sent several lots out, last spring, for trial, to various friends, who are most enthusiastic as to its possibilities. As the quantity is so limited the demand is enormous, and from a sovereign a pound they have risen, in a week, to the unheard-of price of forty pounds a pound. The new-comer promises to live up to its name of Eldorado."

James. We could have done with some of them, Henry. Forty sovereigns for a pound!

Henry. Don't you see, dad—that's the very name. That's what Widow Burrows was trying to say: Fennell's Elder something—Findlay's Eldorado. She's got some!

James [*starting up*]. Do you think so, boy?

Henry. I'm sure of it. The paper says, " Several small lots were sent out for trial," and Japhet Burrows's master, Lord Kyme, as is President of some big Society, would be the first to get them.

James. Well, that's a skelcher. Do you think it's true, Henry?

Henry [*still looking at the paper*]. Here's something else. "As we go to press, we learn that a stone of Eldorados has been sold by a local firm of potato merchants—Messrs. F. Mullen & Son—to Mr. Titus Ambrose of Holt-in-the Marsh at the incredible price of one hundred sovereigns per pound. The cheque for £1,400 is now on view in the window of our fortunate townsmen, and is the centre of the utmost excitement."

James. A hundred sovereigns a pound for potatoes! I shall never believe it.

Henry. The cheque is stuck up in Mullen's office window in Bly market-place. You can't get away from that.

James. Fourteen hundred pounds for a stone of potatoes! [*Suddenly*] Henry! What's Widow Burrows going to do with her two pound?

Henry [*promptly*]. Sell 'em for two hundred pounds, or else do the same as Moses Bellamy did last year with a pound of Northern Stars. He put them in his greenhouse, at Fletton, took the sprouts off into pots, and kept on at that, planting the cuttings out in his garden, till he got two hundredweights from his pound.

James. If I had any, I should *sell*, Henry.

Henry. They'll go dearer yet.

James. We've got to have them Eldorados. That woman couldn't use two hundred pounds: it 'ud be the ruin of her.

Henry. You wouldn't give that price?

James. What do you take me for? She knows nothing about that [*nodding at the paper*] yet.

Henry. She soon will.

James. Then we must move at once. Slip round and say as I've considered to let her have them Early Roses after all. Tell her to come in straightaway and look at 'em—pick her own bag—and then mention her Eldorados, casual-like, and get her to bring them in here to show me.

Henry. She'd smell a rat.

James. Not if you're crafty, Henry. You must be wily with her. Say we reckon we've got some of the same sort and should like to compare 'em. Be quick now, and don't you come back without her. [*Henry hurries out.*] A hundred sovereigns! Two hundred sovereigns! Fourteen hundred sovereigns! It's enough to craze anybody. It's a corker!

[*Betsy comes out of the scullery with a plate of bones.*]

Betsy. Where's them potatoes I asked you for an hour ago?

James [*who is studying the "Chronicle"*]. You don't mean to say as you've never fetched none?

Betsy [*crossing to front door*]. Didn't you promise to see about it?

James. I've plenty to think about, earning your living for you. Why didn't you go and fetch 'em yourself, when you saw it had slipped my memory?

Betsy [*standing on the platform outside the front door, whistling and throwing the bones down into the yard*]. There you are, Jack! [*She comes back into the room without closing the door.*] I'm not going paddling through that mucky yard for nobody.

James. You do what you're told.

Betsy. Why can't I have some of them Early Roses from upstairs? Goodness knows, there's plenty!

James [*looking up from his paper*]. I'll knock your head off if you touch them. They're valuable.

Betsy. I'm tired of this. Nothing but grumbling from morning till night, while I do a servant's work without any pay. I should be better off if I was out at service.

James. You ungrateful mawkin! After all I've done for you! If I hear anything of that again, out you go, neck and crop.

Betsy. That'll suit me down to the ground. I'll go to Doctor Walker's at Bly then. I see in the *Chronicle* that he wants a girl.

James. Think I should have a darter of mine in service ! Just you slip off and get them potatoes.

[*He goes to the door and looks cautiously out.*]

Betsy. I'm not going through all that dirt again for nobody. Just look at my shoes !

[*She holds her foot out, but James takes no notice, so she stamps into the scullery, slamming the door.*]

James. Drat that Henry ! Where's he got to ? I ought to have gone myself. There they come ! She's bringing them !

[*Retreating from the door, he sits down in his armchair, and is poking the fire when Henry and Mrs. Burrows come up the steps. Mrs. Burrows has a paper bag in her hand.*]

Mrs. Burrows. You've changed your mind, then ?

James [*turning round*]. I've considered, Mrs. Burrows, what you said about being neighbourly—and a widow—and I've decided after all, there's something in it.

Mrs. Burrows [*suspiciously*]. I'm to have a bag at my price, am I ?

James. What was your offer ?

Mrs. Burrows [*promptly*]. Five shillings.

James [*staring at the bag in Mrs. Burrows's hand*]. It's fair murder. I wouldn't do it if you wasn't a widow.

Mrs. Burrows. I'll pay for 'em before you change your mind again. Where's my purse ?

[*She puts the bag of potatoes down on the table, and feels for her purse.*]

James. What have you got there ?

Mrs. Burrows [*producing a purse from her pocket*]. Them's the fancy potatoes as brother-in-law Japhet sent me. Your Henry says he thinks you've got some of the same sort, and would like to compare them.

James [*going to the table*]. There isn't two pounds there, surely ?

Mrs. Burrows. They come in separate bags. I didn't bother to bring both. [*She empties the potatoes out on to the table. One rolls over the edge, but Henry catches it, with a horrified face.*] Nice colour, aren't they?

James [*picking up the largest of the five tubers with religious care*]. Nothing to shout about.

Mrs. Burrows. Look at their deep eyes!

James. All the worse for cooking. They waste so much.

Mrs. Burrows. But the shape of them!

James. Wouldn't be many to a root, I lay!

Mrs. Burrows. Don't you like 'em, then?

James. No, I don't. No good at all! [*He turns away, then comes back, fascinated.*] No good at all!

Mrs. Burrows. Brother-in-law Japhet thought they was worth my trying, anyway, and he ought to know his trade.

James. Gardening isn't farming, though. What's all right for the gentry's table wouldn't answer for the likes of us. These wouldn't do for field growing.

Mrs. Burrows [*beginning to put the potatoes back in the bag*]. Deary me!

James [*poking the fire*]. If you take my advice, you'll chuck 'em to the pigs.

Mrs. Burrows. That would be a waste, Mr. Watson.

James. Betsy was bothering me just now for some potatoes for dinner. She might as well cook them, and I'll tell you how they eat.

Mrs. Burrows. I shouldn't like them to be cooked.

James. It's all they're fit for, I assure you.

Mrs. Burrows. Brother-in-law Japhet wouldn't like it.

James [*feeling in his pocket*]. It'll save Betsy getting messed up. I'll give you tuppence for 'em—that's over two shillings a stone.

Henry [*chiming in*]. Nearly twenty pounds a ton!

James [*holding out coppers*]. There's threepence

ha'penny. There you are! I shouldn't do it, only the gel's been worrying me so.

[*He takes the bag from Mrs. Burrows and puts the coppers on the table.*]

Mrs. Burrows. I couldn't, really.

James. Why not?

Mrs. Burrows. Brother-in-law Japhet wanted me to grow 'em, and he wouldn't like it.

James. I'll give you sixpence, then.

Mrs. Burrows. Brother-in-law Ja——

James [*bursting out irritably*]. Confound brother-in-law Japhet! Keep your potatoes!

Mrs. Burrows [*taking the bag from him*]. I think he'd rather I planted 'em. [*She sees the largest tuber in James's hand and reaches out for it.*] Thank you!

James [*waving her off*]. Wait a minute! [*He looks carefully at the Eldorado.*] I don't know, after all, as they mightn't answer in our garden, Henry. I almost think, Mrs. Burrows, as I will set 'em and see how they turn out.

Mrs. Burrows. You said they wasn't any use at all, just now.

James. I think so still, only I like to try new things. Look here! I'll give you a peck of Early Roses in exchange.

[*Mrs. Burrows's suspicions have now come to a head. She looks at James, then at Henry, then at the bag in her hand, and with tightened lips reaches for the largest Eldorado that James still clasps.*]

James. Is that a bargain?

Mrs. Burrows. I'll plant 'em myself. Brother-in-law Japhet sent them on purpose.

James [*edging away from her*]. You've got a pound left, ain't you? We can both try 'em. I'll give you two pecks of Early Roses.

Mrs. Burrows [*still holding her hand out*]. No, I'll keep them. Give us hold of that.

James. Don't be in such a hurry. I'll do you a level

swop—the bag of Early Roses as you want so bad, for this pound.

Mrs. Burrows. Brother-in-law Japhet wouldn't have sent them if they hadn't been something extra special.

James. What *do* you want then, woman ?

Mrs. Burrows. My potato.

[*She seizes the one in old Watson's hand, drops it into the bag, and turns to go. James hurries between her and the door.*]

James. Now look here, Mrs. Burrows ; I'll buy 'em if you'll be ruly and set a price. Come now, what is it ?

Mrs. Burrows [*looking at him for a moment in silence*]. What about them seven young pigs as I tried to buy from you, and you wouldn't part with ?

James. I told you I couldn't sell them. Their father won a prize at Barkston Show.

Mrs. Burrows. I bid you nineteen shillings apiece.

James. But they're not for sale.

Mrs. Burrows. If you offered to give me that sack of Early Roses for this pound [*she holds the bag up, and James puts his hand out eagerly*], and throw in that litter of black pigs, I might consider it.

James. What ! My prize pigs ! You're crazed ! Talk sense, woman. If you'd asked for one now——

Mrs. Burrows. You'd have closed with me, shouldn't you ? You're strange and keen for this pound of potatoes.

[*Henry, who has been making signs to his father behind Mrs. Burrows's back, sits down suddenly, the picture of despair.*]

James. Keen ? Me ? Not a bit ! Keep 'em ! Keep 'em !

Mrs. Burrows. I'm going to.

James [*catching her arm*]. Be reasonable, woman. I'll try and buy them.

Mrs. Burrows. I am reasonable. As you said a bit since : business is business, and if you want my potatoes, you've got to pay my price for them.

James. My prize pigs ! I couldn't.

Mrs. Burrows. Then good-day to you !

[*As she puts her hand on the latch, Henry signals wildly to his father.*]

James. All right ! They're yours.

Mrs. Burrows. Oh no ! Not now. You should have took my offer when I made it.

James. Look here ! Say straight out what you do want.

Mrs. Burrows [*coming back to the table*]. I want that sack of Early Roses, the litter of black pigs, [*she points to the ham hanging from the beam*] that ham, [*she considers for a moment*] . . . and thirty shillings.

James. You never said nothing about a ham and thirty shillings.

Mrs. Burrows. Is it a deal ? I shan't wait.

James [*wildly*]. Yes, drat you !

Mrs. Burrows [*putting the Eldorados on the table*]. There you are, then. Where's the money ?

James [*putting the money on the table*]. You—you—

[*He chokes with spleen.*]

Mrs. Burrows [*calmly*]. Hook my ham down, Henry, and don't bruise it.

James. I'll do that. Fetch a bag of Early Roses down, and then tell young Fox to drive them pigs across.

[*Henry hurries upstairs, whilst James gets on a chair and hooks down the ham.*]

Mrs. Burrows [*taking the ham*]. This is a nice mellow ham, this is. Better'n the scrawdy bacon as I've been having for breakfast lately.

James. You've done me this time, missis.

Mrs. Burrows. You pleased yourself. Do you want to run back ? [*James shakes his head.*] I've been a fool ; that's what I've been ! I see it now. You'd have given more.

James. No, you hard nailer ! You've shaved me clean. My prize pigs !

Scrawdy, Fat, with only a thin streak of lean.

[*The left-hand trap-doors are lifted, and as Henry calls
" Below, there," James walks across to the chain,
which begins to move. As a sack of potatoes
swings into sight, James steadies the chain, and
when the bag reaches the floor, unfastens the slip
hook from its neck and lays the bag over on its
side. Henry closes the trap-doors.*]

James. What about the other pound ?

Mrs. Burrows. I wouldn't sell them for no money.

James. Oh yes, you would !

Mrs. Burrows. I tell you I wouldn't . . . I wouldn't
take twenty pounds for 'em.

James. Twenty pounds !

Mrs. Burrows. No, I wouldn't. Brother-in-law
Japhet——

James. Take ten.

Mrs. Burrows. Now, is it likely ? You've given
me more for *that* pound. [*Henry comes down the steps,
goes over to the zinc plate, takes hold of the bag of Early
Roses, and with an adroit jerk throws them over his
shoulder, and walks out of the door with them.*] You
must think me a fool.

James. All right, then ! Twenty pound !

Mrs. Burrows. Certainly not ! I said I wouldn't
take twenty pounds ; and I won't. They're not for
sale.

James. Oh, we know all about that. Everything
has its price.

Mrs. Burrows [*picking the ham off the table and
going to the door*]. That's just where you're wrong. I
shall keep my pound and see what happens.

James [*contemptuously*]. What do *you* know about
new sorts of potatoes ?

Mrs. Burrows [*turning in the doorway*]. Nothing at
all. But I know a good deal about *you*, Jim Watson.
[*Looking to the left, towards the road.*] There goes my
prize pigs.

James. Thirty pounds, then !

Mrs. Burrows [*shaking her head scornfully*]. I should have took sixpence for them potatoes, only your eyes were so greedy. I may be only a woman, but I can tell when you're anxious. It's nice to get the best of you, just for once.

[*Carrying the ham in front of her, she descends the steps and disappears. James stares after her with a discomfited air ; then recollects himself, goes to the table, picks up the bag, and reads aloud,* FINDLAY'S ELDORADO. *He looks round thoughtfully, and his eye falls on the egg-basket standing on the chair. He takes out the tubers one by one, placing them in the basket.*]

James. I'll fetch my cash-box down and lock 'em in that. I could keep 'em in yon cupboard by the stove : it 'ud be warm there.

[*He goes up the steps. As the trap-door closes behind him the scullery door opens, and Betsy is seen in the doorway, standing in a defiant attitude, with her hands on her hips. But there is no one to defy, so with a toss of her head she makes for the front door, to be brought to a standstill by the sight of the basket of potatoes.*]

Betsy [*with great scorn*]. Five potatoes for three people !

[*Holding up her apron, she tilts the potatoes in and replaces the basket. Its lid falls down. Betsy returns to her stronghold and closes the door. The trap-door opens, and James comes down with a large cash-box under his arm. As he reaches the floor Henry hurries in from the yard.*]

Henry [*excitedly*]. We've got 'em !

James [*pulling out a bunch of keys and trying to find one that will fit the cash-box*]. At a price.

Henry. It was all your own fault. You should have closed with her quicker. [*He sees the empty paper bag that James has replaced on the table.*] Where are they ?

James. In that basket ; but I'm going to lock 'em up in this—if I can find the key. Here ! just see if you've one that'll fit it.

Henry [*producing a bunch*]. It must go under our bed, dad. Suppose anybody stole them.

James. Don't, boy. You make me all of a sweat. I wish I had an iron safe.

Henry. You couldn't get the other pound, then ?

James. No, confound all widows ! Hallo !

[*Mrs. Burrows is seen hurrying up the steps. She enters the room, still carrying the ham, which she plants on the table.*]

James [*uneasily*]. Back again, Mrs. Burrows ?

Mrs. Burrows. You thief. Robbing a poor widow ! But I'll show you up ; I'll expose you if you don't give me my Eldorados back. Where are they ?

[*Henry, at her first word, edged away from the table, and now stands with his back to the egg-basket, hiding it from view.*]

James. What's this all about ?

Mrs. Burrows. What's it all about ? You know very well what it's all about. This telegram was waiting at the door when I got home—from brother-in-law Japhet. [*She holds up a telegram and reads*] JUST HEARD ELDORADOS SENT YOU WORTH TWO HUNDRED POUNDS. LOCK THEM UP. COMING ONE THIRTY-FIVE. — JAPHET. You scanny rascal — you knew it.

James. I don't know what you mean.

Mrs. Burrows. You just give 'em back to me. Where are they ?

James. Bought *and* paid for.

Mrs. Burrows [*pushing the ham across the table towards him*]. You can have your pigs and all the rest of your kelter back again. Where's my Eldorados ?

James. Business is business, Mrs. Burrows. You

Kelter, Rubbish.

thought you'd diddled me—well, you didn't, that's all ! Anyway, you've got one pound left.

Mrs. Burrows. I want them both. What will brother-in-law Japhet say ?

James. I've nothing to do with your brother-in-law Japhet, nor him with me, neither.

Mrs. Burrows. Oh, haven't you ? Wait till he comes : he'll wring your neck—you little ferret !

James. I shall have him locked up if he comes brawling here.

Mrs. Burrows [*a little daunted, remembering Japhet's ungovernable temper*]. We don't want no policemen interfering.

James. Then be ruly ! A bargain's a bargain, and it's no use chuntering. [*He pushes the ham back.*]

Mrs. Burrows. You lied to me so—saying you wanted 'em for your dinner !

James [*pulling his purse out*]. Here ! One—two—three sovereigns. All I've got. I'll throw that in if you hold your noise and call it quits. If you don't, Henry fetches Tom Arch. You know how hot-tempered your brother-in-law is, and if you go and sing a song to him about this, there's bound to be a row, and he'll get locked up as sure as eggs is eggs. [*He holds out the money to her.*] Come on, now ! It's no use roaring.

Mrs. Burrows [*wavering*]. Make it ten pounds.

James [*sharply*]. Not a copper more. Take it or leave it.

Mrs. Burrows [*taking the cash and picking up her ham*]. But I don't know what I shall tell brother-in-law Japhet !

James. You can come away from that chair now, Henry.

Mrs. Burrows. Oh, that's where they was ! [*She steps across and raises the basket lid.*] Why, it's empty !

Chuntering. Grumbling.

Henry and James [*rushing forward and shouting together*]. What !

James. She's took 'em. Hold her, Henry.

Mrs. Burrows. Don't be a fool. How could I, with you gaping at me all the time ?

James. I put 'em in there out of the bag. I'll swear I did. [*The two men search frantically, whilst Mrs. Burrows watches with interest ; but there are so few places in which to look that in a very short time they are staring blankly at each other. The scullery door opens and Betsy appears with a saucepan in her hand, evidently disturbed by the noise.*] Betsy ! I put some potatoes in that basket. Have you seen them ?

Betsy. In that basket ?

James. Yes. Wake up ! Have you moved them ?

Betsy. Of course I moved them.

James [*with an air of enormous relief*]. Where have you put them ? Where are they ?

Betsy. Where are they ? [*Holding the saucepan under James's nose.*] They're here, of course. Where do you think ?

Together {

James. Ruined ! My Eldorados ! My prize pigs !

Henry. Oh, my hat, Betsy. What *have* you done ?

Mrs. Burrows. Well, I never. If she hasn't gone and peeled them !

}

Betsy [*to Mrs. Burrows*]. Of course I peeled them ! [*To her father*] Didn't you put them there for me ?

[*James and Henry are speechless.*]

Mrs. Burrows. Serve you right ! Serve you right ! You said you wanted them for your dinner, and you've got them. [*She opens the door.*] Ten pounds a mouthful ! I HOPE YOU'LL ENJOY YOUR DINNER !

[*She closes the door.*]

CURTAIN

CAMPBELL OF KILMOHR

By J. A. Ferguson

This is the definitive edition of *Campbell of Kilmohr*, with the author's final revisions of the text, made especially for this volume, and his Acting Notes (see page 219). The correct spelling of the title is that given here.

EDITOR'S PREFACE

The scene of the play is the Highlands of Scotland, in the winter of the year 1746. George II. was King of England, but in the Highlands many people still believed that the rightful king was Charles Edward Stuart, grandson of James II., who is known in history as the Young Pretender. He had landed in Scotland with seven followers in July 1745, gathered his Highland supporters, who were charmed by his gallant and attractive personality, entered Edinburgh, and marched south to within a hundred and twenty miles of London before he was compelled to retreat. He won a victory at Falkirk, but in April 1746 his army was overwhelmed at Culloden by the Duke of Cumberland, who had trained his men to meet the terrible charge of the Highlanders. With a reward of £30,000 offered for his capture, and armies searching the country for him, Charles Edward became a fugitive in the Highlands; but through all his adventures and hardships and hairbreadth escapes, the bravery of Flora Macdonald and the passionate loyalty of his friends kept him safe, and he escaped to France at the end of the year 1746. How loyal his followers were, and how they hated Scotsmen who were on the side of King George, we learn in this play from Mary and Dugald Stewart. They are as determined to save their Prince and his friends, who are in hiding not far away, as Campbell of Kilmohr is anxious to get the £30,000 reward.

Produced by the Scottish Repertory Theatre Company at the Royalty Theatre, Glasgow, on Monday, March 23, 1914, with the following cast :

MARY STEWART	Miss Agnes Lowson.
MORAG CAMERON . . .	Miss Rita Thom.
DUGALD STEWART . .	Mr. Nicholas Hannen.
CAPTAIN SANDEMAN . .	Mr. N. N. Wimbush.
ARCHIBALD CAMPBELL .	Mr. W. S. Hartford.
JAMES MACKENZIE . . .	Mr. C. Stewart Robertson.

SCENE.—Interior of a lonely cottage on the road from Struan to Rannoch in North Perthshire.

TIME.—After the Rising of '45.

The Play produced by Mr. Lewis Casson.

CAMPBELL OF KILMOHR

Morag is restlessly moving backwards and forwards. The old woman is seated on a low stool beside the peat fire in the centre of the floor.

The room is scantily furnished and the women are poorly clad. Morag is barefooted. At the back is the door that leads to the outside. On the left of the door is a small window. On the right side of the room there is a door that opens into a barn. Morag stands for a moment at the window, looking out.

Morag. It is the wild night outside.

Mary Stewart. Is the snow still coming down ?

Morag. It is that then—dancing and swirling with the wind too, and never stopping at all. Aye, and so black I cannot see the other side of the road.

Mary Stewart. That is good.

[*Morag moves across the floor and stops irresolutely. She is restless, expectant.*]

Morag. Will I be putting the light in the window ?

Mary Stewart. Why should you be doing that ! You have not heard his call [*turns eagerly*], have you ?

Morag [*with sign of head*]. No, but the light in the window would show him all is well.

Mary Stewart. It would not then ! The light was to be put there *after* we had heard the signal.

Morag. But on a night like this he may have been calling for long and we never hear him.

Mary Stewart. Do not be so anxious, Morag. Keep to what he says. Put more peat on the fire now and sit down.

Morag [*with increasing excitement*]. I canna, I canna! There is that in me that tells me something is going to befall us this night. Oh, that wind, hear to it, sobbing round the house as if it brought some poor lost soul up to the door, and we refusing it shelter.

Mary Stewart. Do not be fretting yourself like that. Do as I bid you. Put more peats to the fire.

Morag [*at the wicker peat-basket*]. Never since I . . . What was that?   [*Both listen for a moment.*]

Mary Stewart. It was just the wind; it is rising more. A sore night for them that are out in the heather.

          [*Morag puts peat on the fire without speaking.*]

Mary Stewart. Did you notice were there many people going by to-day?

Morag. No. After daybreak the redcoats came by from Struan; and there was no more till nine, when an old man like the Catechist from Killichonan passed. At four o'clock, just when the dark was falling, a horseman with a lad holding to the stirrup, and running fast, went by towards Rannoch.

Mary Stewart. But no more redcoats?

Morag [*shaking her head*]. The road has been as quiet as the hills, and they as quiet as the grave. Do you think he will come?

Mary Stewart. Is it you think I have the gift, girl, that you ask me that? All I know is that it is five days since he was here for meat and drink for himself and for the others—five days and five nights, mind you; and little enough he took away; and those in hiding no' used to sore lying I'll be thinking. He must try to get through to-night. But that quietness, with no one to be seen from daylight till dark, I do not like it, Morag. They must know something. They must be watching.

          [*A sound is heard by both women. They stand listening.*]

Mary Stewart. Haste you with the light, Morag.

Morag. But it came from the back of the house—from the hillside.

Mary Stewart. Do as I tell you. The other side may be watched.

[*A candle is lit and placed in the window. Girl goes hurrying to the door.*]

Mary Stewart. Stop, stop! Would you be opening the door with a light like that shining from the house? A man would be seen against it in the doorway for a mile. And who knows what eyes may be watching? Put out the light now and cover the fire.

[*Room is reduced to semi-darkness, and the door unbarred. Some one enters.*]

Morag. You are cold, Dugald!

[*Stewart, very exhausted, signs assent.*]

Morag. And wet, oh, wet through and through!

Stewart. Erricht Brig was guarded, well guarded. I had to win across the water.

[*The old woman has now relit candle and taken away plaid from fire.*]

Mary Stewart. Erricht Brig—then——

Stewart [*nods*]. Yes—in a corrie, on the far side of Dearig, half-way up.

Mary Stewart. Himself is there then?

Stewart. Aye, and Keppoch as well, and another and a greater is with them.

Mary Stewart. Wheest! [*Glances at Morag.*]

Stewart. Mother, is it that you can . . .

Mary Stewart. Yes, yes, Morag will bring out the food for ye to carry back. It is under the hay in the barn, well hid. Morag will bring it. Go, Morag, and bring it.

[*Morag enters other room or barn which opens on right.*]

Stewart. Mother, I wonder at ye; Morag would never tell—never.

Mary Stewart. Morag is only a lass yet. She has

never been tried.   And who knows what she might
be made to tell.

Stewart. Well, well, it is no matter, for I was telling
you where I left them, but not where I am to *find*
them.

Mary Stewart. They are not where you said now ?

Stewart. No ; they left the corrie last night, and I
am to find them [*whispers*] in a quiet part on Rannoch
Moor.

Mary Stewart. It is well for a young lass not to be
knowing.   Do not tell her.

Stewart. Well, well, I will not tell her.   Then she
cannot tell where they are even if she wanted to.

[*He sits down at table ; the old woman ministers to his
      wants.*]

Stewart. A fire is a merry thing on a night like this ;
and a roof over the head is a great comfort.

Mary Stewart. Ye'll no' can stop the night ?

Stewart. No.   I must be many a mile from here
before the day breaks on Ben Dearig.

[*Morag re-enters.*]

Morag. It was hard to get through, Dugald ?

Stewart. You may say that.   I came down Erricht
for three miles, and then when I reached low country
I had to take to walking in the burns because of the
snow that shows a man's steps and tells who he is to
them that can read ; and there's plenty can do that
abroad, God knows.

Morag. But none spied ye ?

Stewart. Who can tell ?   Before dark came, from far
up on the slopes of Dearig I saw soldiers down below ;
and away towards Rannoch Moor they were scattered
all over the country like black flies on a white sheet.
A wild-cat or anything that couldna fly could never
have got through.   And men at every brig and ford
and pass !   I had to strike away up across the slopes
again ; and even so as I turned round the bend beyond Kilrain I ran straight into a sentry sheltering

behind a great rock. But after that it was easy going.

Morag. How could that be ?

Stewart. Well, you see, I took the boots off him, and then I had no need to mind who might see my steps in the snow.

Morag. You took the boots off him !

Stewart [*laughing*]. I did that same. Does that puzzle your bonny head ? How does a lad take the boots off a redcoat ? Find out the answer, my lass, while I will be finishing my meat.

Morag. Maybe he was asleep ?

Stewart. Asleep ! Asleep ! Well, well, he sleeps sound enough now, with the ten toes of him pointed to the sky.

[*The old woman has taken up dirk from table. She puts it down again. Morag sees the action, and pushes dirk away so that it rolls off the table and drops to the floor. She hides her face in her hands.*]

Mary Stewart. Morag, bring in the kebbuck o' — cheese. Now that all is well and safe it is we that will look after his comfort to-night. [*Morag goes into barn.*] I mind well her mother saying to me—it was one day in the black winter that she died, when the frost took the land in its grip and the birds fell stiff from the trees, and the deer came down and put their noses to the door—I mind well her saying just before she died—— [*Loud knocking at the door*].

A Voice. In the King's name ! [*Both rise, startled.*]

Mary Stewart [*recovering first*]. The hay in the barn—quick, my son. [*Knocking continues.*]

A Voice. Open in the King's name !

[*Stewart snatches up such articles as would reveal his presence and hurries into barn. He overlooks dirk on floor. The old woman goes towards door, slowly, to gain time.*]

Mary Stewart. Who is there ? What do you want ?

A Voice. Open, open.

[*Mary Stewart opens door, and Campbell of Kilmohr*
follows Captain Sandeman into the house. Be-
hind Kilmohr comes a man carrying a leather
wallet, James Mackenzie, his clerk. The rear
is brought up by soldiers carrying arms.]

Sandeman. Ha, the bird has flown.

Campbell [*who has struck dirk with his foot and*
picked it up]. But the nest is warm ; look at this.

Sandeman. It seems as if we had disturbed him at
supper. Search the house, men.

Mary Stewart. I'm just a lonely old woman. You
have been misguided. I was getting through my
supper.

Campbell [*holding up dirk*]. And this was your
toothpick, eh ? Na ! na ! We ken whaur we are,
and wha we want, and, by Cruachan, I think we've
got him.

[*Sounds are heard from barn, and soldiers return with*
Morag. She has stayed in hiding from fear, and
she still holds the cheese in her hands.

Sandeman. What have we here !

Campbell. A lass !

Mary Stewart. It's just my dead brother's daughter.
She was getting me the cheese, as you can see.

Campbell. On men, again : the other turtle-doo will
no' be far away. [*Bantering, to the old woman.*] Tut,
tut, Mistress Stewart, and do ye have her wait
upon ye while your leddyship dines alane ! A grand
way to treat your dead brother's daughter ; fie, fie,
upon ye !

[*Soldiers reappear with Stewart, whose arms are*
pinioned.]

Campbell. Did I no' tell ye ! And this, Mrs.
Stewart, will be your dead sister's son, I'm thinking ;
or aiblins your leddyship's butler ! Weel, woman,

Aiblins, Perhaps.

I'll tell ye this : Pharaoh spared ae butler, but
Erchie Campbell will no spare anither. Na ! na !
Pharaoh's case is no' to be taken as forming ony
preceedent. And so if he doesna answer certain
questions we have to speir at him, before morning
he'll hang as high as Haman.

[*Stewart is placed before the table at which Campbell
has seated himself. Two soldiers guard Stewart.
Another is behind Campbell's chair and another
is by the door. The clerk, Mackenzie, is seated
at up corner of table. Sandeman stands by the
fire.*

Campbell [*to Stewart*]. Weel, sir, it is within the
cognizance of the law that you have knowledge and
information of the place of harbour and concealment
used by certain persons who are in a state of proscription. Furthermore, it is known that four days
ago certain other proscribed persons did join with
these, and that they are banded together in an en-
deavour to secure the escape from these dominions
of His Majesty, King George, of certain persons who
by their crimes and treasons lie open to the capital
charge. What say ye ?   [*Stewart makes no reply.*]

Campbell. Ye admit this then ?
[*Stewart as before.*]

Campbell. Come, come, my lad. Ye stand in great
jeopardy. Great affairs of state lie behind this which
are beyond your simple understanding. Speak up,
and it will be the better for ye.
[*Stewart silent as before.*]

Campbell. Look you. I'll be frank with you. No
harm will befall you this night (and I wish all in this
house to note my words)—no harm will befall you
this night if you supply the information required.
[*Stewart as before.*]

Campbell [*with sudden passion*]. Sandeman, put

Speir, Ask.

your sword to the carcass o' this muckle ass and see will it louse his tongue.   [*Sandeman does not move.*]

Stewart. It may be as well then, Mr. Campbell, that I should say a word to save your breath.   It is this : Till you talk Rannoch Loch to the top of Schiehallion ye'll no' talk me into a yea or nay.

Campbell [*quietly*]. Say ye so ?   Noo, I wadna be so very sure if I were you.   I've had a lairge experience o' life, and speaking out of it I would say that only fools and the dead never change their minds.

Stewart [*quietly too*]. Then you'll be adding to your experience to-night, Mr. Campbell, and you'll have something to put on to the other side of it.

Campbell [*tapping his snuff-box*]. Very possibly, young sir, but what I would present for your consideration is this : While ye may be prepared to keep your mouth shut under the condition of a fool, are ye equally prepared to do so in the condition of a dead man ?

[*Campbell waits expectantly.   Stewart silent as before.*]

Campbell. Tut, tut, now if it's afraid ye are, my lad, with my hand on my heart and on my word as a gentleman . . .

Stewart. Afraid !

[*He spits in contempt towards Campbell.*]

Campbell [*enraged*]. Ye damned stubborn Hieland stot . . .   [*To Sandeman*] Have him taken out. We'll get it another way.

[*Campbell rises.   Stewart is moved into barn by soldiers, who remain with him.*]

Campbell [*walking*]. Some puling eediots, Sandeman, would applaud this contumacy and call it constancy.   Constancy !   Now, I've had a lairge experience o' life, and I never saw yet a sensible man insensible to the touch of yellow metal.   If there may

---

Muckle, Great.   *Stot,* Bullock.

be such a man, it is demonstrable that he is no sensible man. Fideelity! quotha, it's sheer obstinacy. They just see that ye want something oot o' them, and they're so damned selfish and thrawn they winna pairt. And with the natural inabeelity o' their brains to hold mair than one idea at a time, they canna see that in return you could put something into their palms far more profitable. [*Sits again at table.*] Aweel, bring Mistress Stewart up.

[*Old woman is placed before him where son had been.*]

Campbell [*more ingratiatingly*]. Weel noo, Mistress Stewart, good woman, this is a sair predeecament for ye to be in. I would jist counsel ye to be candid. Doubtless yer mind is a' in a swirl. Ye kenna what way to turn. Maybe ye are like the Psalmist and say: " I lookit this way and that, and there was no man to peety me, or to have compassion upon my fatherless children." But, see now, ye would be wrong; and, if ye tell me a' ye ken, I'll stand freends wi' ye. Put your trust in Erchie Campbell.

Mary Stewart. I trust no Campbell.

Campbell. Weel, weel, noo, I'm no' jist that set up wi' them myself. There's but ae Campbell that I care muckle aboot, after a'. But, good wife, it's no' the Campbells we're trying the noo; so, as time presses, we'll jist *birze yont*, as they say themselves. Noo then, speak up. [*Mary Stewart is silent.*]

Campbell [*beginning grimly and, passing through astonishment, expostulation, and a feigned contempt for mother and pity for son, to a pretence of sadness which, except at the end, makes his words come haltingly*]. Ah! ye also. I suppose ye understand, woman, how it will go wi' your son? [*To his clerk.*] Here's a fine mother for ye, James! Would you believe it? She kens what would save her son—the very babe she nursed at her breast; but will she save him? Na!

Kenna, Know not.   *Birze yont,* Press forward.

na! Sir, he may look after himself! A mother, a mother! Ha! ha!

[*Campbell laughs. Mackenzie titters foolishly. Campbell pauses to watch effect of his words.*]

Aye, you would think, James, that she would remember the time when he was but little and afraid of all the terrors that walk in darkness, and how he looked up to her as to a tower of safety, and would run to her with outstretched hands, hiding his face from his fear, in her gown. The darkness! It is the dark night and a long journey before him now.

[*He pauses again.*]

You would think, James, that she would mind how she happit him from the cold of winter and sheltered him from the summer heats, and, when he began to find his footing, how she had an eye on a' the beasts of the field, and on the water and the fire that were become her enemies. And to what purpose all this care?—tell me that, my man, to what good, if she is to leave him at the last to dangle from a tree at the end of a hempen rope—to see his flesh to be meat for the fowls of the air—her son, her little son!

Mary Stewart [*softly*]. My son—my little son! . . . Oh, [*more loudly*] but my son he has done no crime.

Campbell. Has he no'? Weel, mistress, as ye'll no' take my word for it, maybe ye'll list to Mr. Mackenzie here. What say ye, James?

Mackenzie. He is guilty of aiding and abetting in the concealment of proscribed persons; likewise with being found in the possession of arms, contrary to statute, both very heinous crimes.

Campbell. Very well said, James! Forby, between ourselves, Mrs. Stewart, the young man in my opeenion is guilty of another crime [*snuffs*]—he is guilty of the heinous crime of not knowing on which side his bread is buttered. Come now. . . .

Happit, Covered.   *Forby*, Besides.

Mary Stewart. Ye durst not lay a finger on the lad, ye durst not hang him.

Mackenzie. And why should the gentleman not hang him if it pleesure him?

[*Campbell taps snuff-box and takes pinch.*]

Mary Stewart [*with intensity*]. Campbell of Kilmohr, lay but one finger on Dugald Stewart and the weight of Ben Cruachan will be light to the weight that will be laid on your soul. I will lay the curse of the seven rings upon your life. I will call up the fires of Ephron, the blue and the green and the grey fires, for the destruction of your soul. I will curse you in your homestead and in the wife it shelters, and in the children that will never bear your name. Yea and ye shall be cursed.

Campbell [*startled, betrays agitation—the snuff is spilt from his trembling hand*]. Hoot toot, woman! ye're, ye're . . . [*Angrily.*] Ye auld beldame, to say such things to me! I'll have ye first whippit and syne droont for a witch. Damn thae stubborn and supersteetious cattle! [*To Sandeman.*] We should have come in here before him and listened in the barn, Sandeman!

Sandeman [*in quick staccato, always cool*]. Ah, listen behind the door you mean! Now I never thought of that!

Campbell. Did ye not! Humph! Well, no doubt there are a good many things in the universe that yet wait for your thought upon them. What would be your objections, now?

Sandeman. There are two objections, Kilmohr, that you would understand.

Campbell. Name them.

Sandeman. Well, in the first place, we have not wings like crows to fly . . . and the footsteps on the snow. . . . Second point: the woman would have told him we were there.

Syne droont, Then drowned.

Campbell. Not if I told her I had the power to clap her in Inverness jail.

Mary Stewart [*in contempt*]. Yes, even if ye had told me ye had power to clap me in hell, Mr. Campbell.

Campbell. Lift me that screeching Jezebel oot o' here ; Sandeman, we'll mak' a quick finish o' this. [*Soldiers take her towards barn.*] No, not there, pitch the old girzie into the snow.

Mary Stewart [*as she is led outside*]. Ye'll never find him, Campbell, never, never !

Campbell [*enraged*]. Find him, aye, by God I'll find him, if I have to keek under every stone on the mountains from the Boar of Badenoch to the Sow of Athole. [*Old woman and soldiers go outside, leaving only Campbell, Mackenzie, Sandeman, and Morag in the room ; Morag huddled up on stool.*] And now, Captain Sandeman, you an' me must have a word or two. I noted your objection to listening ahint doors and so on. Now, I make a' necessary allowances for youth and the grand and magneeficent ideas commonly held, for a little while, in that period. I had them myself. But, man, gin ye had trod the floor of the Parliament Hoose in Edinburry as long as I did, wi' a pair o' thin hands at the bottom o' toom pockets, ye'd ha'e shed your fine notions, as I did. Noo, fine pernickety noansense will no' do in this business——

Sandeman. Sir !

Campbell. Softly, softly, Captain Sandeman, and hear till what I have to say. I have noticed with regret several things in your remarks and bearing which are displeasing to me. I would say just one word in your ear ; it is this : These things, Sandeman, are not conducive to advancement in His Majesty's service.

Sandeman [*after a brief pause in which the two eye*

Girzie, Noisy woman.　　　　　　　*Toom,* Empty.

each other]. Kilmohr, I am a soldier, and if I speak out my mind you must pardon me if my words are blunt : I do not like this work, but I *loathe* your methods.

Campbell. Mislike the methods you may, but the work ye must do ! Methods are my business. Let me tell you the true position. In ae word it is no more and no less than this. You and me are baith here to carry out the proveesions of the Act for the Pacification of the Highlands. That means the cleaning up of a very big mess, Sandeman, a very big mess. Now, what is your special office in this work ? I'll tell ye, man ; you and your men are just beesoms in the hands of the law-officers of the Crown. In this district, I order and ye soop. [*He indicates door of barn.*] Now soop, Captain Sandeman.

Sandeman. What are you after ? I would give something to see into your mind.

Campbell. Ne'er fash aboot my mind : what has a soldier to do with ony mental operations ? It's His Grace's orders that concern you. Oot wi' your man and set him up against the wa'.

Sandeman. Kilmohr, it is murder—murder, Kilmohr !

Campbell. Hoots awa', man, it's a thing o' nae special signeeficence.

Sandeman. I must ask you for a warrant.

Campbell. Quick, then : Mackenzie will bring it out to you.

[*Clerk begins writing as Sandeman goes and orders the soldiers to lead Stewart outside. Campbell sits very still and thoughtful. Clerk finishes writing and places warrant before Campbell for his signature.*

Mackenzie. At this place, sir.

Campbell [*again alert*]. Hoots, I was forgetting.

Mackenzie. It is a great power ye have in your hands, Kilmohr, to be able to send a man to death on the nod, as ye might say.

Campbell [*sitting back, pen in hand*]. Power ! power
say ye ? Man, do ye no' see I've been beaten. Do
ye no' see that ? Archibald Campbell and a' his men
and his money are less to them than the wind blowing
in their faces.

Mackenzie. Well, it's a strange thing that.

Campbell [*throwing down the pen and rising*]. Aye,
it's a strange thing that. It's a thing fit to sicken a
man against the notion that there are probabilities on
this earth. . . . Ye see, James, beforehand I would
have said nothing could be easier.

Mackenzie. Than to get them to tell ?

Campbell. Aye, just that. But you heard what he
said : " You'll be adding to your experience this
night, Mr. Campbell, and you'll have something to
put to the other side of it," says he. [*Paces away,
hands behind back.*] Aye, and I have added something
to it, a thing I like but little. [*Turning to face
Mackenzie with raised hand.*] Do you see what it is,
James ? A dream can be stronger than a strong
man armed. Just a whispered word, a pointed
finger even, would ha'e tell'd us a'. But no ! no !
And so I am powerless before the visions and dreams
of an old woman and a half-grown lad.

Mackenzie [*who now stands waiting for the warrant*].
No' exactly powerless, Kilmohr, for if ye canna open
his mouth ye can shut it ; and there's some satisfaction in that.

Campbell [*sitting down to sign warrant*]. No' to me,
man, no' to me. [*He hands the paper to Mackenzie,
who goes out.*] For I've been beaten. Aye, the pair
o' them have beat me, though it's only a matter o'
seconds till one o' them be dead.

Morag [*her voice coming quickly, in a sharp whisper,
like an echo of Campbell's last word as she sits up to
stare at him*]. Dead !

Campbell [*startled*]. What is that ?

Morag [*slowly*]. Is he dead ?

Campbell [*aloud*]. Oh, it's you. I'd forgotten you were there.

Morag [*in same tone*]. Is he dead ?

Campbell [*grimly*]. Not yet. But if ye'll look through this window preesently ye'll see him gotten ready for death.

[*He picks up hat, gloves, cloak, and is about to go out.*]

Morag [*after a pause, very slowly and brokenly*]. I—will—tell—you.

Campbell [*astounded*]. What !

Morag I will tell you all you are seeking to know.

Campbell [*in a whisper, thunderstruck*]. God, and to think, to think I was on the very act . . . on the very act of . . . [*Recovering.*] Tell me—tell me at once.

Morag. You will promise that he will not be hanged ?

Campbell. He will not. I swear it.

Morag. You will give him back to me ?

Campbell. I will give him back—unhung.

Morag. Then [*Campbell comes near*], in a corrie half-way up the far side of Dearig—God save me !

Campbell [*in exultation*]. Dished after a'. I've clean dished them ! Loard, Loard ! [*With intense solemnity, clasping hands and looking upwards.*] Once more I can believe in the rationality of Thy world. [*Gathers up again his cloak, hat, etc.*] And to think . . . to think . . . I was on the very act of going away like a beaten dog !

Morag. He is safe from hanging now ?

Campbell [*chuckles and looks out at window before replying, and is at door when he speaks*]. Very near it, very near it. Listen !

[*He holds up his hand—a volley of musketry is heard. Kilmohr goes out, leaving door wide open. After a short interval of silence, the old woman enters and advances a few steps towards the girl, who has sunk on her knees at the volley.*]

Mary Stewart. Did you hear, Morag Cameron, **did** you hear ?

[*The girl is sobbing, her face covered by her hands.*]

Mary Stewart. Och ! be quiet now. I would be listening till the last sound of it passes into the great hills and over all the wide world. . . . It is fitting for you to be crying, a child that cannot understand, but water shall never wet eye of mine for Dugald Stewart. Last night I was but the mother of a lad that herded sheep on the Athole hills : this morn it is I that am the mother of a man who is among the great ones of the earth. All over the land they will be telling of Dugald Stewart. Mothers will teach their children to be men by him. High will his name be with the teller of fine tales. . . . The great men came, they came in their pride, terrible like the storm they were, and cunning with the words of guile were they. Death was with them. . . . He was but a lad, a young lad, with great length of days before him, and the grandeur of the world. But he put it all from him. " Speak," said they, " speak, and life and great riches will be for yourself." But he said no word at all ! Loud was the swelling of their wrath ! Let the heart of you rejoice, Morag Cameron, for the snow is red with his blood. There are things greater than death. Let them that are children shed the tears. . . .

[*She comes forward and lays her hand on the girl's shoulder.*]

Mary Stewart. Let us go and lift him into the house, and not be leaving him lie out there alone.

CURTAIN

CATHERINE PARR

By Maurice Baring

HENRY VIII

From a pen-drawing by
E. Heber Thompson

EDITOR'S PREFACE

Here we have King Henry VIII., old and very stout and very hot-tempered, quarrelling with the only one of his wives who contrived to outlive him. If we are not to miss the point of some of her remarks, we have to remember that the other wives were Katharine of Aragon, Anne Bullen (or Boleyn), Jane Seymour, Anne of Cleves, and Catherine Howard. We should remember, too, that Catherine Parr, like Anne of Cleves, was a Protestant, a " Lutheran," and Henry disliked Protestants, although he had broken away from the Church of Rome.

CHARACTERS

King Henry VIII.
Queen Catherine.
A Page.

CATHERINE PARR

OR

ALEXANDER'S HORSE

SCENE.—*London. Breakfast chamber in the palace. King Henry VIII. and Catherine Parr are discovered sitting opposite to each other at the breakfast table. The King has just cracked a boiled egg.*

King Henry. My egg's raw. It really is too bad.

Catherine. Yesterday you complained of their being hard.

King Henry. And so they were. I don't want a hard egg, and I don't want a raw egg. I want them to be cooked just right.

Catherine. You are very difficult to please. The egg was in boiling water for three minutes and a half. I boiled it myself. But give it me. I like them like that. I will boil you another.

King Henry. No, it's too late now. But it is a fact that you have no idea how to boil an egg. I wish you'd let them do them in the kitchen.

Catherine. If they're done in the kitchen you complain because they're not here when you come down, and if they are here, you say they're cold.

King Henry. I never say anything of the kind. The cook boils eggs beautifully.

Catherine. She shall boil them to-morrow.

King Henry. One would have thought that a woman of your experience might at least know how to boil an egg. I hate a watery egg. [*Pensively.*] Poor dear Katie used to boil eggs beautifully.

Catherine. Do you mean Catherine Howard or Katharine of Aragon ?

King Henry. I was alluding to poor, dear, misguided Katie Howard. Katharine of Aragon never was my wife. The marriage was not valid.

Catherine. Well, Catherine Howard ought to have known how to boil eggs, considering her mother was a kitchenmaid.

King Henry. That is utterly untrue. Her mother was a Rochford.

Catherine. You're thinking of Anne Bullen.

King Henry. Yes, yes, to be sure, Katie's mother was a Somerset.

Catherine. You're thinking of Jane Seymour.

King Henry. Not at all. Jane Seymour was a sister of Somerset's.

Catherine. All I know is that Catherine Howard's mother was a kitchenmaid. And I think it's very unkind of you to mention her to me. I suppose you mean that you wish she were alive, and that you loved her better than you love me.

King Henry. I never said anything of the kind. All I said was that she knew how to boil eggs.

Catherine. You clearly meant to say that she had all the qualities which I lack.

King Henry. You are most unfair. I never meant to hint at any such thing. All I said was that I hate a watery egg, and my egg this morning was raw.

Catherine [*rising and going to the door in a temper*]. Well, the best thing you can do is to get rid of me, and to marry some one who knows how to boil an egg.

King Henry. Catherine, come back ! I really didn't mean to offend you. You know how to boil eggs very well.

Catherine [*sitting down*]. One takes an endless amount of trouble, and that's all the thanks one gets.

Don't think that I shall ever boil your eggs for you again, because I shan't.

King Henry. I was thinking we might have a little music this morning. I have composed a new ballad which I should like to try over with you. It's for viol and lute and voice. We might try it.

Catherine. I'm not sure if I have time. What is it called ?

King Henry. It's called " The Triumph of Love," and it begins :

> Come list to Alexander's deed,
> Great Jove's immortal son,
> Who, riding on a snow-white steed
> To Babylon did come.

Catherine. " Son " doesn't rhyme with " come."

King Henry. It's not meant to. It's assonance.

Catherine. Do you mean Alexander the Great ?

King Henry. Yes, of course.

Catherine. The only thing is, his horse was black.

King Henry. No, my dear, you're mistaken ; his horse was white.

Catherine. Black—black as jet.

King Henry. But I know for a fact it was white.

Catherine. Alexander's horse was black. Everybody knows it was black.

King Henry. It was white. You can ask any one you like.

Catherine. It was black. He was famous for his black horse. There are hundreds of pictures of him on his *black* horse—my father has got one.

King Henry. Then the painter made a mistake. Plutarch, Xenophon, Aristotle all mention his *white* horse.

Catherine. Black.

King Henry. But, my dear, how obstinate you are ! I *know* it is white——

Catherine. Black, *coal*-black.

King Henry. Have you read Xenophon ?

Catherine. You are thinking of something else. Even when we were children my father always showed us the picture of Alexander's *black* horse.

King Henry. Well, I can easily prove it to you. There's a Plutarch here in the bookcase.

[*He goes to the bookcase and takes out a book.*]

Catherine. I remember it particularly well, because my brother had a black horse and we called it " Bucephalus," after Alexander's *black* horse.

King Henry [*turning over the leaves of the book*]. If it had been black it would never have been called Bucephalus—it would be absurd to call a black horse Bucephalus.

Catherine. Not so absurd as calling a white horse Bucephalus.

King Henry. He would never have chosen a black horse.   He was superstitious——

Catherine. Just because you're superstitious and believe in saints, and worship images, you think every one else is.   As a matter of fact, he chose a black horse on purpose to show he didn't care a pin about superstitions——

King Henry. Here it is—" χαλεπὸς εἶναι καὶ κομιδῇ δύσχρηστος "—" The horse was wild and extremely difficult to manage."   In fact, he had all the characteristics of the white Thessalian horses of that day.

Catherine. But it doesn't say it was white.   And Thessalian horses are famous for being black.

King Henry. You really are too obstinate for words. I will find you the proofs in Xenophon.   It is distinctly stated that the horse is *white*.   It is an historical fact.   Nobody has ever disputed it.

Catherine. But Plutarch, you see, practically says it was black.

King Henry. Plutarch says nothing of the kind. Besides, I now remember talking about this with Wolsey, who was an excellent scholar.   I distinctly remember his saying one day : " As white as Buce-phalus." It's quite a common phrase among scholars.

Catherine. He must have said, " As black as Buce-phalus."

King Henry. Of course, if you mean to say I tell lies——

Catherine. I don't mean that you tell lies, but you are mistaken—that's all.

King Henry. But I tell you that there is no mistake possible. I know it as well as I know my own name.

Catherine. Your memory plays you tricks. Just now you couldn't remember Catherine Howard's mother's name.

King Henry. That's nothing to do with it. Besides, I did remember it. I made a slip, that's all. But this is an historical fact which I've known all my life.

Catherine. I quite understand your memory failing you. You have so many names to remember. I expect you were confusing Alexander's black horse with King Alfred's white horse—the white horse of Wantage.

King Henry. Good gracious ! If you had a smatter-ing of education you wouldn't say such things ! It comes of having no religion and no education, and of not knowing Latin. A Lutheran education is worse than none. Even Anne of Cleves knew Latin.

Catherine. Thank Heavens, I don't know Latin ! Stupid, superstitious language, fit only for bigots and monks !

King Henry. I suppose you mean I am a bigot.

Catherine. You can turn what one says into mean-ing anything you like. As a matter of fact, all I said was that the horse was black.

King Henry. I'd rather be a bigot than a Lutheran heretic.

Catherine. You know you're wrong and you try to escape the point. That's just like a Tudor. No Tudor could ever listen to reason.

King Henry. I must ask you not to insult **my** family.

Catherine. You've insulted mine, which is a far older one. My family has no blood on its escutcheon.

King Henry. I won't stand this any longer. [*He gets up, opens the door, and calls*] Denny, Butts, Page, who is there ?

[*Enter a Page.*]

Page. Your Majesty.

King Henry. Go and tell the Lord Chamberlain to make the necessary arrangements for transporting the Ex-Queen to the Tower.

Page [*puzzled*]. Yes, your Majesty. Does your Majesty mean the late Queen's remains ?

King Henry. I said the *Ex*-Queen, you stupid boy —Queen Catherine Parr.

Page. Yes, your Majesty.

King Henry. And tell him to give orders to the Governor of the Tower to have everything ready for the Ex-Queen's execution.

Page. Is the same ceremonial to be observed as in the case of Queen Catherine Howard, your Majesty ?

King Henry. Yes ; only there need only be one roll of drums instead of two—at the end. [*The Page goes to the door.*] And on the way ask Dr. Butts whether Alexander the Great's horse was black or white.

Catherine. It was black. [*The Page bows and goes out.*] Well, since I'm to be executed, I daresay you will allow me to go and pack up my things. By the way, you left your lute in my sitting-room yesterday. I will bring it down.

King Henry. Wait a minute, there's no hurry.

Catherine. I beg your pardon, I have very little time, and a great many letters to write.

King Henry [*hesitating*]. And I wanted to have some music.

Catherine. You don't expect me to accompany you now, I suppose ? You had better find some one else.

I have got other things to think about during my last moments on earth.

King Henry [*laughing uneasily*]. I was only joking, of course, my dear. You don't mean to say you took it seriously.

Catherine. I am afraid I don't appreciate that kind of joke.

King Henry. Come, come; let bygones be bygones, and let us have some music. I want to play you my ballad.

[*Enter the Page.*]

Page. If you please, your Majesty, I can't find the Lord Chamberlain, and Dr. Butts says your Majesty was quite correct as to the colour of Alexander the Great's horse.

King Henry [*beaming*]. Very good; you can go. You need not deliver the message to the Lord Chamberlain. [*The Page bows and retires.*] And now, my dear, we'll go and play. You see, I knew I was right.

[*The King opens the door with a bow.*]

Catherine. It was black, all the same.

King Henry [*indulgently, as if speaking to a child*]. Yes, yes, my dear, of course it was black, but let's go and have some music. [*They go out.*]

CURTAIN

MICHAEL

By Miles Malleson

CHARACTERS

Michael was first produced by the students of the Academy of Dramatic Art on Tuesday, April 3, 1917, at the St. James's Theatre, with the following cast:

SIMON	Miss Phyllis Hiller.
MATRYONA	Miss Joan Allen.
ANIUSKA	Miss Noreen Price.
MICHAEL	Miss Gabrielle Clay.
A RUSSIAN NOBLE . . .	Miss Kitty Penberthy.
HIS SERVANT	Miss Phyllis Fenton.
A WOMAN	Miss Molly Wood.
TWO CHILDREN	{ Miss May Taylor. { Miss Ellen Bird.

The play is adapted from the translation by L. and A. Maude of Tolstoy's story, *What Men Live By*.

MICHAEL

SCENE I

A Russian peasant hut. The door into the open air is in the centre of the back wall; there is another door into an inner room on the right as one looks on to the stage. The fireplace is opposite on the left, with a rough wooden bench by it. The room is barely furnished. There is a wooden table and a few wooden stools. On the table are a few tattered clothes and some sewing materials.

An empty stage at the rise of the curtain. A peasant woman enters from out of doors carrying a water-pail. She crosses to look into the inner room, evidently finds it empty, and calls:

Matryona. Aniuska . . . Aniuska! [*A child's voice answers from outside in a loud happy* Oo . . . ee. *The woman crosses to the door and calls out into the open.*] Bring in those sticks you gathered, Aniuska; bring them in for the fire. Now. Now, at once.

[*She returns to the fireplace and for a moment busies herself there. An enormous collection of sticks makes its appearance at the door. The collection begins to advance into the room uneasily and uncannily, and apparently on two little bare feet of its own. However, a child is seen to be supplying the motive power. The sticks are deposited by the fireplace.*]

Matryona. Now make up the fire with them,

Aniuska. Your father will be back soon from the town.

[*The child squats on the floor and begins to break up the sticks. The little ones are easy enough, but she has some hard tussles with the stouter ones. She is busy thus through the following scene. Matryona seats herself at the table and begins to patch a very ragged shirt.*]

Aniuska. Woof! [*A stick is broken at that.*] Mummy—woof——.

Matryona. Yes?

Aniuska. Woof! Why has daddy gone into the town?

Matryona. To buy a warm sheepskin for the winter. We've only one between us, and that's worn to tatters.

Aniuska. Woof! Why doesn't daddy—woof!— go into the town and buy warm sheepskins more often . . . woof! . . . I can't ever remember daddy having been away for the whole day before. . . .

Matryona. There's never a moment to be spared from his work.

Aniuska. Woof!

Matryona. Work's cheap, but bread's dear; and what he earns goes on food; there's little use tramping many weary miles to the town with no money to spend.

Aniuska. Woof! . . . Has daddy got some money now?

Matryona. Little enough. It's taken a year—day in and day out, making boots for the neighbours, to save enough for one sheepskin. And he's got to collect most of it on his way to the town.

Aniuska. Who's he going to collect it from?

Matryona. From the neighbours he's made boots for, silly. [*Matryona continues musing half to herself and half to the child.*] If only the dealer doesn't cheat him—he's much too simple—he cheats nobody, but any child can take him in . . . eight roubles is a lot

Rouble, A coin which was worth about half-a-crown.

of money. He should get a good coat at that price. Not tanned skin, but still, a proper winter coat. It'll be better this winter than last. When he went out he put on our one coat, and I had to stay indoors.

Aniuska [*after a tremendous but vain struggle with a too thick piece of stick*]. Nasty, nasty, nasty, nasty! I can't " woof " it!

Matryona. Tell me how much bread there is, Aniuska. . . . He'll be wanting something when he comes back. [*The child goes to a cupboard and holds up a piece of bread.*] That'll have to do. He'll have had some dinner in the town. Set it out, Aniuska. [*She takes her sewing from the table to the bench by the fire. Aniuska sets out the bread and a bowl or two, dancing and skipping to and fro between the table and the cupboard—singing a little to herself. Matryona continues*] He didn't start very early. It's a long way, and he had to collect the money on his way, but it's time he was back—I only hope he hasn't gone on the spree.

Aniuska [*having set out her father's meal, she has gone to the door. Suddenly*]. Here he comes! Here comes daddy! [*In tremendous excitement she rushes to her mother and then back to the door to run out to meet him ; but instead, she stops short.*] Daddy isn't alone. There's somebody with him.

Matryona. What's that? What sort of a person with him? [*She puts away her work.*]

Aniuska. He must be terribly cold, his arms are all bare, and his feet . . . He looks like a beggar.

Matryona. A beggar!

Aniuska. No. He doesn't look like a beggar.

Matryona. Has your father a sheepskin?

Aniuska. No.

Matryona. No sheepskin! [*She hurries to the door.*] No sheepskin! Nothing! And bringing a beggar home with him. It's as I feared. He's been on the spree. It's vodka the money's gone on, and

Vodka, An intoxicating drink, distilled from rye.

not a sheepskin. [*Her temper begins to rise quickly.*] Here's a nice end to a year's work. My heart could break with disappointment. A year's savings on a drunken spree. [*She vents her rising anger on the child.*] Get off to bed !

Aniuska [*extremely plaintive*]. I want to see daddy.

Matryona. Off with you ! You don't see your father drunk—and you don't hear what I've got to say to him ! Off with you !

Aniuska [*her voice quivering with tears*]. I haven't seen daddy all day.

Matryona. Off with you—and put yourself into your bed. [*Aniuska, her knuckles stuffed into her eyes in an ineffectual attempt to keep back her tears, goes slowly into the inner room. Matryona shuts the door after her, and then shuts the door into the open air. She begins to work herself up into a passionate indignation.*] Oh, it's a nice end to it. One slaves and slaves and slaves, and the money goes on drink, and he brings his good-for-nothing drunken friends home with him. Well, we shall see !

[*She takes up her stand by the fireplace and waits. The door is opened. Simon comes in. He holds the door open for some one else.*]

Simon. Come in, friend. . . . Come in.

[*A young man, apparently of about eighteen, enters. His face is beautiful and his bare limbs wonderfully shaped. Just a piece of coarse material wound round him, and Simon's old cloak across his shoulders, keep out the cold as best they may. Having entered, he stands just inside the door, his head and eyes lowered. Simon is not at all the worse for drink, but evidently very anxious about his reception by his wife.*]

Simon. Well, mother ? [*She does not answer.*] Come, friend. Here by the fire. Sit and warm yourself. [*He sets the bench nearer to the fire, and beckons the stranger to it.*] There ! That's better than the snow outside ! We'll have some supper. Any supper for us, mother ?

Matryona. You shall have your supper when I have my sheepskin.

Simon. Oh, come, mother—that's a poor welcome ! I couldn't get the skin.

Matryona. Why not ?

Simon. I called on neighbour Trifonof on my way to the town, but he couldn't pay me what he owed. He hadn't the money. Hardly enough bread for his wife and children. I couldn't force him. I went on and asked the dealers to let me have a skin on credit, but they wouldn't—so we must go without.

Matryona. Where's the money that you started with ?

Simon. Here. [*He gives her some.*]

Matryona [*counting it*]. It's not all.

Simon. I spent some.

Matryona. On what ?

Simon. On vodka.

Matryona. So ! That's what I thought.

Simon. Just enough to keep out the cold. Many miles through the snow—like this—it's cold work . . . and hungry work, too.

Matryona. There's no supper for drunkards like you.

Simon. Now then, mother.

Matryona. Maybe the cold's sobered you. But you set out to buy a sheepskin, and you come back with nothing but a naked vagabond.

Simon. That's enough, Matryona. Don't wag your tongue without reason. . . .

Matryona. And you ask for supper ! As if nothing had happened. There's only enough bread in the house for a day—we can't feed all the drunkards in the country.

Simon. There now, Matryona, hold your tongue.

Matryona. Hold my tongue indeed ! Yes. I've finished with you. You expect me to slave for another

year, do you ? Then you can get your own supper—
and mind your own house. . . . Here, give that to me !
[*She seizes the cloak from the stranger's shoulders and
throws it round her. She goes to the door, but neither her
husband nor the stranger move, and her curiosity is
roused. She comes back and addresses the stranger.*] If
you haven't been on a drunken spree, how came you
like that ? [*No answer.*] You must be a bad man—
you're afraid. [*No answer ; and she draws a little
nearer to him.*] You're clothed like a beggar, but
your skin is white and your hands are smooth. . . .
Where do you come from ? . . . What do you want ?
[*The stranger shakes his head.*] Haven't you a tongue
in your head ?

Simon. He hasn't spoken a word since I found him.

Matryona. Found him ? Where did you find him ?

Simon. By the roadside. I was passing a shrine at
a bend of the road, and I saw something on the ground
against it, and when I went closer I found him—
naked in the snow. I thought some one must have
stripped him and left him there, and if I meddled I
should get into trouble—so I hurried on. . . . And
then I thought he might be dying of cold and want,
and I was slipping past—afraid ! " Simon," I said to
myself, " have you grown so rich as to be afraid of
robbers ? Shame on you ! " So I went back, and
lifted him up, and put my cloak round him and brought
him home. I questioned him, but he never spoke. . . .
And now you know as much as I.

[*Matryona regards him still more curiously.*]

Matryona. His skin's as white and soft as a nobleman's. In the snow like that ! It's a wonder he's
alive ! Well, we can't let him starve. Here ! Out of
my way ! [*Her voice is kinder. She wishes to reach a
kettle on the fire.*] Here . . . sit here. You'll be
warmer here. [*She sets a chair for him nearer the fire
so that she can reach the kettle. His back is now to the
audience. She fills a cup and gives it to him.*] There.

Drink that. That'll warm you. [*He looks up at her when he takes it ; and suddenly, drawing a little back, she stares at him. As if spellbound and unable to take her eyes from the stranger, she gets closer to Simon. Her voice is full of awed fear.*] Did you see. . . . Simon . . . did you see ?

Simon. What was there to see, mother ?

Matryona. When I handed him the cup, he smiled at me. The strangest smile I've ever seen ! I've never seen a man smile like that. He smiled as if the sun were behind his eyes. Simon, I'm afraid. . . . I'm afraid of him . . . there's something very strange.

Simon. Strange or not—as you say, we can't let him starve. Give him the bread.

Matryona. You.

Simon. Here, friend, take this.

[*Simon gives him the bread. For a moment they both watch him. Then :*]

Matryona. And that's the last food in the house, and you'll be wanting some. Perhaps I can borrow a little from neighbour Martha—I'll go across now. [*By the door she hesitates.*] It's very dark. The stranger's put a spell on me—I'm fearing to go across the black field. . . . Come with me, Simon. He'll be well enough for a while. [*Simon joins her at the door.*] We'd best take the lantern.

Simon. No, mother. We know every step of the way. . . . Take my hand.

[*They go out together. The stranger sits silent on the bench. From the inner room the child's voice calls :*]

Aniuska. Mother . . . Mother . . . Daddy . . . Dad-*dy* . . .

[*The child appears in a tiny little white shirt ; she peeps out into the room. Then she advances into it. When she sees the stranger, she observes him in surprised silence. Slowly she crosses the room to him. He looks up, and she stands taking him*

*in with a solemn, fearless curiosity. She accepts
him and gives him a hand, which he takes. Then,
climbing up on to his lap, she rests her head contentedly against his shoulder. The stage becomes
black.]*

SCENE II

*In a few moments it is light again.
The same Scene. A year has elapsed. Simon sits
shoemaking. Matryona is sewing.*

Matryona. Simon.

Simon. Yes, mother?

Matryona. Do you know what to-day is?

Simon. No. What is to-day?

Matryona. It's a year ago since you brought
Michael home.

Simon. The luckiest day's work I ever did. Never
did I know a man take so readily to his work, or so
easy to teach as Michael. And now no one sews boots
so neatly and strongly in all the district. His fame is
beginning to spread, too. People are coming a long
way to have their boots sewn here. We shall soon be
well off.

Matryona. And yet from that day to this, he's still
as great a mystery as ever. Where is he now?

Simon. He's but taken some boots to a neighbour.

Matryona. It's seldom his bench there is empty.
He seems to work without stopping—silently. It is
strange. He only speaks when necessary, and he does
not joke nor laugh. And—except once, except that
once—I have never seen him smile. Do you know,
father, I often think something very strange will
happen, and we shall lose him.

Simon. God put off the day! He's too good a
workman.

[The door opens, and Michael in peasant dress appears.

He comes in, and going silently to his bench, begins to work. They have only worked a few moments when the bells of a carriage-sledge are heard outside. Matryona goes at once to the door.]

Matryona. Oh, what a carriage! And beautiful horses, and servants! It must belong to a great nobleman . . . it's stopping . . . the servants are getting down . . . the nobleman! . . . he's getting out . . . he's coming here. [*She shuts the door in alarm.*] Simon, a great nobleman is coming up our pathway!

[*Simon rises, and they wait anxiously. Michael works on unconcerned. There is an imperious knock at the door. Matryona opens it timidly. A magnificently dressed noble swaggers in.*]

Nobleman. Are you the master bootmaker?

Simon. I am, your Excellency.

Nobleman [*calling from the door*]. Fedka, bring the leather. . . . [*A servant runs in with some leather.*] Give it to me. . . . Look here, shoemaker. Do you see this leather?

Simon. Yes, your Excellency.

Nobleman. Do you know what sort of leather it is?

Simon. It is good leather.

Nobleman. Good indeed! Why, you fool, you never saw such leather before in your life. It's foreign. It cost me twenty roubles.

Simon [*aghast*]. Twenty roubles! Where should I ever see leather like that?

Nobleman. Just so. Now, can you make it into boots for me?

Simon. Yes, your Excellency, I can.

Nobleman. You can, can you? Well, remember whom you are to make them for, and what the leather is. You must make me boots that will wear for a year, neither losing shape nor coming unsewn. If you can do it, take the leather and cut it up—but if you can't, you'd better say so. I warn you now, if you spoil my leather, I will have you put in prison.

Simon. Your Excellency !

Nobleman. But if you make good boots, as I want them, I will pay you ten roubles for your work.   Will you do it ?

Simon. Ten roubles. . . .

Nobleman. Ten roubles. . . . Well ?

Simon. . . . Yes, your Excellency, I will do it.

Nobleman. Very well.   Take my measure.   [*The Nobleman sits so that his own servant can remove one of his boots.   Simon begins to take the measure.*]   Mind you don't make it too tight !

Simon. No, your Excellency.

[*Aniuska comes skipping, bounding, shouting into the room, unaware of the Nobleman.*]

Matryona [*terrified that such a hullabaloo will annoy the Nobleman*]. Aniuska !

[*The child sees the Nobleman, is overcome, and creeps to hide her head in her mother's skirts.*]

Nobleman. Is that yours ?

Matryona. Yes, your Excellency.

[*The measure has been taken, and the Nobleman rises.*]

Nobleman. There !   And take care, for your own sake, my leather is not spoiled.   [*He notices Michael, who has been working unconcerned.*]   Whom have we here ?

Simon. That is my workman—he will sew the boots.

Nobleman. Oh, he will sew them, will he ?   [*He swaggers across to Michael.*]   Mind !   Remember to make them so that they will last a year.   They must neither lose shape nor come unsewn.

[*Michael rises slowly from his seat.   His back is to the audience.   He stands gazing towards the Nobleman.   Matryona seizes Simon by the arm.*]

Matryona [*whispering*]. Simon !   Look !   Look at Michael !   Michael's face !   He's smiling !

Simon [*under his breath*]. God protect us !

Matryona. . . . As he did when he looked at me a year ago.

Nobleman [*in loud uneasiness*]. . . . What are you grinning at, you fool? Stop! Stop grinning! [*He advances to him threateningly; but as Michael does not move, the Nobleman hesitates, then turns to the door.*] Instead of standing there smiling, if you take my advice you'll sew my boots as I want them, and earn ten roubles for your master. But if the leather's spoiled, you grinning fool, there's prison for you as well as him. Come, Fedka.

[*The Nobleman and his servant go out. Michael stands unmoving, and Simon and his wife watch him, strangely fascinated.*]

Simon [*recalled by the leather*]. It's wonderful leather. You must cut it, Michael—and take care how you cut. If the leather's spoilt, it's ruin for us all. There! [*He gives him the leather with the greatest care.*] Wait now till I give you the measure. [*He turns to fetch the measure.*] Your eye is truer than mine—you must cut as you never cut before, and cut exact.

[*But without waiting for the measure Michael folds the leather and cuts it boldly into two pieces.*]

Simon [*in a terrible state*]. Michael! For God's sake! What have you done? [*Michael deliberately cuts it again.*] The leather's spoiled. O God! We're ruined! We shall be taken off to the prison! Matryona, Aniuska—little one—our home will be broken up!—the nobleman will be enraged, and we shall be helpless against him. . . . Michael, never before have you made a mistake, and now your mistake has ruined us all! [*He examines what Michael has done.*] It's spoiled—utterly spoiled! Oh, mother, mother, we're ruined! No boots could in any way be cut from that now—only soft slippers!

[*The servant of the Nobleman bursts back into the room. He is very excited.*]

Servant. I have been sent back about the boots.
Simon. About the boots.
Servant. My master no longer needs them.

Simon [*repeating slowly*]. Your master no longer needs them ?

Servant. He is dead ! . . . Hardly had he rejoined his lady in the sledge and we'd started off, the horses had been whipped into a gallop, and we were flying across the snow, when we heard a great cry from our mistress for us to stop . . . and before we could get down and go to him, he was dead.   The life was out of him and he rolled over on to the floor of the carriage, like a sack. . . . My mistress has sent me back.   I am to tell you there is no longer any need for the boots, but you are to use the leather to make soft slippers for the corpse.

Simon [*slowly, incredulously*]. Soft slippers for the corpse ? . . .

Servant. I shall return for them to-morrow.   Good-day, masters.   [*Exit.*]

Simon. Soft slippers for the corpse ! . . .

[*Simon and Matryona stare at Michael, who sits down and commences work on the slippers.   The stage becomes black.*]

SCENE III

The light goes up again in a moment on a busy scene. It is towards evening.   Michael and Simon are at work. Aniuska, on the floor, is engrossed with her toys—a number of rough, but brilliantly painted wooden ones. Matryona moves to and fro ceaselessly, busied on household tasks.

A timid knock at the door.   The work in the room stops —the knock is repeated a little louder.

Simon. It's late for customers.

Matryona. See who it is, Aniuska.

[*The child opens the door.   Whoever it was outside has gone a few steps away, and Aniuska disappears.   In a moment she is back again.*]

Aniuska. There's a lady with two little girls, and one of them has a bad leg.

[*Michael's attention has been caught—he rises from his bench. A woman appears in the doorway. She has two little girls with her, of whom one is lame. Michael is evidently deeply moved by them.*]

Woman. Good-evening, good folk.

Simon. Good-evening to you.

Woman. I have come about some shoes for these little girls.

Simon. Pray come in. What sort of shoes do you want?

Woman. I want leather shoes made for them for the spring.

Simon. We can do that. Welted or turned over, linen-lined. My man Michael is a master at the work.

[*Michael has continued to stare at the two little girls excitedly. Realizing now that all eyes are on him he shrinks back into the shadow.*]

Woman. Will you take the measure now?

Simon. Yes.

Woman [*lifting the lame child on to her lap*]. Take the two measures from this little girl. Make one shoe for the lame foot and three for the sound one, and two pairs for the other little girl. They both have the same-sized shoes—they are twins.

Simon [*as he takes the measurement*]. How did it happen to her? She is such a pretty little girl. Was she born so?

Woman. No. Her mother crushed her leg.

Matryona. Aren't you their mother, then?

Woman. No. I am neither their mother nor any relation to them. They were quite strangers to me, but I adopted them.

Matryona. They are not your children, and yet you are so fond of them?

Woman. How can I help being fond of them? I fed

them both—I had a child of my own, but God took him. I was not so fond of him as I am now of these.

Matryona. Whose children are they ?

[*Aniuska has made friends with the other little girl and has taken her to the toys. As soon as the measurement is taken the lame child joins them, and on the floor the three play together.*

The daylight is fading, and the light in the room has grown very dim. There is a lamp on the table which sheds its soft light on the group round it ; but the shadows outside the circle are very deep and black ; Michael in his far corner cannot be seen.]

Woman. Their parents died both in one week. My husband and I lived in the same village. Their father was a lonely man—a woodcutter in the forest. When felling trees one day they let one fall on him. It fell across his body and crushed him. They hardly got him home before he died ; and that same week his wife gave birth to these two little girls. She was poor and alone, she had no one, young or old, with her, and alone she met her death. The next morning I went to see her, but when I entered the hut, poor thing, she was already stark and cold. In dying she had rolled on to one of the children and crushed its leg. The village folk came to the hut, washed the body, laid her out, made a coffin, and buried her. They were good folk. The babies were left alone. What was to be done with them ? I was the only woman there who had a baby at the time, and so I fed my own boy—and these two . . . and God so ordered it, that these grew up, while my own was buried before he was two years old. I had no more children of my own, and how lonely I should be without these two little girls ! How can I help loving them ! They are the joy of my life. . . . [*She rises and watches the children playing on the floor.*] And what a beautiful little one you have ! [*She turns to Matryona.*] We are

very lucky. . . . Come, little ones, say good-bye,
it's late—we should be back.

[*She helps up the lame one.*]

Matryona. You are not from these parts ?

Woman. No. We are staying with a neighbour.
They told me to come to you for the shoes. They will
be ready soon ?

Simon. In two days.

Woman. Thank you, and good-night.

Simon [*opening the door for her*]. Good-night to you.

Matryona. It's dark. Do you know the way ?

Woman. When I get on to the pathway.

Matryona. Simon, show the way. It's rough for
the little one. . . . Good-bye, little ones. [*She kisses
the two little girls.*] Come back to get your shoes and
play again with Aniuska.

Aniuska. Can I go with daddy ?

Matryona. Down to the pathway. . . . Hey, but
it's dark ! Perhaps this will light the way.

[*Matryona takes the lamp from the table and carries
it to the doorway. There she stands with it, high
above her head, to light the others down the pathway. She waves good-bye ; then she herself,
still with the lamp, disappears out of doors. Inside
the room it is dark. Then, from the corner in
which Michael was, a strange light begins to
shine. The light grows gradually brighter until
Michael is seen clearly in the midst of it.*

*Matryona comes back into the room. She
goes straight to the table, upon which she replaces
the lamp. She does not see Michael until she
turns. Then :*]

Matryona [*her voice low with awe and fear*]. Simon !
. . . Simon ! . . . [*Simon, with Aniuska, comes back
into the room.*]

Simon. . . . God protect us ! . . .

Matryona. . . . Michael is smiling . . . I cannot
bear to look !

Simon [*in low awe*]. Michael . . . Michael, we are afraid before you ; we do not know, and we are afraid. Only tell me this : why does your face shine so ?

Michael. Light shines from me because I have been punished, and now I am forgiven.

Simon. And why do you smile so, and why have you smiled so, these three times ?

Michael. I smiled three times, because I was sent to learn three truths, and I have learnt them. . . . One I learned when your wife pitied me, and that is why I smiled the first time. The second I learned when the rich man ordered the boots, and I smiled the second time, and now I have learnt the third truth, and I smiled the third time.

Simon [*with low reverence*]. Tell me, Michael, what were you punished for ? And what were the three truths ? That I, too, may know them.

Michael. I was an angel in heaven, and disobeyed. [*The three figures, of Simon, of Matryona, and Aniuska, can be seen dimly, in a little group, by the light of the lamp on the table : its light seems to burn very low and small beside the great light round Michael. Matryona is seen to kneel, and the child, observing, kneels too.*] God sent me to fetch a woman's soul. I flew to earth and saw a sick woman lying alone, who had just given birth to two little girls. When she saw me she understood, and she wept and said, " Angel of God ! My husband has just been buried—killed by a falling tree. There is no one to care for my babes and set them on their feet before I die. Children cannot live without father or mother."

And I hearkened to her. And I flew to the Lord and said : " Her husband has just been killed, and she has two new-born babes ; I have not taken her soul." And God said : " Go, take the mother's soul, and learn three truths. Learn : WHAT DWELLS IN MAN ; WHAT IS NOT GIVEN TO MAN ; and, WHAT MEN LIVE BY.

When thou hast learnt these three things thou shalt return to heaven."

So I flew again to earth, and took the mother's soul. Her body rolled over and crushed one babe, twisting its leg. I rose above the village, but a wind seized me, and my wings drooped and dropt. Her soul rose alone, while I fell to earth, by the roadside. . . . Never before had I known human needs, but then I was hungry, frozen, and in pain. Suddenly I heard a man coming along the road. [*A movement from Simon. He is seen to be listening with the most intense excitement.*] For the first time since I became a man, I saw the mortal face of a man. And when he saw me he frowned, and seemed terrible to me, and he passed me by on the other side. [*A low cry escapes Simon. He is seen to sink his head into his hands, bowing before the angel.*] I despaired. Suddenly I heard him coming back. I looked up and did not recognize the same man. Before, I had seen death in his face, but now he was alive, and I recognized in him the presence of God. [*Simon is seen to raise his head, and hold himself up straight again.*] He took me to his home—a woman was there. [*The kneeling Matryona is seen to sink low to the ground.*] She was still more terrible than the man had been : the spirit of death came from her ; I could not breathe for the stench of death that spread around her. She wished to drive me out into the cold, and I knew that if she did so, she would die. [*A low cry comes from Matryona.*] But suddenly she changed ; she brought me food, and when I looked at her I saw that Death no longer dwelt in her ; she had become alive, and in her, too, I saw God. And I remembered my first lesson : " LEARN WHAT DWELLS IN MAN." And I understood that in man dwells Love—and I smiled the first time.

A year passed. A man came to order boots that should wear for a year. And I saw behind his shoulder my comrade, the Angel of Death. And I knew before the sun set he would take the rich man's soul. And I remembered my second lesson : " LEARN WHAT IS NOT GIVEN TO MAN." It is not given to man to know his own needs—and I smiled the second time.

A year passed. And there came the girl-children with the woman ; and I heard how they had been kept alive, and I knew that I had learned the third truth —and I smiled the third time. . . . [*The angel's voice begins to ring with a splendid triumph.*) . . . I have learnt that all men live, not by care for themselves, but by Love. I remained alive, when I was a man, not by care of myself, but because Love was present in a passer-by and because he and his wife pitied and loved me. The orphans remained alive, not because of their mother's care, but because there was Love in the heart of a woman—a stranger, who pitied and loved them. . . . It seems to men that they live by care of themselves, but in truth it is Love alone by which they live. [*The angel's arms are stretched out and up.*] I have learnt my third lesson : " WHAT MEN LIVE BY "—it is Love alone by which they live.

> [*Suddenly there is complete darkness. . . . Then, when the light of the lamp seems to steal back into the room, Simon, Matryona, and Aniuska are alone in the cottage.*]

CURTAIN

COMMENTARY

A. A. MILNE: THE PRINCESS AND THE WOODCUTTER

Mr. A. A. Milne is a dramatist of note, a contributor to *Punch*, and the author of *When We Were Very Young*, so it is not surprising that when he sets out to make fun of all the fairy-tale plays it is good fun and very light-hearted. One of the reasons why people enjoy reading his books and seeing his plays—and they do—is that he so obviously enjoys writing them.

Now we daren't be solemn about *The Princess and the Woodcutter*, partly because it would be silly, and partly because Mr. Milne might make us into a joke in *Punch*. To be made into a joke in *Punch* is the height of fame, it means that you really are some one important at last—but it has its drawbacks.

However, we may look through the play again, to make sure that we have not missed any of the smiles, and afterwards, if you can, you should read the whole of *Make-Believe* (of which play this is Act I.) ; if you have any doubts as to whether the love-making of the Princess and the Woodcutter is quite the right thing, you should at least be satisfied with the pirates and cannibals in Act II.

ON TALKING IT OVER

1. Seven-headed bulls have gone out of fashion, but evidently they had their uses. How did this one help

with the suitors ?   And how did he die ?—the Princess is still unmarried !

2. What *is* the Red Prince like ?

3. At which point do you feel that the Yellow Prince ought to be kicked (or smacked) ?

4. What do you think of, " *amazed, as well he may be* " ? (page 28).

5. The author enjoys his stage-directions as much as his dialogue.   Which of the directions do you like best ?

FOR PEN AND PENCIL

6. If you have anticipated the advice of the Princess and " read the history books," you know the stories in which the poor miller's son kills the fiery dragon which has eaten all the Princess's suitors, and then marries the Princess ;   and the little kitchen-wench wins the handsome prince, while the ugly daughters of her cruel stepmother are all turned into centipedes or something equally unpleasant.   They are good stories, and some of them are very old, and some—if we may be almost solemn for a moment, in the hope that Mr. Milne is not looking—are known all over the world ;   they are told in Eskimo huts under the flickering northern lights ;   and repeated by the story-teller to his little crowd of listeners at street corners in Persian bazaars ;   and laughed at by sunburnt boys and girls in the shade of the palm-trees on far Pacific islands.

Choose a fairy-tale or a folk-tale or a legend, and make it into a play, either seriously or in imitation of Mr. Milne. If you do not know a story that will do, you will find ample choice in *Stories from the Arabian Nights*, or *Folk-Tales of the Nations*, or *Tales from Hans Andersen and Grimm* ; they are all in this Series.

7. Draw and paint a brightly-coloured frontispiece for *The Princess and the Woodcutter*.

BOOKS TO READ

8. *Make-Believe*, a three-act play ; *The Boy Comes Home*, and *The Man in the Bowler Hat*, one-act plays, by A. A. Milne.

Peter Pan and Wendy, by J. M. Barrie.

Twice is Too Much, in *Pattern Plays*, by Mary Oakden and E. C. Sturt (T.E.S.).

ALFRED NOYES: ROBIN HOOD

Some historians tell us nowadays that Robin Hood never existed, but whether he lived in the twelfth century or not, we know that he is very much alive now, in the immortal company of Peter Pan and Sherlock Holmes, Long John Silver, Bill Sykes, and Sam Weller, the Pied Piper, Robinson Crusoe, King Arthur, and all the other heroes of story and legend whom we know better than many of our everyday acquaintances. So Robin Hood and his outlaws live merrily in Sherwood Forest near Nottingham, robbing the rich and helping the poor, outwitting the sheriff and defying Prince John, who is ruling England very badly while his famous brother, King Richard I., is away on a crusade against the Saracens in Palestine.

Many stories of Robin Hood have been written, and now Mr. Alfred Noyes has given us a five-act play about him, in which all the well-known characters appear, besides Shadow-of-a-Leaf—a fool who is very wise and brave. The play ends with the death of Robin and Marian, but the ending is not sad, because it is full of beauty and hope. In this book we have only Act III. of the play, but it is sufficiently complete in itself to be read or acted separately.

Mr. Alfred Noyes is well known as a poet. You will probably find some of his short poems in your school poetry-books, and later on you may have a chance to read his longer poems, such as *Tales of the Mermaid Tavern*.

ON TALKING IT OVER

9. What do the words *prologue* and *epilogue* mean? In what way are they alike? How do they differ?

What do you think the separate halves of the words mean ?

10. Some verses from Mr. Noyes's poem *Sherwood* have been given in this book, as a Prologue to his play. The whole poem is in *Mount Helicon, The Golden Book of Modern English Poetry*, and other anthologies. Find it and read it all, or ask your teacher to read it, and then choose a few verses from it to form another Prologue. Can you make an Epilogue in the same way ?

11. What was a maypole ?

12. Why does the Knight wear a red cross on his shield ? What does the red cross stand for nowadays ? Has this any connection with its old meaning ?

13. Why does Robin say that his name *was* Huntingdon ?

14. What do you think Jenny means by calling Widow Scarlet " a mumping mumble-crust " ?

15. Who was Mahound ? Where did the Knight learn to swear by him ?

16. Why does Prince John mutter, ' What ? Thou ? Thou ? Or his ghost ? "

17. What is a visor ?

18. Why does Robin Hood refer to Friar Tuck's " slim waist " ?

19. Note that Robin describes the venison as " borrowed from the King," because all the deer in Sherwood were the King's property. Killing them without permission was a crime punishable by death.

20. What were gauntlets, and why should they prevent the Knight from drinking the toast ?

21. Why should Robin think that a Red Cross Knight might be St. George ?

22. Can you suggest the idea which Shadow-of-a-Leaf has in his mind when he cries, " The King, the King comes home from the Crusade . . . " ?

23. Which do you think is the most exciting moment in the play ?

24. Are Robin and Marian well matched ? If so, why ?

25. Can you suggest a good title for each scene ?

26. What would be the chief difficulties in staging this play if your form were acting it, and how would you overcome them ?

FOR PEN AND PENCIL

27. Describe briefly how you would arrange a small stage for a performance of *Robin Hood*.

28. Write in rhyming verse *either* an Epilogue to the play *or* a song for Friar Tuck to sing in praise of life in Sherwood Forest.

29. Write a short dialogue between Friar Tuck and Little John, in which the Friar tells Little John (who, we will say, was not present) how Will Scarlet was rescued.

30. Write a short story or a one-act play about Robin Hood. If you don't know any of his adventures and can't make one up, then take the story of the archery tournament which the sheriff gave at Nottingham. Robin went in disguise and won the tournament, but when he went to receive his prize he was recognized by the sheriff, who ordered his guards to arrest the outlaw. Thereupon all Robin's men, who were in disguise among the crowd of spectators, came to the rescue—fully armed and in overwhelming numbers. This play should be in one scene only. You have to invent the ending and all the details.

31. Make a careful drawing of a bow, an arrow, and a quiver, and find out what they were made of.* (You must refer to a history book or an encyclopædia for this.)

32. Find a picture of Robin Hood, or Richard I., or a knight of the time in full armour, and copy it.

BOOKS TO READ

33. *Robin Hood*, a play in five acts, by Alfred Noyes. (Blackwood, 5s.)

The Greenwood, edited by Sir Henry Newbolt. (Tales of Robin Hood and English woodland life.) *Robin Hood and Alan-a-dale*, in *Pattern Plays*, by E. C. Oakden and

---

* It is assumed that some books, such as the following, are available in the school library: *Social England*, edited by H. D. Traill. Cassell, 6 vols., out of print. *A History of Everyday Things in England*, by M. and C. H. B. Quennell, Batsford, 16s. *Costume and Fashion*, by Herbert Norris, Dent, Vol. I., 25s., Vol. II., 31s. 6d. Others to follow. All these books are well illustrated.

Mary Sturt. Both volumes are in the " Teaching of English Series."

Robin Hood and the Pedlar. A play by John Drinkwater. (Sidgwick and Jackson.)

W. GRAHAM ROBERTSON : THE SLIPPERS OF CINDERELLA

It was not because suitable plays were not to be found that Mr. Graham Robertson wrote his own plays for young actors. " I came across suitable plays by the score," he writes in the Foreword to *The Slippers of Cinderella,* " plays good and bad, comic and tragic, but all of a uniform and depressing suitability.

" Of what interest to my volcanic leading lady, a strong, emotional actress rising ten and already with an eye on Lady Macbeth, were the pastoral but puny woes of Little Bo-Peep ? What in common had my elegantly fastidious Jeune Premier of eight with Tommy Tucker or Little Jack Horner, whose table manners had long since caused him to drop their acquaintance ? All had left the nursery far, far behind, from the youngest extra lady to the veteran tottering soberly into her teens, and their point of view seemed identical with that of the adult Thespian.

" What they wanted was an unsuitable play, and they looked to me to provide one ; a play that should be neither idyllic, infantine, nor improving. Hang it all—as the troupe very naturally felt—why improvement ?

" Hence therefore the Theatre of the Children's Troupe, of which the three following plays are specimens. Their general tone is low, their language unrefined, they contain no elements of poetry or morality, they could not by any possibility improve anybody ; in a word, they can be confidently recommended to juvenile actors as entirely and absolutely unsuitable."

ON TALKING IT OVER

34. What picture of Elise had you formed before she appeared ?

35. Why is Agatha so " eager " about Lady Errington, and so anxious that the right cards should be to the top in the card plate ?

36. Why should Dolly now understand the feelings of Balaam ? You probably remember that Balaam's ass turned suddenly and spoke to him. (*Numbers*, chap. xxii.)

37. Why should the Fairy think that the twins must be " ugly and cruel, doubtless " ?

38. Which is Belinda's most amusing remark ?

39. If you don't know what homœopathic means, look it up in a dictionary.

40. What do you think of Jane's plan for keeping the police busy ?

41. Is Belinda right about the appointment ?

42. Do you like Agatha ?

43. The charm of this play is due not only to the humorous plot and witty dialogue, but (in spite of the " Foreword ") to its touch of poetry. Which speech would you choose as the best instance of this ?

44. As only a few fortunate people can work magic on the stage, one of the author's chief problems in writing the play must have been to arrange for Myra and Jane and Agatha to change their dresses. How has he solved the problem ?

45. Why is *The Slippers of Cinderella* such a good title for the play ?

FOR PEN AND PENCIL

46. Imagine that Jane is telling a friend of hers all about these extraordinary happenings, and write down what she says. You must imitate her manner of speech, of course, and find out from the play exactly how much she knows. You might allow the friend to get in a word occasionally, when Jane pauses to take breath.

47. Write a spell, in rhyme and in the style of " This

to That and That to This," which the Fairy might speak to undo what she has done.

48. Write a short story or a one-act play in which a boy or girl living in your town finds Aladdin's lamp in a lumber-room, and accidentally discovers its wonderful powers ; or a story or one-act play in which a fairy gives the boy or girl three wishes.

49. Draw and paint the peacock pie or Princess Myra's carriage.

BOOKS TO READ

50. *Alexander the Great* and *Archibald*, one-act plays by W. Graham Robertson. (In *The Slippers of Cinderella*, etc., with the author's illustrations.)

Peter Pan and Wendy, by J. M. Barrie.

Old King Cole, by Clifford Bax.

HERMON OULD : THE DISCOVERY

Mr. Hermon Ould, who has written a number of very interesting plays, has pictured vividly for us the moment of the discovery of America, the greatest discovery in the history of Europe. His " work of imagination " helps us to realize the truth of how that discovery was made.

You may be interested to know that the land which Columbus sighted was one of the Bahamas, probably Watling Island. He went ashore next morning to claim the island as Spanish territory, and was well received by the natives. Then, after visiting other islands, he sailed back to Spain to announce his discovery of the Indies—for he never knew that he had found a new continent.

ON TALKING IT OVER

51. The poop is the raised deck at the stern of the vessel. The quarter-deck is the part of the deck which

lies between the mainmast and the stern, including the poop; it is used by officers only. Why does Columbus go to the poop-head when he is looking for land?

52. What does Diego mean by saying, " We are like bats that fly by day "?

53. The variation of the compass, to which Pedro refers, occurred when the *Santa Maria* had sailed about six hundred miles to westward, and greatly alarmed the superstitious seamen.

54. What do you think of the answer which Francisco makes to Columbus: " There are limits to duty . . ." ? (page 91).

55. Is the stage-direction, *He is paler than his wont, but very calm*, intended for the actor or the reader?

56. Why do the crew call Columbus an Italian renegade "?

57. In what way do all the similes resemble each other in Columbus's speech, ' Loyalty passes . . . at the first contact " ? (page 94). Are they the kind of similes which you would expect him to use?

58. Why does he " peer more earnestly into the darkness " ? (page 95).

59. It seems very easy for the mutinous seamen, thirty to one," to overpower Columbus and turn the ship homewards. Why do they not carry out their plan? (They did actually plan to throw him overboard.)

60. What does Columbus mean by " Your best cannot be bettered " ? (page 95).

61. Why does he send Pepe away before he tells Pedro that he thought he saw a light?

62. Why does he give the order to heave to?

FOR PEN AND PENCIL

63. Imagine that you are Diego Garcia and write a short account of the attempted mutiny and the hailing of the light.

64. " Great men are meteors that consume themselves to light the earth."—Thomas Hardy. Mr. Ould prints this quotation on the title-page of *The Discovery*. How does it apply to Columbus? Do you know any other great men to whom it applies?

65. The character of Columbus has been described by those who knew him well. He was a brave man, not easily turned aside from anything which he had resolved to do. He had a strong imagination, and considerable faith in himself, he was generous, conscientious, and religious ; but he was not a good leader, because he could not handle men well, and being very quick-tempered and impulsive he often did things for which he was afterwards very sorry. His difficulties were due partly to these defects in his character, and partly to Spanish jealousy of him as a foreigner. (He was an Italian, born near Genoa : 1436 ?–1506.)

66. Show how far the play agrees with this description of his character : for example, try to find whether any of the things said and done by Columbus and said about him by others show that he was religious or not religious, brave or cowardly, and so on.

This is not very easy to do, but it is well worth trying. One can imagine Sherlock Holmes doing it with much interest. All the clues are in the play. What can you make of them ?

67. Write a dialogue in which an old sailor tells Columbus of the ancient tradition that the Vikings discovered land across the western ocean centuries before. (This tradition may have been one of the things which made Columbus resolve to set out on the voyage.)

68. Write a one-act play or short story from the following outline. Time: 1580. Scene : Deck of Francis Drake's ship, the *Golden Hind,* lying at anchor at Deptford. Drake has just returned from his three years' voyage round the world, with a shipload of treasure plundered from Spanish galleons and colonies. (Drake was the first Englishman to sail round the world.) Queen Elizabeth visits the ship with her courtiers and asks Drake many questions about his wonderful adventures. She is very pleased. As Spain and England are supposed to be at peace, the Spanish ambassador protests angrily against Drake's piracies, and expects Drake to be punished, for Spain is the richest and most powerful country in Europe, not to be lightly defied. Elizabeth replies by knighting Drake with the sword which she gave him when he left England. (Note that these details are partly imaginary.)

69. Find a picture of Columbus's ship, or of a small ship of his time, and copy it with pencil and water-colours.

70. Draw a map of the Atlantic Ocean, and show the track of Columbus's first voyage : Palos (August 3, 1492); Canary Islands (September 6) ; Bahama Islands (October 12) ; Cuba ; Hayti ; the mouth of the Tagus, near Lisbon (March 4, 1493) ; Palos (March 15).

BOOKS TO READ

71. *Joan the Maid* and *The Pathfinder*, one-act plays by Hermon Ould. (In *Plays of Pioneers*.)

BERNARD GILBERT : ELDORADO

Mr. Gilbert is playing a very fascinating game. Many writers have played it, and probably you have done so occasionally, but few people have been so thorough as Mr. Gilbert. Not content, like most of us, with creating an imaginary island or city in which we can wander and have adventures, he has invented " Bly District "—" a section of three or four hundred square miles, offered as an example of rural England, uncontaminated by English civilization. . . . Reference to the map shows it running up, from the sea, through successive belts of marsh, fen, sand, heath, moor, and limestone, embracing most kinds of soil and methods of cultivation, and nearly all classes of countryman." He has drawn the map of this country and written directories (like that at the head of this play) for every town and village. He knows all the people in his area, and is telling us about them in a succession of novels, plays, and poems.

ON TALKING IT OVER

72. For what purpose did the dramatist put in the opening dialogue between James and his son? (pages 102–104).

73. Why does Henry say, " This isn't fen-land " ?

74. Why is James " scornful " when he says, " Of course not ! That was after I told him I hadn't any to spare " ?

75. Find three or four speeches in which James clearly shows his meanness.

76. Who is Tom Arch ? (page 122).

77. Does the old man really get the better of Mrs. Burrows ?

78. Which is the most enjoyable moment in the play ?

FOR PEN AND PENCIL

79. You have seen only the bottom story of the old windmill as yet. Take a journey to the top story, and then write an account of all you have seen. (Remember Betsy's description, on pages 106–107).

80. Describe the fine view across Caxton Moor to Keal Hill.

81. Write a sequel to *Eldorado*, in the form of a dialogue or a one-act play, in which " Brother-in-law Japhet " learns from Mrs. Burrows what has happened to their potatoes. You have first of all to make up your mind as to what kind of people they are, how each will feel about the matter, and what Japhet is likely to do. You may bring in any characters from *Eldorado*.

82. Make a little rural comedy of your own, in two scenes, about the choir and the vicar in Mr. Thomas Hardy's story, *Under the Greenwood Tree* (Part II, chaps. ii. and iv.). You will have to cut down some of the longer speeches, and make a few additions and alterations. Remember that the story is copyright, which means that your play must not be performed in public without the author's permission, although you can do it as often as you like in the form-room or at home.

83. Draw a plan of an imaginary island or city of your

own, in which you would like to have adventures, and paint it in bright colours.

84. Write a short story or a one-act play about your adventures, keeping the plan in front of you as you write. You need not be your ordinary self, of course: you can be a pirate, or any one interesting.

BOOKS TO READ

85. *The Old Bull*, by Bernard Gilbert, in *Nine Modern Plays* (T.E.S.).

My First Book, by R. L. Stevenson. (It is in the T.E.S. edition of *Treasure Island*.)

There is another very interesting map at the beginning of *Prester John*, an excellent adventure story by John Buchan.

J. A. FERGUSON: CAMPBELL OF KILMOHR

If you live in the south of England you may think that this play is written in " bad English," but this is quite wrong. The characters speak Scots, which has been a distinct form of English for centuries and has a fine literature of its own, including the poems of Robert Burns and (in part at least) the novels of Sir Walter Scott. Now it is developing its own drama too, thanks largely to the Scottish National Players, of Glasgow, who act the best Scottish plays which they can find and act them well. Mr. Ferguson, who has written a number of novels and plays, has given us in *Campbell of Kilmohr* the finest Scottish tragedy, and Mr. John Brandane is now writing excellent comedies.

Campbell of Kilmohr is so good not only because it is cleverly written, but because it is so true to life, so simple and sincere. All the characters in it are real, living people, and the heroism of Mary and Dugald Stewart gives the play a fine nobility of feeling. It is worth reading many times, and well worth acting.

ON TALKING IT OVER

86. The " gift " is the gift of second-sight—of seeing things happening at a distance or in the future.

87. Who is the person to whom Stewart refers as " another and a greater " ?

88. What do you think happened when Stewart ran into the sentry " round the bend beyond Kilrain " ?

89. Why does Morag push the dirk away and hide her face in her hands ?

90. Why did Pharaoh spare the butler ?

91. You will find the story of Haman, and how he came to be hanged on a gallows seventy feet high, in the Old Testament : *Esther*, chaps. iii.–vii.

92. If you do not know the meaning of " proscription " and " contumacy," look them up in a dictionary. The " capital charge " here means punishment by death.

93. Does Campbell really obtain the information which he requires ?

94. When do you most dislike Campbell ?

95. There is one sentence on page 142 which might very well be taken as a motto for the whole play ; and there is another on page 144. Can you find them both ?

96. Is Mary Stewart sad because her son is dead ?

97. In what way does Dugald Stewart resemble Christopher Columbus ?

98. How does this play differ from all the other plays in this book ?

FOR PEN AND PENCIL

99. If you turn back to the paragraph about Columbus's character, No. 65, you will see that it tells you his chief characteristics and then asks you to find things in the play which show these characteristics. Now, do the opposite with Campbell. Read through the play very carefully, making notes about the things which he says and does, and which are said about him. For example, if he says or does something which shows that he is a coward, then make a note of it. When you have been through the whole play in this way, arrange your notes

carefully, and then write a description of Campbell's character.

100. Write a short account of any one who has given his life heroically for a cause in which he believed. If you do not know of any one, you should read Sir Arthur Quiller-Couch's fine book called *The Roll Call of Honour* (T.E.S.).

101. This play is tragic, but not sad. Can you explain why it is not ?

102. Write a paragraph in praise of Dugald Stewart, or Mary Stewart.

BOOKS TO READ

103. *The Escape of Prince Charles Edward*, in *A Book of Escapes and Hurried Journeys*, by John Buchan (T.E.S.).

The Secret of the Heather Ale, by Neil Munro, in *Modern Short Stories* (T.E.S.). A story of a desperate battle between two Highland clans.

Midwinter, by John Buchan (T.E.S.). A tale of the '45 Rebellion.

MAURICE BARING : CATHERINE PARR

Probably you have not read or seen a play like this before. It is one of a number of *Diminutive Dramas* in which the Honourable Maurice Baring makes good-humoured fun of many people who are famous in history and legend—Jason, Odysseus, Julius Cæsar, Alfred the Great, and others. The author has treated history much as Mr. Milne has treated fairy tales, and with the same enjoyable results. This is a very good play to act, and easy to stage.

ON TALKING IT OVER

104. " A woman of your experience " is Henry's unpleasant reminder that Catherine was a widow when he married her. She retorts by reminding him—of what ?

105. Henry was a good musician. He played **several** instruments, sang well, and composed a number of songs. What is assonance ?

106. His pride in his music was equalled by his pride in his learning, which he shows here by referring to the Greek writers, Plutarch, Xenophon, and Aristotle.

107. Bucephalus is pronounced Bū-sĕf'-a-lŭs.

The pronunciation of the Greek which Henry quotes cannot be well represented in English letters, so if you can find no one to tell you exactly how to say it, you had better leave it out when acting the play.

108. " My family has no blood on its escutcheon." Henry had executed two of his wives and many of his enemies. What does " escutcheon " mean, and what does it stand for here ?

109. Dr. Butts, afterwards Sir William Butts, was the King's physician. His reply by the page, " Dr. Butts says your Majesty was quite correct as to the colour of Alexander the Great's horse," is one of the best things in the play. What is the point of it ? What does it tell you about Dr. Butts ?

110. When is Henry (a) most on his dignity, (b) most angry, (c) most good-tempered, (d) most anxious to please his wife ?

111. Which is Catherine's most spiteful remark ?

112. At what point are they quarrelling most furiously?

113. Do you like the people in this play ?

114. Like *The Discovery*, this is a play about people who actually lived in the past, but it is very different. What are the chief differences ? Would you call it a historical play ?

FOR PEN AND PENCIL

115. The dramatist has not given many stage-directions. Copy out the passage from " I suppose you mean I am a bigot " to " a great many letters to write," adding full stage-directions. You may begin like this :

King Henry [*his temper rising again*]. I suppose you mean I am a bigot ?

Catherine [*indignantly*]. You can turn what one says into meaning anything you like. [*Injured and emphatic*]

As a matter of fact, all I said was that the horse was black.

116. Write two short letters from Henry and Catherine respectively, in which they describe the quarrel to friends of theirs. You may be sure that they have very different ideas of what happened, and that each is convinced that the other was altogether in the wrong. Show this as clearly and humorously as you can.

117. Write a one-act play about any historical characters, in the same style as this play. If you choose the incident of King Alfred and the Cakes you may be able to compare your play with the one in *Diminutive Dramas* on the same subject.

118. Find a picture of Henry VIII., and copy it carefully. The best is the famous portrait by Hans Holbein, a great painter of his time. The picture on page 146 is copied from this portrait, but gives only the head and shoulders.

119. Draw a plan of the stage, showing the positions of the table, chairs, bookcase, and entrances, and of the characters when Henry is telling the Page to find the Chamberlain.

BOOKS TO READ

120. *Diminutive Dramas*, by Maurice Baring. Numbers 5, 7, and 18. One of the best of these, *The Rehearsal*, is in *Nine Modern Plays* (T.E.S.).

Shakespeare's *Henry VIII.*, or *The Queen and the Cardinal*, in Evelyn Smith's *Little Plays from Shakespeare*, *Second Series* (T.E.S.).

MILES MALLESON: MICHAEL

Mr. Malleson has made this play from a story by Count Leo Tolstoy (1828–1910), the great Russian novelist, dramatist, thinker, and social reformer. "What Men Live By" is a story with a moral, like so many of Tolstoy's writings, for he gave much thought to the great problem of how men should live so as to make the very best of life, for their fellow-men and for themselves. And he wrote often of the Russian peasants, whom he knew and loved well, even before he gave away all his possessions so that he himself could live the simple life of a peasant. The glimpses of that life which we have in *Michael* are as true as they are vivid.

ON TALKING IT OVER

121. " You must be a bad man—[because] you are afraid," says Matryona. Do you agree with her reasoning ?

122. What do you feel about Michael after Aniuska's behaviour towards him at the end of Scene I. ?

123. What do you think of the nobleman ? What do you learn from the way in which Simon takes orders from him ?

124. When the news comes that the nobleman is dead, what do you think of Michael ?

125. Choose two adjectives to describe the character of each of the following : Simon, Matryona, The Woman.

126. If *Michael* were written in one scene instead of three, how would it be arranged ? Do you think it would be as good ?

127. What would be the chief problem in performing the play, and how would you solve it ?

128. Which is the most striking incident in the play, and which the most impressive moment ?

129. Do you know any sentence in the New Testament which might be taken as a motto for the whole play ?

FOR PEN AND PENCIL

130. Write down a title for each of the three scenes.

131. Explain how the three incidents taught Michael the three great truths which he had to learn.

132. Imagine that you are Simon *or* Matryona, and write a short account of the happenings in the last scene.

133. Say what you have learned from the play about Russian peasant-life.

134. Re-read the stage direction at the head of Scene I., and then draw a picture of the interior of Simon's hut.

BOOKS TO READ

135. *What Men live by, Iván the Fool, The Bear-hunt,* and *Two Old Men,* in *Twenty-three Tales by Tolstoy,* translated by L. and A. Maude. Oxford Press.

Paddly Pools and *The Little White Thought,* one-act plays by Miles Malleson. Henderson.

Brother Wolf and *Sister Gold,* one-act plays by Laurence Housman. Sidgwick and Jackson.

GENERAL

136. Which of the plays in this book do you like most, and which do you like least ? Give your reasons.

137. Describe any amusing incident in the plays.

138. Which character in the plays do you most admire, and why ?

139. Arrange the plays under the following headings : Comedies, Tragedies, Historical Plays, " Moralities."

140. Draw and paint and cut out scenery for any one of the plays, and set it up as it would be on the stage.

141. Draw a stage plan for *The Slippers of Cinderella,* or Scene II. of *Robin Hood,* then choose an exciting moment in the play and show on the plan where you think that the characters would be standing at that moment.

142. Which plays in this book would you choose as most suitable for performance (1) at your school speech-day, (2) at a school concert, given at the end of the Christmas term, (3) by a Scout Troop, (4) by an O. T. C., and (5) by a branch of the League of Nations Union ? Explain the reasons for your choice in each case.

143. Draw up from this book a programme of two, three, or four plays (according to the number of actors available) for performance by your own form or society. Choose and arrange the plays very carefully, to make a good and varied programme. Then cast the plays (that is, choose the actors), giving every person available the part for which he or she is most suited, omitting no one, and in a very few cases giving two parts to one player if this proves necessary. A play which cannot be cast fairly well should not be put in the programme.

144. When you have drawn up this programme of plays, write a short prologue for it, in rhymed verse.

145. Which part would you choose for yourself in your programme, and why?

146. Make a model theatre, with a painted stage-setting for any play in this book, figures of the characters painted and cut out, and electric lighting from " pea-bulbs," and a pocket-lamp battery, if you wish. You can give a performance of the play, preferably with one or two people to help you read the parts ' behind the scenes." Full instructions for all this are to be found in *Everybody's Theatre*, written and illustrated by H. W. Whanslaw. (Wells Gardner, Darton, and Co., 5s.)

A SUGGESTION FOR FORM-ROOM ACTING

147. Elect leaders from the form and make each of them responsible for one of the plays which you wish to act. Having decided how many players are needed for each play, the leaders, taking turns, choose their companies from the form, and then each company prepares a " performance " of its play, to be given with the rest of the form as audience. The leader should act as " producer " in the preliminary rehearsal or rehearsals, and assign parts and positions on the " stage " and suggest movements, etc.

The performances can be very simple, with all the actors reading their parts, or they can be more elaborate, with some or all of the parts learned by heart and costumes improvised or borrowed. In any case simple properties and stage furniture are a great help. Plays acted in this way can be very enjoyable, and there is the advantage that if rehearsals can be held in a large room or in the open air, all the plays can be rehearsed at the same time.

ON WRITING LITTLE PLAYS

148. Having enjoyed the plays in this book, you may like to try your hand as a playwright. To write good plays demands ability of a special kind, and a first-hand knowledge of stage conditions, so you need not be surprised if you do not produce a masterpiece; but the attempt is well worth making, and can be very good fun. You may prefer to begin work on your play without more ado, following your own methods, but if you would like to write a play good enough for performance by your own form or school society, you may find a few hints useful.

149. First of all, for the plot. If you can invent this yourself, so much the better. Perhaps you can write about a historical character in whom you are interested, or an incident in the history of your own town or village or school. Several of these incidents, dramatized by yourself and your friends after you have talked things over, could be put together to make a little pageant, or a " chronicle play " about the life of a great man or woman of the past.

150. If you do not invent your own play, you can follow one of the suggestions already made in this book, or else take an incident from a story and make it into a play, as Mr. Malleson has done with *Michael*. There are many such incidents to be found in novels by Dickens, Sir Walter Scott, R. L. Stevenson, Rudyard Kipling, Sir Arthur Conan Doyle, and other writers. Perhaps your teacher will suggest some incidents from books which are in your school or form library.* A number of books in the " Teaching of English Series " are specially useful. *Pattern Plays*, by E. C. Oakden and Mary Sturt, contains stories, plays made from these stories, and further stories to be made into plays, with hints as to how it should be

---

* Copyright work must not be used in public without special permission from the owner of the copyright.

done.   John Buchan's *A Book of Escapes* and *The Path of the King* are treasure-houses of short, exciting incidents, and the non-copyright books include *The Arabian Nights*, Kingsley's *The Heroes*, Scenes from " *Quentin Durward*," and the stories in Sir Henry Newbolt's *The Greenwood*. Whether you invent your plot or borrow it, you will find it a good plan to write it down briefly before you begin on the play.   It is much better to have your play in one fairly long scene (or act) than in several short scenes, so try to arrange it like this if you can.   For instance, *The Slippers of Cinderella* would not be nearly so good, and would be much harder to stage, if it were written in several scenes—one in which the Tremaines learn that they have lost all their money, and another in which they move into the small house in which we see them, and so on.

151.   Then make up your mind who the people are, and what they are like, and try to make them different from each other.   Notice how different Campbell is from Dugald Stewart, and Columbus from Guillermo Ires, and Myra from Agatha.   They behave differently, and have different ways of talking about the same thing.

152.   The first thing the characters have to do is to let the audience know who they are, and which are friends and which are enemies, and anything important which has been happening.   If you re-read the beginning of *The Slippers of Cinderella* and *Michael* you will see how cleverly the dramatist makes his characters tell the audience all about themselves, by talking to each other. One method is to make a character who has been away ask another to explain what has happened during his absence.   But do not have too much explaining.

153.   Then " the plot thickens " until the play reaches its climax, which is the most exciting part, the highest point, so to speak.   Try to find the climax of *Robin Hood*, Scene II., *Campbell of Kilmohr*, *The Discovery*, and *Michael*.

154.   After the climax the plot is unravelled, the questions which the audience have been asking about the characters are answered, and the play comes to an end. You can learn a great deal by studying the plays in this volume, and by comparing *Michael* with the short story from which it is made.

155. Finally, before you start writing, turn to the beginning of one of the plays and see how it is arranged. Write the title, your name as author, a list of characters, and a short description of the scenery, and then begin the dialogue. Notice where the printer has put capitals, full stops, brackets, and italics, and copy this arrangement. You can't put words in italics when you are writing, so you underline them instead. Take a fresh line for each speech, and write as neatly as you can. It is a good plan to write first on loose sheets of paper, and on one side only, so that alterations can be made easily, and then to copy your work into a book—again leaving alternate pages blank. You will find much more on the subject of play-writing in *Nine Modern Plays*.

SOME BOOKS ON MODERN DRAMA

(Not intended for junior readers)

A Study of the Modern Drama. Barrett H. Clark. Appleton and Co. 15s.

This valuable book, an encyclopædia of facts and critical ideas, is particularly suitable for the school library and for reading circles, because it suggests lines of thought rather than offers definite conclusions. Half the book is given to English, Irish, and American drama ; the other half to the drama of Norway, Russia, France, and other European countries. Exceptionally useful bibliographies and index.

Modern Drama. J. W. Marriott. The " Little Theatre " Series. Nelson. 3s. 6d. net.

An illuminating survey of drama in England, Europe, and America, from the late nineteenth century to the present year. A guide to all the most interesting modern plays and playwrights. Fully indexed.

Drama. Ashley Dukes. Home University Library, 2s.

A very interesting essay, of unusual scope. Chapters on the Nature and Varieties of Drama, The Dramatist, The Actor, The Producer, The Scene, The Playhouse,

The Audience, and Drama Present and Future. Bibliography.

On the Art of the Theatre.   Edward Gordon Craig.
     Heinemann.   10s. 6d.

One of the most stimulating, provocative, and original books ever written on the arts of stage production.

The English Theatre.   Allardyce Nicoll.   Illustrated.
     Nelson.   6s. net.

From Roman times to 1936—the only complete history, by the writer whom the *Times* has recently described as " the foremost historian of the British theatre." With a complete annotated list of London theatres, past and present, bibliography, and index.

ACTING NOTES

THESE brief notes on the plays in this collection are intended for those who know little or nothing of the art of dramatic production. There are several excellent books for the amateur, which teach as much as it is possible to teach of any art in a book, and it is not proposed to attempt to write a complete guide in this limited space, but to attempt instead what none of the books give—a detailed account of the production of a particular play, *The Discovery*. The notes on the other plays, suggestive, not exhaustive, will be merely supplementary to this account.

THE DISCOVERY

We will assume that this play has been chosen because it can be cast fairly well from the actors available, offers a fairly large number of parts (for a one-act play), is not difficult or expensive to dress and stage, and—most important of all—it is worth doing. (For some societies it will have the further attraction that all the characters are men, though one can imagine it performed quite well by a company of girls.)

The Producer.—When the society has organized its activities and finances (see the books recommended on page 226), the producer must set to work.

The producer is to the play what the conductor is to the orchestra. He is responsible for the artistic harmony and unity of the play in all its details. He must have the power of final decision in all matters affecting this artistic harmony, and upon his tact and energy and enthusiasm, his knowledge and imagination, his willingness to experiment and learn, the success of the play will depend to a very large extent.

Casting is the first problem, whether it is done by a small committee or by the producer alone. In the case of untried actors, the best plan is to begin with " auditions " or trial readings, at which the candidates for parts can read in turn various characters in *The Discovery*. The casting authority can then decide from voice, manner, and apparent acting potentialities, how the play is to be cast. Columbus is most important of course, and the actor who is to take this part should have a good presence and ability to assume the dignity and habit of command which are required. Don Pedro is a gentleman also, but of less striking personality. The remaining characters, except the boy Pepe, should be much less cultured in voice and manner.

If the players are juniors, convincing and realistic characterization is obviously not to be expected, but the casting should be done as carefully as with adult players.

Understudies are a valuable insurance against disaster, and some societies choose two casts, which work quite independently of each other, and are responsible for alternate performances.

Permission to perform the play should now be secured, and this must always be done before rehearsals begin, because occasionally a play is not available for amateurs. For *The Discovery*, application must be made to the author's agents, Messrs. Samuel French, 26 Southampton Street, Strand, London, W.C.2, without whose written permission no performance may be given. The royalty for each performance is 10s. 6d., payable in advance. (The play takes about forty minutes.) The society is bound in honour to pay the royalty, which is in many cases the chief source of the dramatist's income, and is simply a payment for the right to use his property. A dramatist should never be asked to waive his royalty because the performance is in aid of charity, for he prefers to choose for himself the charities to which he is to contribute. (Such performances are good for charity and bad for amateur drama ; they suggest that the latter is not on its own account worth paying to see.) An increasing number of dramatists, however, accept percentage royalties instead of fixed fees, on which point inquiries may be made of the British Drama League.

Business arrangements, such as booking a hall, advertising the play, and distributing tickets, should be made well in advance. *The Discovery* will obviously not make a complete programme by itself. Schools and some other educational institutions may get exemption from the entertainment tax by application on the Form E.D.23, which can be obtained from the local Customs and Excise Office.

The Stage.—There is a great deal to be said for the stage simply set with screens or hung with curtains (see the books by Mr. Barrett Clark and Mr. Harold Ridge). At least for those amateurs with no stage of their own, scenery is usually an expense and trouble out of all proportion to its worth, and most amateur scenery is artistically inferior to curtains. *The Discovery* may be played if necessary on a stage draped round with black or dark blue curtains, and bare of properties ; the audience will not resent this simplicity if the acting is good. The great advantage of a simple setting is that it concentrates attention upon the actors and leaves a clearer picture of the play in the mind of the spectator, and the shorter the play the greater is the gain.* For *The Discovery* the setting shown in the stage-plan on p. 205 is suggested as a suitable combination of simplicity and of appeal to the imagination of the audience. It should be possible to most small societies, but if the raised platform for the poop cannot be contrived, the directions for stage movements which are given below can still be used without alteration.

The surround, shown by the wavy line, consists of curtains of black velveteen (or cheaper material), or dark blue serge ; with good lighting they will suggest the night sky excellently. The bulwarks, about four feet high—or less if the actors are short—consists of canvas stretched on wooden frames or, failing this, of a row of butter boxes ; † either can be distempered or painted, to repre-

---

* Mr. Percival Wilde tells the story of a twenty-minutes play of his which was so successful when acted by amateurs on a curtained stage, with very simple dresses and properties, that it was taken up by a millionaire theatre magnate. He spent large sums in giving the play the sumptuous dresses and architectural setting which he thought it needed, and then found that it was a complete failure ; by the time the audience had done looking at the dresses and scenery, and begun to attend to the dialogue, the play was over !

† These boxes are cheap, strong, and very useful to a small society, for they can be distempered any colour and used for many purposes—to make battlements, for instance, or a dais, or the table in *Robin Hood*.

sent the wooden ribs and panels of the ship's side.
(Columbus's vessel was a square-rigged, three-masted
ship of 230 tons, 95 feet long, and $25\frac{1}{2}$ feet wide, with high
poop and forecastle, rounded bow and square stern.
There is a good picture in *A History of Everyday Things in
England*, vol. i., page 155.) If space is limited the raised
platform constituting the poop need not occupy much of
the stage, since little action takes place on it. In this
case the top of the poop is not seen, and the large lantern may be transferred to the place indicated in the
plan. It is not at all difficult to make a beautiful lantern.
On a small stage the poop cannot be high, but eighteen
inches is suggested as a minimum. This gives a flight
of three steps, each of them nine to twelve inches deep.
(Sets of steps, and of small platforms to stand on
trestles, are most useful, for they will serve for many
plays in a variety of combinations and positions. Only
the producer who has worked with them knows what a
boon it is to be able to develop the action of a play in
three dimensions instead of two.) There should be a
rail along the edge of the poop and down both sides of the
steps, low enough and open enough not to obscure the
players at all. The top of this rail and of the bulwarks
may be picked out with a line of white paint if they are
not clear enough in the dim light. The masts, which are
not essential, are made of cylinders of canvas or casement
cloth, sewn firmly to rings at top and bottom and then
drawn taut ; or of tile-battens, nailed at top and bottom,
two or three inches apart, around three-quarters of the
circumference of two wooden discs, this cylindrical cage
being covered with material. To these may be added if
desired a few thick ropes (shrouds), drawn tight so that
they appear to stretch from the bulwarks to the maintop ;
and a strip of light-coloured material, to represent the
lower edge of a sail, curving over the actors' heads, at
right angles to the bulwarks. The sail has no lower yard.
From the foot of the poop to the mainmast is the quarter-
deck. The waist, foremast, and forecastle are off stage to
the right.

Lighting for this play is important, but simple. There
should be an electric bulb or group of bulbs fixed inside
the proscenium, right or right centre, and so shrouded by
setting them in boxes or tin funnels that their light falls

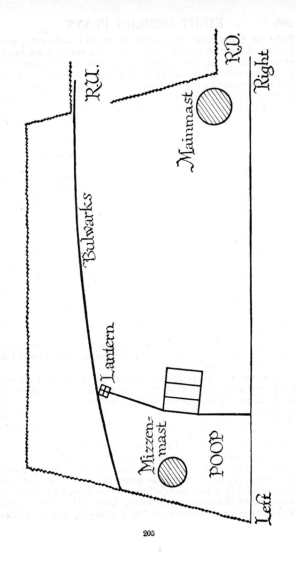

fully on the acting area, slightly on the bulwarks, and not at all on the curtain surround. A small flood-light, costing about £4, 10s. complete, would do for this, and is a valuable acquisition, but a few ordinary electric light bulbs, set in the bottom of a box, make a simple and quite passable substitute. The exact position of the lamps and the intensity of the lighting must be determined by experiment, the safe rule being that people at the back of the hall should see something of the expression of the actors' faces. It may be advisable to supplement the lighting by very dim footlights or by a smaller flood on the left.

Stage Furniture and Properties are not needed for this play. In cases where they are needed, the producer should draw up a full list of the items at the earliest possible moment, for the benefit of the stage-manager, carpenters, etc. Furniture and properties, or rough substitutes for them, are needed in rehearsal from the first.

Costumes for the play must be considered as soon as rehearsals begin. Those societies which cannot make their own costumes for *The Discovery*, with the help of the books recommended on page 226, may hire them at very low rates from the Village Drama Society, 15 Peckham Road, Camberwell, London, S.E.5, or from a firm of costumiers at charges which vary from 7s. 6d. to 25s. for each dress.

Rehearsal.—While all these arrangements are being made, rehearsals of the play must begin, and these the producer controls.

The aim of the producer should be to present to the audience as full and clearly, as beautifully or as humorously as possible, what it is that the dramatist has to say to them; every detail of acting, setting, and lighting should be regulated to this end. So the first thing to do is to study the play.

It will be seen that *The Discovery* depends for its effect upon the dramatic contrast and conflict between Columbus and his crew. Columbus, the visionary, alone but resolute, is following his quest in the strength of his faith and his single-mindedness; the crowd of seamen, who do not share his enthusiasm, though they have some instinctive appreciation of his greatness, are naturally most concerned for their own safety. Though they have the advantage of numbers and the spur of superstitious fear, they are uncertain of themselves and their aims, and lack a good leader, so that Columbus is able to keep them at bay until the sight of land saves the situation. (In all this the play is fairly true to history.) Don Pedro stands between the admiral and the crew, doubting Columbus, but ashamed to oppose him.

The play therefore has to be " worked " to bring out these ideas, and however young the players may be, the performance (and the players) will gain greatly if the producer has a clear conception of the theme of the play.

The stage directions given in the text are inadequate for production, so they must be supplemented. Some producers decide every detail of movement, grouping, and gesture, with a model stage and puppets, before they begin rehearsing ; others decide only the main outlines, and fill in the details with the actors. The producer must work out his own artistic salvation in this as in many other matters, but at least he must go to the first rehearsal with the entrances and exits and important stage movements clear in his mind and on his scrip. A stage-plan is necessary, and smaller plans showing the positions of the characters at important points in the action are a great help. For *The Discovery* we may decide as follows :

When the curtain rises, Diego and Juan are both down stage * to the extreme right, in front of the mast. Diego is standing, facing towards the right, and holding with his left hand a rope which comes down to the deck at his feet from a point above his head and out of sight. Juan, facing left, is kneeling at Diego's feet and fastening the rope to a bolt at the foot of the mast. It should be made as plain as possible that they are not interested in what they are doing, but in what they are saying to each other. Their voices must be low, but with good enunciation they will be clearly heard if, after the curtain rises, they wait a moment until the rustling of the audience subsides.

To emphasize the "*gracious* madman " Juan sits back on his heels. The song of the seamen is heard from the

* " Down stage " means towards the audience, and " up stage " away from the audience, a reminder that stages used to be built sloping up towards the back.

wings to the right; Juan stands up and turns facing front and looking off right when he says, " They ought to stop that." At Diego's " 'Sh!" both kneel and fumble with the rope.

Pedro enters up stage right, going towards the poop steps, and stops short at right centre when he sees the two seamen. Diego stands up and turns to face Pedro at the latter's " Who's that? " " And an uglier deed " is the cue for Juan to rise, salute, and go off, down stage, right, and for Columbus to enter, up stage, right. He is going towards the poop steps, and he too stops short, with a quick suspicious glance, when he sees the two men talking. He is down stage centre. Pedro draws back up stage a step, so that Columbus can speak to Diego. When Columbus " *points off* " Diego makes a movement to confront him in open defiance, hesitates, weakens, and turns away to go off, slowly and with obvious reluctance, down stage right. Columbus looks after him for a second before speaking. When the two have gone on to the poop, Pepe can enter down stage, right, and remain behind the mainmast, in full sight of the audience, but hidden from Columbus and Pedro. (A hatchway is likely to be difficult and is in no way essential.) On the poop Columbus is well down stage, left, looking out over the audience, and Pedro is a pace behind him. He turns on Pedro at " You, too." They are both rigidly attentive during the song, and then as he says, " *Madre de Dios*, they drink too much," Columbus strides purposefully down to the quarter-deck as though he were going to forbid the singing, but pauses centre, and turns, at the words of Pedro, who has followed him more slowly. Both remain centre until Pedro, crossing in front of Columbus, goes off up stage, right. Columbus then paces slowly and thoughtfully to the extreme left of the quarter-deck below the steps, speaking as he goes. He turns abruptly towards Pepe when the latter leaves his place by the mainmast and runs up the steps, to come down again immediately and approach Columbus, who stands his ground. Pedro comes to the centre, up stage a little, and Pepe, when told to go, passes behind Pedro and stands by the bulwarks, up stage right centre. Columbus takes a step towards the right when he cries, " Hallo, there! " and Francisco, entering from the right, down stage, comes to the centre when he says, " Our power of endurance has gone," and Columbus goes to him at " Francisco, let me plead with you." Both look to the right, Francisco half-turning, when " *the song swells up again.*" Columbus's command, " Boy, come here," brings Pepe down stage to him, Francisco stepping back to the right and a little up stage. Columbus turns his back to the audience when he tells Pedro, who is standing at the head of the poop steps, to have Guillermo sent. When the angry seamen crowd on to the quarter-deck from both entrances, right, Pedro pauses half-way down the poop steps, Columbus stands fast, and Francisco draws back up stage to join the other seamen. All these must have their exact positions assigned to them (or they may stand in a straight line) with Guillermo and Diego in the forefront, on either side of the mast, the former up stage of the latter. Guillermo comes down stage to right centre when he " *advances towards Columbus,*" who takes a step forward at " Don Guillermo." Guillermo draws back doubtfully to his former position by the mast at " Now return to your duties," and a moment later Diego starts forward. When Columbus has mounted the poop he turns left and stands a little down stage of the head of the steps, Pedro being on the other side of them. The men crowd forward to centre at " Have him down ! " and when Pepe, " after intervening," goes up the steps, they draw back a little. When Columbus " *looks out at sea* " he looks over the audience, standing rigidly and peering, and evidently forgetting the seamen entirely until their movement recalls his attention. Guillermo " *slinks off* " down stage, right. Francisco speaks from centre, and then follows Guillermo. The others go out slowly and hesitatingly, up stage or down, and Pepe follows them a moment later. Then the wild shout of " Land ! " breaks in with startling suddenness upon the intense but restrained excitement of Pedro and Columbus.

At the first rehearsal the only thing for the actors to do is to " read for position "—reading their parts without expression, and simply learning their movements. After this the actors should make themselves word perfect in their parts as quickly as they can : it is a mistake for actors, especially if they are young and inexperienced, to be set to learn their parts before rehearsals begin.

14

The play then has to be built up at successive rehearsals —twenty or more may be necessary—and when it is in mechanically good " going order " at the right speeds (amateurs are notorious for speaking too slowly or too quickly, without variation of pace), the producer can work for " atmosphere," for all those little subtleties of intonation and movement which make the supreme difference between a living work of art and a mechanical performance.

The actors, as well as the producer, will have much to learn, and the latter should be prepared to give training in speech and movement if it is needed. Every word of the play must be audible to people in the back row of the audience, and this is a question not of shouting, but of correct pitch and clear enunciation. Speech normally should be as pleasant and natural as possible, without any " elocution for elocution's sake."

Actors must speak to the front when they can reasonably do so ; not pass in front of any one who is speaking or distract attention from him ; stand still, when they do stand still, without being stiff and without shuffling about ; and move definitely when they do move. All movements must be natural or made to appear natural, not merely obvious devices for " changing the picture."

The producer should do everything he can to encourage players to " think themselves into " their parts,* to understand as fully as they can what they are doing and saying and feeling, and *to act all the time they are on the stage,* not merely while they are speaking. And they must learn to take their cues very promptly, so that there are no little gaps in between speeches. Every actor should understand the entire play, and regard its success as a whole as a much more important thing than his individual success in his own part ; though he must

* " Unfortunately it is superficially easier to teach by the imitative method than by any other. It is much simpler to say " Copy me " than it is to arouse a sluggish mind to think continually and vividly, or to awaken in minds which are purely intellectual an emotional response. To train and develop the great imaginative faculty of the mind, to balance the emotional response by intellectual thought, and to induce the student to bring his voice, face, and body under his own mental control, requires much more time, patience, and ability from the teacher than exhibiting himself as an example."—LOUIE BAGLEY.

realize that his own part, however small, is vital to the whole.

Make-up.—This fascinating art is dealt with in the books recommended on page 226. The dim lighting of this play may not demand complete make-up (covering the whole face, neck, and ears), in which case a little colour in the cheeks and darkening of the brows will be all the grease-paint needed : but this must be determined by experiment. All the characters except Pepe should wear beards and moustaches, those of the seamen being unkempt. As the appearance of Columbus is not familiar there is no necessity to attempt to reproduce it, but the following description of him, which has been left by his friend and companion, Las Casas, may be of interest : " He had a figure that was above medium height, a countenance long and imposing, an aquiline nose, clear blue eyes, a light complexion tinged with red, beard and hair blonde in youth, but early turned to white." There are several portraits of him in existence, but none that is certainly authentic.

The Dress Rehearsal should be a day or two days before the performance, and should be as much like a performance as possible, with full lighting, stage setting, dresses, and make-up, and a small select audience if desired. The producer should let it go through without interruption or alteration if these can possibly be avoided ; but he may give a few words of final advice to the cast— emphasizing especially that they must keep the play going whatever happens in performance : it is astonishing what audiences will not notice, if the players do not hesitate. If they are to take a " final curtain " this should be rehearsed, or it will almost certainly be muddled.

There is no need for any one to worry if the dress rehearsal is altogether miserable and depressing. Dress rehearsals often are ; but if the play has been faithfully rehearsed it will spring into full life in the performance.

The Programme should give the names of the actors in the order in which they appear or speak. This avoids any question as to precedence, and is an aid to the audience in identifying characters.

The Performance.—The producer's responsibility ends, in theory, with the dress rehearsal, when it passes to the stage manager, who is responsible for the stage setting, furniture, properties, and so on. But the producer will be well advised to remain in the wings to deal with any emergency and help keep the cast in good spirits. They may be comforted with the information that many experienced professional actors are always nervous before they go on!

The chief essentials for an artistic production are good team work, imagination, enthusiasm, loyalty, and an infinite capacity for taking pains. It will be noticed that wealth is not included. One of the most delightful things about amateur dramatic work is the fine results which may be obtained with slender means.

THE PRINCESS AND THE WOODCUTTER

The fee for each and every representation of this play by amateurs is one guinea, payable in advance to Messrs. Samuel French, Ltd., 26 Southampton Street, Strand, W.C.2, or their authorized representatives. No public performance may be given unless this written permission has first been obtained.

The time of acting is about thirty minutes.

The Princess and the Woodcutter is make-believe, and if it is played quickly and lightly, with enjoyment and without hitches, all will be well. If it drags slowly along with careful realism it will probably be very dull indeed. The audience is not asked to take it seriously at all, but only to be amused at the dramatist's lightness and deftness of touch, and the unexpected turns which he gives to a familiar situation. A bright Third or Fourth Form, with that quality of eager alertness which marks young actors of promise, could make the play very amusing, if it were thoroughly rehearsed to secure the lightness and smoothness of movement which are essential.

Staging could hardly be simpler—green curtains, or better still a real glade or a garden, with a bench and a few logs for the woodcutter to chop. Dresses could very well be copied from Heath Robinson's illustrations to Hans Andersen, or the pictures in *Shakespeare for Community Players* or *The Bankside Costume Book*. Both King and Queen should have large crowns, and if they look as though their wearers sleep in them, so much the better. Music for the songs is obtainable from Messrs. Samuel French, but if necessary they can easily be omitted, and so of course can the revels.

ROBIN HOOD

For permission to perform this play application must be made to Messrs. A. P. Watt & Sons, Hastings House, Norfolk Street, Strand, London, W.C.2, and no performance may be given until permission has been obtained. The royalty payable varies with the circumstances.

The play takes about fifteen minutes.

Whether this play is to be acted on the edge of a shrubbery or a wood, or on a stage indoors, it presents little difficulty in staging. Both the gallows and the silver birch at which Marian shoots must be off stage, so that Robin and Marian fire into the wings—which, in the open air, can be simply clumps of bushes or trees. Similarly, both the hut and the cave can be off stage if desired. The oak to which Robin Hood sets his back may be changed into any other tree for open-air performance, or if the play is being given indoors the tree may be dispensed with altogether by omitting Prince John's reference to it. It is easy to dispense with the Knight's horse. For the table a low box or bench or table, completely covered by green turfs or a green material such as serge, will serve very well. If good bows and arrows cannot be borrowed locally, boys will find great pleasure in making them, and should be encouraged to search any available books for information.

For indoor performances a stage draped with green curtains, and set with shrubs (not formal ones) in pots, will be quite adequate.

An open-air performance is likely to be better, and easier to arrange, and the lack of a front curtain presents a problem only at the end of Scene II. It might be solved by the party settling down to their meal after Shadow-of-a-Leaf's concluding speech, while one of the outlaws sings a song : when the song is finished they can all troop away. At the beginning of Scene I. the rustics and townsfolk enter from one direction : at the end the

Knight and outlaws hurry after Robin Hood, and the crowd follows the Sheriff. Then the stage is left empty for a few moments, and the change of scene is sufficiently indicated by Marian's opening speech, as she and the others enter, evidently in great anxiety.

Full instructions for making all the dresses required for the play are to be found in *The Bankside Costume Book* (see page 227), and only the Knight's armour presents any difficulty. The outlaws' dress is particularly simple and graceful : tunics, shorts, and stockings of Lincoln green ; socks with their tops rolled down almost to the ankles, for boots ; felt hats or close-fitting caps decked with feathers. Belts, daggers, etc., can be of bright contrasting colours.

The play is very suitable for young players, for it is so direct and simple ; the keynote is struck by the excellent stage direction, *Enter Robin Hood, disguised as an old beggar, with a green patch on one eye.* There are no subtleties of characterization : Robin Hood is a hero and Prince John is a villain, without qualification. Young actors, believing unreservedly in the play, may well give a more interesting performance than adults. The essentials are speed and vigour, and the fighting, the shooting, and the movements and murmurs of the crowd must not be left to the inspiration of the moment : they must be rehearsed exactly and thoroughly.

THE SLIPPERS OF CINDERELLA

The fee for each representation of this play by amateurs is seven shillings and sixpence, payable in advance to Messrs. Samuel French, 26 Southampton Street, Strand, London, W.C.2, or their authorized representatives, who, upon payment of the fee, will send a written permission for the performance to take place. No public performance may be given unless this written permission has first been obtained.

The play takes about forty minutes in performance.

For this play dark curtains would be too rich in effect, but curtains of hessian or some similar material will serve, or a realistic " box set " may be made—a room complete

except for " fourth wall," through which the audience
views it. Such a set can be made of a wooden framework,
covered with old newspapers or canvas and distempered.
A " practical " casement window is essential, with a small
platform outside, level with the sill, for the Fairy Queen
to stand upon. Behind this hangings are needed, and it
would be an advantage to have two sets—black or dark
blue curtains in front (to represent the night), which can
be drawn aside out of sight, and behind these a surface of
cream or pale grey, which can be lit with red light to represent the glow of the torches. The window-curtains
should be heavy, reach to the floor, hang well out from
the wall, and be arranged so that they can be drawn aside
from behind the scenes. In some cases it will be an
advantage to have the section of scenery or curtain below
the window made removable, so that Agatha can slip
through to put on her dress behind the scenes ; she will
have no time to lose. The window may be near the middle
of the back wall, the door R. up stage, the door L. down
stage, and the table left centre. The fireplace may be
self-contained and constructed to stand by itself. (A
small dramatic society should have several fireplaces,
of different types ; stood against screens or scenery or
curtains, they can be used again and again.) Red paper
and an electric light globe will do for the basis of any fire,
and if flames are specially desired, no doubt some member
of the company will enjoy constructing them with strips
of silk, kept in motion by a small *silent* electric fan con-
cealed in the fire.

The peacock pie is something of a problem. Mr.
Graham Robertson made his of buckram, covered with
real pie-crust and baked, to which were attached a head
made of velvet, stuffed, and a tail of large feathers
painted with peacock colours. For the chestnut, a small
paper-bag may be blown up and burst, off stage. (This
needs rehearsal, to make sure that the sound will be
convincing.) The striking mechanism of the grandfather
clock should not be trusted, but a gong struck behind the
scenes instead. The opening of the clock face, turning of
the hands, and the striking, must be done slowly to give
Agatha time to change.

Myra's dress must be white or silver, beautiful, elaborate, and loaded with jewels (from Woolworth's).

Jane's dress should be gorgeous and ridiculous. The author dressed his Fairy Godmother not as a witch, but in " fairy robes of queer, shimmering green, with a glittering crown, and long grey hair (tow) falling almost to her feet."

All the " noises off " need careful management, especially the murmurs and cheers of the crowd. Probably a Boy Scout can supply the " trumpet " calls. The music must be well chosen, and if it is not possible to have piano or violins behind the scenes, a gramophone will do. Music from *The Immortal Hour* (Columbia Gramophone Co.) is suggested.

The play needs very careful rehearsal, but is not so difficult as it appears, because its stage-craft is so good. It plays even better than it reads. The acting part on which the play hangs is Jimmy's, and this must be well cast. The producer who thinks of attempting the play may be encouraged to learn that the sensation of the first production was the Fairy Godmother—" a really amazing and most eerie performance by a boy of eight or nine."

ELDORADO

The fee for each and every representation of this play by amateurs is one guinea, payable in advance to Messrs. Samuel French, 26 Southampton Street, Strand, London, W.C.2, or their authorized representatives, who, upon payment of the fee, will send a written permission for the performance to take place.

No public performance may be given unless this written permission has first been obtained.

Time for acting, about half an hour.

Mr. Gilbert's stage directions, stage-plan, and descriptions of the characters are so detailed that they leave very little to add in the way of acting notes. It may be advisable to point out, however, that the stage-setting, which at first appears to be very difficult, can be made very simple. A stage hung with curtains will serve very well, and hessian is suggested as a suitable (and cheap) material. If " practical " windows and doors can be included, so much the better, but they are not essential.

EL DORADO

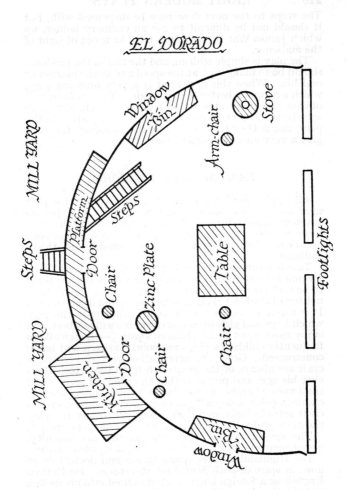

The steps to the next floor may be dispensed with, but it should not be difficult to use an ordinary ladder, up which James Watson can climb until he is out of sight of the audience.

The play is simple realism, and the aim of the producer should be to make it go at the speed and in the manner of real life. When this is done it is a very amusing play, which acts much better than it reads. Young actors will obviously not be able to achieve the convincing characterization which is necessary to do full justice to the play, but if they have rehearsed it thoroughly they can give a very amusing performance.

CAMPBELL OF KILMOHR

All applications for permission to perform this play must be addressed to Messrs. Samuel French, 26 Southampton Street, Strand, London, W.C.2, and no performance may be given unless permission has first been obtained. The fee for each performance is thirty shillings.

This is a difficult play, and not likely to be considered for public presentation by juniors, but there is everything to be said for their attempting it in the form room; it is not too difficult for their understanding and appreciation. It is a not uncommon mistake to think that the play which boys and girls of eleven or twelve will act best, and enjoy most, must be a " children's play "—though all too frequently children's plays are poorly written and badly constructed. Good characterization and clever stage-craft are always of the greatest help to the actor, whatever his age, and provided that the range of feeling and the issues at stake are not beyond their understanding, children enjoy doing a " grown-up play," and sometimes do it astonishingly well. Moreover, the better the play the more profitable are the time and labour spent upon it.

The speech of the characters presents no difficulty. Supplementing his note below, Mr. Ferguson writes: " The Highlander never spoke dialect and doesn't do so now, in spite of both Scott and Stevenson. He learned English as a foreign language, but carried into his spoken use of it the idiom of his own Gaelic. And any player who follows this idiom, supplied for him in the text, can keep to his own pronunciation of the words, and be assured that he is adequately representing the original." Representation is sufficient : exact reproduction is not needed.

AUTHOR'S NOTES

In producing any serious play it is essential to get a clear conception of the characters in it. Here the play turns on the struggle between two sharply contrasted personalities.

Archibald Campbell, a typical eighteenth-century Edinburgh lawyer, knows not only how to browbeat and bully, but also, when occasion calls, how to wheedle and persuade. He is an expert on the baser side of human nature, glib of words and fond of resounding phrases, which he rolls off *ore rotundo*. He has imagination and believes himself free from illusions. As a Campbell he belongs to a clan which never gave itself to unprofitable causes and had a genius for finding itself on the winning side.

Mary Stewart, the old woman, is as much an unconscious idealist as Campbell is a conscious materialist. Simple, uncalculating, unsophisticated peasant as she is, she is a Highland peasant, and therefore quick, sensitive, and passionate.

Out of the conflict between the two comes the tragedy. About that tragedy two things should be carefully noted. First, that Mary Stewart has no sense of defeat, and, second, that Campbell's triumph is far more apparent than real.

But the first is much the more important in the production. Indeed, it is by revealing Mary Stewart's glory in her sacrifice that the play is lifted into the realm of true tragedy. And any failure to make her sense of triumph manifest in her last speech will reduce the play to melodrama, and make it what is called a " sad " play. Tragedy, it may be observed, is never sad or depressing when it shows us the human spirit in some moment of grandeur. On the contrary, it thrills us; and by revealing some particular strength in our common human nature in some imaginary conflict, fortifies us for our own real if smaller distresses.   For these reasons, special care must be given to Mary Stewart's last speech.   It must have exaltation.   Up to the phrase, " High will his name be with the teller of fine tales," she almost declaims the words, a certain proud dignity in her tone.   But after that the pace quickens, with a touch of *wildness*, as if she were " fey," while she recapitulates what has happened. At her summing up of the situation, however, in " There are things greater than death," she returns to the tone with which she began.   The last words of the play, " Let us go out . . . " are quiet, with all the " grandeur " gone out of her voice, as she accepts the fact of death and sees a duty to be done.   Support in this long speech is got if Morag avoids convulsive sobbing and, as was the Celtic habit, lets her sorrow find utterance in a low continuous moan or wail, while rocking herself to the rhythm of the old woman's words.   But this " keening " should cease with " Let them that are children shed the tears."

The second point in the production is to make it evident that Campbell's triumph is more apparent than real. Though of far less importance than the first point, it has much to do with a delicately balanced and finished production of the play.   Can you get your audience to remember that Morag does not really know where the fugitives are, but only *thinks* she knows ?   (Notice how markedly this is emphasized in the scene between mother and son early in the play by the frequent reiteration of the word " tell.")   When Sandeman goes out the girl is sitting huddled up on a low stool, apart.   She sits with her head bent and covered by her shawl.   She should try to get herself forgotten, overlooked.   As far as possible she should blend with her background.   Then when the moment comes when she lifts her face and echoes Campbell's " Dead ! " the audience is as much startled as Campbell himself.   After that her previous rigid stillness will be understood ; inside the girl a silent struggle had been going on as to whether she will tell or not.   Campbell deceives her with his promise, and is himself, innocently, deceived by Morag—though he will only know it later.

Length of Performance.—A good production occupies not less than thirty-five minutes.   It opens very slowly and quietly till Dugald appears.   This leaves scope for the pace to quicken when necessary afterwards. But in a tersely written play like this remember that an audience needs time to take in the points. Therefore the danger is that of being too rapid rather than of being too slow.

Costume.—Archibald Campbell, dark coat and knee breeches of the period, with white cravat and ruffles; tricorn hat, riding cloak, and boots. James Mackenzie, similar, but not so fine; no ruffles or riding boots. Soldiers (usually three), long scarlet coats and white cross-belts, long gaiters, preferably black, tricorn hats. Captain Sandeman, similar, but crimson sash in place of cross-belt, and gold lace on hat, sword and riding boots. Women, skirts of any rough dark stuff with dark tartan shawl crossed in front and tucked into waist. Anything white or fancy is a fatal mistake. The women's " fineness " is internal, not external. Dugald Stewart, kilt of dark tartan, dark plain shirt and hose, leather belt with dirk in sheath.

Lighting.—As a high even lighting will produce a theatrical effect when thrown on so much colour, the lighting should be carefully studied. Where facilities exist throw the roof into shadow. Try to get shadows somewhere, to give depth and atmosphere. For the same reason all who enter from the storm should carry something of it in with them—say a powdering of snow or some sign of fatigue. Avoid the spick and span.

Highland Speech.—The fact that the peculiarities of Highland spoken English lie chiefly in the form of the sentences and the order of the words makes it easy to reproduce, infinitely easier than any English dialect. An occasional slight stressing of sibilants where they occur at the end of a word (" wass " for " was ") would certainly be enough to recall Highland speech to any one familiar with it. Men like Campbell did of course acquire lowland Scots words and expressions such as " birze yont " (" press forward "), but such words of the sort which come in this play have been selected for their phonetic quality—they are, that is, Scots words which are pronounced as written.

J. A. FERGUSON.

CATHERINE PARR

Permission to perform this play must be obtained in advance from The Collection Bureau, The Society of Authors, 11 Gower Street, London, W.C.1. The fee is one guinea for each performance.

The play takes about ten minutes.

For *Catherine Parr* the staging is very simple. Any plain dark background, curtains, panelled wall, or screens, will serve excellently, and the only essential furniture is an antique table and three chairs, all in Tudor style if possible. The third chair can be used as a substitute for the bookcase, provided that the words " in the bookcase " are omitted from King Henry's speech on page 152. The articles required for the table are two boiled eggs in small cups or bowls (not modern egg-cups), antique-looking platters, pewter mugs, and a jug of " beer," a long, tapering loaf of bread (called " Vienna bread " by some bakers), and spoons and knives. Any old printed book will do for the Plutarch, the pages of which need not be seen by the audience. The play can very well be given in the open air, and there is no difficulty about the entry or the final exit.

Dresses are fully described under Shakespeare's *Henry VIII.* in *The Bankside Costume Book* (see page 227), besides appearing in the illustrations of many costume and history books.

A portrait of Catherine Parr can be found and copied, but she is not a well-known figure. In the case of Henry VIII., however, it is important that he should be made up and padded to resemble Hans Holbein's famous portrait. (See frontispiece to *Social England*, Vol. III.) If the actor has a fairly round face the resemblance can be made very close indeed.

The stage movements of the characters are few and simple, but there must be more than those indicated by the dramatist. For instance, King Henry should be asked to decide at what point he will sit down after referring to the Plutarch; and his decision accepted, unless the producer feels strongly that it is wrong. Henry and Catherine should sit sideways to the audience, with the table between them. At the appropriate point an effective movement is for Catherine to fling herself round in her chair so that she faces the audience and speaks almost over her shoulder to Henry. Both spring to their feet, of course, when the quarrel reaches its height.

The play has a particular interest to the producer and to the young actor as an exercise in *tempo*. Success will depend to a large extent upon the producer's discernment in deciding the varying speeds at which the dialogue is to be spoken. And the interruptions must really be interruptions, as they are too rarely with amateur actors. With vigorous performance this play can be most successful.

A word of warning on one point may be useful. In a performance for which the present writer was responsible, Henry VIII. (aged 12) was an almost exact reproduction in miniature of his great original. When the curtain disclosed him cracking his egg, the audience laughed at him so loudly and so long that both he and Catherine (who greatly appreciated the play and their own appearance) broke down, and had to join in the laughter. This had not been anticipated, and naturally the actors had difficulty in recovering their gravity. It would be well to warn young players that this may happen, and provide them with pantomime to keep them busy until the laughter has subsided. In any case it is well for Henry not to crack his egg until the curtain is up, nor to discover its offensive state too quickly. He should peer at it, fling himself back disgustedly in his chair, and then slam down his spoon on the table as he speaks the opening line.

MICHAEL

No performance of this play may be given unless permission has been obtained in advance from the author's agents, Messrs. Curtis Brown, 7 Henrietta Street, Covent Garden, London, W.C. The fee for each performance is ten shillings and sixpence.

The play takes about thirty minutes.

AUTHOR'S NOTE

For the first production of *Michael* special music was
written by Norman O'Neill. In Scenes I. and II., when
Michael smiles, his back is to the audience, and the effect
of the smile is seen on the others in the room ; and it was
then that the string music seemed strangely to fill the air.

In Scene III. it was heard again when Michael is left
alone in the dark room and the light gradually begins to
shine around him. It continued as Michael spoke.

The music was all written for a string quartette, except
that towards the end of the play, after Michael's words,
" It seems to men that they live by care of themselves,
but in truth it is Love alone by which they live," a faint
trumpet call was heard. Michael lifted his arms, spoke
the last words of the play, and the call was repeated,
crashing out, as it were, at the very roof of the cottage.

Application for the original music should be made to
Messrs. Curtis Brown.   MILES MALLESON.

The Author's Note disposes of the prime difficulty of
the play, Michael's smile, and it will be seen that its
effect upon Matryona and Simon will be the measure of
its effect on the audience. There are no difficulties of
characterization in the play, and boys or girls, or any
sincere actors, can do well with it if they have been carefully coached and thoroughly rehearsed. Indeed, the
best rendering will probably be an unsophisticated one,
for the play retains much of that simplicity of spirit
which marks the original story, and which constitutes so
much of the appeal and the greatness of Tolstoy's best
work. Michael's rather exacting part, in particular, demands a player who can act simply and who has an
instinctive sense of poetry. If his long final speech has
the least tone of insincerity or sanctimoniousness or
theatrical straining after effect, it will be ruined. A professional actor may have the technical skill to make
effective a speech which he does not believe in, or understand, but the amateur, young or old, can only com-
pensate to some extent for his technical ignorance by
sincerity and enthusiasm and hard work.

A set of hessian curtains will serve excellently for this

play, and if a " practical " door presents any difficulty it can be dispensed with by having the entrance in one corner, between the curtains, and the knocking "off." Table, bench, and stools should be of plain, unpainted wood (they might all be made in the school workshops), and plates and bowls of earthenware or wood or very plain china.

If accuracy in setting and costumes is desired, reference should be made to Max Tilke's *Costumes of Eastern Europe* (Benn, 1926), which gives coloured illustrations of the garments, and to Russian travel books. There is a useful picture on page 131 of *Folk Tales of the Nations* (T.E.S.). But there is no need for exact reproduction, and, to quote Mr. Malleson, " the clothes and the setting should give scope to producers with a certain amount of creative originality."

For the lighting in Scene III. a dimmer switch is almost essential, though a possible makeshift arrangement would be to have the stage lights wired in small groups, and diminish the lighting by switching off one group at a time. Whatever the method, the light must be very dim by the time the Woman begins to tell her story, and should come from the oil-lamp which is burning on the table, supplemented, if necessary, by an electric bulb, fixed somewhere above the proscenium opening, inside, and set in a funnel of tin so that its light is thrown only in a circle around the oil-lamp. When Matryona takes the lamp away, this electric bulb is dimmed until it is out (or switched off), leaving the room in darkness until the light begins to shine upon Michael, from a powerful lamp or set of lamps focused on his corner—and here again a dimmer switch is almost essential. There is very little difficulty or expense in making such a switch, and full instructions may be found in *Stage Lighting for " Little " Theatres* (see below, page 226).

SOME BOOKS FOR THE AMATEUR

" *Let's do a Play !* " Rodney Bennett. Illustrated by
Hugh Chesterman. Large crown 8vo, cloth gilt.
Nelson. 3s. 6d. net.

Plays, concerts, charades, revues, living marionettes,
mock conjuring, and all kinds of amateur entertain-
ments are dealt with in this book, from the simplest
" show " got up on the spur of the moment, to the full-
dress production in a public hall. Mr. Bennett proves
himself an expert on rehearsal, stage-management, lighting, make-up, scenery, etc., etc., and his wide experience
of amateur work with young players enables him to
explain exactly how to make the best of scanty funds,
very little equipment, and difficult conditions. And his
book is unique because it is as useful to boys and girls
" running a show on their own " as to their elders when
these decide to take charge.

Ample material for a number of programmes is given
in the last 140 pages, which include plays, sketches, and
poems (suitable for young players of various ages from
six to sixteen), by John Drinkwater, Alfred Noyes, Allan
Monkhouse, Rodney Bennett, Ronald Gow, Elizabeth
Fleming, P. Laflin, Rosalind Vallance, John Hampden,
Mary Cousins, John Pearmain, etc., etc.

The Small Stage and its Equipment. R. Angus Wilson :
with an Introduction by Sir Barry Jackson. Allen
and Unwin. 5s.

This deals with all the problems of temporary and
permanent stage-construction, lighting, and scenery, and
is invaluable to the amateur because it offers practicable
solutions.

Stage Lighting. C. Harold Ridge. Heffer. 5s.

An invaluable treatise on the art and technique of the
subject, which every dramatic society should possess.

British Costume during Nineteen Centuries. Mrs. Charles
A. Ashdown. Nelson. 21s.

The best single-volume history : from the time of the
Britons to 1820, with a special section on ecclesiastical
dress. 578 illustrations in colour and line.

A Book of Make-up. Eric Ward. Samuel French.
3s. 6d.

A practical handbook with diagrams.

Mimes and Miming. Isabel Chisman and Gladys Wiles.
Nelson. 2s. 6d. net.

A book for beginners as well as those who have already discovered the delights of miming. It shows *exactly* what to do, and contains fourteen varied mimes without acting fees. Illustrated with stage plans, etc.

A List of Plays for Girls and Women. A List of Plays for Boys and Men. Compiled by the Junior Drama Committee of the British Drama League. Nelson. Each list, 1s. net.

Each list contains full particulars of over two hundred plays of varying length and type, carefully chosen, classified, and indexed. Title, author, publisher, price, fee (if any), agent, number of characters, settings, costumes, and a summary of the play are given.

The Nelson Playbooks, edited by John Hampden, M.A. Nelson. 9d. each.

This comprehensive series includes *Four Modern Plays, Three Modern Plays and a Mime, Five Robin Hood Plays, Caste, Miss in her Teens, She Stoops to Conquer, The Rivals, The School for Scandal, The Critic, The Knight of the Burning Pestle, The Shoemaker's Holiday, Dr. Faustus, Everyman,* etc. ; seven plays of Shakespeare ; Ibsen's *A Doll's House* and *The Master Builder* ; *Mrs. Adis* and *The Mockbeggar,* by Sheila Kaye-Smith and John Hampden ; The *Antigone* of Sophocles and other translations from Greek, French, and German, etc., etc. The plays are carefully edited from good texts, reasonably expurgated, and provided with concise footnotes where necessary. There are several novel features, print and paper are good, and the strong linen covers are of attractive modern design. Lists of these and several hundred other plays for players of all ages and all tastes may be obtained, post free, from Messrs. T. Nelson and Sons, Ltd., 35–36 Paternoster Row, London, E.C.4.

APPENDIX

THE PROCEDURE FOR A MOCK TRIAL

A MOCK TRIAL is a form of dramatic entertainment which can be made interesting, amusing, and instructive at the same time. Most dramatic societies will find it worth while to attempt such a trial occasionally, and since it is easier to stage and needs less rehearsal than a play, while providing much more scope for invention, it can be arranged in the schoolroom or the village hall with the expenditure of little time and, if desired, no money. But it must be arranged. The impromptu mock trial is very rarely a success.

The " crime " should be " discovered " some time in advance—though the " prisoner " must certainly be allowed out on bail !—the most important details of the story decided, and the players instructed in their various parts. If a public performance is to be given, at least one rehearsal is necessary. Speeches, evidence, etc., need not be learned word for word, but each player must know the main facts and ideas which he is to contribute to the progress of the trial, and in most cases notes may be used unobtrusively. Judge and Counsel can have this book open in front of them, with a full " plan " of the trial.

If the whole plot can be invented by the leading players or the organizer, so much the better. If not, it may be based upon a trial in a novel, such as that of Darnay in *A Tale of Two Cities* (for which eighteenth-century costume is needed) or the familiar case of Bardell *v.* Pickwick in *The Pickwick Papers* (which can be given in an adaptation of modern dress). The stories of Sherlock Holmes and other detectives provide very useful material, but public performances based on these cannot be given without permission from the owners of the copyright. Boys and girls greatly enjoy inventing a new Sherlock Holmes mystery, and providing him with a dramatic entry, accompanied by excited witnesses, in the middle of the trial, when the (innocent) prisoner is in grave danger of being convicted by circumstantial evidence. The opportunity for useful classroom work need not be emphasized.

The procedure which is summarized below is approximately that of an Assize Court. This is less familiar and more impressive than the ritual of the " Police Court," and the Assize deals with serious crimes which are suitable for a mock trial—such as arson, burglary, housebreaking, embezzlement, forgery, larceny, and making false coin and banknotes. It is suggested that a mock trial might be very profitably followed or preceded by some work on our legal system and the function of the various courts. The necessary information can be obtained from such books as Mr. F. Swann's *Primer of English Citizenship* (Longmans, Green, and Co.).

The Assize can be arranged simply or elaborately. Though the gilded coach and the javelin-men are not available for " the legal representative of the King," there should be little difficulty in arranging for trumpeters " off " (Boy Scouts with bugles ?) to announce the entry of a Judge resplendent in scarlet and ermine (flannelette and cotton-wool).

If a stage is available, so much the better, but in either case it is necessary to have a dais for the Judge, and advisable to have a lower one for the Clerks. Draped boxes or tables will do. (Dramatic societies will find it a good plan to buy a stock of butter boxes, which are cheap, strong, and portable, and excellent for a dais. For stage use they can be painted and built into a number of different properties.) Two black-boards, a small screen, or a draped towel-horse will do for the witness-box, and two long desks or forms for the Jury. The " bar " to which the prisoner is called can be a thin pole or brass rod lashed to two uprights—chairs will do.

The Judge wears a flowing scarlet robe trimmed with ermine ; the Clerk and Counsel wear university gowns, if available, with stiff collars (but no tie), and bands— *i.e.* two narrow strips of white linen hanging from the

collar in front. If uniforms can be borrowed or improvised for policemen and warders or wardresses, so much
the better, but these are not so important. There should
be as much variety as possible in the dress, make-up, and
manner of the prisoner and witnesses, who can be of
widely different ages, classes, and nationalities.

When everything is ready, and the jury and audience
are seated, the Assize proceeds as follows :

[*Enter the Usher.*]

Usher [*proclaiming loudly*]. Oyez ! Oyez ! Oyez ! All
manner of persons having aught to do before His Majesty
the King and the Lords Justices of Assize draw near and
give their attendance.

[*Enter the Clerk of Assize, the Counsel for the Prosecution, the Counsel for the Defence, and the Judge.
Every one present rises as the Judge enters, and
remains standing until he has taken his seat.*

*Enter the Prisoner, guarded [if a man] by two Warders,
or [if a woman] by two Wardresses.*

Every one except the Judge rises when speaking.]

Clerk of Assize [*rising and reading the charge*]. "John
Doe is charged that on the 8th day of December 1926, at
. . . in the County of . . . he did feloniously . . .
against the peace of our Lord the King his crown and
dignity." Prisoner at the Bar, you have heard the
Charge. Do you plead Guilty or Not Guilty ?

Prisoner. Not Guilty.

Clerk of Assize. John Doe, the names I am about to
call are those of the Jury who will try you. If you object
to any of them, you must do so before they are sworn, and
your objection will be heard.

[*The members of the Jury rise. The Clerk of Assize
reads the twelve names in full, the Foreman's first—
e.g. Thomas Henry Wilkinson, Frederick Jones, etc.
The Prisoner having made no objection,* the Clerk reads
the words of the oath which the Jury are to take.*]

Clerk of Assize. You shall well and truly try the issue
joined between our Sovereign Lord the King and the
Prisoner at the Bar whom you shall have in charge, and
true verdict give according to the evidence.†

---

* If he does object to any juryman it should be for some absurd
reason.

† The words "so help you God" are here omitted.

[*As the last words of the oath are pronounced, the Jury raise their right hands, and then sit. The Counsel for the Prosecution rises.*]

Counsel for Prosecution outlines the crime of which he intends to prove the Prisoner guilty, and then announces the name of his first witness—*e.g.* William Warburton.

Judge's Clerk [*calling*]. William Warburton !

William Warburton enters, and goes into the witness-box. The Judge's Clerk gives him [*and every witness who follows*] *a card on which the words of the oath are printed.*]

William Warburton [*reading the oath slowly and solemnly*].* The evidence that I shall give between our Sovereign Lord the King and the Prisoner at the Bar shall be the truth, the whole truth, and nothing but the truth.*

Counsel for Prosecution proceeds to question the Witness, trying to elicit evidence which will show that the Prisoner is guilty. The Witness answers as clearly and briefly as possible, except when a touch of humour is desired.

[*During the examination the Judge may ask questions on any point which he thinks needs explanation, for his own benefit or that of the audience. When the Counsel for the Prosecution has finished with the Witness he sits down and the Counsel for the Defence rises.*]

Counsel for Defence proceeds to cross-examine the Witness, with a view to weakening or disproving the evidence which he has given previously, and obtaining evidence in favour of the Prisoner.

[*When Counsel for the Defence has finished, he sits, and Counsel for the Prosecution either asks further questions or gives the Witness leave to go. When this is given Witness leaves the box and takes a seat near by. Except when giving evidence no Witness is allowed in court, but this rule need not be enforced.*]

[*When all Witnesses for the Prosecution have been heard :*]

Counsel for Prosecution. That is my case, my Lord.

[*Sits down.*]

Counsel for Defence. I propose to call the Prisoner to give evidence, my Lord.

* The words " I swear by Almighty God " and " so help me God " are here omitted.

[*Witnesses for the Defence are then called, the Prisoner being the first. (He is not compelled to give evidence, but nearly always does so.)*]

[*Prisoner is taken into the witness-box by a Warder, and is sworn as a Witness. After being examined by Counsel for the Defence and cross-examined by Counsel for the Prosecution, Prisoner is taken back into the dock. All Witnesses for the Defence having been examined :*]

Counsel for Defence [*rising*] makes his longest and most important speech, beginning : " My Lord and Gentlemen of the Jury." He sums up all the evidence which tells in favour of the Prisoner, tries to discredit or refute (or passes over in silence) the evidence against him, refers to any past legal decisions which have bearing on the case, and does all in his power to influence the Jury in favour of the Prisoner by an eloquent appeal to their reason and their emotions. [*He sits.*]

Counsel for Prosecution [*rising*] makes a similar speech on the other side. [*Sits.*]

Judge [*remaining seated*]. " Gentlemen of the Jury, you have to decide whether the Prisoner on . . . did . . ." He then proceeds to give the Jury an impartial summing up of the facts which have been established by the evidence, drawing their attention to anything which he considers to be of special importance, and concludes, " Can you decide upon your verdict here, or do you wish to retire to consider it ? "

Foreman, after a brief consultation with the Jury, announces that they wish to retire, or that they do not.

[*If the Jury retire, the Court must wait until they have returned to their places ; but it is better if they can come to their decision (which must be unanimous) without retiring. When they have decided, the Judge proceeds at once.*]

Judge [*to Foreman*]. Are you agreed upon your verdict ?
Foreman. Yes, my Lord.

[*If he says that they have not been able to come to an agreement, the Judge must announce that the case will be tried again at the next Assizes.*]

Judge. Do you find the Prisoner Guilty or Not Guilty ?
[*If the verdict is Not Guilty :*]
Foreman. Not Guilty, my Lord.

Judge. John Doe, I concur in the verdict. You leave the Court without a stain on your character.

[*If the verdict is Guilty ; or Guilty with Recommendation to Mercy :*]

Foreman. Guilty, my Lord, *or* Guilty, my Lord, with Recommendation to Mercy.

Judge. " Prisoner at the Bar, you have been found guilty of a grave offence, which . . ." He points out the evil results of the particular crime, and then, tempering his remarks and sentence accordingly if the Prisoner has been recommended to mercy, he concludes, I sentence you to . . ." [The sentence for burglary should be two years' imprisonment or three or more years' penal servitude ; for arson, penal servitude ; for forgery, imprisonment with or without hard labour, or penal servitude. The shortest period of penal servitude which can be given is three years.]

[*If the Prisoner is Not Guilty, he is free to leave the Court ; if Guilty, he is escorted to his cell by the Warders. The Court then rises, the Clerk of Assize, Counsel, etc., leaving in the order in which they entered.*]

RECORD OF A MOCK TRIAL

held by. . . . . .on. . . . .

The Judge . . . .
Counsel for the Prosecution . . . .
Counsel for the Defence . . . .
Clerk of Assize . . . .
Judge's Clerk . . . .
Usher . . . .
Prisoner (   ) . . . .
First Warder . . . .
Second Warder . . . .
Twelve Jurymen (their real names) :
                Foreman. . . . .

. . . .
. . . .
. . . .
. . . .
. . . .
. . . .

  Witnesses :

. . . .
. . . .
. . . .
. . . .

  The Charge . . . .
. . . .
  The Verdict. . . . .
  The Sentence. . . . .

A CHRISTMAS EPILOGUE

A CHRISTMAS EPILOGUE

CHARACTERS :

Five Boys or Girls, and Father Christmas.

[*The Christmas concert is over.   The lights in the hall are switched on, and the First Boy (or Girl) appears between the curtains.*]

First Boy. Heap on more wood !   The wind is chill ;
But let it whistle as it will,
We'll keep our Christmas merry still.
Each age has deemed——

Second Boy [*standing up at the back of the hall, and shouting*]. Here !   You stop that !

First Boy. Why ?   What for ?

Third Boy [*half-way down the hall, standing up*]. Because that's the Christmas Epilogue !   You know that, don't you ?

First Boy. Well, what about it ?

Fourth and Fifth Boys [*from different points in the audience, speaking together*]. What about it !   Nobody but Father Christmas is allowed to speak that !

Second Boy [*coming up towards the stage*]. And if any one but Father Christmas says it, all the Christmas trees in England will fall down !

[*The other boys also begin to move towards the stage.*]

Fourth Boy. And all the nuts and oranges will go bad !

Third Boy. And all the Christmas puddings will swell up and burst !

Fifth Boy. And Father Christmas will go to Chicago and stay there !

Second Boy. So you'd better be careful, my lad.

[*By this time they have all reached the front, and stand in a group, looking up at the First Boy. He stoops over the footlights to speak to them.*]

First Boy [*aghast*]. But what can we do ? We *must* have an Epilogue !

Fifth Boy. Have you asked Father Christmas to come and say it ?

First Boy. Great Scott !   I never thought of that !

Fourth Boy. Well, you didn't expect him to come if you didn't ask him, did you ?

Third Boy. It's not Christmas yet, and he must be jolly busy, anyway.

Fourth Boy. Come on, you chaps, let's call him !

Second Boy. Good idea.

All [*facing the audience, and calling*]. Father Christmas ! Fa—ther Christmas !   [*They listen intently for a moment.*]

Second Boy. Nothing doing.

First Boy. Perhaps he's offended, and won't come.

Third Boy. Not he !   He's a jolly good sort. He doesn't get offended.

Fifth Boy. Perhaps he's a long way away.   Let's try again.

All. Father Christmas !   Father Christmas !

[*They listen again.*]

First Boy. I can't hear anything—can you ?

Fourth and Fifth Boys. No.

Third Boy. I know. There isn't any chimney in this place.   He can't get in !

[*If there is a chimney, this speech should be, ' I know ! We ought to have shouted up the chimney ! " and the next four speeches should be omitted, and they all go and call up the chimney.*]

Fourth Boy. Well, that's settled it !

Second Boy. I'm not so sure. He must have found other ways of getting in, what with all this central heating and jerry-built houses with chimneys that any one would get stuck in !

Fifth Boy. Oh, let's try once more, anyhow.

First Boy. Oh yes, come on !

All. Father Christmas !   Father Christmas !

[*They listen. There is a faint, far-away tinkle of little bells.*]

First Boy. Hooray !   Listen !

[*They listen again. The bells sound nearer. A voice is heard singing a carol.*]

First Boy. Hooray !   He's coming !

[*All lights are switched off. In the darkness the First
    Boy slips through the curtains and disappears ; the
    others withdraw to the sides of the hall. The curtains
    part and Father Christmas appears, carrying a
    brilliant red lantern which throws its light upon his
    head and shoulders.*]

Father Christmas. Heap on more wood ! the wind is
    chill ; *

But let it whistle as it will,
We'll keep old Christmas merry still.
Each age has deemed the new-born year
The fittest time for festal cheer
E'en, heathen yet, the savage Dane
At Yule more deep the mead did drain ;
And well our Christian sires of old
Loved when the year its course had rolled,
And brought blithe Christmas back again,
With all his hospitable train.
Domestic and religious rite
Gave honour to the holy night ;
On Christmas Eve the bells were rung ;
On Christmas Eve the mass was sung ;
The damsel donned her kirtle sheen ;
The hall was dressed with holly green ;
Forth to the wood did merry men go
To gather in the mistletoe.
Then opened wide the baron's hall
To vassal, tenant, serf, and all ;
Power laid his rod of rule aside,
And Ceremony doffed his pride.
All hailed, with uncontrolled delight,
And general voice, the happy night
That to the cottage, as the crown,
Brought tidings of salvation down.
The huge hall table's oaken face,
Scrubbed till it shone, the day to grace,
Then was brought in the lusty brawn,
By old blue-coated serving-man ;
Then the grim boar's head frowned on high,
Crested with bays and rosemary.
There the huge sirloin reeked ; hard by

* The first forty-nine lines are taken from *Marmion.*

Plum-porridge stood, and Christmas pie ;
Nor failed old England to produce,
At such high tide, her savoury goose.
Then came the merry maskers in,
And carols roared with blithesome din ;
White shirts supplied the masquerade,
And smutted cheeks the visors made ;
But oh ! what maskers richly dight
Can boast of bosoms half so light !
England was merry England, when
Old Christmas brought his sports again.
'Twas Christmas broached the mightiest ale ;
'Twas Christmas told the merriest tale ;
A Christmas gambol oft could cheer
The poor man's heart through half the year.
   So here come I to wish you all
The joys of Christmas festival,
Good cheer as in old days gone by,
Glad hearts, free minds, and good mince-pie,
A happy family round the fire,
And unto each his heart's desire.

                          [The little bells are heard again.]
   My reindeer scents the Lapland snow ;
The sleigh-bells jingle ; I must go,
For many a village, many a town,
Before the Christmas stars go down,
Awaits my blessing on its glee,
That joy may reign from sea to sea.
   Wassail ! Wassail ! To all, good cheer !
Old Father Christmas gives you here
A Happy Christmas, Glad New Year !

CURTAIN

PRINTED IN GREAT BRITAIN AT
THE PRESS OF THE PUBLISHERS